DIAMONDS
in the WATER
A FURNACE AWAITS YOU

DANIEL MCCRIMONS, MD

BALBOA
PRESS
A DIVISION OF HAY HOUSE

Balboa Press books may be ordered through booksellers or by contacting:

Balboa Press
A Division of Hay House
1663 Liberty Drive
Bloomington, IN 47403
www.balboapress.com
1 (877) 407-4847

Because of the dynamic nature of the Internet, any web addresses or links contained in this book may have changed since publication and may no longer be valid. The views expressed in this work are solely those of the author and do not necessarily reflect the views of the publisher, and the publisher hereby disclaims any responsibility for them.

The author of this book does not dispense medical advice or prescribe the use of any technique as a form of treatment for physical, emotional, or medical problems without the advice of a physician, either directly or indirectly. The intent of the author is only to offer information of a general nature to help you in your quest for emotional and spiritual well-being. In the event you use any of the information in this book for yourself, which is your constitutional right, the author and the publisher assume no responsibility for your actions.

KJV:
Scripture taken from the King James Version of the Bible.

Any people depicted in stock imagery provided by Thinkstock are models, and such images are being used for illustrative purposes only. Certain stock imagery © Thinkstock.

Printed in the USA.

ISBN: 978-1-5043-8876-4 (sc)
ISBN: 978-1-5043-8877-1 (hc)
ISBN: 978-1-5043-8909-9 (e)

Library of Congress Control Number: 2017914613

Balboa Press rev. date: 10/20/2017

To "Sallie Ann" and like-minded soldiers of humanity whose spirits "must have nightly floated free," colorless and eternal, like diamonds in the water

Contents

Acknowledgements

The task of creating this literary work required a dedicated team seasoned with broad experience and immeasurable wisdom. They were kind to share their time and energy, and they suggested many ideas to make the story impacting and memorable. I could stand by the edge of a precipice and shout out the individual names of these gracious assistants, echoing loudly throughout the mountains, valleys and hillsides, but I will just mention them quietly for they already know my true feelings.

I would like to express my gratitude to the late Reverend Madeleine Renner, minister at the Science of Mind Church in Sacramento, whose sermon triggered the idea for the principal character's life story. I would also like to thank my friend and colleague, Dr. Gregory Douglas, for introducing me to the late Dr. Sondra Wilson who listened to my ideas for a book 13 years ago, and helped me create a background and characters to make an exciting life adventure for my protagonist. My mentor at college, the late Dr. Michael Brown-Beasley, was instrumental in unfolding so many valuable historic references and many of the great living individuals mentioned throughout the story. The late William St. John, whose personal accounts of his experience at boarding school in the 1930's and 1940's, helped me develop ideas for the life of the protagonist. The late Dr. Carl Camras and the late Carl Holmes, respected friends and community servants, formed the model for me to create my principal character. The late Howard K. Gray, Jr., whose personal remembrances added so much color to the story line. My longtime friend, Dr. Margaret Haynes, introduced me to the late Dr. Vincent Cordice and his wife, Marguerite Cordice who gave me so many suggestions about the medical school experiences in the 1920's. John Noble, my roommate at college, who obtained many references and took me to the Plimoth Plantation to meet the Wampanoag Indians. My friend, Brad Cutler, whose personal experience gave me the background to the Maine summer home. To my brother, Raymond McCrimons, who suggested using Plato's "Allegory of the Cave", sincere thanks for such a valuable reference for the story. To Maxwell Collard, my former patient and aspiring scientist/physician, whose initial critical review broadened my understanding of what the readers would need to be satisfied and willing to read on. To all of the insightful reference librarians, particularly Ms. Mariah Sakrejda-Leavitt, archivist at the Rare Books Collection, Frost Library, Amherst College, Amherst, MA; Ms. Tevis Kimball, curator of special collections, The Jones Library, Amherst, MA; Ms. Jessica Murphy, reference archivist, Center for the History of Medicine, Francis Countway Library of Medicine, Harvard Medical School, Boston, MA, and all the others at the New York Public Libraries, the Sacramento Central Library and the University of California- Davis Medical Library, Sacramento, CA. To the Ethical Cultural School representatives in Manhattan, New York, my thanks for the background information for my principal character's schooling and camp experience. To my friend and supporter, Dr. Bradley Chipps.

To Spiritual Life Center- Unity Church in Sacramento with Reverend James Trapp and associates, whose weekly spiritual messages, meditations and music were inspirational in guiding my hand and thoughts to produce many of the written pages.

And to my 'inner circle' of confidantes, who conjured their magic to help me with their time and sacrificed to build the story line, and other character development, do the editing, the book cover design, the painstaking detail to format the entire project, and allow me the opportunity to get this work completed while I still performed my pediatric duties in my clinic and the hospitals- Dr. Jerome Wright, Jack Metzen, Fred and Lori Cooper, and Marcia Sund.

I would like to distinctly mention my parents, Marion and Mary Alice McCrimons, and extended family who encouraged and nurtured my burning interests to become an avid lover of music, science, literature, and history and remain a lifetime student of learning, my mother whose spirituality and wisdom carried me through the aches and pains as well as the triumphs and glory of life's lessons, and other earthly and heavenly angels who lead me to the literary resources and personal remembrances that rounded out the story line with the historical events.

And finally, to my friends at Balboa Press- Senior Editor Robert Colon and Publishing Services Associate Mary Oxley who put it in book form and helped me spread the word about reading it.

Disclaimer

All characters appearing in this work, whether they truly lived or were originally fictitious, are mentioned in historic context only, and not with the intention of character defamation or praise, but rather a perspective taken by the analysis of the fictitious narrator.

Any resemblance of opinions to real persons, from the author's perspective, living or otherwise able to take legal action against him, is purely coincidental.

Nature is plebian; she demands that one work; she prefers callused hands and will reveal herself only to those with careworn brows.

—Louis Pasteur
Louis Pasteur: Free Lance of Science
Rene Dubos

Food alone is not enough. Man has a mind, which also requires sustenance. Sensing a personal duty to follow a divinely instituted natural order of things gives man hope and keeps him actively seeking a clearer understanding of life's essential nourishment (lessons).

—Dr. Bhimrao R. Ambedkar (paraphrased)

That you may know from the rising of the sun to the place of its setting in the west, people, know, I am the Lord, and there is none besides me; there is no other. I form the light and create darkness; I make peace and create hardship and evil; I the Lord do all these things.

—Isaiah 45:6–7 (paraphrased)

Diamonds in the Water

Diamonds in the water,
Sparkling with delight,
Rare and distinctively exceptional,
Fervently admired, but only appreciated through conscious insight.

There's a lot of preparation for a diamond
To be made true.
It takes time, withstanding great pressure for the quality to stand out and
be counted as a part amongst the few.

Diamonds, like the seeds anticipating growth with the promise of spring,
Have their potential buried deep within their core.
Some seeds blossom into mighty trees bearing sweet, flavored fruit,
While the carbon molecules of diamonds transform to a beauty forevermore.

Those carbon molecules that remain carbon have no luster to express,
But it is that same carbon backbone that forms the diamond, no different
than the rest.
Unlike the actual diamond that is formed confined in the depths of the
earth,
Being a human made of carbon particles, we are given a choice to make
that could or couldn't be for our worth.

So make your decision a commitment with intent,
And not flounder in excuses when the outcome is something to resent.
It's either the graphite or the diamond that you are planning to mine,
But the latter search has its dark, grueling moments to abide, in order to
reveal precious peace of mind.

These "living" diamonds scattered throughout the worldly waters,
Always calm and still with lustrous shine,
In raging storms and forceful waves,
Stay faithful, ever vigilant to the flow of the deep blue-green brine.

Though visible from above, they reside beneath the surface
Where turbulence and confusion reign,
They observe the fear, the anger, and the shame,
As they constantly try to show a simpler, wiser choice to maintain.

There's a message to take notice that rings loud yet not heard by all,
That the diamond offers hope and shares a virtuous voice to reach the big
and small.
Strive to think good thoughts, to act good deeds, and share a conscience
good and clear,
And the rewards of living will be worth their weight in diamonds for
Everyone throughout each and every new year.

Diamonds in the water,
Sparkling with delight,
Rare and distinctively exceptional,
Fervently admired, but only appreciated through conscious insight.

List of Fictitious Characters

- ➤ Windsor Langford Waterbury III and Family Members
- ➤ Soulange Micheaux
- ➤ Hope Lightener
- ➤ Jasper Hardy
- ➤ Minnie Bel Mar
- ➤ Windsor Langford Waterbury Sr. (aka Walter Williams)
- ➤ Sallie Ann Williams
- ➤ Charlotte Williams McPhee
- ➤ Tavish McPhee
- ➤ Charlotte McPhee's Family Members
- ➤ Uncle Bennett
- ➤ Uncle John (a real person who lived in Baltimore but is a member of a fictitious family)
- ➤ Lizzy
- ➤ Zeke and Isaac
- ➤ Lucy and Sadie
- ➤ Mrs. Caldwell and her nephew
- ➤ Reverend F. W. White
- ➤ Andrew
- ➤ Mr. Fulton
- ➤ Confederate soldiers on the train
- ➤ Elizabeth Adams Cameron Waterbury (aka Mumsie)
- ➤ Herbert Horace Huntington (HHH)
- ➤ Windsor Langford Waterbury II (Deuce)
- ➤ Thaddeus Waterbury
- ➤ Rose Brewster Waterbury
- ➤ Walter and his mother at Coney Island
- ➤ Salvatore Cantolini
- ➤ Eugenia Brewster Duke
- ➤ Henry Spencer Duke
- ➤ John Harmon
- ➤ Anne Farwell
- ➤ Judge John Farwell
- ➤ Sterling Bentley

- ➢ Tyrone
- ➢ Gus Ruff
- ➢ Nelson Buckworthy
- ➢ Qing King So
- ➢ Tillman Merritt
- ➢ Bessie
- ➢ Talize Morningstar
- ➢ Victoria Donelson

All the other names in the story are real people who lived and were quoted accurately—except for their interactive commentaries with fictitious characters.

Introduction to Book I

By all outward appearances, I was given a successful life. I've had monetary fortune, a regarded professional career, a privileged social upbringing, and a loving family.

But what is apparent may not always be the truth. Secrets unveiled during or after a lifetime may alter the perceptions of success. A person can rise to the top; he or she is revered and held in the highest esteem. Later, a secret may reveal a truth, and the image can become tarnished and shamed. On the other hand, a person may have been discredited and ridiculed unfairly at some point, but if an unexpected secret unfolds, he or she could then be rightfully deemed worthy of adulation and respect.

So what truly defines a successful life? My success did not come from my wealth, position of authority, or ambition. Success was not outwardly acclaimed; it evolved as an ongoing journey of review within me. My experiences and relationships helped build a solid foundation of growth by continually searching, sharing, questioning, and remembering.

The *real* success I felt in my life materialized after I clearly understood the importance of soulful thought. Soulful, dynamic thought provides the compass for navigating the way through darkness, raging storms, and all treacherous pathways faced since birth—as well as days of sunshine and peace. Sometimes, acquiring soulful thought may demand a waiting period; one has to learn an appreciation of time and patience to bring that choice of thinking to fruition. I was reminded of a lucid definition of patience that was told to me: "Patience is loving the questions for which you don't have the answer yet." Still, during that critical interval, we need to actively participate—to do our part to reduce the confusion, the cynicism, and the errors—and elevate our hope for improved health, simple living, and a closer tie to earth and all its inhabitants.

In my individual circumstance, a secret that became known around my sixty-fourth birthday precipitated a very detailed review of my life and the influences that made me who I am. It was this review, this introspective examination, which prompted me to share my story with you, the reader, and to emphasize that nothing could have made my life more successful or meaningful.

This soul-searching endeavor reminded me of the entry written in the back cover of my grandfather's memoir:

Furthermore, my son, take heed … let us hear the conclusion of the matter … Be aligned with God and keep His commandments for this is the whole duty of man. For God shall bring every work into proper judgment, with every secret thing, whether it be good or whether it be evil. —Ecclesiastes 12:12–14 (paraphrased)

Maybe, in time, we can all consider the conclusion of any matter; by seeking soulful thought, we shall discover our true answers and give ourselves a sense of satisfaction for a life well lived.

My God! Why was Grandfather's secret so tardy to my ears? Why was it not spoken from his own lips? I was in a state of sadness, agitation, isolation, and shock as overwhelming feelings of betrayal preoccupied my thoughts. I had been wrestling with the revelation of his secret for a little over a month, as I was about to celebrate my sixty-fourth birthday and witness the births of my first two grandchildren within three weeks of each other. Rationally, I knew I needed time to allow more clarity to evolve, placing the secret in proper perspective. I had already been given objective insight and comfort from two special, trusted, and endearing friends whose support I had relied upon for countless occasions over the years. Even though I was told it was for my "protection," I allowed my insecure feelings of pride and a false understanding of a betrayal of trust to haunt my better judgment.

Fortunately, my thoughts drifted in a more pleasant direction while walking down Fifth Avenue in Manhattan, observing the decorated stores, Rockefeller Center skaters, the familiar bell of a Salvation Army worker, and the first snow flurries of the season.

It was exactly seven days before Christmas of 1965, a time of wonderful memories in my life, and I needed to snap out of this fog, if even for a few special moments, to remind myself of the blessings of the season.

The bells of Saint Patrick's Cathedral rang out gloriously, signaling the start of a new hour. I felt a temporary tranquility as my thoughts shifted to Henry Wadsworth Longfellow's "Christmas Bells." The poem had offered a beacon of light and hope amidst the gloom of senseless death and suffering in the winter of 1864 during the cruel Civil War:

I heard the bells on Christmas Day
Their old, familiar carols play,
And wild and sweet
The words repeat
Of peace on earth, good-will to men!
Then from each black, accursed mouth
The cannon thundered in the South,
And with the sound
The carols drowned
Of peace on earth, good-will to men!
And in despair I bowed my head;
"There is no peace on earth," I said:
"For hate is strong,
And mocks the song
Of peace on earth, good-will to men!"
Then pealed the bells more loud and deep:
"God is not dead; nor doth he sleep!
The Wrong shall fail,
The Right prevail
With peace on earth, good-will to men!"

I must have walked off the curb to cross the street when a taxicab's horn startled me, bringing me back from my reverie to the harshness of hurt feelings. Those laboring thoughts taunted me further while I tried to get home. I barely remembered going through Central Park, passing the Dakota building and my house on Seventy-Third Street. In my careless dismay, I accidentally knocked over the vendor selling chestnuts at the corner of Seventy-Fourth Street and Central Park West.

I was embarrassed and concerned about the poor fellow.

He looked up at me with a smile and said, "Oh, Dr. Waterbury. I didn't recognize you at first. Are you okay?"

I looked at this man curiously as I helped him to his feet and then smiled. "Yes, but what about you?"

"Oh, I'm fine. Doc, I have to thank you again for the medicine you gave me for my wife last year. You made her feel as good as new. Here, have some chestnuts to take home to your family. God bless you. Merry Christmas!"

This man was so gracious to me after I knocked him over. Frankly, I didn't remember him until he reminded me of the medicine.

As a matter of fact, I didn't remember anything along the way from Fifth Avenue to that corner of Seventy-Fourth Street and Central Park West. As time proceeded, my senses refocused, and I went back to Seventy-Third Street. While walking up the stairs, I looked next door, where Joel Spingarn and his family lived while I was growing up. They were such good people and great friends of my family.

As a child and through the years as a young man and adult, I understood the Spingarn family's sense of community responsibility. They gave their financial, personal, and emotional support graciously to promote human welfare. In their home, they were simple and genial, offering the wealthy and poor visitors equal hospitality and regard. They cherished the ideals of democracy and remained quite puzzled at how America could go forward if any contributing segment of its population were left behind; they embodied the true spirit of Christmas and Hanukkah.

I opened the door, and while walking in, I could hear little Sallie Ann crying. I took off my coat and was about to enter my library when I heard the bathwater running and my daughter Elizabeth speaking down the hallway. When I peeked around the door, she was giving little Charlotte a bath. Her eyes were open wide, and the peaceful expression on her face was sobering. I went to touch her dainty little hand; it reminded me how Grandfather used to hold mine so gently, as though he was stroking a treasured heirloom gem.

I left and returned to the library. As I slipped into my overstuffed chair, my thoughts were redirected to the secret hidden in my grandfather's memoirs. I had vivid memories of Grandfather writing in that old, yellow-paged journal when I was twelve years old and telling me that it contained "important information" that would be valuable to me when I became a grandfather. He said, quoting the poet John Burroughs, that "time does not become sacred to us until we have lived it." Now, in my sixty-fifth year, and still feeling somewhat betrayed, his words carried a prophetic meaning. The secret itself created an obvious omission to my identity, but after it was recently revealed, I thought I would have accepted it—even at the age of twelve.

The story in his writings was verified by the only living person who knew my grandparents and father intimately—my governess, trusted friend, ardent supporter, and guiding light, Soulange Micheaux, who at the age of eighty-four, was still spry and clear-minded. She explained why the secret was kept from me. She assured me that it had nothing to do with betrayal or lack of confidence in my ability to accept the truth. It was a practical decision for me to learn who I truly was by my own definition, and not by the judgment or misperceived opinion of others. I felt deep empathy for Grandfather's plight, but it took time for me to realize he was even more of a man to be idolized, respected, and emulated.

After reviewing what Soulange had said, I returned to my immediate thoughts, surrounded by the portraits of my grandfather, grandmother, and father on the walls, and the framed pictures of my close friends and extended family members on my desk. I reread his memoirs, trying to comprehend and appreciate the greater meaning of his life—his sacrifice, his tireless effort, and his pursuit of fulfilling his own mother's vision and dreams. I took Soulange's words to heart as I pondered the births of my two grandchildren. In time, they needed to know this great testimonial. Little Charlotte was born on my birthday, November 28, and little Sallie Ann was born on December 13.

I also reflected on the conversation I had with Hope Lightener two weeks ago. She has been my confidante, friend, and spiritual soul mate—a pillar of strength over the past twelve years. Her husband had recently died, and I had flown to Paris to provide support for her. While there, I spoke about Grandfather's secret as well. She had a much more settling understanding as to why its truths were not disclosed earlier. She suggested having the whole family and close friends over for Christmas and giving them Grandfather's family story as a gift for all. I held her recommendation in the back of my mind since I was still trying to sort through my emotional reaction. Both Soulange and Hope presented the circumstances and broader picture in understanding why I had to wait for this information. Surely, the story needed to be shared with my family and loved ones. I gazed once more on Grandfather's portrait, and it was as if he was smiling back, refocusing my thoughts. What did Christmas mean to us?

Christmas had always been a particularly important part of the winter season for us, not just a celebration of the Nativity of Jesus, but also the connective human feelings expressed in fellowship, family, and friendship through festive gatherings, places of worship, or friendly exchanges. I remembered learning about the customs, traditions, and celebrations of Christmases past at our family's Christmas festivities in 1912. I thought I should share those meaningful memories since they only reinforced why Hope's suggestion of reading my grandfather's memoirs would be appropriate for a Christmas gathering.

There is no definite account of the date of Jesus's birth, but Clement of Alexandria wrote about the religious feast of the Epiphany commemorating the arrival of the three wise men in Bethlehem in the company of Mary, Joseph, and baby Jesus. On the eve of the Epiphany, the twelfth night after Jesus's birth, the springs and rivers were blessed and water was drawn to be stored—"holy" water—and used throughout the year for baptisms or other ceremonial purifications. This feast of the three kings, considered a feast of baptism, was acknowledged on January 6. It was also called the Day of Lights, or *Natalis Invicti Solis* (the "birthday of the unconquered sun"). The Greek origin of the word epiphany is *epiphaneia*, meaning *manifestation* or *appearance*.

In the early part of the fourth century AD, the December 25 date became the "official" birthday of Jesus, paralleling the pagan festival Saturnalia in Rome around the end of the first century. This festival honored the god Saturn and the spring planting to come. There was no religious inference in these celebrations. The English derivation of Christmas was around AD 1000. The reference in Old English was Christes Maesse, meaning the Mass of Christ. It was later shortened to Christemass and then Christmas.

Throughout the first twelve centuries AD, Christmas was celebrated in the church with rigid, ceremonial rites and very little festivity. But in the

5

town of Greccho, Italy, an insightful Saint Francis of Assisi was given the opportunity to conduct midnight Mass with the pope, and he encouraged the townspeople to celebrate Christmas as a reenactment of the birth of Jesus, similar to the familiar Nativity scene, with singing carols of the glory of the birth. This joyous celebration of the "Creche" (French for the manger) would evolve in France as well, and permanently change the experience of Christmas.

The general themes of all the carols—derived from Germany, France, Austria, England, the Nordic countries, and America—are love, peace, and joy. The religious "purists" of the 1600s (the Puritans in England and America) denounced the carols, considering the music a distraction from God for the worshipper. Throughout this time, the Dutch, French, and German Episcopalians continued writing and singing carols at festive celebrations of Christmas.

In the mid-nineteenth century, England had great changes in the attitudes of both music and overall customs. German-born Prince Albert, new husband to Queen Victoria, brought his home tradition of a Christmas tree to Windsor Castle. Many favorite Christmas carols were written from 1818 through the 1850s.

American author Washington Irving, noted for his legendary *Sleepy Hollow*, wrote several essays supporting the ideas of Christmas after his visit to England during the late 1810s. Charles Dickens wrote his favorite classic *A Christmas Carol* in 1843, later becoming a theatrical play and winning great public acclaim. The Episcopalian minister, Clement Moore, wrote *A visit From Saint Nicholas* in 1822, featuring the Dutch "Sinta Klaes" (Saint Nicholas). The first greeting cards came from England, and Louis Prang perfected the art of a more detailed greeting card in Boston in 1873. With illustrations of Santa Claus from Thomas Nast, Frank Woolworth's commercial interest in decorations for the tree, electricity giving "light" to the ornaments, and more and more public interest in the spectacle of Christmas, the whole tradition evolved in the twentieth century to the current dazzling display of excitement and magic.

After remembering some of these highlights about Christmas past, I thought about two special considerations that my father and grandfather shared with me that same 1912 Christmas night.

The custom honoring the twelve days of Christmas, starting on December 25 and finishing the night of January 5 (the Eve of the Epiphany) had distinct significance. The twelve days symbolically represent the twelve months of the full year. The time spent and the active participation in the church and homes of families and friends offered an introspective review, reminding us what we could use throughout the year to sustain ourselves during the trials and tribulations as well as our serene and good times. The twelve days provided an active process to create a "storage supply," like the farmers did as they prepared for the lean months of winter so they wouldn't starve.

Those days also provided a time of reflection to consider the needs and circumstances of poorer, less fortunate people who are part of this life. Grandfather was emphatic when he said, "It is through their eyes and ears that we can see ourselves more clearly and listen to our hearts more openly. It is not the alms that we conveniently give to satisfy our conscience while addressing their needs. It is their plea for routine regard and their hope for comfort that remains unaddressed when we don't take that extra step to offer time and interest with direct involvement. We don't want to walk away from our given opportunities."

There have been individuals, even leaders of nations, who have embraced the plight of those less fortunate. Saint Vaclav, better known as Stephen Wenceslaus, Duke of Bohemia, was ruler from AD 925–929. In that short period of time, he provided his people with peace and compassion. The account recorded by one of his biographers stated:

> Prince Vaclav not only mastered letters, but he was perfected by faith. He rendered good unto all the poor, clothed the naked, fed the hungry, and received wayfarers. He defended widows, had mercy on people, the wanting and the wealthy, and served those who worked for God … he did as much as he could, all manner of good things in his life. [1]

He was assassinated by his evil younger brother who conspired with their mother and others. After his death, Vaclav was made a martyr and saint, and his influence was felt throughout his country because of the exemplary life he lived. A Czech holiday is celebrated on the second day of the twelve days of Christmas: the feast of Saint Stephen. His influence was so great that a carol was written in 1853, describing his good deeds.

The second point to share from that 1912 Christmas was a reading from Washington Irving's *Old Christmas*, which was written in 1820. The following lines from that introspective essay have been etched in my thoughts of Christmas since Grandfather recited them, and I take time each year to meditate on its comprehensive lessons:

> Christmas awakens the strongest and most heartfelt associations. There is a tone of solemn and sacred feeling that blends with our conviviality, and lifts the spirit to a state of hallowed and elevated enjoyment. The services of the church about this season are extremely tender and inspiring. They dwell on the beautiful story of the origin of our faith, and the pastoral scenes that accompanied its announcement. They gradually increase in fervor and pathos during the season of Advent, until they break forth in full jubilee on the morning that brought peace and good-will to men. I do not know a grander effect of music on the moral feelings than to hear the full choir and the pealing organ performing a Christmas anthem in a cathedral, and filling every part of the vast pile with triumphant harmony. It is a beautiful arrangement, also derived from days of yore, that this festival, which commemorates the announcement of the religion of peace and love, has been made the season for gathering together of family connections, and drawing closer again those bands of kindred hearts which the cares and pleasures and sorrows of the world are continually operating to cast loose; of calling back the children of a family who have launched forth in life, and wandered widely asunder, once more to assemble about the paternal hearth, that rallying-place of the affections, there to grow young and loving again among the endearing mementoes of childhood … But now, the world has become more worldly. There is

more of dissipation and less of enjoyment. Pleasure has expanded into a broader, but a shallower stream, and has forsaken many of those deep and quiet channels where it flowed sweetly through the calm bosom of domestic life. Society has acquired a more enlightened and elegant tone but it has lost many of its homebred feelings and its honest fireside delights ... Shorn as it is of its ancient and festive honors, Christmas is still a period of delightful excitement ... It is indeed the season of regenerated feeling—the season for kindling, not merely the fire of hospitality in the hall, but the genial flame of charity in the heart.[2]

Irving's use of the word *charity* was not the alms mentioned by Grandfather. He was referring to the unconditional love for our fellow man, being mindful of our blessing through the eyes and ears of the poor.

I thought about those insights from my father and grandfather and realized if we took a moment, whether you are a Christian, any other religion or even an atheist, we could appreciate and actively practice the message of the Christmas *spirit*, for anyone could then envision a "reservoir of water," offering a full supply of "remindings" to spread hope and regard throughout the year. During those twelve precious days, a transparent message, like the epiphany of Ebenezer Scrooge, could reveal the root of the spirit of Christmas. If others would embrace that choice, or at least think about it, maybe we could be a little happier, maybe more content with life.

All at once, I felt anchored in peace as I looked at Grandfather and the adjoining faces and thanked them for the gift. Hope did suggest that I have the family and close friends by at Christmas and share Grandfather's secret as a *gift* for all of them. What better time or place to discuss these memories and reveal his true identity? How could I further my grandfather and great grandmother Sallie Ann's living beliefs to emulate their regard for the next human being? I called Hope that night and told her the plan. She was very pleased, and at the same time, she was disappointed she could not be in New York to see everyone's face and hear their responses; she had to stay in Paris to finish all the legal matters regarding her husband's will.

The week went by quickly, and before I knew it, Christmas Eve was here. It was our special routine to go to the orphanage to hand out toys and clothes to the children and go to the shelter to serve food. It was particularly meaningful this year because I would soon be able to share this tradition with my grandchildren as my grandparents and father had done when I was a boy.

Christmas Day arrived, and as we enjoyed our splendid breakfast, we were drawn to the wonderful background music and captivating voice of Johnny Mathis singing Percy Faith's arrangement of "The Christmas Song." It was a fitting introduction for the gift that Grandfather's memoirs would bring to the entire family. We all moved into the library where the story would be told. Most of my remaining loved ones were here: Soulange, my dear friends Jasper and Minnie Hardy, Elizabeth, my son Hugo and his wife Pamela, and of course the two cherubs, Charlotte and Sallie Ann.

While sitting, truly reflective, with people who influenced, guided, and supported me through many of the difficult, painful challenges in my life, I wanted to find a way of honoring the women whose names were given to my new granddaughters and offer an understanding of why they played such an important part in the life of my grandfather. Grandfather would be most pleased if he was here to witness the continuity of his life goals.

I began by saying the memoirs provided an amazing, incredible, and at times, mystical journey of Grandfather and how he was directed by two extraordinary women: his aunt, whose insight and understanding of truth gave her a clear appreciation of grandfather's potential, and his mother, a simple, yet strong-willed woman of sound character and heightened spiritual freedom awareness, which guided her daily through the darkest conditions that she endured.

The first entry was dated in September 1864, when Grandfather had just arrived in New York from Baltimore.

Dear bittersweet memories, I am not who I appear to be, but I will be who I need to be until my final breath is released. I have a clear purpose and direction in my life. I have a mission that supersedes race, social order, or economic difference. I will offer no pretense, games, or illusions, but I will wear a mask. Unlike the typical ornate veil worn at a masquerade ball to conceal an obvious identity, mine will be colorless, custom fit—a permanent fixture to my heart and soul. I wear it and accomplish deeds that need to be done for the poor brethren and other downtrodden souls who suffer life's injustices and do not have the opportunity to live in harmony.

Today, my life has a new name and a new social identity, but its core remains vital and intact with old reliable glue—a lingering reminder in my conscience of who nourished my foundation and encouraged me to make this inevitable, critical transformation.

My name is Windsor Langford Waterbury, and I am a free man living in New York City, New York, with all the privileges and rights endowed by the Constitution of the United States to all white men who live on this soil. But I was born a slave, with the given name of Walter Lee Williams, to a proud and steadfast Negro mother, Sallie Ann Williams in Dallas County, Valdosta, Georgia. For the past two years, I have assumed July 1 as my date of birth; I had only heard my birth took place in the summer of 1844. We lived in the slave quarters on the plantation of Tavish McPhee, a wealthy, flint-hearted, despised, and nefarious master. He was also my father, and I loathe the fact that his blood will flow through the veins of my heirs.

I am a bit ahead of myself, and this is my first journal entry. I must say that my explicit recollection of events, quotations, and emotions from the time I left Valdosta in October 1861 to present were preserved on notes that I wrote continually since that time, and all the previous memories were too unforgettable. I am recalling these experiences more as a narrative memoir after giving time and thought with each entry to explain the circumstances and outcomes more clearly.

If I have the good fortune of settling down and raising a family, I want them to know these truths and to know I am not ashamed of revealing the truth to close members. No one else would believe it, and I know that no one outside would accept me as I am now.

With that clarification being made, I need to set the stage for that painful and haunting October night that is etched on my mind and heart with the same intense burn that I feel from the scar that has disfigured my left hand.

The life of a slave on the McPhee plantation is best described as a yoke around our necks, and a whip cracked upon our backs; there was endless hard labor using toughened hands, hands that sacrificed everything without a glimmer of reward. I read what one fugitive slave, Jermain Loguen, wrote: "No day ever dawns for the slave nor is it looked for. For the slave, it is all night-all night forever."

It seemed like our temporary relief was on Sunday mornings, and Christmas Day would never come soon enough. They were the only times we were able to share a particle of light and hope through the spirituals and Bible reading. I guess I should have considered myself fortunate that my mother and I worked at times in the house, caring for the needs of the rancid master himself, but that was a very difficult thing to do as I carried the painful knowledge that Tavish McPhee was my father. He had raped Momma repeatedly before and after I was born; when I was older, I had to listen to that animal attack my mother, and hearing her cries—her helpless cries all those long nights—I became more and more embittered.

By the time I was seventeen, I had grown to become a few inches taller than McPhee and quite strong from all my labors. Although we had somewhat similar facial features, thank goodness, I didn't have that cursed devil's red hair. I looked more like my mother, and many people said that I had her loving disposition. The workload varied from chore to chore, day to day. I fed and groomed all of the horses, plowed the fields, and repaired the farm tools, the fences, and any other woodwork in the house or on the property. I helped all the other slaves with the heaviest labor; I was called away from my own work to help many times.

It was 1861: times were changing. War was on, and McPhee began to worry incessantly. He drank more, he abused more, and became more of a tyrant as each day passed. He struck fear in all the slaves and threatened that he would kill us all first before he let us go free if that "nigger-lovin' Lincoln" put an end to slavery. This irrational behavior continued until an unexpected course of events happened in harvest time in the middle of October.

The moon was nearly full, and it was time to put out all the kerosene lamps. Not all of the fireplaces were glowing since the house was warm from the Indian summer days. It was quiet at first, but I was awakened when I heard the horses become restless out in the stable. As I approached the door, I could hear Momma saying, "No more. Please no more." It was a familiar sound. I heard McPhee say, "Still resisting my pleasures, you black bitch? I come in here to get what I want. How dare you tell me what I can and can't do? I own all of you darkies. You keep resisting me, and I'll put that bastard son of yours on the block tomorrow and make sure you never see him again." I was so numbed by the thought of being separated from Momma. God only knows what misery would prevail on the plantation— let alone what that devil would do to her. At that moment, he walked out of the barn with Momma and headed for the big house. I followed close behind without either of them seeing me. They went to his room, and suddenly, there were the forceful sounds of bedsprings squeaking. I could not let him harm my mother any more. I opened the door and saw him naked on top of her: drunk, violent, laughing hysterically, with both hands squeezing her breasts. I saw the look of terror in her reaching, helpless eyes. The kerosene lamp reflected off her almost lifeless, naked, middle-sized frame, revealing the many black-and-blue bruises she had endured. I looked at this huge wild bear, taunting its captive prey, salivating with fangs exposed, waiting to deliver a blow from his mighty claw.

There was a moment's pause before he realized I had entered the room. He glared at me with those cold slate eyes, and with a ruthless tone, he said, "Get outta here, you black bastard. How dare you enter this room?" Before he could say another word, anger flashed before my eyes. I ran toward him like a charging rhinoceros. My right fist squared off against his jaw, and while he was stunned, I dragged him off Momma as best as

I could. That drunken old man fought back, knocking me down with a swift kick to my shin.

Momma tried to separate us, but his violence escalated with a powerful backhanded blow that sent Momma to the floor. Her head struck the bedpost, and she was stunned. At that moment, every whipping and every drop of slave's blood that had been spilled at the hand of this crazed being rushed into my consciousness, giving me energy and purpose. I would never let him have another opportunity to raise his hand to anyone.

I glared at McPhee and wrestled him down onto the open floor. We rolled near the flames of a lit fireplace. He lifted one of the fire irons and attempted to brand me. Fortunately, it missed my face, his intended mark, but he did manage to burn the back of my left hand. I could feel no pain. Momma had tried to recover enough to help me, but she was struck on her hand by the poker as it flung from McPhee's grip.

I paused for a moment to look around the room. Everyone's facial expression showed wide eyes and anticipation as the drama unfolded. I returned to the reading; the adrenaline rush was eminent.

Now it was my turn. As McPhee fell to the floor, I attacked him fiercely as if I was a ravenous fox about to strike a helpless chicken. I grabbed his neck. I was relentless. The flames reflected a look of horror in his frightened eyes. He went limp, and then his eyes were empty. All movement stopped. Quiet returned once again.

I quickly recovered to check on Momma and saw her hand was burned and her head was still bleeding. I went to the closet to get a clean cloth to hold over her wounds and brought her a clean sheet to cover her body. I held her in my lap and cried out that McPhee was dead. The smell of burnt flesh filled my nostrils. I looked at Momma's hand and my own. We were a pair: we had suffered, but won't suffer any more.

She spoke softly, deliberately, and at times in a mere whisper. I can still hear her words in my head. I will paraphrase our conversation. "My son, I knew this day would come when we would be free from the menace, McPhee."

"But Momma," I interrupted. "I killed a white man. I killed a white man."

"Hush, child," Momma said. "You didn't do anything wrong. It was a blessing from God. You put a rabid dog to rest for his own sake. That man was born never to live. He is of no importance right now. Listen carefully, Walter. I have a lot to say. I thought about escaping with you and your Uncle Bennett's two children since he died. But they were so small, and there was no way they would keep quiet. Besides, the trip would have been too dangerous. But I had a dream this day would come, and we would all be free of that monster. I prayed to God daily for this day to come. Miss Charlotte and I have talked about escaping since that time."

A look of surprise came to my face with the mention of McPhee's wife.

Momma continued, "Yes, Miss Charlotte. She has always cared for us. She knew my big brother John lived in Baltimore, and it would be the place to reach." Momma paused, trying to clear her throat, and she reached out her burned hand to hold mine. "When you were born, Walter, I knew all my hopes and dreams of living with a family on a small farm with some animals and a free day to greet us in the morning would someday come true. I looked at you in the tub and as you lay peacefully in the water, and my thoughts went away from all the wrong, the tortures, and the injustice, and I clearly saw a precious jewel in the water. As you grew, I became more convinced that you would remain the shining light; even as the storm raged, you would still shine. You would have renewed strength with each test in life.

You were born with a caring soul. You have looked out for all the slaves here. Remember just last year when you and a few of the others were carrying supplies from the general store? You had loaded the wagon, and the overseer was paying the bill. You were joking and laughing when a white lady passed by and thought one of them had whistled at her. There was going to be trouble when the overseer returned. The lady didn't see you until you said, "No, ma'am. We wasn't whistlin' at you. We was imitating the sounds of the brown thrasher bird. We didn't mean no harm."

She responded, "Well, keep your nigger boys more quiet." You were so upset that you lied, but you saved them from severe punishment.

And this past summer, you saved Lizzy from certain rape after some of the Confederate soldiers came by the house and saw Lizzy cooking. McPhee was away, and one of the soldiers tried to force himself upon her. You saw the whole thing and interrupted him. You took one of McPhee's guns and told them to get off your property if they wanted to live. I was behind the door, listening to the whole conversation. You are colorless, like the diamond. No stranger can tell if you are white or Negro. You fooled those Confederate soldiers completely. You even fooled that white lady at the general store. Your blue-green eyes, light brown hair, and big frame will allow you to be who you need to be to follow your destiny."

Momma's voice was getting weaker and more muffled. I could barely hear her words.

"Promise me you'll try to live as a white man, and with Miss Charlotte's help, take your cousins safely to Baltimore and stay with Uncle John. You can take McPhee's suits and clothing and his carriage. He has some money somewhere in his room. I have a map showing the route to take."

"But, Momma, I won't go without you. Besides, I can't pretend to be a white man. That ain't very Christian-like. How could you ask such a thing?"

Momma continued, "Most of the time, we don't know why we are put on this earth to face so many struggles, so much pain. We just do enough to survive as long as possible, and then, we are forgotten. But the Lord made you this way by design. God sent you to me this way. He has a special duty for you. You are going to do great things for the Negro race. I had a vision that said you would go forward because of the way you looked, and you would go forward as a white man.

"You are one of God's messengers of hope, and therefore, a true beacon on this earth. You will not be able to achieve your task in the shackles of slavery. You have a passion to learn, a passion to help others less fortunate, and a passion to sacrifice."

Momma stopped for a moment and rubbed my hands against hers ever so gently and with such profound soothing.

"These hands were willing to sacrifice your life to protect mine, and mine were willing to protect your life as well. God's will gave us these hands to protect. God's will gave you a clear skin to protect you. Use these gifts and perform God's work."

I looked in Momma's eyes and saw the gray highlights turn blue; for that special moment, she smiled and radiated a glow that the older slaves told me she possessed on the Williams" plantation, the previous slave owner. "The Gullah told me you can do this and make a difference for many less fortunate people. God has spoken to me and said you will do great things. And your children and grandchildren will also do great things and their children too. Go to the bottom of my clothes box underneath my garments, and you will find my keepsake box. It has the Bible that Miss Charlotte's mother gave me, the little boy doll of corn husk that I made for you as a baby, the map showing you the way to Baltimore, and Uncle John's address on Stirling Street. Be strong, Walter, and fear not. Maintain faith; God will see you through and guide you on a colorless journey. Watch the girls on the trip; tell them I love them. And I love you, Walter. Keep the light of hope burning in your heart. I am always with you."

Her hand no longer moved, and I knew she was gone. She was so peaceful and so strong. Tears ran down my face as I ran my fingers through Momma's hair and smelled it; it had a fragrance of lilac. She was still smiling and glowing; her soul remained fragrant.

As I looked up from my reading, I noticed Elizabeth and my daughter-in-law, Pamela, were both in tears. They knew that Sallie Ann had convinced her son to do great things, and they both remarked about the prophecy that his children and grandchildren would also do great things and their children.

Elizabeth said, "Father, look what you have done and how you have fulfilled Sallie Ann's vision. This wonderful woman was our great-great-grandmother, and now we understand why great-grandfather was such an outstanding man."

Jasper, my dear friend, on a lighter note, said, "Water Pump, I always said you had some brother in you."

Minnie, his wife, stated with disgust, "Stop your lying, Jasper. You never said anything like that."

I continued with the reading.

So many things filled my head. I would bury Momma next to Uncle Bennett. I had to dispose of McPhee someplace. I had to awaken the girls, and I had to change clothes. What if someone caught me with the dead bodies? I looked up from Momma, and through the mirror above the fireplace, I gazed upon a silhouette of a wheelchair with Miss Charlotte sitting in it. My heart jumped, and the look of shock on her face put a quick end to any plans of escape. Her eyes were cold, glaring at McPhee's body. There was no one else I would have wanted to see, but she was the master's wife, and truthfully, my mother's half-sister. She remained silent for a few eternal moments; my heart was racing with anxiety and fear. Her somber voice drew my attention to her words.

"You don't know how many nights I heard the screams of your mother. I hated that man, and God forgive me, I am glad he's gone. He was the devil walking this earth."

She told me that I had lifted a burden off all the slaves and her as well. Then she applauded my bravery and my sacrifice. She saw me fighting and heard some of the conversation and some of the instructions that Momma had given me. "Whatever she told you to do, you must do. Follow her vision, and I will help you."

I was so overwhelmed by her unexpected response.

Miss Charlotte had always been kind and partial to me ever since I was a little boy. But she also had a strong attachment to Momma that went back many years. She had made it a point to tell me a detailed history of her family in one of our conversations while McPhee was away on business, just weeks before this unexpected confrontation.

She told me that her father was John Langford Williams, born in 1780 to a prominent southern family. After marriage, they had two daughters: Abigail, born in 1818, and Charlotte, in 1823. Her mother and Abigail would travel to England frequently, leaving Miss Charlotte on the plantation with her father. Miss Charlotte and her father were very close, and after Momma was born in 1828, they became close to her as well; they did have the same father. She taught Momma how to read the Bible and other books. Momma's oldest brother, John, had been freed by her father in 1839 and traveled to Baltimore to live.

She told me that her father was caring to all of his slaves and treated them as if they were part of his family. There was never any abuse or hunger. Everything was happy until one day in the summer of 1841. Mr. Williams was sitting on his porch, and he suddenly started choking, gagging, and turning blue. He dropped dead without any obvious cause. Momma and Miss Charlotte rushed by his side, but they were unable to help him. Sorrow surrounded the plantation, and Miss Charlotte had to make decisions she had never made before. Mrs. Williams had died five years earlier, and Abigail was married and living in England. Miss Charlotte could not run the plantation by herself for long.

One day, a visitor came to discuss the business of selling the plantation. Miss Charlotte refused to hear such a proposal. She knew the slaves would be sold by traders to unpredictable cruelty. She thought it would be better if she married a promising gentleman and kept the plantation intact. A smooth-talking suitor—Momma called him a "buzzard in a hummingbird's disguise"—kept calling on her with persistent and persuasive charm. Finally, Miss Charlotte, still grieving over her father's death, weakened to the point of accepting the marriage to the widowed Tavish McPhee. Momma couldn't see what Miss Charlotte saw in old McPhee and told her never to trust him. When Momma first met him, he was a relatively good-looking and well-mannered man, but she knew then, deep down within herself, that McPhee was a no-good, smooth-talking, crafty fox.

The marriage took place in 1843, and on that fateful day of their return from their honeymoon, the evil, ruthless, and inhumane treatment began like thunder cracking the air during a dreary rainstorm. The Williams" land was sold, and only some of the slaves were brought to his home in Valdosta, including Momma, Uncle Bennett, and the other "fit" slaves. They were unaccustomed to a whip; they had always worked hard, but now they were forced to harsh privations and overseers who treated them worse each day. Many of the slaves became ill and died, which made McPhee more hardened and more despised.

Momma had already told me how McPhee had been abusive to Miss Charlotte. Miss Charlotte became very despondent. One day, about five years after their marriage, Momma overheard her arguing with McPhee about the abusive treatment of the slaves. McPhee slapped Miss Charlotte and told her never to question his handling of "those stupid niggers." He told her that those lazy fools were here to pick his cotton and take care of his needs, and he didn't give a "God-damn" what Miss Charlotte thought he ought to do for us "critters."

Miss Charlotte was so upset, crying and shaken by this unreasonable beast. She went to the stable to ride her favorite horse just to get away, and then Momma described what unfortunately happened after that. Instead of her usual pathway, Miss Charlotte decided to jump over the property fence. The horse came over successfully, but it landed forcefully. Miss Charlotte was thrown off, and her lower back slammed against a jutted stone. At the age of twenty-five, Miss Charlotte became paralyzed.

McPhee blamed Miss Charlotte and had nothing to do with her after the accident. She was confined to a separate section of the house, and as far as he was concerned, she might as well have died from her injury. There was never a moment of peace on the Tavish McPhee plantation when he was there. Momma would take care of Miss Charlotte and was the only friend she had.

Miss Charlotte was the first white person to care about me and treat me as a human being. She would encourage her nephew to play with me when he visited, and she taught me how to read and write secretly when McPhee was away. Miss Charlotte's older sister, Miss Abigail, had a son, Windsor Waterbury, who was one year older than me. He and his mother came to see Miss Charlotte every summer, and I can remember all the fun I had when Miss Charlotte would read to us or tell us stories about growing up on the Williams" plantation with her sister and Momma.

Little Windsor was the second white person who regarded me as a person and a friend. I called him "Windy" and he called me "Walty." He said we were the "W brothers." We would pretend we were pirates looking for buried treasure, but we never did anything when McPhee was around.

We waited, and then Windy would say, "Let's have a good time."

When he left to return to England, I was so sad and would have to be patient until my secret "brother" returned the following summer. But tragedy struck in 1854 when he and his father were on a ship that capsized in the middle of a storm; there were no survivors. Miss Abigail came one final time to see Miss Charlotte. She was not the same woman; she barely spoke. From what Momma said, she died less than a year later, but she had spiritually and emotionally died after that awful storm had taken her family. I cried many nights longing to see my Windy.

As I looked in Miss Charlotte's eyes after telling me to listen to Momma's instructions, still thinking about Miss Charlotte's family, I felt as if she was talking to me like a family member rather than a slave on her husband's plantation. I told Miss Charlotte that Momma had instructed me to escape and live my life as a white man. She affirmed Momma's reasons.

"Your mother knew the truth of what was important to achieve in this lifetime, and she knew you would not be able to accomplish anything in the skin of a Negro. She understood what was given to you and how to use it for good." She looked at McPhee with a sense of disgrace. "Whatever feeling I had developed for Tavish died many years ago. You have freed both your mother and me. You have done what was necessary to do." She then proceeded to help me plan the proper escape.

We had to get the clothes, suits, and travel bag organized. I was told to wake up Zeke and Isaac, two slaves who Miss Charlotte felt could be trusted, to help bury Momma by Uncle Bennett, her brother, and to drag McPhee's body down by the river. She would tell everyone that McPhee went on a business trip to Richmond, Virginia, for ten days and would bring the slaves back to Valdosta on his return.

Miss Charlotte went over the papers I would carry throughout the trip. I was the son of the late Mrs. Windsor Waterbury and the nephew of Mrs. Tavish McPhee, visiting for a few weeks and now heading back to Baltimore. I would be traveling with two of McPhee's slaves to tend to my chores. She instructed me on how to answer a white man's questioning.

"These slaves will obey Mr. Waterbury. I understand the ways of a good Southern gentleman." She added that I would have to justify why I was not fighting as a Confederate soldier, and she told me to say, "I am not a fighting soldier due to a hunting accident, damaging my vision. I would be risky on the battlefield without my full sight. I squint regularly to see and have to wear glasses to see things far away. But I still wanted to enlist—the call to arms, defense of the women of the South, and ensure the integrity of the slave labor and pride of the Southern traditions, but my family knew I would be a potential liability."

Aunt Charlotte gave me McPhee's reading glasses to wear during the trip and told me to squint regularly. If anyone questioned her about any part of their well-intentioned "plot," she knew how to handle it.

Isaac went to the slave quarters to awaken Lucy and Sadie to come to the house to prepare for the trip. They brought two outfits that gave the appearance that they were boys; their hair was cut, and hats were placed on their heads. They were only eight and ten years old, and a great responsibility would be placed on them on this long sojourn. They would be called Luke and Sam, and they were instructed by Miss Charlotte to call me Mr. Waterbury and to say "Yes, sir" or "No, sir" and only answer to Mr. Waterbury. Miss Charlotte told them to start whistling or singing when they felt frightened; it would be a good signal for me to respond.

After burying Momma, Isaac and I placed the slave chains around McPhee's ankles, wrists, and chest, and we threw him in the deep part of the river where the alligators and water snakes could feast on him until he was a bony carcass going straight to hell.

I did everything we had to do and went to get cleaned, and after I had packed the carriage with food, supplies, a few of McPhee's guns, a whip, and all the clothes, I found Momma's keepsake box and went to Miss Charlotte to say good-bye.

Tears of memories gone by swelled in Miss Charlotte's eyes. She held my hand and left me with words and feelings that only Momma had expressed to me.

"You have a great promise to fulfill. I am certain it will not be deterred. You helped me many years ago without realizing it when you ran up to the house to get the medical care I needed after the accident, and you showed me much capability and caring for others, just like your mother. You questioned everything while we read poetry and books, and you were very attached to my nephew. He adored you and would have grown up to be a strong, fine gentleman like you. He always wanted to give you something special every time he left. So now, I can give it to you. You will no longer be Walter Williams. You will be Windsor Langford Waterbury, a name he would want you to carry with distinction and honor. You were like a son to me, as Windsor was. He loved you like a brother. You must promise me to carry Windsor's legacy of love and peace as well as your mother's dream."

What a gift to have bestowed upon me. Holding back my own tears, I asked if she would come with us and start a new life. She wished she could come; she would take us to New York City. She had been there when her father was still alive. But she realized her place was on the plantation. She needed to protect the slaves. The war was on, but she would not be afraid. Zeke and Isaac were her longtime slaves; she would arm them if the time came to defend her. She reminded me again to fulfill my destiny.

"You will be guided accordingly, Windsor. Use your common sense as your mother taught you to use."

Miss Charlotte reached down to give me the letter she had written on McPhee's stationary and handed me some extra gold coins. Then she opened another package containing her father's pocket watch, Windy's copy of *Uncle Tom's Cabin*, and a leather pouch of bright, flawless diamonds. She told me her father had bought these diamonds in 1815 from some desperate peddler on the streets in London. He told Mr. Williams that they were part of the crown necklace jewels that were smuggled out of Paris during the French Revolution in 1790. It cost Marie Antoinette her life, and he could have a part of history for a price. Mr. Williams didn't know to believe him or not, but the diamonds were blue-white, ranging in size from one to three carats, roughly the size of a pea to a small filbert nut. There were eight stones, and her father never had them appraised. He gave them to Miss Abigail as a wedding gift. After her husband and son's untimely deaths, she gave them to Miss Charlotte along with Windsor's personal books.

Miss Charlotte continued, "All these things would have eventually been given to Windsor. You are Windsor, and they belong to you. Your mother called you her diamond in the water. Please take this gift and remember both of us. Fulfill your mother's dream. Go in peace. God be with you. Stay strong and never abandon yourself."

I bent over to hug Miss Charlotte, and she sent me tearfully on my way.

As I left the big house, turning around one final time to see Miss Charlotte waving, I said a prayer to Momma. "You gave me a fearful task, Momma. But I have a job that has to be done, and I will not fail your wishes. I have two cousins who need to be safe from harm, and whatever I have to do, I will have to accept the challenge."

It was ten miles to the train station. With the war on, I would have to be more careful, especially getting on the train in a few hours. As Zeke and I followed the deserted roads with a full moon leading the way, the back of my left hand felt like it was on fire, even with the dressing Miss

Charlotte made for me, reminding me the days ahead were going to get worse before they got better.

We finally arrived at the station; Zeke waved good-bye and wished me good luck. He whispered, "God will watch you on your journey."

As I stared into the final hour of night, I gazed on his image floating peacefully back toward the plantation, but I had to go on. There was no turning around. My new identity would unfold shortly; would I have the strength and courage to make it last?

The first entry was complete, and I looked around at everyone's faces. They were intrigued and so amazed at Grandfather's bravery, resourcefulness, and his commitment to his mother, Miss Charlotte, and his two nieces—as well as Miss Charlotte's attentiveness and loving regard for Grandfather.

Memoir Entry 2
Remembrance from October 1864 Trip from Valdosta to Baltimore

That whole night of events leading to my departure with my two younger cousins seemed like a bad dream. I was numbed by Mother's death, frightened after killing McPhee, unexpectedly supported by Miss Charlotte, Zeke, and Isaac, and finally counseled to be someone I would never want to pretend to be. If I was still asleep, how would I deal with these thoughts when I awakened, still a slave on McPhee's plantation?

The wait to get the tickets for the two "slaves" and myself seemed endless, but I had to be patient and strong. I started thinking about Momma as a young woman. Some of the slaves who were brought from the Williams home told me that they wished I could have seen how beautiful and happy Momma was as a young lady. They said even Miss Charlotte appeared jealous at times. Momma had long, light brown hair tucked into a chignon and skin like the cream on the top of milk, smooth and silky. She had a radiant smile, and her eyes reflected the blue of the sky. She was so caring, organized, and helpful to all the slaves and to the Williams family that everyone thought she was running the plantation herself. When Momma spoke, you instinctively knew to listen. She was deeply spiritual, and her kindness and touch would make any circumstance tolerable. Momma took charge without being in charge.

I thought about Windsor and how I was entrusted to keep some of his personal possessions, in particular the copy of *Uncle Tom's Cabin*. Of all the books and poetry of Longfellow, Hawthorne, Emerson, Thoreau, and Melville, the literary piece that influenced me the most was *Uncle Tom's Cabin*. Although it was banned in the South, Miss Charlotte had it and read it to me from cover to cover when I was twelve years old—after Windsor came to visit for the last time. On the page opposite the frontispiece, the following words were inscribed:

> If I died tomorrow for a cause as noble as helping the Negro out of slavery, America's most hypocritical stain on its founding principles of democracy, and into freedom, I would know my fervor was not in vain.[3]

In the last chapter of the novel, the "concluding remarks" were particularly meaningful and penetrating:

> To you, generous, noble-minded men and women of the South … to you is her appeal. Have you not, in your own secret souls … felt that here are woes and evils in this accursed system, far beyond what are here shadowed or can be shadowed? And does not the slave system by denying the slave all legal right of testimony make every individual owner an irresponsible despot? … Both North and South have been guilty before God … The Union will be saved only by repentance, justice, and mercy or suffer the Wrath of Almighty God![4]

It was during these times with Miss Charlotte—those secret sessions to discuss ideas from those authors—that a passion for knowledge, an unquenchable thirst for more stirred in my conscience, and I will be grateful to Miss Charlotte for kindling that flame forever. I also thought Miss Charlotte was a "slave" with us. She wasn't whipped physically, but she was mentally.

The pain from the burn I received from McPhee shifted my thoughts back to that evil man. McPhee had acquired his wealth by the "great croppin' soil" in the cotton fields inherited from his former wife and Miss Charlotte's families, according to Momma. He was hated for his disposition most of his life.

Momma heard from one of the older field hands who remembered when McPhee was still a young man and how he used to come and check on the slaves in the field to make sure they were working hard all the time. He always came with his favorite dog, Black Jack.

One day in the hottest part of summer, the overseer had said there was a water break. McPhee went up to one of the slaves he resented most and told him that Jack, his dog, was thirsty and needed a drink from his cup.

The old field hand told Momma that the slave hesitated, and McPhee struck his hands with the butt of his rifle and apparently said, "You black baboon, if Jack can't get any of your water, you don't need it now either."

McPhee walked away as if his cruelty was a routine part of any given day. With his bright red hair, his cold-steel gray eyes, his mouth fixed in a frown, and his evil soul, the slaves had nicknamed him "the red serpent."

And how could I forget what happened to Uncle Bennett? He came to the plantation with Momma back in 1843. He was about to get his freedom on the Williams plantation, but Mr. Williams died before that happened. He was a hardworking man who had hated McPhee for as long as I could remember. And McPhee hated him also. Uncle Bennett was whipped mercilessly for not having a grin or a satisfied look on his face while he worked. He had two daughters, and when the youngest one was born in 1853, his wife lost a lot of blood and was weaker than she was with the first delivery.

Old McPhee couldn't care less and wanted her back out in the field within hours after the baby was born. When she went to the field, she started to work and passed out. McPhee was enraged and went out to the field to whip her himself.

Seeing her brutal treatment, Uncle Bennett picked up a shovel and charged at McPhee.

Within a split second, McPhee had pulled his revolver and shot Uncle Bennett between the eyes. That evening, there were two burials—for Uncle

Bennett and his wife. I felt numb and speechless for days. All I could think about was these pointless killings and sufferings by a madman from hell.

The railroad ticket office finally opened, and I purchased my ticket for Charleston, with a stop at Savannah. There was no questioning from the white-haired, slow-moving clerk. He wished me well on my trip, and I smiled and thanked him. Once I placed Sam and Luke in the colored car, I went to the front of the train and sat next to a window. A newspaper was left in the seat, and I perused it, occasionally looking out the window and finally seeing the steam of the locomotive engine. I realized the train was on its way.

As the train built up speed, I thought about some other things Miss Charlotte reviewed before I left. She had to teach me what to expect on the train as well as go over "appropriate" responses when questioned. I had to learn how to sign my newly acquired name in the registry at the customs house at Charleston, and I had to know the value of each of the gold and silver coins. She had added some fake gold coins that she told me to keep separate. She said, "If you need them, use them cautiously. If someone tries to rob your money, give them these coins. They will be fooled." We had to go over the train route and the steamer route to Virginia; farther north, I would have to wait and figure out how to advance. With the war in full force, the conductors and crewmen could be detoured or stopped by Southern or Northern troops.

"Be prepared for any situation. Use your head. Be alert. And never quarrel or disagree with anyone. Remember you are a white man living in a white world now. Don't look back. Look forward. You will be guided. Your mother will watch over you. Mind your own business, but when you are dragged into someone else's business, maintain your good sense and never show your fear—even when you are scared out of your mind. You have seen cruelty, and you will see and hear more from Southerners and Northerners alike. Very few will be sincere, but you will have to use your judgment wisely as to whom you can and cannot trust.

Miss Charlotte continued to offer her sage thoughts. "When my father died, I was very upset and unable to make good decisions on my own. Your mother put her arms around me and gave me the best advice, repeating it daily for several weeks, to get me through the sorrow. 'Charlotte, things last just as long as they should.' He was a good man, but he is in a better place now. He would want you to have an understanding thought about his departure. Be strong and carry his memory until you can join him to share it again. When you arrive in Baltimore, and I believe you will get there, mail this letter already addressed to me. I left the envelope open for you to read before you seal and send it. After the children are safe and settled with Uncle John, you are going to have to find a place to stay in the white section of town. Ask your uncle where to get a room. Visit your family discreetly; they will understand everything."

I will never forget her words of wisdom.

Miss Charlotte also gave me a letter to mail when I arrive in Richmond. It said that McPhee was there in his hotel, and while eating his dinner, he choked on a chicken bone, suffocated, and died. The body could not be sent back to Valdosta because of wartime activity. She placed McPhee's wallet and ring in the envelope with the letter. I would have to write a hotel name on the front side just before mailing it; hopefully I could inquire which hotel was reputable from a local resident.

The sway of the train and my exhaustion from the all-night ordeal put me to sleep until I heard the conductor call out loudly, "Tebeauville! Tebeauville, next stop!"

After opening my eyes, I was surprised to see a middle aged, well-dressed woman sitting next to me, staring at me with a scowl that warranted some explanation. The first thing I could think to say was "Good morning, ma'am."

She remained stern and replied, "What's a healthy young man like you doing in civilian clothes when you should be out supporting our boys on the battlefield for the cause? I saw you when you got on the train in Valdosta and wanted to talk to you sooner, but you fell asleep. I wasn't going to awaken you. So what do you have to say for yourself?"

I started to squint while she was speaking, and it obviously annoyed her more.

"What is wrong with your eyes, young man? Do you see something that I'm not seeing?"

"No, ma'am. I apologize for my squinting." I reached for my glasses and remembered the words that Miss Charlotte wrote on the letter. I told her I was in a hunting accident two years ago where the gunpowder exploded in my face and two pieces landed in my eyes. My eyes healed, but my vision was damaged. I went to sign up, but the Confederate recruitment officer told me that I would be too risky in battle without full sight. I still wanted to enlist to defend the women of the South.

Her face softened slightly, which meant she did not detect my true identity, but I still had to pay the price of listening to her harsh words and accepting her upper-class manners. There was a lesson to learn, and I was willing to take it.

Her name was Mrs. Caldwell, and she was originally from Charleston. She had graying hair up in two buns, piercing eyes that stared at me while she spoke, and tight thin lips that were engraved in a frown. She wore a very fine black wool dress and white gloves. She was married to a successful cotton plantation owner in Albany, Georgia, a market center for shipping cotton by steamers on the Flint River. She was a close friend of Mr. Nelson Tift, founder of the city.

She went on telling me she attended Madame Talvandes's French School for Young Ladies in Charleston, a very proper place to be educated. She felt she was, as idealized in Madame Talvandes's manual, "a woman who is defined by the man she married and the father who reared her to be a good Southern gentleman's wife."

By marriage, she was a distant cousin to Governor—and later Senator—John Calhoun, and she reveled in that association. She fondled the pearls wrapped around her neck as she shared with me that Calhoun was regarded as one of the five most respected senators in the nation's history. She asked if I was familiar with his speech in the Senate in 1837, and when I told her I wasn't, she insisted that I make it my business to find a copy to memorize. He foresaw this Civil War, and the North should have heeded his words. In discussing abolition, he said:

> As widely as this incendiary spirit has spread, unless it be speedily stopped, it will spread and work upwards till it brings the two great sections of the Union into deadly conflict … But let me not be understood as admitting, even by implication, that the existing relations between the two races in the slaveholding states is an evil—far otherwise, I hold it to be a good, a positive good, as it has thus far proved itself to be to both (races), and will

31

> continue to prove so if not disturbed by the fell spirit of
> abolition. I appeal to facts. Never before has the black race
> of Central Africa, from the dawn of history to the present
> day, attained a condition so civilized and so improved,
> not only physically, but morally and intellectually. I speak
> with full knowledge and a thorough examination of the
> subject, and for one see my way clearly.[5]

Without a pause, she continued to say why she was on the train in the first place. She was heading back home to Charleston to see her younger brother's family who was mourning the loss of their oldest son. He died of complications from wounds sustained in the Battle of Manassas in Virginia just a few weeks before. Her nephew had been under the command of General Thomas Jackson, nicknamed "Stonewall" because of his bravery and ability to hold the line. It was a victorious moment for the Confederacy, but her nephew was hit by enemy fire.

She told me her nephew was a courageous and honorable soldier. She blamed his death on Lincoln: "Who does he think he is to say we are wrong in maintaining slavery? If he had let us take care of our own affairs, there would be no need for war. Why should good white blood be shed on account of some niggers? Any slave would have no idea what to do with himself if he was free. He'd get in trouble and ruin everything we have spent years developing. If I ever saw a nigger try to think he was good enough to be white, I would look him in the eye, take my nephew's rifle and bayonet, and run it through his throat. And while he was dying, I would tell him, 'You wretched beast, who do you think you are, trying to be someone you were not born to be?' That is simple South Carolina ethics!"

I sat there, expressionless, holding back the shock that permeated my gut. This woman would no doubt do exactly what she claimed if the opportunity ever arose. The look coming from her eyes as she spoke would have frightened all the eggs out of the hens in the coop. I kept listening.

"And Mr. Calhoun, bless his departed soul, made it very clear when he said about the mixing of the races: 'The God of Nature, by the differences of color and physical constitution, has decreed against it.'"

Over the next long and tedious thirty minutes, she rambled on about how "dangerously unpredictable a nigger is," how all black people harbored contagious diseases, and how a Dr. Benjamin Rush, one of the original signers of the Declaration of Independence, had said that Negroes were black because the entire race had been afflicted with leprosy or "some other form of pollution." She bristled at the notion of Northern men or women criticizing the social order of the South. And then I had to hear about that "nigger-lovin" Harriet Beecher Stowe writing *Uncle Tom's Cabin*. "The book should be banished to Hell."

She changed the subject and asked me where I was going, and I told her back to Fredericksburg, Virginia. I dared not tell her I was going any further north. She asked if I had any interest in courting, and I told her no. She continued to ask what my parents did and what I was looking for in a woman since I was getting of age to think about these things. As the conductor was calling out the next train station, Satilla, she leaned over, patted my head, and said, "You are a nice young man, Windsor. You remind me of my nephew. I hope you live a good, long life."

I have no words to describe what I felt then. If she only knew the "wretched beast" she was complimenting.

As the new passengers boarded, I was impressed with a young gentleman in his twenties with blond hair and soft blue eyes. He had deep scars on his neck and both cheeks, which I later found out were from smallpox. He walked with a cane and had an obvious deformity in his left foot. As he was about to board, the conductor came off the train to personally assist him to his seat. He sat directly in front of me so I could only see the back of his head.

The gentleman said, "Thank you, John."

The conductor responded, "Is there anything else I can do for you, sir?"

"Not at this time."

The conductor went back to the front of the coach, and the passenger sat there quietly and unassuming.

The rest of the passengers came on board, and a portly man sat opposite Mrs. Caldwell. He was wearing a minister's collar and appeared to be in his forties. He spoke serenely, "Good afternoon. I'm Reverend F. W. White. Beautiful October day we're having, don't you agree?"

We all introduced ourselves, and Mrs. Caldwell took it upon herself to tell the reverend my circumstances—the hunting accident, that I wasn't married, and so on. After all the pleasantries were exchanged, the reverend told us that he was heading to Charleston to give a sermon to one of the city's largest congregations as a guest speaker. He and the regular minister were friends from growing up in Macon, where his current church was located. He told us his topic for the sermon was "showing mercy to the poor unfortunate souls of the community."

I inquired innocently, "Oh, are you talking about the slaves on the plantation?"

"Definitely not, young man," he said, showing an uneasiness and a sudden transformation in tone and facial expression. "I am talking about the poor white men and women who live in dilapidated homes and have little to no money to live. The slaves are under the jurisdiction of their masters."

He said that the Dred Scott decision was made in 1857 by the highest court in America. It laid down the law of the land. No black man would ever have a right that any upstanding white citizen would ever have to respect. The white man, including the poor and the uneducated white man, is "inherently superior and therefore, dutifully bound to be the Negro's master."

I was dumbfounded once again. "I didn't mean any disrespect, Reverend," I said.

He gave a historic commentary, saying that in 1844, the Baptist General Convention had told their members and congregations to come to their own conclusion on how to handle their slaves. More than three hundred delegates met in Augusta the following year to organize a separate Southern Baptist Convention, and he was a proud member of that group. He quoted Reverend Stringfellow from Virginia, who in 1856 said:

> Jesus Christ recognized this institution (of slavery) as one that was lawful among men. I affirm that Jesus Christ has not abolished slavery by a prohibitory command and he has introduced no new moral principle which can work its destruction.[6]

He went on quoting in the New Testament, giving specific references that *justified* the status of the slave. Ephesians 6:5 says, "Servants, be obedient to them that are your masters according to the flesh." Colossians 3:22 says, "Servants, obey in all things your masters according to the flesh." First Peter 2:18 says, "Servant, be subject to your masters with all fear, not only to the good and gentle, but also to the forward."

Senator James Henry Hammond, in his famous speech in the US Senate said:

> In all social systems, there must be a class to do the menial duties, to perform the drudgery of life. Its requisites are vigor, docility and fidelity. It constitutes the very mud-sill of society … Fortunately for the South we have found a race adapted to that purpose to her hand. Our slaves are black of another inferior race. The states we have placed them is an elevation. They are elevated from the condition that God first created them by being made our slaves.[7]

All during this time, Mrs. Caldwell kept interjecting, "Preach on, Reverend White. You know your Bible—and you know the ways of the South."

He never once offered to mention what he was going to say at the Charleston service, but somehow, I knew I wouldn't want to sit in the congregation and listen to this hypocrite's garble.

By the time we arrived in Walthourville, the train was getting more crowded. Another man in his late twenties with dark, unkempt hair and a harelip sat down opposite me. At first, he didn't appear very friendly, and no one offered greetings to him. Eventually, he opened his mouth and asked if any of us knew of any "niggers" that were in need of selling. He said his name was Andrew, and he was one of the overseers on the large, wealthy plantation of George Washington Walthour, son of the town's namesake. Mr. Walthour owned more than three hundred slaves picking cotton crop on a thousand acres of land. Mr. Walthour wanted some more slaves and sent Andrew to buy some in Savannah.

He talked freely and proudly of his harsh punishment of any slave who did not do his full day's job with a smile on his face. There was no second chance. If someone looked cross-eyed, he'd pull out his whip and let him feel the wrath of hard leather on his back. He just kept talking about how much all the slaves smelled.

"I can tell a nigger a mile away just by the disgusting odor coming from his skin. He can't help it. He don't know how to smell another way. And since the war started, there is always a nigger trying to escape every day. Who do they think they are? As long as there's cotton to pick, they have no place to be except in the field. If they were any other place, they'd try to be alone with a white woman and attack her like a wild beast." His speech was slurred by his harelip as well as the huge chunk of chewing tobacco that had yellowed his corroding, crooked teeth.

Soon, he turned his conversation to me. "Stranger, where are you going?"

I told him Fredericksburg, and he asked if I was traveling alone. I told him I was taking my two young slaves as well.

He perked right up. "Stranger, today is your lucky day. I'm in the right mood to offer you a good price for them niggers."

I told him I wasn't interested in selling, but he insisted. "Good money is worth more than those niggers will ever be. Reconsider my offer."

I repeated to him that I wasn't interested, and at that point, the blond gentleman who was sitting behind him turned around and said, "Who are you to come on this train and make demands of any of these passengers?"

Andrew was not very tolerant of that question. "This conversation ain't including you—so keep your mouth shut."

The blond gentleman was quite direct in his response. "No, sir. It will be you keeping his mouth shut. I'm not one of your slaves who you can order around. Besides, I'm tired of listening to your cruel and crude talk about those hardworking folks."

Andrew became redder and redder till it looked like his head was going to burst. "Boy, this train ain't fit for the likes of nigger-lovers like you. When the train stops, you better get off before you lose …"

By that time, the conversation had become so loud that the conductor had come back to investigate.

Andrew said, "It's a good thing you are here, Mr. Conductor. This boy thinks that slavery is a bad thing, and he should be dropped off this train at the next stop."

The conductor gave Andrew a firm look. "Do you know who you are talking to?"

Andrew, appearing more agitated, said, "Yes, a spineless critter that don't know when to keep his mouth out of other people's business."

The conductor replied "Well, for your information, Mr. Fulton will decide on letting you stay on this train or not. His father is the superintendent of the Savannah, Albany, and Gulf Railroad."

Andrew slowly sat down in his seat, steaming like a pot of fresh gumbo served at a Saturday night meal. He did not say a word for the remaining two hours to Savannah. Both the reverend and Mrs. Caldwell remained silent as well.

As we passed over the Altamaha River at Doctortown, I saw the Confederate troops securing the bridge. I realized this journey was going to be a rough one every step of the way. There was a war going on, but the battles were not confined to the fields.

I had an opportunity to think about all that I had learned in these first encounters after leaving Valdosta. First, I was accepted as a white man even though I had no prior experience talking to white adults like that before. Here were four different people, with different experiences and yet, three out of the four had very similar negative attitudes about race and slavery, and another saved me from further ridicule. This conversation was not going to end in either Savannah or Baltimore. It was a beginning—and a rough one at that.

When we arrived in Savannah, I went to see how Lucy and Sadie were doing. They told me no one had bothered them, and I was grateful. It was already after six in the evening, and we would stay in the waiting room at the train station and get tickets to the Savannah-Charleston Railroad departing early the next day. I found a place to get some food that was close to the station and came back and rested in an inconspicuous corner.

The following morning, the sounds of the other passengers and the workers aroused me. I went back to the same place to get some breakfast before our departure. As we were returning to the train station, and before I could go anywhere, Andrew and another man were standing in front of me, smiling. "Well, stranger. I see your two niggers are young, and they look pretty able. I didn't get a chance to make you an offer on the train on account of that mama's boy interfering with me. But I have your attention now, so I'll make it simple. I'm willing to give you ten pieces of silver for them."

I could see the frightened look on my cousins' faces, but I spoke without hesitation. "I told you on the train that I wasn't interested."

"Stranger, I see you are a sharp businessman, so I'm going to make the deal a little sweeter. I'm willing to give you twenty pieces of silver for them—ten pieces for each buck. That's a mighty good deal, if I say so myself."

At that point, I knew I was facing a man who wasn't going to accept no for an answer. I recalled the Pharisee high priests offering Judas thirty pieces of silver to betray Jesus. I said, "Now, don't get me wrong, because twenty pieces of silver is a good offer, but I'm not in the position to sell them. They belong to my uncle who will meet us in Fredericksburg on business, and he's expecting to bring them back to his plantation when he leaves."

Andrew said, "Stranger, you don't come through these parts and not take a good deal when it is offered. You just never know what can happen in the next turn."

I had my cousins grab a piece of luggage, and I went back into the waiting room.

The men departed, and I waited fifteen minutes or so before getting in line to purchase our tickets.

I had told Lucy and Sadie to alert me if anything or anyone was bothering them or causing trouble. We had a secret code; they would clap their hands three times quickly in a rhythmic manner three times in a row. If one couldn't do it, the other would try. As I was receiving our tickets, I heard the clapping code. As I looked around, I could see Andrew taking them toward the exit of the station.

I moved swiftly, hiding behind the other passengers as I moved closer. I kept my eyes steady on them every step. When I finally reached them, they were about to go outside where Andrew's associate was waiting. I said, "I don't recall telling you these slaves were for sale."

Andrew's associate opened his coat, letting me know he had a gun and wasn't afraid to use it.

Andrew looked at me, smiling slyly, spit a wad of tobacco juice by the edge of the street, and said, "I recall you being told you had a good deal—and you turned it down. Besides, I saw these two niggers just sitting in the station. They didn't appear to be going anyplace, so I thought it was my duty to take them to a safe, new home. We don't want any trouble, so you just get back on your train and keep going."

I had to think quickly, in terms that an ignorant poor white overseer might find personally beneficial. "Well, Andrew, I know I can't change your mind for me not taking your offer before, but I'm willing to make an offer to you that might make you and your friend some unexpected money."

"You have my ear, stranger."

I continued, "If you were going to give me twenty pieces of silver for the two of them, what if I told you I'd be willing to give you a piece of gold worth a hundred pieces of silver? Then, you can buy ten slaves for the price you were offering—and still keep your money."

Their eyes opened wide when I pulled out the gold that Aunt Charlotte told me I might use in an emergency situation.

"Stranger, if these darkies mean that much to you, you have a deal." As I gave them the gold, they released my cousins, and we walked away toward the Charleston train.

When I got them settled in their car, I went up front and took my seat. The train departed after fifteen minutes, and I breathed a sigh of relief. I didn't see Mrs. Caldwell or Reverend White in my car. Andrew and his buddy would get some disappointing news when they tried to exchange the fake gold for money. I had to stay on guard; Momma and Miss Charlotte were watching my back.

Once we got to Charleston, we boarded a steamer that took us to Wilmington, North Carolina. From there, we took the train through Weldon, North Carolina, and then Petersburg, Virginia, and on to Richmond.

About fifteen minutes into the trip between Petersburg and Richmond, the train was stopped by a troop of Confederate soldiers. They got word that the Union Army was sending a unit to the area, and they needed a civilian to help secretly operate their handcar so they could scout the Union's position. As the lieutenant was walking through the passenger cars, he spotted me and asked where I was going. When I told him Baltimore, he looked a little apprehensive. He asked if I was alone, and I told him I had two colored boys who were tending to my chores. He said he needed my help and inquired if I knew how to operate a handcar.

I told him I had no experience but was willing to do whatever I could "for the cause."

He replied, "Thank you, sir. And don't worry. Your niggers will be staying safe on the train."

The lieutenant sent for his sergeant who rode on the handcar with me and a few of his men. By the time we were prepared, the sun was setting. After we had been gone for thirty minutes, we stopped.

The sergeant said, "It's getting dark, and we won't be able to see anything. We might as well head back to the train."

I told him that the troops would have to have horses with them. If a horse got lost at night down on the plantation, they would be afraid of the nighthawks that were out looking for some mice or other small animals. The hawk made a scary sound in the trees. The horses would neigh loudly when they heard the sound. I told them that one of my slaves taught me how to make the sound of that hawk. Perhaps, we could alarm the horses to neigh. At least we could get some idea where the unit might be. If there were any horses around within a few miles, they would make noise and we would hear them.

I let out a loud, piercing sound that traveled in the evening air. All was quiet at first, but I repeated the sound a few times. The plan worked. The horses started neighing a few miles to the east.

One of the soldiers looked at me and said, "You say one of your good-for-nothin' niggers teach you to do that there noise?"

I replied, "Yes."

He said, "Well, I never heard of any nigger that did anything good."

I answered, "My colla'ds are loyal and hardworking."

"But that's what they supposed to do. They niggers, ain't they? Don't give them any credit for nothin'."

We placed a large piece of wood with a white X painted on it as a marker and returned to the train. The sergeant told the lieutenant the whole story, and they planned their surprise attack. We had to stay on the train all night; the Confederate soldiers would awaken before dawn, follow the tracks to the marker, and head east from there. The train would leave for Richmond in the morning after eight o'clock.

The lieutenant was so pleased that he had one of his soldiers accompany me to Richmond and make sure my "slaves" and I were safely on the train to Fredericksburg.

The soldier told me he was from the Richmond area.

I asked him where a good hotel was located, and he said the Ballard Hotel, at the corner of Franklin and Fourteenth Street. Mr. John Ballard was the proprietor.

When we arrived, I went to the post office and finished the letter that Miss Charlotte instructed me to return with McPhee's watch and wallet. I signed the letter with Mr. Ballard's name to validate McPhee's death there and printed his hotel name to make it look legitimate.

When I returned to the train station, the soldier who was watching my cousins told me that he would have to go back to his unit. He paused for a moment and said, "Your trip north of Fredericksburg is going to be a little more dangerous than you figured. There is no train that goes from Fredericksburg direct to Washington, DC since the war began. But I do know a way."

My heart sank below my knees; the escape was in vain. I paused for a moment. *Did he say he knew a way?*

He said, "There's a railroad line in Fredericksburg that heads northeast to Aquia, where boats are docked to carry passengers north up the Potomac River to Alexandria. Alexandria had been occupied by Union Army troops for a few years."

He couldn't cross over the Long Bridge to Washington with us, but he was given a paper from his lieutenant for me to travel to Baltimore with my two slaves to visit a dying uncle whose last request was to see his only living relative. It was the "right" thing to do to grant this young man permission to cross the enemy line.

After accompanying us to Aquia for the boat to Alexandria, he wished me well and a safe journey. As I was departing, he said, "The lieutenant felt he owed you a debt of gratitude for your help. I agreed. You sure set a fine example for a good Southern gentleman. But the way you handle your slaves, if I didn't know better, I would have thought you lived with them and knew what they were thinking."

I smiled and said, "I've learned a lot of things from a lot of people, and they all told me to just be myself."

He laughed and waved good-bye.

I went to my seat, believing we were going to make it.

They allowed me to cross into Washington, DC, and from there, we barely made it to the connecting train to Baltimore. Once we arrived, I was able to get a local deliveryman to take us to Stirling Street where I finally let out a quiet Hallelujah and knocked on Uncle John's door.

I arrived in Baltimore five days after leaving Valdosta. It was a big moment in my life. We were greeted by Uncle John and his family, singing freedom hymns. They were grateful we had made it. There was great joy in the family getting together for the first time. Uncle John was crying, feeling somewhat guilty about leaving the relatives behind with that cruel McPhee. He knew about the abuse through Momma and Miss Charlotte's correspondence.

That first night, I stayed at Uncle John's house and went over the plans as Miss Charlotte had discussed. Uncle John said there would be no problem getting me situated in the white section of town the next morning. I slept in a real bed for the first time in my life. I reviewed the long, dangerous trip and realized that we had made it safely. *We did it.* I took time to appreciate how happy Uncle John and his family were to see us. My new identity allowed me to change the lives of my two cousins. I was able to give them freedom because I was "white." I now understood why Momma and Miss Charlotte concurred that I would make a difference. *I did this—I won't let either of them down.*

Early the next morning, I remembered that I had another letter to send back to Miss Charlotte when I arrived in Baltimore. I opened and read it as tears swelled in my eyes:

> Dear Aunt Charlotte,
>
> I enjoyed my visit and wished I could have stayed longer to take care of you. But like my mother said, things last just as long as they should. Stay safe. Be courageous. Keep the memory until we can share it again.

I signed it: "Your nephew, Windsor Langford Waterbury."

Memoir Entry 3
Baltimore to New York, Christmas 1864

In Baltimore, I was able to get a job in spite of my apparent limited vision. I visited Uncle John often and had the pleasure of getting to know his son, John Bennett Nail. My identity remained effectively concealed; things continued to go well for me at the job.

I wanted to get further academic training, so I attended night school and was befriended by my teacher who was from New York. He spent more and more individual time with me; over the two and a half years, we had such an extraordinary experience of engaging discussions. I asked him so many questions, and he always had answers that precipitated another inquiry. Without realizing it, he was also helpful in guiding me to pronounce words with a northern intonation. He was an alumnus of Columbia College, and during our personal talks, he would take time to tell me about New York and his alma mater.

One day, he approached me and said I had great potential and needed to pursue a higher degree at Columbia. He would help me with a letter of recommendation.

I received my acceptance letter from Columbia last spring. I couldn't believe my good fortune. Miss Charlotte had always talked about the opportunities in New York and knew I should get there somehow. But to attend Columbia? That was a real prize. My teacher told me he would help me financially if I needed it. I appreciated his generous offer, but declined. I would find some job, go to school, and not let him down. He said, "You could not let anyone down. You are too focused on fulfilling your ambition." Had Momma whispered in his ear to help her son? I was convinced she remained by my side.

Before I made the trip to New York, I wanted to know the thinking of the city so I could prepare myself to face any unexpected, subtle mannerisms. I did not want my guard down for one moment. I knew where I stood in Georgia, but I was not sure in a big northern city. I quickly learned the bitter truth, and I was disgusted by it all.

Slavery was "officially" abolished in 1827 in New York. Over the ensuing years, raw cotton was the number one US commodity, averaging at least sixty percent of the nation's total exports. The South supplied almost 90 percent of the raw cotton utilized. The New York businessmen became the middlemen, distributing the "white gold" crop to the cloth-making mills in the Northeast as well as the manufacturers in France and Great Britain. The immense profits steered politics, journalism, and public opinion in favor of the South before, and during, the Civil War.

Before the war, the British manufacturers would export metal products and fine cloth, including silks and wools, and import the slave-picked cotton. Raw sugar became the other commodity of interest in the transatlantic trade. The sugar was grown in Louisiana, Cuba, and Haiti and arrived in New York for distribution to all states and Europe.

True to its economic interests, the Democratic Party ruled New York from 1832 to the current time. Lincoln received less than 35 percent of the popular vote in both the 1860 and 1864 elections.

New York's most important newspapers, the *Herald*, the *Courier*, and the *Enquirer* often supported the ways of Southern life. Even the former Mayor, Fernando Wood, was labeled as a "Northern man with Southern principles."

American publishing companies produced "suitable" images for wealthy New Yorkers—and their Southern white guests—of the happy slave and his benevolent master, supporting the institution of slavery as a "valuable" tradition. Currier and Ives, as well as other New York-based printing offices, regularly distributed these convincing impressions.

P. T. Barnum's American Museum had exhibits that depicted all nonwhite people as "non-people." One attraction showed Joice Heth, the alleged 161-year-old Negro nurse of George Washington. No Negroes were allowed admission to his museum. One New York merchant summed up the prevailing social customs in the city leading up to the Civil War:

> We are not such fools as not to know that slavery is a great evil, a great wrong. But a great portion of the property of the Southerners is invested under its sanction; and the business of the North, as well as the South, has become adjusted to it … We cannot afford to let slavery be overthrown … It is a matter of business necessity … our merchants have for sale on their shelves their principles together with their merchandise.[8]

The theaters and lecture halls held forums further promoting the public sentiment toward accepting the Negroes as inferior. There was also a great deal of local conflict about this issue that escalated during the Civil War. Throughout the war, New York supplied the most troops, money, ammunition, and food and lost the most soldiers of any state in the Union or Confederacy.

New York was an important and powerful influence on public thinking across the Union. By 1863, there was a serious need for more troops—and voluntary recruitment efforts were not meeting expectations. Congress passed the Conscription Act in March, and New York City was failing to meet its recruitment quotas. The act would force New York's poor white immigrants to enlist, threatening the small economic opportunities available to them but allowing the Negroes to take their places while away. The Emancipation Proclamation, issued in September 1862, also marked a transition in thought from the political struggle to restore the Union to a moral conflict to eliminate slavery.

The Irish reacted violently to the draft on Monday, July 13, 1863. Anger and resentment poured into the streets of Manhattan when thousands of rioters set the draft building on fire. Over the next four days, beatings, tortuous killings, lynchings, looting, and mass chaos erupted with minimal police protection. In the end, the well-to-do businesses and the Negroes suffered huge losses. The Brooks Brothers clothing store was burned, and the police superintendent was beaten mercilessly and dragged through the streets of the city. Even the president of Columbia College was approached at his own front door. The Colored Orphan Asylum on Fifth Avenue and Forty-Third Street had been a four-story facility to house more than two hundred children with food and supplies donated by the white community. When the mob approached the asylum, they broke in, stole all the bedding, clothing, and food, and set the building on fire, shouting, "Burn the nigger's nest!" The 233 children escaped to the local police precinct by the kindness of caregivers and other sympathetic bystanders.

When the riots finally ended, 120 people lay dead—mostly Negroes— and property damage exceeded two and a half million dollars. Many of the Negroes who resided in New York left, dropping their total number within the city below ten thousand.

Although the riots were physically over, the public's attitude in New York remained divided. This was a Northern city, home to much of the abolitionist movement. Horace Greeley and his New York *Tribune* wrote overt sentiment against slavery, and political cartoonist Thomas Nast with *Harper's Weekly* depicted the horrors and injustice of slavery. But there was living racism supporting the Southern codes and ideologies too.

The 1863 Draft Riot was itself a civil war, with an outcome of lawlessness, property destruction, uncivilized, bestial behavior, and human loss. No more than sixty-seven of the thousands of rioters received convictions, and all of them served minimal prison sentences. The prosecuting attorney as well as the presiding judge, both Tammany Hall Democrats, conducted what they called a "rigorous yet fair trial." If no retribution was delivered in New York, what would be tolerated in America at the end of this national "civil" war between the North and South?

I knew it was going to be a tremendous challenge every step of the way to maintain my composure and outward indifference. But I knew I would be guided, while at school—or when I finished—by some friend who would genuinely accept me and support my dream of fulfilling Momma's vision.

Memoir Entry 4
Meeting Elizabeth, Christmas 1866

Two years have gone by since my last entry, and I have adjusted to Columbia's rigorous schedule and learned how to face life in New York. I had been lonely—missing Momma, Miss Charlotte, and my relatives in Baltimore—until fate placed Elizabeth in front of me while going to class in the fall of 1866, my junior year.

I was walking through the Columbia campus one day to get to my next class when I noticed her handing out flyers, telling the people passing by about the Frederick Douglass rally to be held in town hall that following Saturday evening. I was impressed by her courage, and I thought she was a bit intrepid to be distributing flyers openly endorsing such a controversial national figure like Douglass when the Civil War had ended only eighteen months before. I continued to walk to my class, but she left a definite imprint on me.

To my good fortune, she was in the same spot the following day, handing out the flyers about the rally with the same zeal. I walked toward her and asked for a flyer and details about the meeting, and I was struck by her demeanor and confidence. She told me she was a student at Oberlin

College, majoring in French and Italian, and currently on a break to help her father.

While trying to tell her I wanted to see Mr. Douglass and inquire if I could see her again, a man suddenly walked up to us, interrupting and yelling that we had no business encouraging anybody to listen to some "no-good nigger."

Before I could think of an appropriate response, Elizabeth let him know there would be no need for a speech to waste anyone's time if the country addressed the inequality problem directly. Before the man had a chance to react, he looked up and saw my size and cold, angered stare and thought it best to go away. Misfortune followed him. While walking away disgusted, he slipped, dropping all his papers. The incident turned comical as we watched him desperately trying to retrieve each sheet while the wind kept blowing everything farther away.

Elizabeth and I chuckled, thinking it served him right. At that moment, I realized that a natural and inextinguishable fire existed in Elizabeth's heart. Before leaving, I made sure I knew her name—Elizabeth Adams Cameron—and I gave her mine.

The town hall meeting came, and I waited in the audience, hopeful to get a glimpse of Elizabeth. A very distinguished gentleman in a top hat and fine suit walked up to the front of the stage, thanking everyone who attended. He said his name was Archibald Cameron, and he introduced Mr. Douglass as a personal friend and social justice champion.

In the speech, Mr. Douglass repeated some of the highlights of a message he delivered to the Massachusetts Anti-Slavery Society at the close of the Civil War around the time of President Lincoln's assassination. I took careful notes to paraphrase the important points he delivered:

> What I ask for the Negro is not benevolence, not pity, not sympathy but simple justice. The American people have always been anxious to know what they shall do with us … I have but one answer … Do nothing with us. If the apples will not remain on the tree of their own strength … let them fall. And if a Negro cannot stand on his own legs, let him fall, also. All I ask is give him a chance to stand on his own legs! Let him alone. If you see him on his way to

school, let him alone, don't disturb him … If you see him
going to the ballot-box, let him alone, don't disturb him.
If the Negro cannot live by the line of eternal justice … it
will be his who made the Negro, and established that line
for his government. If you will only untie his hands, and
give him a chance, I think he will live. [9]

I was captured by Mr. Douglass's insightful wisdom and powerful words of
truth. I thought, *Just give those hands a chance to be untied and work—they
would then start clapping, living, and rejoicing.*

After the speech ended, I saw Elizabeth standing with a man who
appeared to be her father as well as the guest speaker. As I approached
them, she was kind enough to introduce me to both of them. She
remembered that I was studying history at Columbia, but her father was
neither impressed nor interested in listening. Before departing, I asked
Elizabeth if I could see her again.

While looking into my eyes, she told me "maybe," paused, and with a
memorable twinkle, added "hopefully." I was an excited man.

To my good fortune, Elizabeth was available. I helped her with other
rallies and engagements. I learned that she was the only child of Archibald
York Cameron, an extremely wealthy man in shipping and real estate. Mr.
Cameron claimed he was a distant cousin to Queen Victoria, and his wife
was a descendant of the Adams family of Massachusetts, who had two very
familiar members, the second and sixth presidents of the United States.

I was surprised to find out Mr. Cameron had been an abolitionist for
the past thirty years. Their home in Maine was only a few miles from one of
the Underground Railroad stations, and he served as a captain to help the
escaped slaves get to Canada before and during the Civil War. Elizabeth
shared his interest in working with various causes, including the Henry
Street Settlement and the Woman's Suffrage Movement.

Even with all his work and outside humanitarian activities, Mr.
Cameron's priority was his family. They were a close-knit group, and
Elizabeth was their pride and joy. He maintained suspicion and was
resistant to getting to know me. I realized I had no upper-class background
and no family in the North (except for Uncle John in Baltimore). I could
only say I had an aunt by marriage, Miss Charlotte McPhee, down on

the plantation in Valdosta, Georgia, when queried by Mr. Cameron. I found out later that he sent a private investigator to Valdosta to find "my supposed" aunt to verify my story, and it was confirmed.

Time passed, and I wondered if my interest in Elizabeth could ever manifest into a long-term relationship. Mr. Cameron knew I had no name or money. They had very strong family ties, and I had no direct ties since everyone else had "died" during the war down in Georgia. When Mr. Cameron asked why I left the South, I told him I thought I would have a better opportunity to get educated and find a job.

As intimidated as I was by all these apparent "differences," I was still impressed by all the genuine efforts his family had made with the Underground Railroad and their open support of the education and economic improvement of the less fortunate. I deeply wanted to share with this family in all their forthright humanitarian interests.

Memoir Entry 5
Getting Close to Elizabeth, Christmas 1869

I gathered the courage one day to tell Elizabeth the truth about my background. I told her about Momma's vision and what Miss Charlotte had done to help me escape. I told her about my adopted name, about the teacher in Baltimore who encouraged me to apply to Columbia, and about my overall fortune to meet her. It was as if Momma had brought her into my life to help guide me along the way.

When I finished, I looked into her sweet face—and she was crying. She held my scarred hand, rubbed it gently, and said, "Windy, I was attracted to you when we laughed at that miserable fellow chasing his papers and when I sensed your genuine interest in all these worthy social causes. The truths you just shared with me do not change any of my thoughts about you. If anything, I see more of the man I have come to admire. You sacrificed a great deal to get to this point in your life. You remain yourself, Windy. I know Father will come around at the right time."

Elizabeth's heart could not have been more gracious to accept me as I was. She was special—a gift from God to cherish and adore. Elizabeth gave me that nickname, "Windy," months after that fellow was chasing his papers, without realizing that I had called my cousin that name as a boy.

After two and a half long years, an unexpected course of events evolved that changed Mr. Cameron's mind. Elizabeth and her mother had traveled to Paris in the spring of 1869. Mr. Cameron had stayed in Maine and had sent his servants back to New York to prepare for the arrival of his family. He had arranged for me to come to Maine to help him chop wood and perform other tasks around the place.

One afternoon, when Mr. Cameron was returning from a walk, he started feeling sick and weak. He collapsed near the doorway to his home. I arrived later that day and found him on the ground, completely helpless. I carried Mr. Cameron into the house, nursed him, and cared for him over the next week. Mr. Cameron watched me give him care, staying up around the clock, attentive to all his needs. He told me I went "beyond the call of duty."

When Elizabeth and her mother arrived in New York, Mr. Cameron told them the whole incident and said he was grateful that he saw another side of me. He granted his blessing for Elizabeth and me to marry. I had the biggest diamond given to me by Miss Charlotte cut into diamond earrings, rings, a necklace, and hairpin for Elizabeth as her engagement gift. Mr. Cameron was very pleased, but he was most impressed when I told him the diamonds had not been appraised. He told me to never have them appraised; they would be more valuable without a "price." He had some diamonds that were never appraised, and he appreciated them the most.

We were married in September 1869 at the Trinity Church in Lower Manhattan. There could be no greater love that God could have given me on this earth. Elizabeth was influential in opening many doors and ideas for me. I gave her full credit for guiding me toward a greater understanding of what issues needed to be addressed and what realistic outcomes needed to be advocated. She introduced me to Felix Adler, founder of the Ethical Cultural School, Frederick Douglass, and Senator Charles Sumner. Let it be written in stone that Elizabeth is the rudder, the ballast, and the anchor.

I paused for a moment to look around the room, and everyone continued to be amazed by Grandfather's story.

Memoir Entry 6
News about my Baltimore relatives, 1872

It has been eleven years since my sojourn to Baltimore, and I needed to note their current endeavors. Although I did not stay under Uncle John's roof at night, I was spiritually close and never felt separated. He enrolled the girls in school, and both of them excelled in their studies. Lucy was accepted at Howard University and is working toward a degree in teaching, and Sadie is interested in nursing.

Sadie had demonstrated her passion in healing throughout our trip north. She was so concerned, and every moment we were alone, she would ask if my hand was all right, or if she could get something that would make it feel better. Her words were very comforting, and I knew I would be in competent hands if I needed her services after she finished her training.

Uncle John's son (Cousin John) and I were very close, and after I came to New York, he decided to move here as well. He was always good with business and finance, and after my marriage to Elizabeth, we bought an apartment building together, with the total cost around $60,000. Elizabeth and I lived on the third floor, and John came and visited us regularly.

Most people who met John did not realize he was a Negro; he was very light-skinned. He was able to continue making successful financial deals, but he never told anyone my secret—even after he got married and had a family of his own. None of them (Uncle John, Cousin John, Lucy, or Sadie) ever mentioned our ties because they all felt it was too risky to disclose. I have corresponded with Uncle John, and he and Cousin John have kept me posted on all their endeavors.

Chapter

8

Memoir Entry 7
Papa C's Guidance, Friendship, and Saddening Death, 1874

I have never felt a fatherly influence. McPhee was the most offensive creature on the planet, although I could not deny his hereditary attachment to me. Momma had instilled her spiritual wisdom and vision within me and set my course over these thirteen years. And I was gratefully supported and encouraged by my teacher in Baltimore and other professors at Columbia who helped keep me steady. But after Elizabeth and Frederick Douglass introduced me to Senator Charles Sumner, there was a bond—an unmistakable bond—that existed between us. He was the primary facilitator for bridging my growth from a youth to a fully matured man. He asked me to call him "Papa C," and I gladly did.

We had conversations about history, law, the Bible, philosophy, and other topics "to cultivate our minds." We spoke in depth about his burning passion to promote social justice, equality, and civil rights to all men. His speech on the "Equal Rights of All" stated:

> Show me a creature with lifted countenance looking to
> heaven, made in the image of God, and I show you a Man,

> who, of whatever country or race, whether darkened by
> equatorial sun or blanched by northern cold, is with you
> a child of the Heavenly Father, and equal with you in
> all the rights of Human Nature. You cannot deny these
> rights without impiety ... you cannot deny these rights
> without peril to the Republic ... What is Equality without
> Liberty? What is Liberty without Equality? One is the
> complement of the other ... They are the two lobes of
> the mighty lungs through which the people breathe the
> breath of life.[10]

After his election to the Senate in 1851, he began his outspoken campaign against slavery, much to the chagrin of his Southern constituents and some of his Northern counterparts in the Senate as well. But Sumner had two choices as a politician who felt he represented the public and the common good of his country. He could have become "famous" in the eyes of his colleagues and white scholars who would later write nineteenth-century American history with a delivery of compromise or be a ridiculed, disparaged, "perpetual burden to his political allies." Sumner chose the latter—the higher moral ground as a man of reason—sealing his fate to become known as an "idealist and a pedantic."

In Sumner's mind, a compromise would only appease the capricious whims of the time. He paid an enormous price for his unwavering sense of morality and good will; in a heated discussion with one of the irascible Southern senators from South Carolina, a defenseless Sumner was knocked unconscious by his heavy cane in the Senate chambers. He never fully recovered from his injury. Nevertheless, he remained true to his beliefs. He was more committed to reason and sustaining the value of enlightenment. "The true Grandeur of Humanity is in moral elevation, sustained, enlightened, and decorated by the intellect of man."

Charles Sumner was a man who understood his options well: deal or no deal. His reasoning concluded that there was no deal that would bring a true solution to the problems.

He told me several months before he died that he wished his fellow senators and other appointed government officials would reexamine their positions as responsible policymakers for their communities, states, and nation. "I have said enough on paper and in oration. I have tried to do the deed to match the word. I have not been as successful as I wanted to be. I wanted the Thirteenth Amendment to state, 'Everywhere within the limits of the United States and of each state or territory thereof, all persons are equal before the law, so that no person can hold another as slave.' But it is a fight worth fighting and a struggle worthy of your participation. You understand me. You'll accept the challenge as well. But it is ongoing, and the tide is not in our favor. Just keep your head above the roaring waters and navigate toward that lighthouse that has no extinguishable flame. There is no other journey that promotes you to higher ground. If you have any choice of ground to walk, why not walk on the safest, the surest, the most protected, and the most sacred? Windy, remember, we have to strive for and seek within ourselves, a hopeful understanding of the universal representation of our fellow man. But more clearly, we, as individuals, must be responsible and mindful while we work for the public and our individual good."

On his deathbed, I told him about my secret and Momma's vision. I had only shared that truth with Elizabeth and Uncle John Nail. He looked at me with his eyes wide open, appearing like two shining lights guiding my thoughts and said, "You, above those unfortunate, undisciplined beings that I have tried to persuade for these twenty-three long years, get the point. Your secret will sustain your mission. Your mother was a wise and strong woman. Elizabeth will stay by your side and assist you unhesitatingly. Go in peace–and let God pave your way."

"Papa C" died on March 11, and was laid in the US Capitol rotunda, the first senator to ever be so honored. Remembrances were held in the Senate chamber and the House of Representatives on March 13, and his body was brought via train to Boston where he laid in public view.

As Elizabeth and I attended the service at King's Chapel in Boston on March 16, we observed the emotions on the faces of tens of thousands of mourners. It reminded me that I, too, had sunken deeply in the mire of despair surrounding my own thoughts. I spent two frustrating and agonizing days trying to sort through my sorrow for this great statesman whose wisdom, insight, scholarship, and ideals would not be expressed from his mouth again. But during the service, I did feel somewhat uplifted as I heard and read several of the tributes given at the memorial:

What happy fortune, to close his mortal eyes on the crowning steps of justice to the cause his whole life has pursued.

The nation mourns. Today humanity mourns the world over ... God, in His infinite wisdom, has blotted out the brightest star of the American firmament ... But he has left behind him a noble heritage ... He possessed honesty of purpose and unquestioned spotless integrity, persistent and unfaltering devotion to the great principles of freedom and human rights which characterized and under laid all his actions ... When stricken down and felled to earth by the minions of slavery, uncomplainingly he bore upon his person the effects of the brutal assault which finally brought him to the grave; but within his soul faith and hope, and confidence in the righteousness of the cause which he had espoused sustained him through long years of bodily suffering.[11]

It is not to detract from the respect and gratitude due to President Lincoln that I emphasize the difference of their principles and note that one said, "Union with or without emancipation, but the Union at all events." The other said, "Salvation of the Union through justice to the slave." Let the memorial monuments say what they may, but it was more due to Senator Sumner than to President Lincoln that the Edict of Emancipation came at last: the fruit of his entreaties, of his undiscouraged, persistent will.[12]

Sumner's contribution as a voice of reason, not so much as an advocate of utopic principles, but more deeply about his uncompromising conscious awareness of responsibility for the common public good. I had read his speeches and talked to many people who knew him, but I was fortunate enough to have known this man personally, and over the seven years of friendship, our thoughts became more and more aligned, and he mentored me with the devoted love of a father.

He has passed on, but the tributes still reverberate within my mind. He was a big man in stature (six feet four) with a big cause. Even with his unquestionably committed efforts, the politics—the "pragmatic" way of handling issues—still prevailed and the pre-Civil war thinking prevailed. Sumner had given me a broad review of the general feelings and sentiment that surrounded the Civil War and the postwar years.

In the time leading to the war, the South maintained a strong inclination of state's rights over federal jurisdiction and felt "violated" that anyone could deny them the right to do whatever they wanted to do with their "property" and go wherever they chose to take it. And the North had its own stake in the matter. The Republican platform in 1860 clearly "denounced those threats of disunion as denying the vital principles of a free government and as an avowal of contemplated treason."

During the ensuing four years, the country witnessed all the destructive effects that Sumner stated with prescience about war, itself, back on July 4, 1845:

> War crushes, with a bloody heel, all beneficence, all happiness, all justice, all that is God-like in man. It sets at naught every principle of the Gospel. It silences all law, human as well as divine, except only the blasphemous code of its own, the Laws of War … War, like a poisonous tree … though watered by nectar and covered with roses, can only produce the fruit of death! As man is higher than the beasts of the field; as the angels are higher than man; as Christ is higher than Mars; as he that ruleth his spirit is higher than he that taketh a city, so are the victories of Peace higher than the victories of War.[13]

And the Civil War did crush our nation as such. Classmates at West Point who had taken an oath to serve and protect their country were divided in loyalty and abandoned their codes. Even when Robert E. Lee was approached by President Lincoln and the commanding general of the army Winfield Scott to take the top command of the Union Army, Lee resigned his commission. As a West Point graduate and superintendent of the Academy for three years, it seemed quite puzzling that he would resume a command and fight in this war against his previous comrades.

Aside from the waste and horrible suffering and death allegedly ignited, as I understand it, by Northern and Southern difference in handling the slave problem and the economic and social implications of "freedom" for the slave, the Civil War was far from civil, and the lessons in the aftermath of supposed "Reconstruction" were not embraced with equality in mind. The truth of the tragedy was witnessed and displayed on the battlefield and had to have crossed the eyes of each soldier as he sighed his last bloody breath, but was not examined on the floor of the Senate or House of Representatives, nor the White House of Andrew Johnson or the chambers of the Supreme Court. Amendments 13, 14, and 15 of the Constitution were passed with vague enough wording to interpret as the need suited.

Sumner understood the underlying imbalance of the written laws and their real day-to-day practice. He recognized the hypocrisy and the opportunistic rhetoric displayed on the Senate floor when they created the Fugitive Slave Act of 1850, the Supreme Court with the Dred Scott decision, and the White House itself with Andrew Johnson's ongoing veto of all equal rights bills. And yet, he pressed on, undaunted, fearless, and focused on an outcome that would maximize humanity and repair the deep wounds that were draining the blood out of this country. His visionary words fell on many deaf ears and closed minds—sadly, some of the most educated and intelligent men that America had produced. He did, however, leave his imprint on the country; his legacy will one day be appreciated by scholarly historians, and his good name will be uttered with the reverence it deserves.

Even the eulogy Sumner wrote on the assassination of President Lincoln was a testimony to his virtuous thought:

> In the universe of God there are no accidents. From the fall of a sparrow to the fall of an empire or the sweep of a planet, all is according to Divine Providence, where laws are everlasting. It was no accident which gave to his country the patriot we now honor. It was no accident which snatched this patriot so suddenly and so cruelly

from his sublime duties. The Lord giveth, and the Lord taketh away; blessed be the name of the Lord.[14]

My personal view of the Civil War is more philosophical than historical. The Civil War took away so many lives and etched permanent scars on those who lived; it polarized the country even further at a time it was supposed to be healing. It produced some of the most revolutionary and progressive thinking in our country during the late 1860s that was cast aside intentionally, and in many ways, it evolved into even more detrimental thought and deed against those who were not white. There was no justice and no retribution assigned to the secession states. Most of the former senators and congressmen retained their jobs. Even the president of the United States, Andrew Johnson from Tennessee, recommended quick pardoning and tolerated allowing matters to rest. The truth, that there would not be equality by law or manner, was blurred deliberately. I think back to what Momma told me when things didn't seem right: "God doesn't always have a straight answer readily at hand. You have to wait and hope for one, sooner than later. In the meantime, don't give up doing right. The truth of the matter will reveal itself in its own time."

Papa C frequently repeated a stanza from William Cullen Bryant's poem, "The Battlefield." He told me he thought about it nightly throughout the four years the war raged:

Truth though crushed to Earth, shall rise again
The eternal years of God are hers.
But Error, wounded, writhes in pain
And dies among his worshippers.[15]

I hear both voices now, Momma's and Papa C's, one a slave, the other an educated and distinguished white man, both aligned in wisdom and spirit. Both understood the humanity of man and set a steadfast example of how to conduct affairs. My devoted wife, Elizabeth, will remind me who to be at all times. God could not have been more beneficent to me. I will not disappoint Momma, Papa C, Elizabeth, or anyone else I know and love as long as my heart beats and my mind stays sound.

I have to also mention the influence of Thaddeus Stevens on Elizabeth and the Cameron family, on the passage of the thirteenth and fourteenth amendments to the Constitution, and the years following the war. Mr. Stevens had been a family friend for many years, and like Sumner, he was an outspoken voice in the House of Representatives during the 1860s. He was intolerant of inequality and unaccepting of the compromises that were given to him. Criticizing his fellow House members who opposed granting voting rights to the former slaves, he responded:

> The whole Copperhead party, pandering to the lowest prejudices of the ignorant, repeat the Cuckoo cry.
>
> This is a white man's Government ... What is implied by this? That one race of men are to have the exclusive right forever to rule this nation, and to exercise all acts of sovereignty, while all other races and nations and colors are to be their subjects, and have no voice in making the laws and choosing the rulers by whom they are to be governed. Wherein does this differ from slavery except in degree?[16]

After the Fourteenth Amendment was ratified, he still remained disappointed. He knew the language was made vague enough to ensure limited enforcement. He stated:

> I have fondly dreamed that when any fortunate chance could have broken up for a while the foundation of our institutions and released us from obligations the most tyrannical that man ever imposed in the name of freedom, that the intelligent, pure and just men of this Republic, true to their professions and their conscience, would have so remodeled all our institutions as to have freed them from every vestige of human oppression, of inequality of rights, of the recognized degradation of the poor, and the superior caste of the rich ... This bright dream has vanished "like a baseless fabric of a vision."[17]

Regrettably, he died just weeks after addressing the House to impeach President Andrew Johnson in the summer of 1868. Elizabeth and the Cameron family attended his funeral services. They had been dear friends fighting for the same cause. I had just become a part of the family when he became ill. Elizabeth spoke of him with the highest praise.

Memoir Entry 8
Our Two Sons, 1884

Our first son was born in 1870. He was a beautiful child, healthy and robust, and Elizabeth wanted him named after me, Windsor Langford Waterbury II. We called him Deuce. We were so grateful to God for bringing a new life and new hope in our lives. Thaddeus, born in 1872, was premature and very sickly during the first year of life; we weren't sure if he was going to survive during that time, but he did. His full name was a tribute to three important men in our lives: his godfather, Charles Sumner, Thaddeus Stevens, and his Uncle Bennett. His name is Thaddeus Charles Bennett Waterbury.

We could only hope that both of our boys would grow and aspire to be just men, honorable men, and exemplary leaders in their time as well. Elizabeth and I encouraged the boys to grow up never taking anything for granted and doing their best to help others with fewer privileges. The boys and I understood that Elizabeth knew how to make good decisions and she was designated the "queen" of the house. To create a personal name, Deuce, at the age of four, thought it appropriate to call her Mumsie; it still had a regal resonance to it. We all called her Mumsie afterward.

We became involved in the Ethical Cultural School and Society through Mumsie's personal ties to their founder, Felix Adler. Dr. Adler had studied at Columbia, and after completing a PhD at the University of Heidelberg, he returned to New York and created the society in 1876. The school followed in 1880, originally called the Workingmen's School, and both Deuce and Thaddeus were enrolled.

The Society for Ethical Culture was a nonsectarian group, emphasizing the importance of moral training—in addition to academic excellence—and reaching out to embrace all races and religions to represent a universal philosophy of practical concern. Dr. Adler was also involved in many reform movements, including the abolition of child labor and advocacy for model tenement buildings. Mumsie and I gave financial and personal support to Dr. Adler, and recently, I became a history teacher in the upper school.

The environment at home and school was ideal for the two growing boys, but Deuce was the only one who consistently accepted the principles shown by us and the Ethical School.

Mumsie and I queried over Thaddeus many times during his childhood, and young adulthood; he was like no one we would ever imagine growing up under our influence. It seems strange that he was named after those three great gentlemen. Deuce had achieved academic excellence, demonstrated athletic prowess in fencing and football, played the violin masterfully, and understood and supported our efforts to bring social, economic, political, and educational justice to this country. Thaddeus, on the other hand, outright defied the family's beliefs. These memories stir great anguish and disappointment in me as I write them.

As a boy, he displayed open resentment to attending the Ethical Cultural School. I had to come to his class one day because Thaddeus did not like the Jews, Negroes, or Chinese, and he boldly told them to go home to their own kind. He was asked to leave the school, much to our chagrin. Instead, he wanted to go to school in England where he could be with the "elite" and well to do in the world. He spent the next eight years in school at Eton, and when he came home every year, he would brag about some invitation he had received to ride horses with one of Queen Victoria's relatives, or go pheasant hunting with the younger brothers of members of the Bullingdon Club. He came home wearing his school cape and expected all the servants to bow to him. What was even more disturbing was that his limited capabilities gave him no justification to assume arrogance. He was a mediocre student, had no athleticism, had no musical talent, and had no interest other than to be rich and appear "better" than the next person. He was, however, a very cunning youngster and felt he could outwit any of us.

One day, Mumsie and I had to go to the hospital to see a friend unexpectedly and left both of the boys at home. I knew we were having a delivery around the time of our return. I left ten dollars in cash on the dining room table so it would be ready to give to the deliveryman. When we returned, the man came, and when I went to get the money, it was gone. I looked for some additional cash, paid the man, and wondered what happened.

I spoke to Deuce, and he looked puzzled and said he didn't know anything about it, but when I approached Thaddeus, he was incensed. "How should I know where your money is? Are you sure you left it there? Don't go accusing me of taking it!" He left abruptly. I knew he couldn't be trusted; it was too easy for him to lie to my face. When I told Mumsie, she just looked at me and did not appear surprised.

Another thought about Thaddeus had to be considered. Deuce quietly discussed several things that Thaddeus had done that I never knew. He would take his towel and snap it to hear the sound. Deuce warned him it was dangerous, and Thaddeus said to mind his own business. A few minutes later, Deuce heard the sound of shattered glass. When Deuce asked him about it, he claimed he heard it, too, but "couldn't figure out" what happened; it was one of Mumsie's crystal glasses.

When they walked through the park, he would go out of his way to kick a stray cat or dog or step on its tail and start laughing. He would throw rocks at the squirrels or the peaceful ducks swimming on the pond. Deuce was so outraged that he wanted to pick up Thaddeus and hold his head under the water in the pond.

Deuce asked me, probing for an answer. "What can be done to punish him, Father? He needs to learn a lesson."

I replied, "Mumsie and I have tried to restrict his allowance, even though he would cry and act remorseful; we knew he was not. We tried to punish him physically, tried to wash his mouth with soap or quinine. Nothing has helped; he acts as if he has done nothing wrong. He is never culpable and never responsible, except when the talk concerns acquiring money, and then he is focused on what he needs to do to make another dollar. He is obsessed with money, and we can't convince him that it is better to give than to receive. He would say we were losers to give and winners to receive. Mumsie, you, and I don't like the way Thaddeus is, but we cannot change that personality. He is his own decision maker. We have to wish him well and tolerate his peculiarities. Maybe, someday, he will put it all together before it is too late.

10

Memoir Entry 9
My Friend, Herbert Horace Huntington, 1891

I had been teaching at the Ethical School, and within a few years, I was selected to the nominating committee for all newly hired faculty. In the spring of 1886, a very distinguished gentleman applied for a position in the upper division. From the outset, he displayed a unique presence, not just on a physical level, but remarkably, that keen mind that I learned to appreciate more and more as the years went by.

Dr. Huntington was a man of medium stature, but everything about him was tailored and precise. From his white forelock always angled to the left side of his head to his well-groomed beard, custom-made suits, and perfectly polished shoes, he was a man you could not ever forget. He had been an assistant professor of classics at Yale and then took some time to look for a job all over the United States as well as Europe. He spoke fluent Latin and Greek, and he had taught philosophy and history as well.

Trying to be facetious, I inquired of Dr. Huntington, "Oh, I see you have qualifications to teach history as well as your classics background. Should I be worried that you might be capable of replacing me?"

He looked at me with a slight tilt to his head and quite calmly replied, "I have done a thorough investigation of you and your associates, and unless you plan to withhold the adroit capabilities you have demonstrated to your students since your original appointment and have maintained in your job thus far, I wouldn't have an inkling of a chance."

I got the response that made me want to know this man more.

After his unanimous acceptance, we became friends and found we had much in common. Our interests in history, music, nature, philosophy, the Bible, literature, and teaching were at the same time passionate and freely shared. He would regularly weave a Greek myth or classical thinker into our conversation.

One day, I interjected that he really knew himself.

He said that he always tried to live by the Roman poet Juvenal's advice from his "Eleventh Satire": "From the heavens descends 'know thyself.' It should be fixed upon the mind and wielded by the memory."

I continue to be in awe of his powerful gift of thought.

By 1891, he was a frequent visitor to our home and was well acquainted with the humanitarian efforts of both Mumsie and me. He also knew what a powerful influence my mother had on me and that her spiritual guidance was still infused in my daily living. He was astute to notice the scar on my left hand, but he never asked me how it got there.

One afternoon, we were enjoying tea, and a discussion arose on the higher educational opportunities denied to people of color. As the conversation lengthened, he kept reminding me of the grave injustice.

I snapped, slammed my fisted left hand on the end table, and said, "It has torn me in ways you would not understand."

Herbert looked at the back of my left hand, looked deep into my eyes, and with his usual quick wit, responded with two stories revealing the incompetency of man's decision-making when authority and arrogance blind the most practical decision to be made.

Frederick the Great, patron of the arts and tactical genius of warfare, had a sophomoric approach to some of his decisions. He possessed a grove of beautiful cherry trees, and the story goes that, after seeing some of the local birds eating his prized fruit, he ordered all of those birds nesting within the Prussian borders to be killed. The following spring, no cherries blossomed on any of the trees. It became clear that the birds did not eat the nascent cherries themselves, but instead would eat the insects that were eating the fruit. The farmers also lost many of their crops to the uncontrolled insect infestation.

Shakespeare also points out the carelessness of man's authority in *Measure for Measure*. Vienna's acting administrator, Angelo, has rekindled the enforcement of laws that had been ignored for quite some time, with one particular law condemning adulterers to death. Isabella, an apprentice at the local convent, comes to Angelo to beg for her brother's pardon. He is condemned to die for his promiscuous ways. Angelo coldly refuses to change his egregious decision even as Isabella points out the obvious flaws in his fantasies of absolute power:

> Could great men thunder,
> as Jove himself does, Jove would ne'er be quiet,
> For every pelting petty officer
> would use his heaven for thunder,
> Nothing but thunder. Merciful Heaven,
> thou rather with thy sharp and sulphurous bolt,
> Split'st the unwedgeable and gnarled oak
> than the soft myrtle: but man,
> proud man, Drest in a little brief authority,
> Most ignorant of what he is most assured,
> His glassy essence, like an angry ape,
> Plays such fantastic tricks before high heaven
> As makes the angels weep; who with our spleens,
> Would all themselves laugh mortal.
> Man, with all his pride, and temporary power, makes decisions irrationally, conveniently forgetting the fragile qualities of his own mortality, enough to make the angels and God Himself weep.[18]

Herbert continued, "Thank God there are men like you who see the need to know yourself and do as much as one can to make a positive impact on a world surrounded by errors and illusions of grandeur. But you, my friend, took a higher road and have been able to accomplish more, much more. God gave you an invisible shield. Keep the faith, keep the shield held high, and keep your dreams close at heart. You have my complete admiration and devotion; I will never let you down."

I was taken aback by his remarks. I couldn't tell if I should thank him or question what he meant by his statement.

He left, and I thought he knew my secret. How did he see it? I had been so careful, so clearly cautious, in my display to everyone. What did he see? What if he told someone else? I went to Mumsie, and she quickly assured me that she felt he was too good a person to dismantle our work.

The following day, I went to Herbert in private, quite pensive, and he recognized my troubled mien. I asked, "How did you unveil my secret?"

Herbert was his usual analytical self and said that I possessed an experience and an aura, something more than any white man, scholar, or dullard that he had ever met.

He had traveled to several islands in the South Pacific as well as South America. He found the people vibrant, happy, considerate, helpful, and inquisitive. They were called "natives," primitives, and wild beings, but they were more hospitable and genuinely civilized than any written commentary ever stated. Then prior to his appointment at the Ethical Cultural School, he went down South on a tour of the Negro preparatory schools in Augusta, Savannah, and Atlanta, Georgia, as well as Nashville's Roger Williams University. The students were bright, articulate, and willing to meet the academic standards of higher learning. He was introduced to several of the communities' prominent Negro families at an annual church bazaar who appeared quite fair and displayed aristocratic graces and mannerisms that could equal or better any of his Yale colleagues in their faculty club. But even with the possibility of passing for white, with many of these families having the blondest hair and bluest eyes, it amazed him that they had no desire to pretend to be white.

He said, "You, on the other hand, chose a different road to walk. You have chosen to be a man who would sacrifice his personal comfort and gain to help so many in need but do it as a 'white' man, knowing you would have more opportunities given to accomplish your deeds and further the advancement of those less privileged. You could have done so much as an active educator amongst the socially elite families of color in Augusta, Raleigh, Washington, or even New York City, but you knew there would be too many trivial roadblocks to scale.

"I knew you were a distinct human being the moment I met you during our interview. You seek open thought, you know yourself, and you know what it takes to leave a positive imprint on your fellow man—no matter what station he or she has been assigned. All of mankind fits into your understanding of the equation of life. That insight can only be drawn from an inner awareness that God gave you to use. You were also given two strong women to guide you: your mother and dear Elizabeth. They have nurtured you into a true man, a thinking man, a caring man, and a spiritual man.

"But I did not have any recognition of your identity until last evening when the fire in your heart burned so brightly while discussing the lack of educational opportunities and you told me, 'It has torn me in ways you would not understand.' I then looked at the scar on your hand and at your face and realized you had suffered."

I became very emotional; tears suffused onto my cheeks and into my handkerchief as I told him about the night Momma died and the promise I made to her, Miss Charlotte's support, and the unforgettable journey North with my two cousins. I told him that Uncle John and his son, my two cousins, Miss Charlotte, and Elizabeth were the only other people who knew my secret. I was going to tell my two sons but no one else.

Herbert held my left hand, and with a tear in his eye, he said, "Your secret is safe with me; I swear on your mother's spirit. Most of God's work remains a mystery to all of humanity. We will keep this conversation between you, me, your mother, and Him."

The conclusion of this whole experience reminds me of the final three verses of the last chapter in Ecclesiastes: "Furthermore, my son, take heed … let us hear the conclusion of the matter … Be aligned with God and keep his commandments for this is the whole duty of man. For God shall bring every work into proper judgment, with every secret thing, whether it be good or whether it be evil."

I hugged Herbert and told him that I could not want a finer brother, a finer friend, or a finer human being in my life. "God was kind in giving me Momma and Miss Charlotte, and then my relatives in Baltimore, Elizabeth and her family, and now you. You told me two great stories yesterday. I was not focused to appreciate them. Would you repeat them for me?"

Herbert smiled, "Yes, and I'll even restate the remarks I made about you afterward."

Our friendship would grow, and his presence would continue to inspire me. "For God shall bring every work into proper judgment, with every secret thing, whether it be good or whether it be evil." Those words would recapitulate Momma's vision and instill hope in me.

I put the journal down for a moment and spoke to everyone. "Words cannot do justice to describe the wondrous impact that Uncle Herbert had on my grandfather, my father, and me. His mind soared to Parnassus daily, and he was infused with the intellectual capability to place so many thoughts into proper perspective."

Memoir Entry 10
The Regrettable Evolution of Thaddeus, 1894

I began reading again.

And now, I must come back to the painful reality of Thaddeus. We were hosting a party in June 1886 to discuss ways in which the Ethical Cultural Society could help Negroes gain opportunities to get further education. The guests included Frederick Douglass, Fanny Garrison, Alexander Crummell, Henry Villard, John B. Nail, and the founder of the school, Jacob Adler.

Deuce was sixteen, and Thaddeus was fourteen. Right in the middle of our discussion at the dinner table, Thaddeus stood up, threw down his napkin, and shouted, "I'm sick of this nigger-loving family. Have all of you lost your minds? All this talk about making a nigger equal to me is sickening. And sitting at this table with all these niggers and a Jew isn't right, either. I'm leaving."

I thought I was going to beat that boy into the ground until I couldn't see his head anymore. We apologized for his rudeness and continued our discussion.

Deuce was irate with Thaddeus for his disrespect to the family and followed him upstairs.

Before Thaddeus could lock his door, Deuce lifted him up.

Thaddeus screamed, "Don't drop me out my window. Are you crazy?"

After graduating from Eton, he went to college at Vanderbilt University in Nashville, Tennessee, where he became more embittered and felt more entitled. He relished in the Southern segregated life. Each conversation, each disrespecting word, and each disregarding act would plant grave doubt about Thaddeus ever learning his lesson. He was so distinct from all the rest of us; I had not considered that he was the only one with a full head of red hair.

But nothing that Thaddeus had done was more emotionally devastating than his response when I revealed my true identity to him. When I told Deuce, he was surprised, and yet very supportive, very understanding. He took my scarred left hand, placing his right hand over it, as if it were a Bible and pledged that he would do whatever he had to do to keep Grandmother Sally Ann's vision a reality and the family name honorable.

Mumsie and I waited two long years to tell Thaddeus, and though I hesitated with a prudent awareness that he could have a negative reaction, we felt it best to tell him also. Good fortune had Deuce back from school on break when I told Thaddeus about Momma and my secret.

Thaddeus kept interrupting me, saying, "Why are you telling me this?"

He was even more livid when I told him I wished his grandmother was still alive so he could know her. I felt a cold shudder run down my spine. It was as if McPhee himself had come from his grave in hell and spoke through Thaddeus.

"You are not my father. You are just some nigger pretending to be somebody. Mother, how could you knowingly accept this slave into your family? Don't consider me a member of this family. I want no part of this. I'm leaving. I can't stand it any longer."

I stood frozen, helpless, unable to respond outwardly, but Mumsie, with all of her usual charm, tolerance, and acceptance of most matters, slapped Thaddeus so hard that he dropped to the floor. Mumsie glared at him, saying that if he ever spoke that way to his father or family again, she would personally go to all his "high-society" friends and tell them he was adopted from an orphanage in the lowest slum in New York City. As he looked at Mumsie, he knew it wasn't an empty threat.

Thaddeus left for several weeks. When he returned, he acted as if nothing had ever happened. He was accepted at the University of Michigan Law School. After completing school, he started working in the financial district on Wall Street. He expected to take over the management of the family fortune, but Mumsie directly informed him, in a private conversation, that he would never handle the family money and investments.

He was quite shaken by her decision and blamed it on me.

Mumsie retorted, "On the contrary, Thaddeus. It was your own distorted perception of money that forced me to deny you having any influence on the Waterbury funding."

Thaddeus said, "That is Cameron money—not some impostor's."

Mumsie firmly countered, "If you are going to chastise me, you better keep your facts straight. That money is Waterbury money today, tomorrow, and long after you have left this earth. And since you have such an aversion to the Waterbury assets, you can count on it never 'darkening' your pathway."

Thaddeus was enraged. "What are you saying?"

Mumsie quite clearly responded, "Well, you won't have to worry about the money because Deuce will oversee its distribution after we have died. And I doubt he will be as tolerant or understanding about you as your father and I are."

The subject of money was never discussed again, but for all his shortcomings, Thaddeus "charmed" his way into managing other society member's finances and developed a "favorable" reputation amongst them. By that time, he had changed his name to T. Hamilton Waterbury. All of his society friends called him Ham for short.

As I finished this memoir, I paused for a moment, going over this passage again in my thoughts. After all these weeks of disappointment and feelings of neglect, I could now clearly come to terms, appreciating why Grandfather felt justified in not sharing his secret with me or anyone else after Thaddeus's reaction. I could not have made a bigger error in my personal judgment. I finally looked around at everyone, but I was most pleased to see Soulange's supportive smile; she always had an intuitive sense of what was in my best interest.

Jasper interjected, "Hey, Water Pump, your grandfather carried a great load on his shoulders for a long time. You have got to be proud of him."

"I am, Jasper. I truly am—more than I've ever been before."

Chapter

12

Memoir Entry 11
Deuce's Dilemma, Christmas 1901

I started reading the diary again.

With as much of an enigma as Thaddeus was, Mumsie and I could not have been more content with the accomplishments of Deuce. He had gone to Harvard College and Harvard Medical School and completed his training at the newly built Johns Hopkins Hospital, working closely with Dr. William Osler, learning all the cutting-edge medical practice standards and research skills available in this country.

Shortly after moving into a new house at 9 West Seventy-Third Street in 1898, Deuce became engaged to Rose Brewster, the daughter of one of our longtime friends. The Brewsters were a family of like-minded progressive thinkers. Deuce did not know Rose very well before 1897, but he felt she would follow her family traditions. Rose had her own agenda to marry into a socially prestigious position to carry on her social club ties and continue a life of privilege. They were married in the spring of 1899.

Rose knew about Deuce's strong ties to social justice and active participation in civil rights and women's rights, and he told her the family secret before they got engaged. She told him she could overlook that fact and would do whatever she should as the lady of the house. But she deliberately deceived Deuce by pretending to show interest in helping people, knowing it was all a lie right up to the day they were married.

In the summer of 1899, Deuce took the opportunity to do public health work in New Orleans. Within a few months, he met Soulange Micheaux at the clinic there. She became his nursing assistant, and Deuce had great fulfillment in treating the patients and implementing better hygiene. After coming back to New York for short visits, Deuce would return to the New Orleans clinic regularly.

I paused at this point, and Elizabeth must have observed a puzzled look on my face when she said, "Father, is everything all right?"

"Yes, but there seems to be a remnant of a missing page that I hadn't noticed in my previous readings. Well, let me continue."

Mumsie and I were so thrilled to meet our new grandson after Deuce and Rose returned from New Orleans. He was a beautiful, healthy boy. Mumsie and I thought he looked like me. We sensed there was something special about him from the moment we laid eyes on him. It was as if Momma was standing next to me, saying he would carry forth the legacy.

After my birth, the diary focused on events and feelings about the relationship that Grandfather and I shared. I was already quite familiar with these notes, but as I read them, wonderful recollections flashed in front of my thoughts. I smiled. They were golden memories, but there were a few more entries to read.

Chapter

13

Memoir Entry 12
Mumsie's Death, 1910

Mumsie's departure was a contemplative time for me. She had made my dreams come true, and she had worked diligently over our forty years together to live the good life, to care about the next human being without judgment or expectation. She had been physically compromised to the point of disintegration, yet her inner spirit remained unbroken—and her heart continued resonating with the concern and regard that struck me so when I first saw her handing out those flyers on the Columbia campus.

What can I possibly say about this angel sent from up above? When I came to her frustrated about the injustice in the world or the vast power of evil steadily influencing our second son and others, she remarked with a steadfast conviction, "Good and evil forces are expressed as they are intended to be expressed. You can say that someone didn't live their life in a kind or helpful way, but that person's life is not for us to judge. It is for us to note and observe, but not to judge. Our judgment is always limited to what is apparent at hand.

"We have chosen to take on a life to spread kindness and offer help to the next person. Sometimes this choice may interfere with the way of the world. And going against the tide creates unfavorable or threatening times. My dear father's friends, Arthur and Lewis Tappan, suffered tremendous ridicule for their outspoken disapproval of slavery and inequality, and for their financial support of the abolition movement. Yet, I don't think they regretted their decision to speak out. Neither did my parents, Charles Sumner, Thaddeus Stevens, or any of the other like-minded thinkers.

"We are all allowed to play out our roles in life as they are intended to be played out. I am happy that I chose the life I have lived, and that the man I married shared a similar choice."

Metaphorically speaking, Mumsie conducted the orchestra (the people who knew and loved her) with such a tremendous familiarity with all the music in life. She knew the harmonious and the dissonant, yet she conducted with highest respect to all the musicians and their chosen instruments. It finally came time for her to put down the baton.

My sweet Maestro, continue your earthly song in heaven where you and Momma can join hands and sing eternally.

Chapter

14

Memoir Entry 13
Biography of an Ex-Colored Man, Book of Substance, 1912

This book was given to me by a friend, James Weldon Johnson. Although the title was printed on the front cover, there was no author's name underneath. I know that James Weldon wrote it, but he chose to use appropriate discretion in not using his name.

James Weldon was recently married to Cousin John's daughter, Grace Nail, and he had just finished his assignment as the US Consul to Venezuela. The book reminded me of my own "biologic offspring." He, like the main character, "knows not who or what he is."

It was a pity to have raised him. I felt I could have done so much more if I had another supportive child.

Memoir Entry 14
Moving On and Saying Good-Bye, 1914

This is the last entry in 1914, one month before his death.

I know I will die soon and join Mumsie on the eternal side. But I will leave you this wish, son and grandson: that you both continue the hard work that Mumsie and I tried to accomplish against the tide during our lifetime. It remains an uphill battle and a never-ending one. But you both have the fortitude, the motivation, and the clear thinking. Keep going! Don't let Momma down!

A prophetic biblical quotation was written on the back cover of the journal, the one given to me by Uncle Herbert:

> Furthermore, my son, take heed … let us hear the conclusion of the matter … Be aligned with God and keep his commandments for this is the whole duty of man. For God shall bring every work into (proper) judgment, with every secret thing, whether it be good or whether it be evil.

(Ecclesiastes 12:12–14)

The box, and most of its contents that Grandfather brought from Valdosta, Georgia to Baltimore, still survived after 104 years. The remains included a lock of Sallie Ann's hair, entries of family member's births and deaths in Sallie Ann's Bible, the map to Baltimore, the toy doll made by Sallie Ann out of cornhusk for Grandfather when he was a little boy, John Nail's address in Baltimore on Stirling Street, a copy of *Uncle Tom's Cabin* from Charlotte's nephew, and the train ticket stubs on each of the transfers north.

Elizabeth looked up at me and said, "After all the courage and strength displayed by Great-Grandfather through all those challenges, it is no wonder that you have had a very similar life, following in his footsteps. The two of you were one in so many ways, yet there was a great difference in the conditions surrounding you during your formative and young adult years. He was born into darkness, but he was given a guiding light to walk out. You, Father, were encouraged, regarded, and directed from the beginning and given opportunities that only a few were privileged to receive. In spite of appearances, you had to face evolving circumstances that placed you in a *furnace*. You, however, carried the torch of Great-Great Grandmother Sallie Ann, as she had envisioned it.

"You finished Great-Grandfather's memoirs, so now, we have to learn about your formative and young adult experiences as well. What memories can you recapture—and how did you face your setbacks? What drove you on? Did you realize you had the help of an *invisible* torch?"

Everyone agreed with Elizabeth; they wanted to hear my earlier remembrances, and they wouldn't take no for an answer.

I was stunned, surprisingly apprehensive for a moment. First, how could my recollections measure up to the trials and sufferings of Grandfather? He was in a *furnace* and got out. He had to look over his shoulder constantly and worry. What if his identity was revealed? What consequences would manifest for Mumsie and the entire family? And second, I had painful reflections that haunted me at times. I knew my family and friends would all understand, but would I be strong enough to share these thoughts? Would I feel intimidation or dismay?

As I looked at all their wonderful, caring faces, I was given a sense of assurance that it would be a good thing to share. The recollection would bring old memories a breath of vitality, maybe even a deeper appreciation of what they did to make me the man I am today.

Chapter

15

I went to my desk drawer and pulled out my own journal.

"In retrospect, many of the entries in Grandfather's notes were *told* to me indirectly throughout my life. My writings contain many events and people who have influenced me over the years. I will try to limit my discussion to particular experiences in my earlier life that will broaden your awareness of what has made me the man I am today and what has motivated me to grow further both introspectively as well as outwardly.

"As I recall these events, I will speak as if I were telling them to you during this past summer, before I knew about Grandfather's secret. It will become clear that I was not, in fact, as unaware of his circumstance as it would seem."

Soulange nodded in agreement. On all of the earlier entries, Soulange was helpful in assisting my recall and remembrance of the lesson-filled experiences.

Early Childhood Memories (Event 1)

My childhood bear sits on my study as it usually does every winter holiday since I can remember. It is most fitting to start my story with that bear.

When I was two years old, Father purchased one of the first teddy bears, made in honor of President Theodore Roosevelt. I was told that I carried the bear wherever I went, but I was most excited to have it with me while listening to the wonderful bedtime tales, children's stories, and good-night prayers shared by Soulange.

I looked at Soulange with a smile and then sternly said, "And don't interrupt my praises for you."

Soulange, who I affectionately called "Sue-Lee," treated me with guidance, friendship, regard, and unconditional love. She came to live with us in the spring of 1902 when she was almost twenty-one years old. Though born of Creole descent, in impoverished conditions, she was determined to take advantage of the opportunity to be the only member of her family to earn a high school equivalency diploma.

I enjoyed her immensely as a young boy. I was at peace with her warm smile and gentle way. I remembered the smell of vanilla and jasmine lingering in the air when I was by her side. She was tall, thin, and strikingly beautiful. She had long dark brown hair that she wore up, supported by two favorite combs that Father had brought her from the Orient: one horn comb and one ivory comb, depicting the Chinese year of the snake with an intricate, lacy background.

"Sue-Lee was born in the year of the snake," Jasper said, asking what animal I was in the Chinese calendar.

I told him I was an ox.

Sue-Lee and I used to say, when I grew up, I would be a great ox to help and protect people—and she would bite anyone who tried to harm me.

When she read stories or told me tales at night, I would hold teddy in one hand, and with the other hand, I would rub her smooth, silky arm or her right hand that showed a birthmark. I had a similar birthmark on my left hand. I asked her where she got her mark, and she told me God gave it to both of us. I then inquired further, asking why He didn't give a mark to Father or Mother.

Sue-Lee said God gave us a special mark to have something that would link us as friends for life. She read Longfellow's children's poems, Hans Christian Andersen's stories, "Ali Baba and the Forty Thieves" from *1001 Arabian Nights*, and Grimm's fairy tales, but the most fun were the southern tales she learned as a girl in New Orleans.

One of my favorites was the story telling the reason why "turtles ain't the most handsome critters in the world." She would always use her southern dialect. She was so good at imitating the barn animals and all the noises on the farm or in the woods."

"Please share the story with us," pleaded Elizabeth.

I told her I would try, but no one can tell a story like Sue-Lee.

"The turkle ain't handsome like the other critters; he ain't got no hair like most of them, and he ain't got but mighty little hide, and some of his family can go inside and shut the front door and the back door, and you can't see neither their hands nor their tails. But they wasn't always that way. They used to be a good-looking family, and it all come about in the early days playing with fire.

"In them times, the turkles had soft skin and hair all over them just like the other animals. But one day, the turkle family got into a wheat field. They were all in there eating the wheat, but they left two of the children by the picnic fire, and they told them not to play in the fire. Well, sir, pretty soon them children forget all about not playing in the fire, and they begin to make red ribbons with the chunks, and the first thing you know, the fire catch the wheat and the wind blowed it.

"Well, sir, them there turkles never was much of a family for running, but they tried in vain to escape. The fire caught up with them, and it was so hot that it burnt their hides and shrunk them all out of shape. They hurted so bad that they all crawled to the creek and got into the water to ease the pain. And when they done that, the bubbles come to the top and the water sizzled and made their hides hard like a piece of hot iron when the blacksmith puts it in the water. And ever since that time, the turkles has all stayed in the water or mighty close to it where they can drop in and get out of the way if any trouble comes along. And that's what makes me tell you, honey, if you want to grow up handsome, don't never play with fire."[19]

She could also tell me the same story in French; she was my first French teacher. There were times when she would read a story using both languages—whichever she thought sounded nicer for a particular passage.

After the story was finished, we would hold hands, close our eyes, and share good-night prayers. Soulange is deeply spiritual, as you already know, reading her Bible daily and providing positive feelings, encouragement, bonding, self-worth, and love through those prayers. I relied on them many times in the darkest moments of my life as well as the happiest ones. The biblical quotes would be soothing for my fears. One time, Teddy was misplaced, and I cried hysterically, thinking he was lost. Soulange kept reassuring me he would be found. "Be patient, my little Chip," which is what everyone called me as a boy. "Paul tells the people in Hebrews, 'Let us run with patience the race that is set before us.' Teddy didn't wander far." I remember how patient she was and how strong her faith has been throughout my life.

That night, before I went to sleep, she sang the Schubert "Lieder" with her sonorous voice and lulled me to a peaceful slumber. She sang it every night afterward for many years. The song became a tradition, and I soon learned the words as well.

Another one of her frequent quotations from the Bible was from Deuteronomy 4:9. It was a verse that offered a clear reminder to keep at the forefront of our consciousness: "Only take heed for yourselves, and keep your soul diligently, lest you forget the things which your eyes have seen, and lest they depart from your heart all the days of your life, but declare them to your children and your children's children."

Her understanding and wisdom remained a pillar of strength during my life, reminding me to keep my soul diligent and to look forward, past the storm.

Soulange smiled and said, "You did learn how to follow that advice."

Pamela inquired, "Since it is December 25, was Christmas a special time for the Waterbury family when you were a boy?"

Christmas 1907 (Event 2)

The holidays in the Waterbury family were very traditional and promoted the gathering of friends and extended family to share the wonderful and glorious tidings of good cheer, as well as reflect on our offerings to others. My grandfather, grandmother, father, and Soulange would go to the Henry Street Settlement on the Lower East Side of Manhattan to serve the less fortunate people a meal and bring them gifts every Christmas Eve. I was included in that Christmas of 1907, participating in that meaningful event. I brought some of the toys that I no longer used and helped everybody with the meal serving. I saw men, women, and children with tattered clothes and desolate expressions on their thin faces. When they saw my family, they briefly, but definitively, changed expressions. Their smiles would glow with appreciation and thankfulness. It was an experience I would treasure each year—no matter how cold or snowy it was.

Grandfather was a dear friend, a great influence, and a man I have tried to emulate throughout my life for the standards he set and his uncompromising belief in humanity. He was a big man, at six feet two inches, with a neat, bushy mustache, extended sideburns, wavy silver hair, and an old scar on his left hand that he said was an accident as a young man. He was a history teacher at the Ethical Cultural School and a world traveler. He had artifacts and books from all over the world and had the most fascinating stories to share about every piece. He walked with a cane that had a Chinese symbol, meaning life, on the top. He smoked Cuban Havana cigars, and he cleared his throat regularly. He wore his pocket watch attached to a gold chain in his vest daily. I can picture him now with his jovial laugh, walking with his cane and answering my incessant questions.

Mumsie was a strong, nurturing woman who devoted her life to support Grandfather's visions and achievements, and she showered me with kindness, encouragement, and unconditional love. She had very soft, green eyes, light gray hair, and a serene face. After her sturdy frame was riddled with arthritis, particularly her hands, legs, and feet, she moved about slowly, humming cheerfully and always caring for the next soul. One of her favorite books was *The Simple Life* by Charles Wagner. It was published in French in 1895. She had first-edition copies on her nightstand in both French and English. She and Grandfather were the best grandparents I could have ever wanted.

Father was a dear friend also, but because of his busy schedule with patients, I was not able to spend as much time with him as I did with my grandparents or Soulange. He was a big-framed man at six feet two inches. His dark brown hair was parted in the middle, and he wore thin wire-rimmed glasses. After a long day at the office, he would approach my room, whistling some opera aria or a Mozart melody. I would pretend to be asleep, wait until he was close to my bed, and try to scare him. It never worked, but we did have a fun moment every night.

After our return home from the shelter, we would routinely get our hot chocolate, sit by the fire, and listen to Grandfather reciting Dickens's *A Christmas Carol*. At Christmas of 1907, however, he added a story from the supplement of the New York Sunday World Magazine. It was "The Gift of the Magi," which was written by one of his friends, William Porter, better known as O. Henry. Grandfather went on to discuss the true meaning of Christmas. He talked about the origin of the mistletoe that hung over the entrance of the front door. Centuries ago, the mistletoe plant was considered a miracle plant for its ability to grow during winter's harshest days when all other plant life ceased. It offered color, life, and hope.

Christians at that time viewed the mistletoe as nature's representation of how mankind should understand its relationship with God: Man is made to survive in the most daunting times, as the mistletoe can survive the cruelest winter storms, by never abandoning your faith. Mistletoe was considered a peacemaker, a protector, and a symbol of love.

After gathering around our special Christmas red candle, we would talk about the meaning of light and the message of Christmas to carry in our lives daily throughout the year. We would recite Matthew 5:14–16: "Ye are the light of the world ... Neither do men light a candle and put it under a bushel, but on a candlestick; and it giveth light unto all that are in the house. Let your light so shine before men, that they may see your good works, and glorify your Father which is in heaven." Christmas was understood to be about giving—not receiving—in our household.

Afterward, I would go to my room to get ready for Christmas morning. Before I went to sleep, however, I would go to Mumsie's room and listen to the wonderful old Olympia music box, playing an enchanting Christmas work called "The Holy City" by Stephen Adams. After kissing Mumsie goodnight, I would go to bed. Soulange would tuck me in nice and tight. How spoiled I feel with such wonderful memories of Christmases past. I want to share one other special Christmas experience.

I reviewed Christmas in 1912 with everyone.

Let me not forget the special occasion of Christmas Day at the Waterburys' home. After a big sit-down breakfast, we would come around the tree and open the few gifts that were wrapped before the lovely music would start. Grandfather, Mumsie, Father, and Sue-Lee were accomplished musicians: Grandfather played the piano; Mumsie, the harp; Father, the violin, and Sue-Lee would accompany them with her beautiful voice. I was taught the piano early; we would all have our turn in a solo part, and then we would all play the Christmas hymns together with Sue-Lee singing like a nightingale. When Sue-Lee accompanied Father on the violin, her voice seemed to be even more harmonious. It was a delightful experience whenever we played for each other.

After the music was finished, Grandfather took me aside and said he had another gift for me. They were seven Christmas letters, all addressed to me. He told me he had written one each year of my life, starting in 1901. He said they reviewed what I had accomplished in that year and his projections for a new and exciting year to come. He waited until my seventh Christmas to show me what each year meant to him so I could appreciate their meaning a little more. "One day we will write these letters together, Chip. And you can follow this tradition with your own children." Even though I didn't know the significance of the letters at that time, I eventually read each one with deep gratitude.

I must have gone into a momentary trance when Pamela inquired, "What was your mother's participation in the Christmas tradition?" They all sensed the change in my face and tone of voice.

"Well, to be honest, Mother never got involved in too many of the family activities." I went on amplifying what they already knew.

My mother, Rose Brewster Waterbury, had a different "point of reference" about life and a very limited alliance with my father and the rest of us. Mother was reared in a wealthy family and was affiliated with all the social clubs. She once told me, in her familiar high shrill voice, that it was your "social duty" to remember those worthy of your time and interest. "Your father will never accept that obligation, but then again, he is his parents' son." She had a genuinely cold personality, but she would display a warm veneer when the opportunity presented itself. Every hair was in place, and she dressed impeccably. Mother did not like to touch anyone; she was manipulating, self-indulging, and easily bothered when queried. Her fingers were long and thin, and her hands were always cold, just like her personality.

She spent most of her time at the social clubs with her elite friends. She was obsessed with leaving a "good impression" on them about everything that all "well-bred, upper-class" individuals sought to maintain. She found the activities and charitable offerings we participated in to be boring. She was more interested in traveling to Paris or London to dine with some nobleman's family. One year, she missed the Christmas holiday with us completely. I didn't understand why she remained so distant, but the rest of us went ahead and enjoyed ourselves without her.

On a brighter note, we also enjoyed the visits and social activities shared with our neighbors. The relationship my grandfather and father had with the Spingarns was long and enriched with like-minded endeavors and dreams. They had met "Uncle Joel" through Grandfather's friendship with Dr. George Woodberry—literary critic, poet, and professor at Columbia University—in the early 1890s. Uncle Joel was one of his protégés and developed his own nurturing bond with Grandfather and Father over the years. Father had moved into our Seventy-Third Street home in 1897, and through good fortune, the Spingarns moved next door a few years later.

We have shared so many wonderful things together. Uncle Joel and Aunt Amy would accompany us to serve the Thanksgiving and Christmas meals down at the Henry Street Settlement, and Aunt Amy would help me practice French and some German. As the years went by, I enjoyed their beautiful children as well. The Spingarn family always had scholarly discussions with Father and Grandfather.

I must not forget our early Christmas afternoon visit from Grandfather's dear friend and my godfather, Herbert Horace Huntington. He was Grandfather's close friend, a teacher of public speaking, and a classics scholar at the Ethical Cultural School. He was a distinguished man with an air of sophistication. He had a white forelock, very formal British enunciation, wore a bow tie, and had a monocle. He had a mild hearing loss; Grandfather told me to speak loudly so Godfather Herbert could hear me. Unknown to me at that time, he would have a powerful influence on my life after Grandfather died. He always gave me an insightful book for a Christmas gift, and then he would go off to talk with Grandfather.

We also had our yearly visit from Uncle Thaddeus in the later afternoon on Christmas Day. Thaddeus Hamilton Waterbury would show up in a grand carriage, wearing a fancy suit, top hat, and satin cravat. He was the senior partner of the Waterbury, Fendersen, and Whitetower law firm down on Wall Street. He was very wealthy and quite arrogant, even when I was a little boy. He was several inches shorter than Father, and he had thick bright red hair.

Uncle Thaddeus would stay for a short visit only, but in that time, he would talk about his recent expensive trips, his acquaintances down at the Knickerbocker and Metropolitan Clubs, and even his social activities; it was the only time I saw Mother smiling. He would give me a five-dollar gold coin every year and tell me to save it and become rich like him. He would say, "Here's a gold coin, Nephew. Hopefully, you won't waste the family fortune like your father and grandparents, on Negroes, poor people, and cripples. The prestige of the Waterbury name can only be increased as the money increases. Listen to me, Nephew: if you expect to get anywhere in this life, you had better have money and power next to your name."

I would dutifully nod my head in agreement and thank him for the money. "Thank you, Uncle Thaddeus, for the gold coin."

He scowled at me and said, "Don't call me that name. Address me as Uncle Hamilton or sir."

"Yes, sir." It seemed like Grandfather, Mumsie, and Father ignored him completely and continued to call him Thaddeus. In my mind, those kinds of comments upset me, and it took everything in me not to hate him.

Looking back, the holiday meals were very special to my family. Everyone had his or her place at a table for ten. The gathering was very connected, although Uncle Thaddeus insisted on sitting at the opposite end of the table, away from Father and Grandfather. Grandfather sat at the head of the table, and Mumsie sat across from him. Going clockwise, there was Grandfather, Uncle Herbert, myself, Uncle Joel, Aunt Amy, Mumsie, an empty seat, Uncle Thaddeus (if he stayed), Mother, and Father, who sat on Grandfather's right side. We held hands to bless the table before meals.

Mother never extended her hand to Mumsie and barely held Father's hand; it was just part of her usual unaffectionate way. Father never admitted the strained relation between Thaddeus and himself openly, but it was apparent even in my youth, and only got clearer with age.

Uncle Thaddeus usually left before the meal began, and he did not return until the following Christmas with the same look, the same talk, and the same plutocratic thinking. Once he left, the atmosphere of the holiday became bright again. We continued having fun; I listened to Mumsie's music box and went to sleep with Teddy. I felt my world was surrounded by peace and love, and the holiday spirit glowed in my heart.

Chapter

17

Trip to Washington, DC, September 1908 (Event 3)

I told everyone that the entire family went on a trip to Washington, DC, to stay at the White House with President Theodore Roosevelt. Godfather Herbert was a personal friend of his, even before Roosevelt was police commissioner in New York City. We were invited along with Godfather Herbert to visit after Roosevelt's family returned from their summer vacation in Oyster Bay, Long Island. Godfather Herbert wasn't able to come due to illness, and I saw the deep disappointment in Grandfather's face that he could not attend with them.

We boarded the wonderful train leaving Pennsylvania Central Station. A tall and broad-shouldered porter by the name of Evander greeted us with a warm smile upon entering our coach. As we were traveling, I could hear most of the passengers call him "George" and call the other porters "George" as well. I found that misnomer very puzzling. I watched Evander shine Father's shoes so diligently and so easily. I asked him why the people called him and the other porters "George."

He smiled with a warm expression on his face and said, "Sometimes, people just don't take time to know people. But I's happy you takin' the time to care."

I shook his large hand and said good-bye when we pulled into the brand new Union Station in Washington, DC.

We arrived on September 10, 1908, and a carriage took us from the station to the White House. We were greeted by all of the children and Mrs. Roosevelt. Mother started talking to their oldest daughter, Alice, to discuss the social activities in Washington and ignored the rest of us. The president's sons—Quentin and Archie, ages eleven and fourteen—made me feel like one of the family. We roller-skated in the basement, and we played with all their wonderful animals. There was Eli, Ted Jr.'s macaw, with beautiful multicolored feathers; Josiah, Archie's pet badger; and Quentin's pet pony that he let me ride. We blew soap bubbles on the White House lawn, and they allowed me to join them and President Roosevelt in wrestling and pillow fighting. The president hit Archie so hard that all the goose feathers came out of the seam, and it looked like it was snowing in the room. Quentin was especially kind to me. I liked his nickname, Quenty-Quee, given by his father.

Mother was invited to attend a party hosted by Alice that evening, and she wanted Father to accompany her. Father, however, had already planned a special meeting with the president and Grandfather and told her to go by herself. Mother was irate and told Father it would be embarrassing for her if he didn't go. Father stated firmly that his meeting was too important to cancel. He was sorry that she couldn't understand his circumstances. Mother dressed and left very upset.

Grandfather, Father, and I were given a tour of the White House—including the executive office—by Mr. Roosevelt, and I was left to play in the adjoining room of his secretary.

The door was not fully closed, and they must have thought I was preoccupied, playing, but I overheard them discussing a serious concern that needed President Roosevelt's influence to "not let this atrocity occur again."

I had not seen Grandfather so upset. He was pounding the table, and Father had to calm him down at one point.

The president said he would look into the matter and do what he could.

Years later, my father told me about their discussion. The Springfield Race Riots had occurred from August 14–16, 1908, as Springfield, Illinois, was preparing for the hundredth anniversary of the birth of Abraham

Lincoln. A white mob lynched two Negroes senselessly, killed four white men, and injured almost another hundred people. A distinguished writer, William Walling, went to Springfield to gather the facts as best he could. His findings were reported in the *Springfield Independent* newspaper on September 3. Grandfather, Mumsie, and Father got a call from their friend, Mary White Ovington, about a meeting she wanted to organize to address the valid question that Walling had proposed in that article.

The issues were clear and blunt. I read the entire article when I was in college; here is an excerpt:

> We have closed our eyes to the whole awful and menacing truth that a large part of the white population of Lincoln's home … has initiated a permanent warfare with the Negro race. Its significance is threefold. First, that it occurred in an important and historical Northern town; then that the Negroes, constituting 10 percent of the population, could not possibly endanger the "supremacy" of the white; and finally, public opinion of the North, not withstanding the insane hatred of the Negro, is satisfied that there were "mitigating circumstances" for the race hatred which is the cause of it all … Either the spirit of the abolitionists, or of Lincoln must be revived and we must come to treat the Negro on a plane of absolute political and social equality or … every hope of political democracy will be dead, other weaker races and classes will be persecuted in the North as well as the South, public education will undergo an eclipse, and American civilization will await either a rapid degeneration or another profounder and more revolutionary civil war. Yet who realizes the seriousness of this situation and what large and powerful body of citizens is ready to come to their aid?[20]

Grandfather and Father were very disappointed that TR did not address this matter openly. But Mary Ovington's meeting did lead to my family's active involvement in the newly founded National Association for the Advancement of Colored People, the NAACP. Grandfather, Mumsie, and

Father poured their money, devotion, and commitment into supporting organizations that aided the denied, the unjustly treated, and the unequal to give those neglected people the opportunity to receive the freedom, the justice, and the equality that all Americans should share together.

Grandfather and Father never blamed President Roosevelt and remained in contact with their family even after his presidency ended. I remember a Christmas card addressed to the Waterbury family with regards from the Roosevelts every year.

Introduction to Medicine, Fall of 1909 (Event 4)

Everyone's eyes remained bright and interested in each event as I continued with the story.

Pamela inquired, "Your grandfather, godfather, and father's respected professions had to influence you deeply. You apparently had a great interest in history, philosophy, science, Romance languages, and medicine yourself. How did you choose medicine?"

I heard a good story every day in my childhood from family or friends, whether it was an interpretation of an historical event, listening to a bedtime story, discussing issues in French or German, or hearing Father talk about his medical cases with Grandfather or Mumsie. I remember Father describing the sidewalks piled high with daily waste, including horse manure, coal dust, kitchen slop, and putrid raw garbage down on the Lower East Side near his clinic. He said he had to walk through it, and it was even more disgusting during the summer months and rainy days. His office was down on Broome Street, and every day he came home, he would take off his clothes and change because he smelled like the environment he worked in.

One day, he had to go to one of his patients' homes because she could not get to his office, and he made the mistake of putting his coat down on her bed. When he got home, he brought the bedbugs and chiggers with him. We had to wash all the linens twice to eradicate the infestation. Those bedbugs have a painful bite. Father told me to appreciate that we did not have to deal with that burden every day, as so many poor people do.

When I was seven or eight years old, I had fever, sore throat, and hoarseness. He was particularly worried and waited on me more attentively with Soulange's help. After I was better, Soulange told me that he had a recent case of an eight-year-old boy with hoarseness and sore throat caused by a serious infection, diphtheria. The boy had gotten sick, and developed a gray-brown membrane covering the back of his throat that caused him to have difficulty swallowing. His throat dramatically swelled and the boy's neck enlarged to look like a bull's. Within two weeks, the swelling was so overwhelming that he suffocated to death, and Father was helpless trying to relieve his symptoms. The whole experience showed that my father's care for his patients was no different than the care he would give me. He offered his service to them as if they were extended family.

Soulange interjected, "Do you remember what you said to your father and how you pronounced the word *diphtheria*?"

"Yes, I do. I said, 'Father, you need to look that bull in the eye and scare him away the next time you see a patient with the *ditderia.*'"

Father was well trained, as mentioned in Grandfather's journal. After graduating from Harvard College and Harvard Medical School, he trained at Johns Hopkins in Baltimore and worked with Dr. William Osler. He was very familiar with the diverse population of patients he had; he had worked at the New Orleans Shelter for the Indigent and Poor, where he met Soulange.

As capable a clinician as he was, it was more impressive that he showed such tremendous passion and caring for all those people.

Mother complained constantly about his absence. He never attended the social functions that were so important to her. But as busy as Father was, working the long hours that he did, he never said he was tired and never spoke negatively about any aspect of his work, except that he wanted conditions to be improved for all of his patients. He had talked to the officials at the Department of Health to work on improving sanitation and housing conditions.

Overcrowding and malnutrition were regularly discussed at dinnertime, and Mother was always trying to change the subject. "You can't help every poor, miserable life. Why do you keep trying?"

As frustrated as Father was with Mother's indifference, he remained consistent with his offerings to all of his patients. He was noticeably happier one night, and I asked Soulange what sparked his joy. She showed me a letter of gratitude that one of his patients had written and read it to me. "We thank God that our daughter came to see you with her ailments and troubles, and like the Great Physician, Himself, above, you healed her soul while saving her life."

In the fall of 1909, I accompanied Father to his office for the first time. It was filled with immigrants, Negroes, Jews, and Chinese. I glanced around at his patients' faces in the waiting room. They had worn, desperate looks, their clothing was tattered, the smell was like the sidewalks, and several of them were constantly coughing. They were basically unhappy while waiting for Father.

Then, while walking to the exam room, I saw a little joy—briefly felt, but genuinely displayed—as my father held their hands and led them to be examined. He had wealthy patients as well whose reimbursements helped Father pay for the facility and all the care for people who had no means to pay for his service, and who obviously needed him most.

During that first visit to Father's office, while watching him place a bandage on an elderly lady's arm, an unexpected incident aroused my interest in medicine. Father had a patient who had advanced syphilis, and he had failed to cure him with repeated mercury injections. Several months after his last clinical visit with Father, he suddenly came through the front door—with the office filled with patients—waving a sharp knife and screaming that he was going to kill "Uncle Charlie."

My father reacted quickly to get the knife from him, but the deranged man cut deeply into the back of Father's left hand. Father was able to control a very serious situation. The police were summoned, and the patient was taken away to Bellevue Hospital.

Father's hand healed, but I told Father I was frightened. That madman could have seriously harmed or killed him.

Father replied in his usual unassuming way, saying he didn't know whether the man was suffering from the disease or the poison given to attempt a cure. It didn't matter. He couldn't blame the man for not knowing what he was doing. Syphilis was such a penetrating disease in all parts of the body, including the mind. His teacher, Dr. Osler, had said, "Seek ye first the knowledge of syphilis, and all the other things clinical will be added unto you." But Father had to protect his patients and me at all costs.

I will never forget his lesson about a person's hands. He said, "Son, it is what you do with them that will inevitably plot the journey of your life. Hands are God's tools for helping, touching, healing, sacrificing, working, and holding one another. All offering hands have some mark, some reminder, and some record of our lives. The longer the journey of those who utilize their hands in some offering capacity, the more it is etched on their hands. Use your hands to help your fellow man throughout your life."

Father told me the story behind the great art masterpiece, *The Praying Hands*, by Albrecht Durer. He recalled that Durer and his close friend were both interested in attending art classes to become professional painters, but they didn't have enough money to matriculate. They decided to help each other: one would go to work and send money to the other while he was in school, and once he finished, he, in turn, would work to send the first worker to school. They drew straws, and Durer would attend school first. The faithful friend would send money until Durer had completed his apprenticeship. Upon returning home, ready to reciprocate, Durer learned his friend had been a blacksmith all those years and the labor had ruined his hands to become an artist. The sacrifice moved Durer to paint his masterpiece for his friend as a gesture of appreciation and a permanent memorial to their bond.

That experience at my first visit to Father's clinic as well as his lesson about the priceless service of our hands imprinted an indelible calling within my consciousness to follow in Father's footsteps and become a physician to do my life's work.

Trip to Coney Island, Dreamland, 1910 (Event 5)

As I was thumbing through the pages of the diary, I opened to the ticket stub from my trip to Coney Island with Grandfather and Soulange in June 1910.

I looked at everyone with a big smile and told them that people can talk about the fascination of Disneyland and how impressive the 1939 or 1964 New York World's Fair really were, but if you ask anyone who visited Dreamland at Coney Island, no matter their age, they will convince you assuredly that the marvel and splendor of all those wonderful exhibits and buildings were the best real-life fantasy on this planet.

Jasper became extremely fascinated. "I remember the Steeplechase and Luna Park when I came to Harlem after World War I. They were such fun. I didn't know there was another part of Coney Island."

I gave them some background about the place that was described as the "Gibraltar of the Amusement World."

The most noticeable was the landmark Tower, 375 feet tall. You could see it from the Atlantic Ocean at fifty miles away, especially at night when it was fully illuminated. Throughout the entire park, all the fifty-foot-wide walkways were level or inclined, and on any given day, they could accommodate 250,000 patrons moving about and able to see any of the exhibits without crowding.

There was the fabulous "Trip through Switzerland," sitting in a car that would take you on a panoramic view of Switzerland, including the snow-peaked Alps, valleys, and other natural scenery that makes Switzerland such a beautiful landscape. There was an "Incubator Building" with the latest technology, and the largest incubator ever made. Nurses and doctors came to see this display for small infant care.

In the "Fighting the Flame" exhibit, four thousand people were employed to help with the fire department in action. They enacted a real fire with the flames jumping from one floor to the next with real hoses used to put out the flames. The "Leap-Frog Railway" had a rail car carrying thirty-two people going full speed toward an oncoming rail car with thirty-two people riding at the same speed. At that moment when you would expect impact, one of the cars would ride above the other, thus creating a paradox of sorts. I still wonder how the inventor of the system created such a fascinating work.

I can't forget Frank Bostock's "Animal Show," with his vast numbers of different species of wild animals from around the world. The performing elephants, polar bears, jaguars, and the lions were all spectacular as well. The place was simply amazing. And all those bright, colorful lights!

While enjoying the rides, I had an unexpected experience of meeting another boy who touched Grandfather and me more deeply than Coney Island itself. As we were about to enter the "Venetian Building," a Negro mother was speaking loudly to her son who was about my age.

Grandfather, Soulange, and I were close enough to hear them.

"Walter, Walter, get back here before you get lost! I told you we don't have no money for the amusements. I brought you here just so you could see all the lights. Now come on, son. It's going to take time for us to get home."

I looked at Grandfather, and he was staring at them, suspended for a moment. He walked up to the mother, introduced himself, and after a short conversation, the boy and his mother joined us for the rest of our visit.

Walter was nine years old and a victim of polio since the age of five. I had seen patients with polio in Father's office, but they were older. Walter was the first child I knew with this awful disease. As much effort as it took for him to manipulate his crutches, he had the biggest smile and he kept thanking Grandfather repeatedly, as if he had never experienced wonderment like this ever in his life.

Watching Walter's face brought more satisfying joy than the rides or the other attractions. He maneuvered himself on the "Chute Ride" as well as any child I had seen, despite his obvious limitations. He didn't complain about anything. He told us that he wanted to be an inventor, to create some electrical device to help people with polio or other muscular diseases get around easier. He said that his doctor was amazed that he walked so quickly after recovering from the first stages of polio and that he had such remarkable strength in his arms and hands. I saw him swing the mallet to hit the bell, and surprisingly, he hit it three times in a row.

Grandfather looked at him with sheer delight and held all his prizes with a special pride; it appeared as if Grandfather had acquired a new grandson.

We shared an exciting moment with Walter in the "Lilliputian Village," where three hundred small people were employed to create their own circus, theater, fire department, and homes. After Walter was helped onto one of the saddle ponies, the band and one of the tall guides marched around behind him as if he was a prince being honored for the day. The smile on Walter's face was priceless. When I looked over at Grandfather, he mirrored the same expression of joy as if he was a young child all over again.

When the Coney Island experience was over, we walked Walter and his mother to the gate, powerfully illuminated by all the lights that surrounded us.

Walter's mother kept thanking Grandfather. "Thank you, sir. Thank you. You made my Walter a happy boy."

Grandfather replied, "I can't thank you enough for letting us enjoy Walter as much as we did."

When Walter's mother told Grandfather that he made her son a "happy boy," he responded that her son had made him a "happy boy," giving him the privilege of such a worthwhile memory.

Grandfather held his right hand midline on his chest, slightly bowed, and expressed to her how Walter's dream of helping other polio victims would come true. "I will see to it."

Walter shook Grandfather's hand and then mine. In all the excitement, he gave me such a powerful handshake that I thought my hand would break. And the feel of his callused hand reminded me a lot of Grandfather's hand—years of laboring hard work.

Grandfather kept in touch with Walter. Walter eventually went to New York University on a scholarship given by Grandfather. He studied physics and mathematics, and in spite of his malady, he went on to become the scientist that he wanted to be. He sent a Christmas card every year faithfully until he died in 1941 due to complications of pneumonia. I will always remember this great, driven soul and those strong, weather-worn hands.

Elizabeth, in all her innate wisdom, looked at me and said, "Great-Grandfather truly saw himself in Walter. They had the same name, similar challenges. Both were Negroes, one a former slave child with no opportunity to aspire to dreams, and the other, a 'freed' child with a physical setback that could have denied his dreams, yet both had a common core determination that no obstacle or outer force would limit."

Death of Mumsie and Her Request to Have the Fisk Jubilee Singers at Her Funeral (Event 6)

Everyone's eyes reflected the moments at Dreamland as if they were with me in 1910.

"I only wish Mumsie had been able to share this memorable experience, but by then, she was unable to walk without assistance or pain."

Hugo's facial expression noticeably changed from obvious delight to a more reflective state. "I'm sure your father and Mumsie were sorry they missed that experience with you. You previously shared the wonderful joy Mumsie gave you in the Christmas remembrance, but what about her overall influence?"

I looked at him and everyone else and paused a moment to speak.

I could not offer an appropriate verbal tribute to Mumsie's influence because words would only reveal a mere fraction of her guidance, strength, and love for all of us. Although Grandfather, along with Mumsie, Father, and Soulange were teaching me the principles, there would be no Waterbury tradition without her financial and spiritual encouragement. She backed

Grandfather and Father 100 percent on their journeys in life, helping to reduce the obstacles that came their way, and it was very clear that we all depended on Mumsie. She held the seat of highest regard in our eyes.

She was the contributor to many social causes, including women's rights, Negro colleges, orphanages, hospital services, and the Hull House Center for neglected and poor immigrants, and she was an outspoken advocate for civil rights, world peace, and the fight against hunger. She was a woman way ahead of her time. She worked with Jane Addams, Florence Henley, Julia Ward, and Mary White Ovington, helping plan the care and feeding of the mothers and children in the Hull House and Henry Street Settlement facilities. She helped write beautifully inspiring speeches for the woman's suffrage groups. She and Grandfather were a working team, and it was only reinforced at her funeral how special her humanity and kind way were to the community and her friends. Even after she developed crippling arthritis in 1898—which Father had said eventually caused her death in August 1910—she wore her warm smile and participated in all our activities until she was no longer capable.

When I was growing up, I remember the awful and painful progression of the disease that deformed her hands and wrists, and gradually her knees and feet. Her disease advanced more quickly over the last two years of her life. I would help open her mail or cut articles from the daily newspaper. I even cracked her favorite walnuts and pecans during holiday season of 1909. I realized the impact of her limitation completely when she was unable to accompany me on her harp after my piano lessons. She used to look forward to this with great excitement every week. Even though she must have felt saddened by this disappointment, she never showed it. She continued to sit with me while I played the piano, and she encouraged me wholeheartedly.

Eventually, I would try to ease her discomfort by massaging her hands and feet, but I could not do as effective a job as Father or Soulange. Every night, after a long day at work, Father would come home and faithfully rub Mumsie's hands and feet with special salves from his office. Even though Grandfather became distraught at times, he tried to remain attentive. He and Soulange were willing to do whatever Father told them to do to make Mumsie more comfortable. In spite of her malady, this woman never complained and did as much as she could to be the wonderful matriarch that she truly was.

During the summer of 1910, her pain worsened, and she became increasingly frail. She knew her time was near. She called me into her room one day and told me to listen carefully. She was forced to sit in a wheelchair by this point, and the deformity of her hands and wrists had taken away her ability to open and close her fingers when trying to grasp or hold anything. Even though her voice had dropped to just above a whisper, her mind stayed sharp and her wisdom poured from her soul. "Look at my hands and then hold them, young Chip!" she instructed with an air of tranquility. She went on to say that her hands had lost their ability to perform as they once did. She missed her creative writing, playing her beloved harp, and giving herself a bath, but she missed holding me most of all.

She went on to say that she thought I had been diligent in trying to comfort her, and it was during her most painful moments that she would stop and dwell on thoughts of a loving memory we shared together—and relief would come at the right time. Finally, she shared how Grandfather had tirelessly tried to find some cure, any cure. He even took Mumsie to Lourdes in France to find a powerful healing from the waters of the grotto of Massabielle. The experience was soothing, but the remedy was short-lived.

I kept staring and rubbing Mumsie's hands. *Why had she suffered so? Why can't Father cure her disease—as he does for his patients? Why didn't that healing water in France perform a miracle?* I started to cry, and Mumsie separated her hands from mine and started wiping my tears away. "Please don't despair, my child. Your warmth and love have always had the distinct ability to lighten the burden of my pain. I feel your sympathy, and I know your heart will always remain in the right place. I have a special gift to give you." Mumsie tried to reach for an aged black wood box with the letter C embossed in an Old English text style on its top, but she was having difficulty grabbing hold of it.

I brought it to her lap.

"Open the box, Chip."

As I opened the box, there was a leather pouch, which I took out to examine. Mumsie instructed me to pour the contents of the pouch into my hand. As I did, my eyes must have become as wide as saucers. The sunlight came through the windows just at the right angle and reflected brilliantly on Mumsie's personal jewelry collection. There were two diamond rings and two other diamond pieces. She pointed to one of the rings and said that Grandfather had given it to her when they were engaged, and the other one was given to her own mother from her father. She added that both rings were handed down from several generations; rumor was that the Cameron ring, like the Williams ring, was part of the French crown jewels that were stolen at the beginning of the eighteenth century. It was probably worn by King Louis XIV himself. They were supposed to be given to Mother, but I was told they did not fit her fingers. Since they could not be worn by Mother, Mumsie felt they should be given to me. "Your father will hold them for you until you are older." She stressed the point that the note at the bottom of the box was far more valuable than the gems themselves. "Over time, I think you will appreciate its message, and hopefully, you will remember me most when you do." Mumsie had me help her put on her glasses, and she began reading her letter, which appeared to be written by Soulange.

Dearest Chip,

Your grandfather and I have been together for over forty years as partners and friends. In this time, we have built our endeavors on a foundation of love, peace, hard work, and caring about our fellow man. There has been no discord between us, but rather a lasting trust. That trust helped us face the many obstacles that together we overcame. But that is what life involves—a series of burdens, obstacles, challenges, injustices, imbalances; in other words, a series of errors that need to be corrected. We could not change them all, but with our strong bond of love and friendship, we've made an effort.

These jewels are symbols of love and commitment to basically reach that goal. They have no monetary value to us. As far as Grandfather and I are concerned, they are priceless. They have never been appraised, but the message and reminder of the diamonds is clearly as bright as the stars that shine nightly. The diamonds represent that worthy post that we have not abandoned all these years. It has not been an easy task. Too many people do not understand the true meaning of this post, but it didn't matter to us. Our focus remained to nurture a more steadfast character in each other these forty-plus years.

Your grandfather and I have been a good team, like the two wheels of a bicycle, making our journey through life less burdensome, simpler, and more sustaining. It has been our duty.

Mumsie paused for a moment and put down the letter. She asked me to get the book on her nightstand. It was worn, but she opened the English copy to page 65. She had to read a quotation from Charles Wagner's *The Simple Life* to make a special point:

However simple duty may be, there is still need of strength to do it … Alas! The officer, though he finally collars the thief, can only conduct him to the station, not along the right road. Before man is able to accomplish his duty, he must fall into the hands of another power … the power of love. When a man … goes about his work with indifference, all the forces of earth cannot make him follow it with enthusiasm. But he who loves his office moves of himself … and this is true of everybody. The great thing is to have … been led by a series of experiences to love this life for its griefs and its hopes, to love men for their weakness and their greatness, and to belong to humanity through the heart, the intelligence and the soul. Then an unknown power takes possession of us, as the wind of the sails of a ship, and bears us toward pity and justice. And yielding to its irresistible impulse … men of all times and places have designated a power that is above humanity, but which may dwell in men's hearts. And everything truly lofty within us appears to us as a manifestation of this mystery beyond. Noble feelings, like great thoughts and deeds, are things of inspiration. When the tree buds and bears fruit, it is because it draws vital forces from the soil, and receives light and warmth from the sun … This central force manifests itself under a thousand forms … All that it touches bears its seal, and the men it inspires know that through it we live and have our being. To serve it is their pleasure and reward. They are satisfied to be its instruments, and they no longer look at the outward glory of their office, well knowing that nothing is great, nothing small, but that our life and our deeds are only of worth because of the spirit which breathes through them.[21]

She began reading from the letter again:

Your grandfather and I have shared a blossoming, growing love as a team. We believe and abide by Monsieur Wagner's insight on simple duty. But our journey together is nearing its end. Your father has done an outstanding job in maintaining that post of honor, and he carries this message daily in his interactions with patients, friends, and all of his family. But he will need your help someday.

And know that Soulange continues to maintain that station in life as well. Her spirit and genuine caring live up to every standard your grandfather and I aspire to attain. Just as the lighthouse directs the tired sailors in their journey toward the shore, she remains an excellent friend and guide for all of us. Stay close to her and listen to her sage advice.

Chip, you have shown us your great potential to follow this important path. Your attendance to me during this illness, and to the people at the shelters during holiday time, as well as your interest in your father's work and your genuine heart, which speaks loudest of all your attributes, demonstrates your willingness to join God's "crusade" and march in accord. When you look at these diamonds, let them remind you that you are to report to duty to that treasured position daily, focusing on refining that steadfast character and no matter what forces there are that will attempt to distort or falsify the truth about the meaning of this important mission, you will stand tall. Truth, like the cutting process needed to create these colorless diamonds, requires patience, painful moments, and frequent unsettling, but eventually, it rises to the top and remains a beacon of hope. Truth can overcome ignorance, fear, and apparent beliefs that are proven false over time. Whatever you do, whatever may happen to you during this lifetime, be faithful and unyielding. The truth will see you through.

Be "colorless," Chip. The most valuable diamonds are the colorless diamonds. They are the clearest and the most desirable. Like the colorless diamond, the most valuable quality of character in a human is to be colorless and truthful to yourself and others. This quality promotes the clear thinker, the clear learner, and the clear being.

When you are of age, young Chip, I am counting on you to find someone special to give these jewels as a token of your teamwork, and to build a foundation on each other's strength and purpose. Listen to Paul's advice to the People of Corinth in the First Book of Corinthians, chapter 3 verse 10: "According to the grace of God which is given unto me, as a wise builder, I have laid the foundation and another buildeth thereon. But let every man take heed how he buildeth thereon." Remember, she must be worthy of the diamonds. They are our loving reminder of our ties to that foundation. Pass them on judiciously.

I will love you always,
Mumsie

I looked at Mumsie's sweet smile and tried to hug her.

She reached out with her hands, unable to grasp anymore. I told Mumsie, "I won't let you or any of the family down. I will remember to report to duty."

"That's my boy," replied Mumsie, "Be a diamond, at all times." Her eyes sparkled for those moments with me. They mirrored the diamonds in the box. I kept hearing the words, "their value is priceless; their value is priceless" resonating in my head. Having Mumsie in my life was priceless.

Within weeks, Mumsie passed away, and for the first time in my life, I had to face the pain of death. At the funeral, however, the eulogies brought solace to the family as we listened to the tributes given by her friends at the Trinity Church downtown.

It was Mumsie's wish to have her service at Trinity Church, an Episcopalian parish of notable historic deeds since its founding in 1697. The current church was consecrated in 1846 and its familiar Neo-Gothic spire, its daily worship, and its outreach to the needs of the poor, the disadvantaged, and the infirmed truly represented the lifework of Mumsie and all her ideals.

Several of her close friends—Jane Addams, Helen Keller, Florence Kelly, Mary White Ovington, and Julia Ward—presented praiseworthy tributes, but Miss Keller delivered one of the most memorable. Miss Keller said that she and Mumsie held many common beliefs, but one specific was distinctly worth mentioning. She quoted from her essay "Optimism":

A man must understand evil and be acquainted with sorrow before he can write himself an optimist and expect others to believe that he has reason for the faith that is in him. I know what evil is. For a time, I felt its chilling touch on my life; so I speak with knowledge when I say that evil is of no consequence, except as a sort of mental gymnastic … the struggle which evil necessitates is one of the greatest blessings. It makes us strong, patient, helpful men and women. It lets us into the soul of things and teaches us that although the world is full of suffering, it is full also of the overcoming of it. My optimism, then, does not rest on the absence of evil, but on a glad belief in the preponderance of good and a willing effort always to cooperate with the good, that it may prevail.[22]

I'm sure Mumsie was quite acquainted with its darkness as well. She lived with a "willing effort always to cooperate with the good." I could feel her optimism and "see" it when I held her hand in mine.

"The world is sown with good; but unless I turn my glad thoughts into practical living and till my own field, I cannot reap a kernel of the good." Mumsie had an abundant harvest of good that she shared with the whole world.

The Fisk Jubilee Singers graciously accepted the invitation to sing at Mumsie's service, as a personal request by her. She had been a financial supporter of Fisk University, went to their concerts in New York, and even heard them in London and Paris on their world travels.

I sat next to Grandfather and Father during the service; Godfather Herbert sat on the other side of Grandfather. After the remarks were made by the minister and friends, the Jubilee Singers stood and sang the Negro Spiritual, "I's Gwine to Bear the Burden in the Heat of the Day."

Throughout the remembrances, Grandfather's shoulders were slumped, and his eyes were saddened, but when the first note rang out, he appeared fixed, as if he was part of the choir, mouthing the song and drawn to the power of the words. It was as if the message of the spiritual fortified his very being; it consoled him as if Mumsie, herself, was standing up and joining the service. Although he was tearful, there was a glow, a sense of serenity inside Grandfather while they sang. At that moment, he had more life in him than I had seen since Mumsie's death.

One thing I could never forget was the look on the faces of Mother and Uncle Thaddeus as they sat in the middle of the service with no expression. There was no sadness or grieving expressed by them during the eulogy or the personal tributes of Mumsie's friends, but they scowled in disgust quietly when the Fisk Jubilee Singers started their music. Mother did ride to the cemetery with Father, Grandfather, and me, while Thaddeus had his own transportation arranged.

On the ride from the church across the Brooklyn Bridge to the Greenwood Cemetery where Mumsie was laid to rest, I sat thinking about some important observations. I could not understand why Sue-Lee wasn't able to sit with us during the service. Grandfather and Father needed her comforting like she had given me over these past few days.

It was my first time at the cemetery when we arrived at Greenwood. I was so impressed with the size of the plots, the old headstones, and the mausoleums that blended in a place that looked like a meadow out in the country. The trees, flowers, and grass enclosed the area, leaving New York City a distant place just a few hundred feet inside Greenwood. I felt a gentle breeze flow through my hair, and I knew at that moment that Mumsie would truly be at peace.

As they were gathering around the gravesite for Mumsie, I saw Uncle Thaddeus pull Father aside, showing his outrage and bitterness at Father for allowing Mumsie to give the family diamonds to an eight-year-old boy. Thaddeus angrily stated, "She was in a weakened state. Those diamonds are too valuable to be in the hands of a child. He has no understanding of their worth."

Father gave Thaddeus a look that could have stopped a train going full speed and responded, "You self-glorified imbecile. Mumsie made her decision. And you will not say any more about that decision to me or anyone else. Be grateful I won't disturb Father with these blasphemous remarks."

Uncle Thaddeus walked away with his face as red as his hair. He left shortly after the burial in his carriage, alone. I never understood how this man could have been raised by Grandfather and Mumsie and be so deliberately contrary to their beliefs and actions.

After we left the cemetery, I watched Grandfather closely. There he sat, solemn and obviously in despair, but I reached over to hug him. I told him that Mumsie would have been pleased with all the tributes given to her, especially the music.

Grandfather placed his large hand on my shoulder and said, "Thank you, Chip, for caring as you do. Mumsie talked to me about the letter she gave you. She told you to be faithful to the post. That will be a lifetime commitment."

That night, I was alone, but I was not very lonely. Father did not come home, and it was Sue-Lee's day off. I sneaked into Mumsie's room and went to the drawer in her dresser where the wooden box was placed. I opened the box and looked at the diamonds. I carried them over to Mumsie's bed and laid my head on her pillow as I slid the diamonds underneath. I felt so close to her at that moment. I don't know if it was a dream or a pre-sleep vision, but I thought I saw Mumsie smiling without being in pain. She was reaching to hold me. Her hands appeared to be normal, not disfigured. "Hold on to the truth … truth rises to the top," she said and then vanished. I looked at the diamonds again and returned them under my pillow. As painful, dark, and unpleasant feelings evolved through the night, I knew I was given an inextinguishable light to operate, and I needed to understand how it worked more clearly.

The following morning, I awakened to Father calling me in a concerned voice. He appeared emotionally unsettled. He had to make all the funeral arrangements and had to comfort Grandfather, and I was convinced that Uncle Thaddeus made matters worse with his remarks to Father. He asked me how I was doing, and I told him how Mumsie came to me in a vision and said to hold on to the truth. I had a big responsibility. I also told him that I was protecting the diamonds under the pillow. I reiterated to Father that I would never disappoint Mumsie, but as I looked up in his face, I became more concerned about him. I placed my arm around him and said, "Mumsie told me that I will need to help you someday. But I want to help you now. We are going to stick together as Mumsie would have wanted. We are going to find the sun even if we have to look through every cloud."

Father sat there, quiet for a moment, and then he told me how much he appreciated me supporting him at a time when he needed it the most. He told me that Grandfather and Mumsie had been very impressed with my understanding of my attachment to humanity and my capability to accept responsibility. He reminded me of a time when I was a small baby being bathed. He looked at me sitting in the water calmly, and I glowed right before his eyes. I appeared "as a diamond in the water" he said; the image was so powerful to him. He went on to say that the image remained as strong over the years as it did then. "And, Chip, you are correct. We will find the sun, even if we have to look behind every cloud in the sky." Father kissed me on the head and returned the diamonds to Mumsie's drawer.

I had not looked at Mumsie's letter or thought about my reactions to her death in many years, and I realized how necessary it was to review it now. Truth does rise to the top, but is accompanied by painful moments and unsettling feelings frequently. I need to remain patient and open.

Minnie said, "Mumsie's heart and wisdom served your family during pleasant and worrisome times, and her letter lives forever within you. That is why letters are intended to be read and reread. We have to return to their content, especially when it is so replenishing."

Chip's Tenth Birthday and a Gift from Grandfather, November 28, 1911 (Event 7)

Minnie said, "You were very passionate in your recollection of Mumsie. How did your grandfather manage after her death?"

As her illness worsened, they came and lived on the fourth floor of our home at 9 West Seventy-Third Street. When I wasn't there for Grandfather, he had frequent visits from Godfather Herbert, who tried regularly to reassure him and lift his spirits.

Grandfather and I had been good friends always, but it seemed like we needed each other more after her death. We found comfort in sharing stories about Mumsie, what we did to make her happy, and the things that upset her the most.

He said I would respond to questions the same way that Mumsie did on several occasions. He thought I had many of her mannerisms as well. Sometimes we laughed out loud, and sometimes we would sit and cry, but we managed to get through the sadness and grief with each other's support.

Grandfather expressed his gratitude for our friendship regularly, but on my tenth birthday, he gave me a special "gift," which, in addition to the diamonds, reminds me of both of my grandparents.

I removed my watch and fob from my vest pocket and handed them to Jasper to show everyone what that gift truly meant.

This gift represented Grandfather and Mumsie so distinctively and indelibly. The watch was originally bought by Mumsie's grandfather nearly one hundred years earlier—around 1810—from a European collector, and it was handed down through the generations. Mumsie surprised Grandfather with the watch after having a new dustcover with his initials engraved and a diamond chip in the middle on their first anniversary. Over time, the mechanism needed major repair. Grandfather had it redesigned in 1886.

Everyone was fascinated with the details of the watch, beginning with the face.

The watchmakers preserved the enamel filling depicting a man who resembles Moses. He is striking the rock open to let out the water to quench the thirsting Hebrews, also depicted near the rock. The water is made of revolving twisted glass. Moses closes the flow of water in a second position. The scene is brightened by a gold raised area of rock on an enameled ground showing the Hebrew people as well as the Almighty Eye of God and a cherubic angel in a cloudy sky looking down. On the bottom of the watch, there are two cupids striking a bell to sound the hour and quarter hour.[23]

I admired the watch so much as a young child, and I was so surprised to open the box and see it. I felt somewhat reluctant to accept it.

Grandfather had waited until the evening of my birthday and I had gone into his room to say good night. Our routine of exchanging good nights was one of the best times for us.

"Chip, my boy, climb on in the bed. I have some important business to share with you."

After we got comfortable, Grandfather reached under his pillow and pulled out a box and letter. "This is for you."

It reminded me of the box of diamonds that Mumsie had given me.

"Open the box, and I will read the letter to you." To my amazement, I found the watch and fob and remained speechless in disbelief. He started to read before I could reply.

> Dearest Chip,
>
> The watch, representing time, has had a deep impact on your grandmother and me, and we both felt it should be passed on to you now to learn its hidden meaning. Time is short, but what you do with your time, is etched indelibly in stone or wasted in shifting sand. You must make a choice. It is not the quantity, but the quality of time that makes your presence on earth worthwhile or ignored. Michel Montagne stated simply, "Wherever your life ends, it is all there … Some men have lived long and lived little. Attend to it while you are in it."
>
> You have shown Mumsie and me that you are already etching your presence on this earth in stone. The watch is a visible reminder, but I wanted to add two new items to it that would spruce it up for this occasion."

He then described the background of the fob, which is a caricature figure of the Fate, Lachesis, carrying her distaff. Grandfather could never forget the useful message of mythology. He referred to Plato's *Republic* with Er, a soldier who was killed in battle, but returned to life and told what he had witnessed after his own death.

Er watched as the souls were judged by their conduct during life. If they were just and caring, they went to the heavens to benefit from various experiences and return refreshed at the place of judgment. If they were unjust, they went to the underworld, punished for their misguided ways and then, they would return refreshed as well. Souls considered irredeemable would not have an opportunity to leave the underworld. Soon, all of the "cleansed" souls would travel toward a spindle carrying the threads of life. The spindle was operated by Anake (Goddess of Necessity) and her daughters, the three Fates—Clotho, Lachesis, and Atropos. They sang with the sirens who were assigned to each of the eight planets (one siren per planet) singing one continuous note together, making a complete scale and creating harmony. Lachesis, the sustainer of life, assigned the destinies of the souls. Choose wisely during your life, they were told, for you alone are responsible, not God. Once chosen, they were given a spirit to be its guardian.

Er saw souls who chose avarice and tyranny and they were destined to have a miserable outcome. Once the soul was assigned a spirit, they were taken to the River Lethe (the waters of forgetfulness) to drink and forget their memories. They were then swept back to Earth to their new lives. [24]

So the fob was carved into the image of Lachesis to remind you to stay on course and that in time, destiny would lead you to a greater truth.

While Pamela was admiring the fob, she asked, "What was the second item besides the fob?" I told them that Grandfather had a quotation engraved on the dustcover for me. I continued reading the letter.

> There will be times in your life that will be sad and painful, not well understood, and even unbelievable, as well as joyful and peaceful, but over time, healing and pleasant memories should prevail. The quote is from Virgil's *Aeneid*, line 203: "Forsan et haec olim meminisse iuvabit" which translates in English: "Perhaps, in future times, it would be pleasant to have remembered these things."

> Remember these things and remember me every time you look at the watch and open the dustcover. I will look back and smile at all your good deeds and intentions.

> Always,
> Grandfather

I was so emotionally aroused that I had to sit in his bed, holding the watch, thinking about both Grandfather and Mumsie, and wondering how would I ever measure up to their aspirations of me.

He must have been reading my mind when he leaned over and said, "Don't try to figure things out tonight. You will have a lifetime to do that. Be happy and just be you."

Rekindling the moment became as impacting as it was fifty-four years ago. I looked at Soulange because she would fully understand all the feelings that swelled within me thinking about Grandfather and Mumsie. She was there. I ran to show her and Father the watch when I returned to my room that night. She was smiling tonight as she did then, with a tear and great satisfaction.

I then mentioned that the gift from Grandfather was also significant because the front of the watch has three generations of Waterburys' initials engraved on it. When I drift off in thought, at times, we are the Three Musketeers: "All for one and one for all."

My family attached a great importance to my birthday regarding Thanksgiving Day. I was born on November 28, 1901, which happened to fall on Thanksgiving Day. My birthday was always celebrated on Thanksgiving Day. Grandfather, Mumsie, and Father did not mention the Pilgrims or any connection to the 1621 feast. They recognized me as a part of their thankfulness for the opportunity to serve others.

We had a cornucopia display on the table, but Grandfather and Mumsie told me we were blessed with an overflowing abundance of God's treasures—friendship, love, peace, goodwill, and brotherhood. They would all wish me happy birthday, and we would hold hands and recite Robert Louis Stevenson's "Prayer for Thanksgiving."

> Lord, behold our family here assembled. We thank thee for this place in which we dwell, for the peace accorded us this day, for the hope with which we expect tomorrow, for the health, the work the food and the bright skies that make our lives delighted, for our friends in all parts of the earth and our friendly helpers ... Let peace abound in our small company.

Looking back over my first ten years, I was truly blessed with great memories.

The clock struck five o'clock. I had been talking since late morning, and it was time for dinner. I had only expected to talk about Grandfather's journal, but I was urged to add my early years as well.

Elizabeth looked at me and said, "You must finish telling us more of your story. We all want to hear about those subsequent events. We can extend the Christmas spirit throughout the week with Father's gift to all of us."

Jasper was first to agree with Elizabeth. "If anyone doesn't want to hear Water Pump's stories, don't bother coming around until next year because I definitely want to hear it all."

Minnie said, "Jasper, who put you in charge of making the decisions around here?"

Everyone laughed and agreed to meet the following evening to continue where I had left off.

Trip to Troutbeck with Grandfather, Uncle Herbert, and the Spingarns, August 1913 (Event 8)

The following night, after a wonderful dinner, we all gathered in the library again.

Pamela said, "I loved all those riveting stories about Soulange, Great-Grandfather, Mumsie, Grandfather, and even the questionable antics of your mother and Uncle Thaddeus and how you revealed them last night in vivid detail. I'm excited to hear about Uncle Herbert's influence on you and his close relationship with Great-Grandfather, especially after Mumsie's death."

Uncle Herbert was not very tall in physical stature, but in Grandfather's eyes, he was a giant friend and guidance counselor. They knew each other's thoughts, and they both looked to each other for inner strength and hope. They were both outspoken and very logical in their thinking. They were tireless readers. Mumsie told me that Uncle Herbert brought a spark to his life. Their friendship started in 1886 when Uncle Herbert joined Grandfather on the faculty at the Ethical Cultural School. Their bond continually grew stronger and stronger.

Uncle Herbert was a great nature lover—the plants, trees, and wildlife of the forests and the birds, insects, mammals, and rodents. It was a passionate hobby outside of his academic study. He was personal friends with John Muir, a founding member of the Sierra Club, and a lifetime member off the Audubon Society and the Museum of Natural History.

My most memorable conversation about nature was when Uncle Herbert joined Grandfather and me on a trip to Uncle Joel's summer home, affectionately called Troutbeck, in upstate New York (Amenia) on a sunny August day in 1913.

The Spingarns had owned Troutbeck since 1910. It was more than 350 acres of beautiful land south of the Berkshire Hills that could be seen from the high grounds. The property had rocky hills, many winding brooks, and several hiking trails, with my favorite trail leading down to a private lake. The lands were filled with sprawling trees, many species of plants, and numerous woodland creatures giving you a moment to escape the doldrums of the city and enter a world of paradise—an open wilderness filled with all of its majestic trimmings.

On this particular day, Uncle Herbert was quite absorbed in the surroundings and openly offered his insights for me to appreciate as we walked with Grandfather and Uncle Joel. Let me paraphrase what I recalled him saying: This wooded forest is replete with such grand species of trees, particularly the white pine, the stretching oaks, and the noble chestnuts. These wonders, nature's disciples of God, took a relatively short time to grow to their fullest potential and lasted for ages. The young chestnut, bearing its first burr somewhere at the point where it is fifteen to twenty feet tall, will be unassumingly approached by a squirrel or bird to gather the nascent seeds and plant them at a distance from the growing tree amongst the pines or oaks to manifest the rest of the chestnut tree population. According to Henry Thoreau, who spent enormous time observing the happenings in the woods, the men who came to shake or club the chestnut trees to gather the nuts had great dissent from the blue jays screaming or the red squirrel *scolding* their tactics as if to say these wood lots are the result of our hard efforts and labor; we need to preserve and maintain their continuity.

And now, all of the forests are in jeopardy because of disease and the further development and commercialism of man. The chestnut, in particular, has a gloomy future since the invasion of the Asian fungus first observed in the Bronx Zoo in 1904. The trees that reached one hundred feet in length with a nine-foot girth and had their gorgeous canopies immortalized in Longfellow's *The Village Blacksmith* may be decimated within our lifetime. Look at these trees now, young Chip, for they won't look like this for long. The oncoming blight is near, crippling the growth of new trees. Once the spores infiltrate the bark, the tree is diseased and destined to die within one year.

The bigger problem has been the myopic attitude that the land and its wildlife provide unlimited resources in this United States for man to arbitrarily take. As a result of this unconscionable rationale, the widespread destruction of habitat (the forest) and its unsuspecting residents (the wildlife—birds and ground dwellers) has diminished the populations of both to near extinction in several species. Thank God, we are blessed with strong-willed advocates who have pleaded with government officials to do something right to protect and preserve these natural wonders.

John Muir was successful in holding off the damming of Hetch Hetchy Valley in Yosemite National Park in California, and his strong words still echo within me. I carry them with me and read them out loud to remind myself how valuable God's gardens are and forever will be for all of us:

> Hetch Hetchy Valley, far from being a plain, common rock bound meadow … is a grand landscape garden. As in Yosemite, the sublime rocks of its walks … give welcome to storms, and calms alike, their brows in the sky, their feet set in the groves and gay flowery meadows, while birds, bees and butterflies help the river and waterfalls, to stir all the air into music … in our magnificent National Parks … Nature's sublime wonderlands, we have the admiration and joy of the world. Nevertheless, like anything else worthwhile, from the very beginning, however well guarded, they have always been subject to attack by despoiling gain seekers and mischief makers of every degree from Satan to senators, eagerly trying to make

everything immediately and selfishly commercial … These temple destroyers, devotees of ravaging commercialism, seem to have a perfect contempt for Nature, and instead of lifting their eyes to the God of the mountains, lift theirs to the Almighty Dollar.[25]

Take note and observe, young Chip! You are witnessing God's creation. Breathe it in. Let it stir your deepest thoughts of life and then exhale with the satisfaction you were so privileged to celebrate.

There was complete silence from Grandfather, Uncle Joel, and Uncle Herbert as we continued walking. A bee buzzed near my ear, a woodpecker was tapping a Morse code on the distant tree, and the brook seemed to lend support to Uncle Herbert's words as it meandered along the trail. As we came near the clearing, the sounds muffled—and we were surrounded by a blanket of peaceful solitude. The fragrance of the wild sweet peas was intoxicating.

I was in awe of the entire experience. Uncle Joel then talked a bit about his prize clematis collection and what a favorable blossoming he had this season. We stopped at the end of the trail down by the lake and held hands together, giving thanks to be a part of God's creation and "instruments to do His work."

While marveling at the brightness and clarity of the day, Grandfather said, "I hope you appreciate the poignant words your Uncle Herbert shared about nature's design because it is an important consideration for all mankind during their lifetime. What else is important in life, Chip?"

I thought for a moment and answered, "Love, friendship, hard work, helping others, and happiness."

He agreed with me, and he wanted me to consider other concepts as we walked. He reiterated that I had enjoyed a privileged life with opportunities most of the people of the world would never see. I was privileged to be born into the majority "class" with a key to open any door I chose and explore without denial or refusal to enter. However, a "great majority of the majority" assumed their superiority and, through legal and social customs, has prevented others labeled "different, inferior, and unworthy" from sharing those privileges. Grandfather emphasized never taking privilege for granted or expecting someone who appears "different" to be less of a person than myself.

In truth, I was not any better, even if I lived my life believing that I was. He illustrated his point with Uncle Joel who was asked to join the local Duchess County Country Club by one of its members, but when some other member found out about his Jewish heritage, the club members collectively rescinded his invitation. His money, education, and worldwide reputation as an authority on literary criticism could not influence their final decision.

I became noticeably unsettled.

Uncle Joel put his arm around my shoulder and told me not to be upset, to study my battles, and know when to fight and when to remain unaffected. Grandfather reassured me that Uncle Joel did not want to belong to a group of "pretenders" anyway. Grandfather, Uncle Joel, and Uncle Herbert laughed and eased my mind considerably.

Uncle Joel went on to say that I would have my challenges in life, but it was my duty to uphold my principles against all odds and keep on course with diligence. "Chip, your unwavering efforts will be the only thing to bring you true honor."

I thought about another conversation Uncle Joel and I had with regard to honor and his reference to Edmund Spenser's masterpiece, *The Faerie Queene. She* is Spenser's reference to honor:

> In woods, in waves, in war she wants to dwell,
> And will be found with peril and with pain.
> Nor can the man that moulds in idle cell,
> Unto her happy mansion attain.[26]

Grandfather emphasized to reexamine who I am, keep clear thoughts, and maintain an ongoing search for truth as part of each day's routine. I can only truly be happy, content, loved, and befriended when I am living my life to help others. Hard work and caring for the next person will offer me a greater understanding of who I am. He repeated himself, saying hard work and the recognition to use my hands to do good deeds was so important. He told me how pleased the family was that I was a student at the Ethical

Cultural School, where they reinforced hard work and the use of the mind and hands to accomplish all endeavors.

As we approached the Indian Lake, the sunlight glistened on the calm waters and made the lake appear more regal and bejeweled.

Grandfather seemed transfixed as he watched the stillness. We held hands as usual, and I distinctly remember the reflective look in his eyes and the gentle touch of his large hand on my shoulder. "You have been given much, Chip. Mumsie and I are counting on you to continue to help others and to always remember what this *privilege*—helping others—has meant to the Waterbury family."

As Grandfather, Uncle Joe, Uncle Herbert, and I walked back to the house, I was distracted from my usual admiration of the bird's nests and other fascinations of nature by the reminder of Grandfather's declining health. It was a slower walk back with Grandfather stopping along the way several times to catch his breath and needing Uncle Joel and Uncle Herbert to help support him as well as his cane. He had started to look older and was moving slower since the previous summer, and little did I know we would not experience that special summer trip together again.

Chapter

23

Grandfather's Death—May 3, 1914 (Event 9)

An overwhelming sense of peace filled the library, and the tranquility of the room was heightened by everyone's consciousness of nature's plan, as it was described in my 1913 trip to Troutbeck.

Elizabeth spoke first with thoughts and reflections of a sacred meditation. "It was as if Great-Grandfather, Uncle Joel, and Uncle Herbert were guiding you in the wilderness, and as you paused, absorbing all their wisdom and caring, you were intuitively envisioning the burning bush, and hearing the answers you would always rely upon for your forthcoming challenges. You felt God's presence with them, and Great-Grandfather knew you could not have been more blessed."

Everyone was emotionally moved by these insightful words, and a tear came to my eyes as I began telling them about Grandfather's death.

One can clearly see that Grandfather's greatest desire for me was to impart a greater understanding of life while he was alive. But his health steadily failed throughout that fall, and during the winter in early 1914, he became ill. He had developed long-standing irregular fevers and bright red dots on his fingers and toes. The spots were very sore when I tried to hold Grandfather's hands, but I never knew I hurt him because he wanted me by his side as often as I could be.

By April, he was too weak to get out of bed. Father, Soulange, and I would apply cool washcloths over his hands and forehead for the fever.

Father told me he wasn't talking very much, but he mumbled Mumsie's name frequently. Whenever I came into the room, he always managed to put on a smile and rub my face and ear.

One time when I walked in, he was resting, but he was speaking out loud: "Get off Momma! Leave Momma alone!" He appeared agitated, his fists clinched and face reddened. I ran to get Father to help, and he gave Grandfather a sedative. I asked Father about the outburst, but instead of answering, he asked me if I had heard him say anything else. When I said no, he didn't discuss it any further.

I went on a school field trip on May 1 and didn't return home until Sunday morning, May 3. When Father picked me up from school, he told me Grandfather had slipped into a coma and had not spoken for two days. I was so anxious to see him. When I saw Grandfather so helpless and appearing lifeless in his bed, I ran to his side and rubbed his face and ear the same way he had with me.

After a few minutes, to the surprise of Father, HHH, Soulange, and the Spingarns who were present at the time, a miracle happened. Grandfather sat up, opened his eyes, and looked at me. He whispered, "Chip, take care of the family. You are our hope and dream. Momma, he's here. Your dream has come true. He's our diamond in the water." He smiled, closed his eyes, laid his head down, and appeared very peaceful.

Father checked his heart, and he had gone. Years later, Father told me that he died from complications of bacterial endocarditis from an earlier rheumatic fever illness as well as chronic lung problems; he had been coughing for several months. The first patient I examined in medical school had the same disease, and I felt equally as helpless trying to care for him, knowing the inevitable.

It was hard enough to watch Mumsie, lying in Trinity Church, but now I had to accept Grandfather being there as well. Father and Mother sat with HHH, the Spingarns, and me while the minister read the prayers. I sat next to Father to hold his hand.

After the prayers, Father went to the lectern and gave the eulogy. He talked about Grandfather's strength and guidance and said, "He was a man who dared to dream. He was a man who served the public, never ignored the cause of justice and humanity, and carried a mighty shield—but no visible weapon except commitment, caring, and love for his fellow man. He had lost all his family members during the Civil War in Georgia, and he had left to seek a better life in New York. After marrying Mumsie, they worked effortlessly to champion social injustice and the ills of poverty together for nearly forty years. And now they are united once again in eternal peace and happiness. May their memory live long—and their dream never die."

The choir sang Grandfather's favorite hymn.

I looked at Father—who had to stay strong through Grandfather's illness and death—and I felt the grief that we shared. I then looked at Mother, and she appeared indifferent about his death and Father's sorrow. She showed no support during the service; she seemed to be off in her own world. She was "perturbed" that her trip to Paris was interrupted by the funeral services. She pleaded with Father, insisting that he alter the time of the service one day earlier so she would not miss her scheduled departure. Father was too sad to argue with her; he held the services earlier in the day just to keep the peace.

At the end of the service, Mother found Uncle Thaddeus who chose not to sit with us. He appeared dressed to attend an evening at the Ziegfeld Follies on opening night. The two of them were talking as if they were out dining instead of showing any remorse. *Did they belong in someone else's family?*

As we were leaving the church, I saw a man and two colored women sitting with Soulange in the back row. I didn't recognize them, and I wondered who they were. They left quickly, but they were visibly unsettled by Grandfather's loss.

As I was retelling the incident, Soulange interrupted, saying it was his cousin, John Bennett Nail, and his two younger cousins who he brought to freedom on that train ride from Valdosta to Baltimore. They never forgot his courage or his devotion to their welfare. He had regularly sent money to the family and kept in contact with all of them over the years.

I returned to the story.

While driving through the opening gate at Greenwood Cemetery, I was in awe of the details and impressive size of its structure for the second time. Built during the Civil War, the Gothic-style high-arched gate at the north entrance towers above all the surrounding trees.

Just before the burial service, I saw Uncle Thaddeus step out of his fancy new automobile and approach Father to speak to him about something that enraged him immediately, like the private conversation they had at Greenwood during Mumsie's burial. I did remember a few of the choice words that Father said to Uncle Thaddeus.

"Don't ask about the box or the books. They are of no concern to you. Never bring that up to me again. I won't tolerate your disrespect for Father. Not another word!"

Uncle Thaddeus left sheepishly, almost as fast as he came. Mother departed with him to go on her trip. After they were gone, things seemed to be more in order. HHH came along and put his arm around Father's shoulder and led him back to the rest of the grieving family and friends. HHH was trying to stay strong, but it was obvious that he had lost a very important part of his life. Uncle Herbert only looked at me once that day, as if making eye contact would make matters much worse.

That evening, I was home without Soulange, who was visiting a sick friend, and Father who was beside himself and needed time away to ponder the whole ordeal. I lay in my bed tearful, thinking about Grandfather's parting words and holding the wonderful watch that he had given me. Every time I wound that timepiece, I listened to the beautiful music that it played, reread the words on the dustcover, and as time went by, realized that I carried Grandfather with me wherever I went. I could not let Grandfather or Mumsie down.

I walked into Grandfather's room and lay quietly under the quilt that Mumsie had made for him years ago. I thought about the conversation on the trail, walking at Troutbeck, and the discussion that Mumsie gave me about the diamonds. I didn't understand fully why Grandfather had called me the diamond in the water on two different occasions, but it must have had some clear significance. I felt that all of our time and talks together were connected. I looked over on his nightstand and saw a beautiful picture of Mumsie smiling when she was a younger woman. I loved that picture; it always reminded me of good times with her. I also saw an old book that I had not seen before. It looked like it was *Uncle Tom's Cabin* in fancy old English, but my mind and body were tired and I went to sleep.

The next morning, Father came into the room, put his arm around me, and asked how I was doing. I was too concerned about him. I could tell he needed time to get his thoughts together. I told him I was hanging in there, and he put on a smile as best as he could. He had done so much to help Mumsie and Grandfather. It seemed like all the family responsibilities fell on him. Mother and Uncle Thaddeus offered aggravation rather than support for Father. He was so strong, just like Mumsie and Grandfather.

He mentioned he had a letter for me written by Grandfather around New Year's. I had received my customary Christmas letter, which I treasured always, but this was still sealed. I opened it and read it with Father.

As I was telling everyone, I reached into my wallet and opened a yellowed, worn but legible note, dated January 2, 1914:

In the dooryard fronting an old farm-house near the
whitewash'd palings, stands the lilac bush tall-growing with
heart-shaped leaves of rich green, with many a pointed
blossom rising delicate, with the perfume strong I love,
with every leaf a miracle—and from this bush in the
dooryard, with delicate-color'd blossoms and heart-shaped
leaves of rich green, a sprig with its flower I break.
—Walt Whitman
"When Lilacs Last in the Dooryard Bloom'd" [27]

My dearest Chip,

I am sorry that I am no longer physically with you. And I cannot recapture each year's events in our annual Christmas letter. However, this final letter of remembrance is given with all my heartfelt joy in having you as a beloved grandson, dear friend, and namesake. As much as you may grieve my departure, and wonder why our splendid times together couldn't last, we both should be grateful for the memories we shared.

You enriched my life in so many ways. Your inquisitive mind allowed me to renew my thoughts daily. As a young boy, your insistence on an explanation of everything amazed me and humbled me to realize how much I needed to learn. Your love of history always gave me a special pride to know that we shared a common interest. Your outstanding performance in academics, athletics, and music shows how you have taken full advantage of the opportunities you are given.

You appreciated all the things I gave you and enjoyed all the events and places we traveled together. I especially know how much the pocket watch means; when you carry it, you are carrying a part of me.

I stopped to smile. Every time I read that sentence, he couldn't have been more truthful. I continued with the letter.

Time will go by and experiences will unfold: some triumphant, some defeating, some predictable, and some unforeseeable. But never forget, something in all your experiences, obvious or concealed, will always teach you a lesson. I have some advice that I hope lingers inside of you and offers reinforcement to the foundation that is developing strongly within you now. These are thoughts that helped me face my life experiences with less confusion and less regret. These axioms will hopefully assist you in your life's journey and bring me back, now and then, for a while. Utilize them with your best judgment.

1) Think openly and dynamically. An open mind is the essential tool. All of the great spokesmen throughout the centuries, men and women, recorded or unknown, continually maintained flexible thinking and questioned themselves. With an open mind comes clearer thought, learning new lessons to gain wisdom, but never quite learning the final lesson ("the tower, but not the spire, we build"). Ironically, an open mind provokes those who do not choose to think openly. Galileo, Joan of Arc, Socrates, and Jesus thought openly and were punished to death because they were not understood and not accepted. But their thoughts will always be remembered.

2) Memorize Cicero's proposed "Six Mistakes of Man" mindfully:
- The delusion that personal gain is made by crushing others.
- The tendency to worry about things that cannot be changed or corrected.
- Insisting that a thing is impossible because we cannot accomplish it.
- Refusing to set aside trivial preferences.
- Neglecting development and refinement of the mind and not acquiring the habit of reading and study.
- Attempting to compel others to believe and live as we do.[28]
- There is no need to expound on these truths; they speak for themselves.

3) Offer your best unconditionally. Be like the sun shining equally on the rain forest and the desert sands. The sun's rays on fertile soil provide beautiful foliage. The sands, however, remain barren and lifeless. No distinction is made by the sun; all energies used are self-regenerated, no matter how they affect the receiver.

4) Practice the Golden Rule faithfully. Do unto others as you want (hope) them to do unto you, not as you expect them to do unto you. If you want their best, you better give your best—first. Be happy, knowing that when you offer yourself unconditionally, you can only give your best, and you can only feel your best.

5) Talk with God daily. Each conversation is a continuing journey to understand yourself better, to understand the next person better, to express yourself more deeply, and to gain a greater insight, connecting your life with His. Challenges are solved with prayer. Patience is learned through prayer. Love and joy are manifested by prayer. Prayer is a force as real as gravity and the air we breathe. My mother instilled that point in me as a boy, and I leave you with that point with the same conviction. Never summon God for personal convenience or illusionary gratification. Call Him humbly to supplicate and link into an infinite source of power and sustenance.

6) Be yourself earnestly. Know your shortcomings and strengths. Follow Polonius's advice to Laertes in Shakespeare's *Hamlet*: "To thine own self be true. And it must follow, as the night the day, thou canst not then be false to any man."

7) Forgive yourself and others unceasingly. Try to accept weakness, vulnerabilities, fears, and mistakes in people. But in your acceptance, actively separate from

these limited thinkers, lest you forget their detrimental offerings. It remains one of the greatest challenges our hearts and minds face. Keep trying, Chip! Time heals in many ways; practice patience.

Do not forget the lessons learned in life. Keep the things worth keeping alive in your mind and bury the anger, frustration, confusion, and denial. When you forget the lessons, you can't think openly, you will repeat any or all of the six mistakes of man, your offering will be conditional, and not your best, your talks with God will be linked with uncertainty and disbelief, you will not be yourself, and the meaning of forgiveness will remain elusive.

In a tribute to President Lincoln, Walt Whitman uses the lasting fragrance of lilacs to represent a perennial keepsake. My sprig has been broken from the bush, but I pray the fragrance is remembered with these words of encouragement.

Be strong, young man, and may God grant you the awareness and growing understanding of and reverence for life. Come speak with me from time to time, and "perhaps, it would be pleasant to have remembered these things."

I will miss you …
With all of my love and devotion,
Grandfather

What inspiration, what hope, and what love for me to treasure always. I was pensive for a moment, absorbed in each piece of advice, which I still feel is helpful and insightful today, but I wanted to be honest with myself then. Could I live up to what Grandfather and Mumsie wanted? I doubted myself, but I still had "to make every effort."

I looked at Father and asked if he thought I could measure up to their dream, and he assured me with a confident yes. He felt that we would do all the things that Mumsie and Grandfather felt we needed to do. I shared with him that I truly wanted to be a doctor. I wanted to use my hands and touch people's lives through medicine. I could discover what privilege really meant.

Father kissed me on my forehead and said he had a lot to be grateful for. I didn't know why he didn't say that I should be the one to be grateful, but the purposeful look in his tearful eyes was enough of a clear message that we would make it through.

As he continued to hold me, I looked at the nightstand—and that old book was no longer there. I never saw it again until Grandfather's secret was revealed, and I had not thought about it until then. I always felt Grandfather came back to get it, to read to Mumsie.

Ethical Cultural School Years, September 1915–June 1919 (Event 10)

Soulange said, "It was a sad day for all of us close to Windy, but the world lost a dear friend as well. He was beloved by the poor, needing food and shelter, the strong and weak, the helpless and privileged. He discerned no distinction amongst races, religions, or cultural persuasions; he was too occupied with offering himself to any humanitarian cause. He and Mumsie were a team, and he greatly missed their time together after she passed away, but he and HHH were conjoined. When Uncle Herbert didn't call Grandfather 'Windy,' there were personal times he would call him 'Odysseus.' Grandfather called him 'Mentor.' HHH suffered more than any of us, but he would hide most of his pain and continue on. He was not the same for a number of years, but then a ray of hope renewed his spirits."

Pamela asked, "What happened?"

Soulange replied, "Let Windy continue with his school years at the Ethical Cultural School, and that question will be answered."

After Grandfather's death, we all had a tough time trying to adjust to his absence. It was hard following Mumsie's death, but Grandfather gave me the emotional support that made it feel as if she was still with us. But I was older in 1914, and more responsibility was placed on me to learn and do my best to help others.

I transferred to the upper division at the Ethical Cultural School in September 1915. I knew I was walking the halls where Grandfather had taught history, and there was a tradition that he, Mumsie, and Father embraced since Father enrolled in the first class in 1878 when it was called the Workingman's School.

At that time, the school was the dream of Dr. Felix Adler who envisioned the development of the moral character of the student accompanying his or her mental growth with an ethical training focus as well as learning by doing. It was Dr. Adler's hope to also acquire a diverse student body, thereby bridging the classes and upon graduation, become "not only *working* men and *working* women, but working *men* and working *women*" (Augustus Paine, Secretary of the New York Society, 1878).

They also made a concerted effort to promote the integration of the use of the hands and brain; besides the core curriculum, the students were required to learn artwork, various metal and wood shops, and weaving. It was during my father's formative years at Workingman's School that his interest in medicine developed through the emphasis on the manual use of his hands and having his first contact with patient care accompanying Mumsie to the New York Almshouse.

Mumsie had worked in voluntary hospitals caring for the orphaned, the blind, and the mentally insane as well as the Civil War veterans who were too poor to receive appropriate care for their battle wounds and infections from malnutrition and poor sanitation. She would patiently rub the liniments for painful limbs and spend time with the homeless children who had no one to provide any hope from despair.

Father accompanied Mumsie when he was eleven years old for the first time to the Almshouse and watched Mumsie rubbing the legs of a ten-year-old girl, who according to the staff, had not spoken for two years. Mumsie had shown Father the technique of her care with her strong, meticulous fingers. She rubbed her leg like she was playing each note on her harp—determined, patient, and effortless.

Father tried to imitate her with careful gestures of his fingers. When they had finished, the patient smiled, and to the surprise of both Mumsie and Father, she verbally thanked Mumsie for all of her kindness and caring. They were both moved by the girl's response. Mumsie told me that Father was profoundly influenced by that experience—so much so that at dinnertime that evening, he announced his intent and commitment to becoming a doctor. He was struck by the glow in her eyes, the joy and happiness in her face, and the way she rubbed Mumsie's face with her little hand to show appreciation. He would devote his life to aiding the infirm and helping improve public health conditions.

Grandfather was on the faculty in the upper division of the Ethical Cultural School from 1882 through 1909. According to Father, he was highly regarded by his students as well as fellow members of the faculty. He inspired learning, and I would have loved being a pupil in his class. I did have the privilege of learning some of the best lessons in life from Uncle Herbert, although when I was a student there, he was the strictest, most demanding, and most challenging teacher I had in all my school years.

Herbert Horace Huntington was a professor of classics, public speaking, mythology, and world religion. He was a scholar and a true Renaissance man. Grandfather had told me that he was a child prodigy. He could read at the age of three, recite long passages from a Julius Caesar speech at the age of five by memory, and was fluent in Greek and Latin by ten.

He was one of my teachers in the fall of 1915 and each subsequent year at the school. He was no longer Uncle Herbert, but Professor Huntington. I didn't recognize him the first day of class; he was unimaginable. He belonged on Mount Olympus. He wore an academic cape, had his gold pince-nez glasses with a black silk ribbon attached around his neck, and every hair—the gray-and-black mixture accented by his trademark white forelock—was in place.

The first class I had with him was public speaking. He began the class every day in front on a small lectern, walked down the two steps, and started moving to the back of the room, peering over his glasses at every student. With an imperious, sarcastic tone, he would say, "Eyes front, mouths shut, minds opened, and focused on me now!" Nervous would be a euphemistic way of expressing our inward and outward anxiety from the moment we walked through the door to his class until we were saved by the school bell.

The first student to recite in front of the class, having made it up the short stairs to the podium, positioned himself carefully, opened his mouth to deliver his painstakingly prepared speech, and was struck wordless. So great was his fright that he could not utter one syllable; he could not even stammer. A minute passed, maybe two. Not a word from the rest of the class, only an occasional uneasy shuffle from someone impatient.

While the classmate stood still, his mouth opening and closing like a guppy fish, a deep, modulated yet elegant and articulate voice rose from the recesses of the back of the room: "Don't just stand there, mammering like a petrified scarecrow, boy. Out with it!"

The poor lad just threw up.

Another time, it was my turn to speak. I had rushed to get to class from a delay in my previous lecture, and my thoughts were a little scattered. And so was my necktie. Before I began, Professor Huntington remarked, "Boy, your tie is askew."

As I was fixing it and starting my speech, I became slightly nervous and began slurring my words.

He interrupted, saying, "Boy, be more lucid!'

The following year, he taught Greek mythology, Homer's *Odyssey* and Virgil's *Aeneid* from his notes, which were in Greek and Latin. One day, I walked in the class, and someone had drawn a caricature of Professor Huntington on the blackboard with the caption: "Eyes front, mouths shut, or else Medusa will turn you all into stone."

Needless to say, the professor was not pleased and demanded the artist's name. "What rampallian princox shows such disrespect for me?"

No one said a word, but the student sitting next to me passed a message that said, "Look how beet red the old boy looks."

I could not help but smile, and that was further fuel for his wrath.

"Since some of you find this so amusing, and no one is admitting ownership, you will all study and memorize the great funeral oration in Thucydides "History of the Peloponnesian War." Be prepared for tomorrow's class, if you know what is good for you."

I didn't know if he thought I made the artwork or not, but he remained hardest on me throughout the year.

I talked with Father, and he told me to be patient. He asked if I was learning something, and I told him I was. As time went by, I understood I had to perform well, and then I wouldn't have to feel so uncomfortable.

By my junior year, I adjusted and did well in his class. On one occasion, I instilled the scorn of a jealous classmate. Salvatore Cantolini was one of the students on scholarship. He was a tough Italian kid who bullied many of the younger students. We were in class together, and when the test scores were returned, he had received a C minus while I had an A.

Something upset him enough to come up to me during recess and try to pick a fight.

I told him I didn't want to hurt him, but he kept insisting that I thought I was better than him, and he was going to teach "the rich kid" a lesson.

I was already six feet, and Grandfather had prepared me to take care of myself with boxing training in the event of any unexpected altercation. I started to walk away from Sal, but he picked up a book and hurled it at me. I saw the book coming and ducked to avoid getting hit. Then he came at me with the first punch. He missed me, but I hit him straight in the eye and knocked him down. He got up and tried to hit me again, but this time, I was so angry at his inconsiderate treatment of the younger-class students that I decked him in the nose and blood started pouring out. It was the first time I had to defend myself in my life. I looked at my fist, not realizing how strong I had become, and was frightened for a moment to think I could have caused serious bodily harm to that kid.

Grandfather and Father were just preparing me to deal with all the people I would encounter—some nice, some not so nice. They had told me that hands could be soothing and gentle, and in a moment, they could be used to hurt to protect in self-defense. They could also save your life from harm. "Realize the hands can do much good as well as damage."

One of the faculty members saw me, and I was brought to the principal's office and suspended. When Father arrived, the principal told him that the school would not tolerate violence to answer any disagreement. I told Father what happened, and he said he was glad I didn't start it, but he was sorry for Sal not heeding my warning. He added that I needed to abide by the school's rules and codes—but never let any man take advantage of my fairness or sense of decency.

After I returned to class, Salvatore never said another thing about the incident. As a matter of fact, he asked me to tutor him in math—and I remember that he was much kinder to the younger classmen.

Time went by quickly, and graduation finally came. I had been accepted at Amherst College and would start in the fall. The morning before the graduation exercises, Professor Huntington came by the house to congratulate me personally. He admitted that he had been extremely harsh and demanding of me all four years, but he was well aware of my grandparents' hopes and promised them that he would help prepare me to face the world and be ready to go against life's adversities. He did his "best" to toughen and strengthen me and that Grandfather and Mumsie would have to be very proud looking upon me today.

"I will tell you something that I only need say once. I could not look at you at your grandfather's funeral because you reminded me too much of him, and I would have cried uncontrollably at the time. I needed to stay strong and show you discipline, even under the worst conditions. You are a man now, going off to college, and you have lived up to your grandparents' hopes. You have represented your grandfather's name well. You will no longer be called Chip. I would like to call you Windy, as I proudly called your grandfather. I could not bestow a higher honor on you or show you greater respect. And please call me Mentor." He apologized for being the martinet, but he would not have done anything less. He finished by adding that, as I went off to college, I would be directed accordingly and should keep up the hard work. We would stay in touch.

I was in disbelief. This man had tested me, scrutinized each detail, and would tolerate nothing less than perfection so that I could stand up to anyone or anything and still get the job done. It was a hell of a lesson. It definitely made me more of the man that I needed to be. I was conscious of a spiritual bond between Mentor and me that I had not appreciated since I was at Troutbeck.

We hugged, and I felt his genuine love and regard in that moment. I was so puzzled for four years how he and Grandfather were such good friends, and now I understood why they were. I also understood that we would nurture a friendship that lasted until his death and resonates to this day.

"Thank you, Godfather."

He handed me an inscribed copy of Plato's *Republic* and said we would enjoy several conversations discussing its content. He accompanied my family back to Ethical Cultural School for the graduation. I received the top school prize for academics and athletics as well as a special prize for leadership and handicraft for carpentry.

I knew that Father, Godfather, and Soulange were very pleased that day, and I wouldn't say anything to spoil their joy. But as I went to bed that evening, I had concerns about my own doubts of measuring up to Mumsie and Grandfather. I also had to live up to Dr. Adler's similar wish for all of his students to leave his school to "contribute our share towards the development of a better social order, and that only by attempting to lift the heavy weight of these public questions can our own moral fiber grow strong and firm."

As I listened to Dr. Adler's voice in my head, I could see how Father, Mumsie, and Grandfather had given their best efforts to help change the world for better living. I took a deep breath and knew I would have to take life one day at a time, but I would eventually be a part of that change.

As I packed my bags to start at Amherst in September 1919, I knew that I would go with the idea of changing conditions and devote my learning to becoming a humanitarian to help the disenfranchised and less fortunate. Mumsie, Grandfather, Father, Soulange, and Godfather clearly understood that living in this world as a man with a conscience meant you had to have an internal purpose, an offering to help others, with an outcome of fulfillment.

Most people assume that you need an education for the purpose of a "better" job and more money. However, I agree with my family's tradition of acquiring an education to become a more enlightened humanitarian. Although my doubts about my capability of doing what I needed to do lingered for nearly another decade, I was motivated toward that goal, and I was convinced I was doing the right thing.

Chapter 25

The World War and Influenza Epidemic, 1918 (Event 11)

Jasper was his usual colorful self. "Man, Water Pump, you had a real eye-opening experience during your school years. You had to face a tough professor, the tough Italian kid, and a tough principal who all tried to teach you a lesson, some good, some bad. But it made you all the stronger still. If I had been in the class with you, I don't know if I could have handled the professor. He would have been giving his lecture, and I would be lost after the first sentence. We would have had to memorize the whole 'Penelope' War. I ain't never knew anything about that war. Anyway, I knew something about the Great War, but you didn't ever mention it. Did you forget about the Spanish flu too?"

Minnie interrupted, "There you go, Jasper, with one of your assumptions again. Let Windy continue with his story."

"Ah, Minnie, I'm just trying to keep the story straight. I don't want to miss anything."

I smiled and said, "Well, Jasper, the war and Spanish flu need to be included."

In the fall of 1918, as a senior at the Ethical Cultural School, I witnessed what would be the deadliest "plague" in recorded history, and the most defining moment of my Father's life, right before my eyes. School had begun, and US troops were fighting against Germany in the "War to End All Wars."

The spread of the Spanish Influenza proved even more deadly, more fearful, and more devastating than the tragedy of the war itself. Father had been in communication with his friends William Park and Anna Williams at the New York City Department of Health, and he knew about the impending flu months before it came to New York. But the politics to mobilize patriotism and support for the war effort interfered with the rational plea of the public health experts and knowledgeable physicians who knew that early quarantine and masking would be a helpful course of action.

The first reported death in New York City occurred on September 15. Within days, panic and terror reigned as the disease struck with fury, spreading quickly throughout the city, the country, and the world.

Father had affiliation at both Bellevue and Harlem Hospitals, and he found himself immersed in a wave of illness and despair he had never imagined. He had treated patients during epidemics of cholera and diphtheria before, and he had managed to stay healthy, but now, he would face a scourge that all of the diseases combined would have less mortality than the influenza alone during that particular season.

Mother had been in Europe on her usual summer vacation and was expected to return in late September. She had written in July, letting us know that she was "safe" despite the war, and that she had the pleasure of meeting and dining with the Princess of Luxembourg and attending the Royal Ball Affair for fund-raising in the war effort ("French and British aristocracy, of course"). While she was sipping champagne and the finest French wines, Father was diligent in taking care of the poorest and most vulnerable victims in New York.

After Father became so heavily involved in the flu-care clinics, Soulange volunteered to assist in any capacity, as she had helped Father in New Orleans, twenty years earlier. They would awaken to be at either hospital by five thirty and stay as late as nine o'clock at night. Soon, they would come home with the most depressed mood I had ever seen either of them in. Usually, even on a demanding day, Father's spirit was upbeat and positive. But now he was down, and it seemed that his only moment of pleasure was listening to me practicing the piano and his favorite Enrico Caruso or the young violinist, Jascha Heifitz, playing on his Victrola.

During this time, we received another letter from Mother addressed to Father and me. She had heard about the developing illness and had decided to leave France in August. Instead of coming home, she left for Australia where the epidemic was not present. She arranged her stay with friends there through her connection in the State Department. She said she wouldn't leave there until the flu was gone here. How typical of Mother: selfish, cowardly, and manipulating. Why did she even bother to write at all? It was obvious that Father was upset.

I worried about Father and Soulange, and I begged them to let me volunteer on the weekends to help. Father and Soulange were adamant against my participation though they knew I was concerned about them and their patients. I continued to insist and argue with them for the first time in my life. The next weekend, I saw one of the most gloomy and emotionally painful experiences I could ever imagine.

After putting on a white gown and mask, I followed Father and listened carefully to his discussion as well as trying to help in my own way. I was immediately overwhelmed by the stench of urine and feces with so many of the patients unable to get up to go to the toilet because of their weakness and delirium—not to mention the pain and suffering I felt while listening to the horrible screaming and hysteric outbursts.

I saw Soulange trying to clean the patients and sanitize the area as best as she could, under the circumstances. I saw Father use his special case where he kept all his medicines that he used whenever he saw patients. He only had aspirin for fever, and ipecac and opium to attempt to relieve the coughing and pain with little to no success. I saw Father holding their hands and trying to soothe their souls when he knew they were about to die. As awful as the experience could be, watching Father and Soulange sacrifice and stand courageous against the threat of death to themselves, I was convinced that I would follow in his pathway and try to measure up to the principles he set to medicine and to life itself.

To my surprise, I watched Father take care of Salvatore, my classmate who had since become my friend. He looked as if the illness was beating him in the worst way. Father had already talked about the speed and spread that the illness brought to the individual patient and the rest of the community. The incubation period was twenty-four to seventy-two hours, and within two hours of feeling feverish, achy, and coughing, a small but significant percentage of the victims would develop brown spots on their cheeks that would coalesce, making the white patients look almost like Negroes. Some of the patients were a dreadful dark blue in their coloring due to the extreme lack of oxygen.

Salvatore had been in class yesterday, appearing fine without any complaints. Now, as I watched in disbelief, I saw him progress with coughing, high fever, difficulty breathing, and a sudden onset of uncontrollable bleeding from the nose. In one hour, his skin coloring became that unforgettable deep indigo blue, almost midnight in appearance. He was so weak and disoriented. I know he didn't recognize me behind my mask. As he attempted to roll over in the makeshift bed, there was a crackling sound, like stepping on a pile of raked leaves in late autumn, coming from his chest. Father allowed me to listen through his stethoscope, and there was barely any air moving—just that awful crunching noise. A short while later, his ashen face looked at Father and me with fear and a sullen expression, and finally he died in Father's arms, the icy-cold look of death lingering in my memory. Father told me he started having symptoms last night, sixteen hours ago.

I was numbed, and I knew I had to leave. We had been classmates since kindergarten. I couldn't understand how he was such a healthy guy and rarely out of school with illness. Even though Father and Soulange were at their busiest time with patients, they both made time to help me get through Salvatore's death. No words were expressed, but Father left those needy patients, knowing that I needed him right then.

When we got home, I hugged him and asked, "When is this all going to end? How is Salvatore's family going to handle such a tragic and early death? And all those other poor people suffering?"

Father tried to hold my hands and offer some explanation, but as I rested against his chest, I heard the familiar sounds of coughing. The routine had been demanding for Father, and after working four weeks, seven days each week, the exhaustion and exposure took its toll on him.

He continued coughing, and by Monday morning, I woke up and saw Father's door still closed at seven-thirty. Soulange tried to hurry me off to school, but I threw my books down and opened the door. Father was in bed, coughing and barely able to speak. He pleaded with me not to enter the room and said that Soulange would take care of him. School was the furthest thing from my mind. I was going to help Soulange do whatever was needed to do.

Over the next twelve hours, Father looked like he might die that night. His temperature was elevated, he had a tremendous headache, and his coloring was looking bluer. He kept calling for Mumsie and Grandfather and making other incoherent statements.

Soulange and I took turns changing the cool cloth on his forehead and trying to make him as comfortable as we could under the circumstances. There were several times when I returned to relieve Soulange, and she was whispering in his ear and supporting him. He appeared most calm during those moments. She would hold his hand, rubbing his face and ear gently and consistently. Watching Soulange take care of Father so faithfully and with such uncompromising devotion, I thought it was sad that Father did not have a wife like her. They would have been the same team as Grandfather and Mumsie.

The room remained silent. I could hear nothing but the tick, tick, tick of the clock at the end of the hall as if an impending shadow was waiting to come to take Father to join Grandfather and Mumsie.

Time went by slowly, but Father eventually appeared in less pain, less blue, and less ill. He eventually recovered. However, he did have a residual cough and intermittent headaches that would haunt him until his death. To this day, I believe Soulange saved Father's life during that epidemic.

Soulange smiled as I continued.

There were others who were not as fortunate in facing this pandemic scourge. In early December 1918, we received a phone call from Mother's younger sister, Eugenia Brewster Duke, saying that her husband, Henry

Spencer Duke, had died from the complications of influenza. I did not know Eugenia very well. I called her "Aunt Genie" and only remember seeing her three or four times in my life. They lived in a large home in Greenwich, Connecticut. They had no children.

On those few visits, we would have to walk up a long stone stairway to get to the front door and they had a large German shepherd that they had to put in the yard when I came because he would bark and they didn't know if he would be friendly or bite me. Uncle Henry would come to the door and greet us, and then when we got inside, he would close the huge wooden door and the room would appear dark.

All of the shades were drawn in the middle of the day, and we would go through the living room and dining room and finally see Aunt Genie knitting a quilt in her rocking chair. The house was always hot, summer or winter, and the black-and-white photographs along the walls that were hanging above the radiator had been faded and discolored by the continual steam.

Aunt Genie would frighten me with her thick glasses; they were so thick you could barely see her eyes. And her body was so extraordinarily thin; she couldn't have weighed more than ninety pounds, and she was not a short woman. She always drank her cup of coffee with ten teaspoons of sugar, and she drank at least ten cups daily. I thought she was aloof and not very caring. She reminded me of my mother and had a similar coldhearted manner. I had very little interaction with her since.

Father recuperated from October 21 through January 1919, when he was strong enough to resume working. The war had ended, and the troops came home that February to a hero's parade down Fifth Avenue, including the "Hell Fighters of Harlem," the 369th Colored Infantry Regiment, who were decorated with France's highest medal of honor for valor and gallantry. In spite of their unit not being given the appropriate time or place to train properly as well as the least available equipment for training—they had to use broomsticks and pretend they were rifles—they served the longest time on the front in the trenches of any American regiment during the war. They never had a single man captured alive by the German soldiers, and they were the only unit that was denied serving under the United States command. They were assigned under French command—using French uniforms and French weaponry—and were taught how to use them by

French-speaking troops. Most of these soldiers had not spoken French or had any familiarization with any of the equipment. When they turned to finish their seven-mile march past 110th Street in Harlem, everything returned to the same condition as they were before they returned home as "patriots."

Many of the 369th fighters had permanent lung damage or injuries resulting in blindness, hearing loss, or severe internal organ damage from the mustard gas, the bullets, or the shells released in the trenches by the German soldiers. Once they returned after the war, they needed medical care. Many of them couldn't afford it—or it was conveniently "unavailable." There weren't enough doctors, and Father was appalled at the conditions at Harlem Hospital. The influenza had lost much of its devastating fury, and although it did linger, it wasn't nearly as fatal.

Father and I regularly discussed the cases of these poor patients at dinnertime. Two soldiers' tales stand out quite vividly; their valor and genuine caring struck Father noticeably. He spoke so often about them that they were like Father's friends, and I felt I knew them personally, although I had not met either of them at the time.

The first was a private who received the company's Croix de Guerre medal and the American Distinguished Service Cross. He was a messenger on the battlefield, risking his life to carry vital information to the soldiers in the trenches. He had to run on the open field and return with their replies. After making the trip safely, he was sent out there again to dodge the machine gun bullets, but this time, he was asked to carry a can of coffee to give to one of the units that needed it. Upon his return, his trousers and the coffee can had several bullet holes, but no flesh wounds. The best part was to hear him say, "I jumped into shell holes and got back safely. And what do you think? When I got back into our own trenches, I stumbled and spilled the coffee."

In the next thirty minutes, he was back out there in no man's land, helping to bring back wounded comrades. Even though he was badly gassed, he repeatedly refused to take cover and went again to aid the wounded, still facing the deadly attack of bullets. He was more concerned about the welfare of the men and bringing that coffee can to the captain than he was about his own life or personal wounds. I heard that coffee story so many times that I thought the can and his trousers had no more metal or thread left to be recognizable.

Another soldier came home wounded from a few shots to the leg during shellfire. He had refused medical attention at the time to remain with his fellow soldiers who were wounded more severely and keep the German unit from advancing. Complications set in, and there was little hope to save his leg from amputation. He was sent back to New York with the leg still questionable. Father saw him at Harlem Hospital, and his left leg was almost twice the size of his right. He had to drain the abscess, and after several days, the circulation started to improve. The swelling eventually resolved, but the leg was never fully functional. He would limp and drag his foot when he was tired, but Father was pleased with his recovery.

The soldier had many visits with Father and was grateful for saving his leg. He told Father he could fix any watch, new or old, cheap or expensive, with any problem. Father was willing to give him one of his finest and favorite watches that needed servicing, but he got called to see another patient with an emergency and inadvertently left the watch on his desk. Father didn't even remember placing the watch down, but a few days later, the soldier returned the watch, and he had fixed it perfectly. Father said he must have been born a watchman because his own jeweler couldn't repair the watch, and it was returned like new with a precise timing mechanism. Father was so happy that he gave the watch to the soldier and invited him to service all the family watches and clocks. He called the soldier Mr. Watchman.

It's important to keep in mind how much these watches meant to Father, sentimentally. They were as important as the pocket watch that Grandfather had given me. There were heirloom clocks from the Cameron family as well as those purchased by Mumsie and imported from Switzerland. It meant a big deal to both of us that Father entrusted Mr. Watchman. Unfortunately, every time he came by the house, I was either at school or away elsewhere. I can see Father laughing out loud about some joke they shared. I did not meet this man until many years later.

"Who was it?" asked Hugo.

"You'll find out—no need to spoil the suspense."

With the war and the influenza somewhat behind us, the time that Father, Soulange, and I spent together in conversation and after dinner with our music during Father's convalescence was one of the most memorable and comforting times growing up. He was always so busy with the patients routinely, but those months were just the best. After dinner, we would go to the library, and Father would play his violin with me in a duet, and then I would play the piano with Soulange's nightingale voice accompanying me and filling the house with joy. Father was most relaxed, laughing and smiling like he did on special occasions only.

Father remained with this cheerful, jubilant demeanor until Mother finally returned to New York from her extended trip in April 1919. The chauffeur was sent, and when she got home, there were countless pieces of luggage to be emptied. I went out to help, but Father stayed inside.

As she walked to the door, she acted as if nothing was wrong. She offered no apology or explanation and showed no concern about Father or me. She brought Father a new navy blue sweater, making a point to tell us it was pure cashmere and a personal gift from the Duke of Portland, William Cavendish-Bentinck. Mother gave me a book of George Bernard Shaw's plays, personally signed by the author and also given to her by the duke.

As I was thanking Mother, Father dropped his gift on the chair. We were in Mother's room, and Father asked me to leave the room so he could discuss a few matters with her. Looking at Father's face, I knew that he was extremely upset. He nearly slammed the door once I was outside.

I stayed right outside, hoping to hear a few words, but Father's voice reverberated. I could hear the strain of anger with each word. "How dare you parade around Paris and Australia during wartime and not have the decency to come home to see how your son was doing, especially during the epidemic? What made you think you could *escape* the influenza in Australia? Only a selfish coward would think like you. If the ship bound for Australia had been torpedoed by an enemy submarine, you would be the first one in the lifeboat and demand a seat even before the children."

Mother interrupted him sternly, "Are you finished? I just came home, gave both of you thoughtful gifts, and now you act as if you needed me home. I'm sure you got along quite well. You, your father, mother, and precious son have always gotten along without me. You act as if I haven't existed since he was born. You are only happy around him. You are even happier around the hired help than you are around me."

Even though I couldn't see through that closed door, I have only seen Father that angry when Uncle Thaddeus came to Mumsie's and Grandfather's funerals.

"Since you are so convinced that my allegiance was to my parents and now to Chip, let me inform you that, starting this moment, you will receive one-half of your allowance that you have always taken for granted. I will make this point perfectly clear. When you die, you will have arrangements made to be buried in another plot—not the Waterbury plot. I have spent the last twenty years of my life with you, regretting the day I married you, but I'll be damned if I have to spend an eternity with the likes of you. The thought of it makes me sick. Think about your future. It looks pretty grim to me.'

I could hear Father's steps coming toward the door, and I quickly moved toward my own room.

Mother came out a few minutes after Father left, looking for a servant to help her unpack. She didn't see me, but I saw that cold, stoic face, dark and disconnected, as if nothing had happened after Father left her room.

She did not join us for dinner that evening, but she did come to my room when I was getting ready for bed. She asked how I liked the book, and I told her I was pleased and thanked her again. She reminded me to write a thank-you note to the duke for the book, and she also asked me to write one for Father's gift.

She left quickly, but I faintly heard her on the telephone with her friends, talking about her trip, her time with the duke, and giggling about how those who were *unworthy* would never have the privilege of dining with the aristocracy of Europe, but she did.

Whatever anger she may have had toward cutting her allowance, she never showed it during the rest of my formative years, but things were very different between them after that talk.

Pamela asked what was going through my mind after that nasty confrontation.

That night, I pondered their conversation, especially when Father said he regretted the day they got married. If they were never compatible, how could they have taken the time and produced a son when that union of love should be harmonious and joyful? I could understand why I was an only child.

I felt concern for Father—but more pity for Mother. She was obviously an unhappy woman. Neither of them was happy with the other, and both appeared quite miserable, even in conversation. It was a relationship that seemed doomed from the start. I knew Father loved medicine, the philanthropic side of his work, and the genuine friends he had, but Mother loved nothing except the imitation relationships she established and the illusions of grandeur she displayed to all of them.

Chapter

26

Amherst Experience 1919–1923 (Event 12)

My college years at Amherst were both a broadening learning experience as well as an academic milestone. After acceptances at several schools, I chose Amherst for three reasons. It carried a tradition and philosophy similar to the Ethical Cultural School, the campus and its surroundings were so irresistibly beautiful, and it was Uncle Herbert's personal preference for overall excellence and his close friendship with the school's president, Alexander Meiklejohn.

Although the school is somewhat remote in the heart of the western section of Massachusetts, the lovely fertile meadows and glorious mountain ranges would be best described by anyone who witnessed it as a picturesque vicinity of "nature at its best," through all four seasons, all year long. The town sits in the Connecticut Valley, bordered by the Connecticut River, and Mount Toby and Sugar Loaf are viewed to the north while Mount Tom and the Holyoke bluffs border to the south.

After arriving on the Boston and Maine Railroad for the beginning of school in September 1919, I stayed in South College, "home" to all the entering freshmen. After a few days of orientation, we heard a welcoming talk by President Meiklejohn at the Johnson Chapel, stating our responsibilities and willingness to continue the proud tradition of seeking intellect "fitted to forge the anchor or spin the gossamers of thought." As I looked around the chapel, there were flags of the Amherst Ambulance Corps, one of the first American units called to the European battlegrounds, decorated with the Croix de Guerre and the fourragère as well as the American flag and Massachusetts state flag. I was painfully aware that we were the first freshmen class matriculating after the end of the Great War.

My overall day-to-day support and "re-connector" was my roommate, John Harmon, who I met that first day. He was a farm boy from the Battenkill Valley in upstate New York. He was the first member of his family to attend college. I will never forget his initial greeting. With a smile as wide as the Hudson River, he shook my hand—and I wasn't prepared for his exceptionally powerful grip. After my painful wince, he apologized, telling me that he used his hands daily, milking the cows and lifting the hundred-plus-pound farm equipment. Although he was a few inches shorter than me, he was a solid 220 pounds. His gentle mannerisms and obvious strength led me to eventually nickname him "Babe" after Paul Bunyan's blue ox.

We had some classes together, ate together, played varsity baseball together, ran down to the Connecticut River and back, and went into town when we had a free moment.

Every night, he would wait for a short while after we went to sleep, and in the silence of the moment, maybe while the stairs were creaking if someone was walking back to their room, he would ask the same question, the same way for the next four years. "Windy, you awake?"

And I would mumble, "Well, now I am."

"Good, I needed to talk to you for a minute." He would tell me some particular story, good or bad, of what happened that day and what I thought about it or some activity he did on his farm that he missed doing. He'd talk for five minutes or so, and then he'd say good night. I would drift off, pleased that I had such a great friend and roommate. We stayed together all four years, and his friendship and presence in my life could not have been more nurturing for my growth and peace of mind.

At the end of my sophomore year, Amherst celebrated its hundredth anniversary. During that festive gathering of alumni and friends, I gave one of my piano recitals. Professor William Bigelow, head of the music department, had arranged for me to perform at five o'clock on June 20, 1921, the first of three days of celebration. It was my first solo performance at Amherst, and I had prepared throughout the spring semester between my academic obligations as well as varsity baseball. The pressure was on, but I was focused to handle it.

Music had been such a nourishing passion since I was a boy. I began lessons at the New York Music School Settlement on East Third Street at the age of six. I was quite immersed in the whole training they offered us. I took music theory from Miss Angela Diller and piano instruction from Miss Elizabeth Quaile. They were both demanding of their students, but they gave more of their insightful and encouraging tips in playing each new piece with greater personal expression to those of us who practiced diligently. I remember those repetitive scales and arpeggios, those Czerny exercises, and those outbursts: "Less pounding of the keys, more life from them. Hold your hands straighter to the keyboard." All those expectations made me more determined to deliver what I was capable of feeling—an ongoing need to raise my artistic capability.

I gave my first recital at the Ethical Cultural School at age eleven, and I continued performing each year until I graduated. Misses Diller and Quaile's advice lingered in the back of my head. "Always be your own severest critic. Always listen while you are playing. Concentrate on each passage whether you are going over technical exercises or an eight-bar stanza of a piece. Always pay attention to detail, and always take time to perform each note well." The great pianist, Busoni, once said, "I never neglect the opportunity to improve, no matter how perfect a previous interpretation seemed to me."

My music teachers wanted me to pursue a career in music after I left the Ethical School. They introduced me to Olga Samaroff, the gifted pianist, and she was kind enough to attend my final recital at Ethical Cultural School. Afterward, told me that she would personally train me to perform in Philadelphia Hall under the baton of her ex-husband, Leopold Stokowski. My interest in music still burns brightly, but I knew I could not make a career of entertaining audiences. I had a more pressing calling to be a physician.

I continued practicing piano after I came to Amherst, but I could not keep up the lessons with the greater demands of biology and athletics. I did want to give another recital. After meeting and enjoying the time spent with Professor Bigelow in my freshman year, he encouraged me to play some of the pieces I had performed previously.

As I rehearsed that week prior to my recital, my teacher's voice filled my thoughts. The piano is the most non-expressive instrument in the entire orchestra. Once the note is struck, it can no longer be sustained, except partially by virtue of the pedal; that is still incomparable to the bow on a stringed instrument or the reed vibrating a woodwind. The piano is expressed more deeply when it is musically interpreted and stroked harmoniously. You don't want to play the keys when sitting at the bench. You want to clarify by sounding the piano—as the Italian pianists would say, "Suono il pianoforte"—by making the notes sing to the listener. Think about these things while doing other activities when you are not actually playing. Rachmaninoff, the great composer, pianist, and conductor, once remarked, "Fine playing requires much deep thought away from the keyboards."

June 20 arrived, and I felt ready for the concert. Father, Uncle Herbert, and an added surprise—Soulange—came on the train to hear me perform three of J. S. Bach's Preludes and Fugues from his *Well-Tempered Clavier, Books I and II*. I always included a composition by Bach whenever I played for an audience, Robert Schumann's Kinderszenen, Op. 15 and Frederic Chopin's Ballade #3 in A flat major, Op. 47.

I played in the College Hall, the gathering place for nearly all of the commencement exercises and musical events at Amherst. The school had recently remodeled the nearly hundred-year-old building with a new portico and six colonial columns, and it housed a Steinway Model D concert grand piano. This instrument had a gorgeous sound, and it reverberated with vivid acoustic balance.

After my introduction by Professor Bigelow, I walked out on the stage, realizing that the hall was filled to capacity. The sunlight shone brightly through the western windows. It was warm and humid, but the fans created a tolerable breeze. I started the Prelude and Fugue, #2, in C minor, keeping in mind that Bach did not have the privilege of performing his work on a Steinway, but rather a number of keyboard instruments much smaller in size and breath. The word *Clavier* in contemporary 1720–1730

Germany meant a generic grouping of all the keyboards, including his favorite organ.

Even though he was at his prime as cantor/director for all musical activities in the four churches in Leipzig, Germany (the "capital" for music in Europe at that time), Bach was never concerned with the instruments themselves, but more importantly with the spiritual essence of each of his compositions. I played each selection, feeling my spiritual tie to his music.

Next was the Schumann "Kinderszenen," thirteen pieces of music composed to provide various scenes reminiscing through his childhood memories. My favorite is "Traumerei" or dreaming. I have a music box at home that plays the unforgettable melody. With its simplistic yet tranquilizing beauty, I never tire hearing it, playing it, and enjoying its richness.

What better way to end the concert with a composition written by a composer whose primary contribution to the musical world was pieces written for the piano. The Ballade, a musical form in its own class, was created by Chopin. Although all four ballades are technically challenging, the #3 is a profoundly joyful piece, harmonic, vibrant, and a great testimony to the soulfulness of Chopin.

When it was over, I was given a standing ovation with applause lasting several minutes. I was humbled by their generous receipt of my playing. As I looked around, I could see President Mciklcjohn, several faculty members, my family, and the wonderful surprise of my teammates who left practice in their baseball uniforms and spikes, standing in the front entrance, waving their caps, and cheering me loudly. It was a grand day; one I will never forget.

After brief conversations with several of the alumni, and speaking with Uncle Herbert who sat next to President Meiklejohn, everyone left to attend their class dinner and other events set for that evening. Because of my focus on the preparation for my recital, I didn't realize that the town of Amherst had swollen nearly one and a half times its normal population with the influx of the alumni and other dignitaries.

The next morning, I could see the display of all the tents, banners, flags, and colors throughout the usually quiet campus, offering quite a boom of business for the town and general excitement all over. Even Vice President Calvin Coolidge, class of 1895, was persuaded to come to present one of the featured speeches. Not to be facetious, but he probably spoke more that day than he did in his entire five years during his presidential administration.

On a more serious note, speaking of presidents, our school president gave quite an arousing address on the final day, Centennial Day, of the alumni's gathering. His talk was entitled "What does the college hope to be during the next hundred years?" I only wish more ears could have truly heard its message and acted on its sincere request:

> What will the college see in its next century? I have three prophecies to make: 1) We are an Anglo-Saxon college ... yet we are Americans. We may not keep ourselves apart either from persons or cultures not our own. Our undergraduate life must represent the country which it serves ... People who rule tend to know more of ruling life than living it. We need the wealth of spirit which the other people have to give. And they need us. 2) We cannot cultivate our youth unless their teachers have themselves been cultivated. Here is the essential weakness of our national scheme of teaching. We are vainly trying to pay for education rather than to give it. 3) Men lose their poise in days like these, grow frightened by events which they themselves cannot control, take desperate means to save the situation by a single stroke, are willing "just this once" to put their faith aside, to save it for all future time. And colleges must tell them what the ages have to tell, that single strokes do not save worlds except for single moments. And if the faith is sacrificed today, it will cost more to win it back tomorrow.[29]

After his speech, I became pensive. This was not a man who came to speak about milestones, or ceremonial camaraderie. Here was an open plea to consider a broader, loftier responsibility of a college and its students, faculty, and daresay, trustees and administrators to take and reexamine the true fiber of leaders and thinkers, directing them to move toward a more nurturing and refining life experience for all.

167

On the train ride home, as the bucolic meadows, creeks, and forest greens went darting past my passenger window and the murmuring sounds of faint conversations shared by my fellow passengers, I remained mindful of my final two years ahead and what I needed to do to be a responsible and faithful graduate servant to my fellow man.

During the summer of 1921, Babe invited me to his farm in Battenkill Valley for a four-day weekend visit. I developed a deeper appreciation of dairy and agricultural farm life, the strong family and community ties, as well as a new, invaluable hands-on experience with hard physical labor.

Every member of the family had chores daily, before and after school for the children. The cows, a combination of Jerseys and Holsteins, were milked at five in the morning and five in the evening every day, taken out to pasture, and then brought back. The horses were fed and harnessed for work, the eggs gathered, the outhouse needed to be cleaned, the weeds cultivated, and the annoying insects (beetles, potato bugs, grasshoppers), and gophers controlled regularly. The weather offered its usual mix of sunshine and rain, but there were droughts, thunderstorms, and blizzards that had to be faced. Unpredictable accidents and illnesses set back the opportunity to complete tasks that needed to be done.

I helped Babe with all the work. One of the most physical tasks was hauling the ice from the icehouse to the milk-storage area to keep the milk chilled before transport. The blocks of ice weighed forty to fifty pounds for the smaller blocks and up to one hundred pounds and had to be lifted by hand. The storage area required 250–300 pounds of ice daily. While helping Babe, I quickly discovered that it was grueling work. I was also impressed that nothing gathered, from the eggs to the apples, went to waste. If any of the produce had a bruise or crack in it, these items would be used as fillers in pies or other baked or canned goods.

His family's relations with neighbors and the community were exemplary. They would regularly ride their horses to neighboring farms to help with their chores. Sometimes an illness produced a shortage of manpower. And the neighbors, in turn, would assist the Harmon family with their work. Sunday congregation at church was a central part of life in the farm community. There were fund-raising activities to help other families in need.

Although his parents did not have formal education beyond eighth grade, they had common sense and the understanding that their son had great academic promise. They encouraged him toward his dream of attending college. Mrs. Harmon was a seamstress and made all the family clothes as well as cooking meals like Soulange, and I had not tasted anyone's cooking measuring up to the standards of Soulange. Mrs. Harmon had an advantage of preparing the freshest and finest vegetables and meat that I had ever eaten.

Mr. Harmon was a quiet, hardworking man, but he was openly proud of his family traditions and son's achievements. He had already showed me his collection of tools that had been passed down for four generations and were still used daily. Before I left, he took me aside and told me how grateful he was that we were roommates. He was worried that Babe would not have any friends and the other students would laugh at him coming from a farm and being a country boy. I assured him that he and his wife had raised a confident, scholarly gentleman. Considering all of the privileges and opportunities given to me, his son had no less competence navigating the toughest academic challenges. If someone was rude enough to state an unkind or sarcastic remark to him, that would only reflect their ignorance and impairment—not his.

When the visit came to a close, I thanked them all for one of the most refreshing and revealing experiences in my life. The farm visits to my grandfather's friends in Virginia were exciting and always filled with happy moments, but time spent with Babe's family at his home was priceless.

Father's schedule still demanded his time with his patients, but occasionally—and enthusiastically—he would come to one of the football or baseball games. Mother never came to any of my games or piano recitals. In fact, she only set foot on the campus once: graduation. She felt it would be "awkward" in her social circle if she had not gone at all.

Uncle Herbert retired in 1920 and came to see me several times through my upperclassmen years. He had shown the interest in me that Grandfather had given, and his sage advice and mentorship were invaluable. It was particularly beneficial at the beginning of my junior year, in the fall of 1921. I had met my first girlfriend, Anne Farwell, a sophomore from Smith College, at a school dance in the spring of 1921.

Jasper in his usual form, interrupted, "Uh, Water Pump, you never told me you were a Rudolph Valentino type."

"Jasper, did I ever claim to be a Casanova?"

"Is he a movie star? I never seen him on the picture show."

"No!"

I continued.

We started dating that fall after we returned to school. She was quite attractive, friendly, personable, and popular. She was the daughter of John Farwell, a prominent Saint Louis judge. We did not get to spend a lot of time together because of my commitments to studies and varsity football.

Coach Englehorn had selected me to start as the team's fullback, and I was considered one of the leaders of the team. There was a promising sophomore who had joined the team by the name of Sterling Bentley, a Negro from New London, Connecticut. When he came to the first few practices, some of the teammates jeered him for his color, but I would not tolerate such insensitivity. I told all of them if anyone had a "problem" playing with Sterling, they also had a problem with me. There were no further remarks.

There was an extra game, an exhibition game scheduled on a Wednesday in October against the University of Virginia. One week before the game was to be played in Amherst, a letter of protest was sent to Coach Englehorn from the Virginia coach stating they would not play against a team with a "nigger" player.

I couldn't believe it! I was infuriated and told our coach that I wouldn't play in that game to protest their bigotry. I went directly back to my room, simmering with the thought that anyone would even accept the idea that Virginia was justified with their "school policy" in the first place. Since Babe was at some school function, I couldn't really get a comforting word to help settle me.

That evening, I was still in a dampened mood. Anne asked why I appeared so low. Reluctant to discuss the matter, I finally shared the whole story. Her acidic response troubled me deeper than I was already feeling. "How dare you consider not playing? My father is coming all the way from Saint Louis to see you in that game. You have to play. I bought a new outfit to wear. If you aren't there, Amherst may lose—and Virginia's team will think our star fullback is a coward. Is that Negro's removal from the game more important to you than my happiness or helping the team to win?"

Her cold and self-glorifying conversation had nothing to do with sportsmanship or principle. I chose not to play because Sterling had every right to play no different than myself. If he was injured or had been pulled out due to academic failure, I could see why he couldn't be in the game. I said good-bye and left her, numbed with disappointment on top of the notion that Sterling was unfairly banned.

That night, I went back to my room and told Babe what happened. He was very consoling and told me to do the right thing and not worry about Anne's "hang-up." He said to talk to Sterling, and the two of us would work everything out. Instead of his usual "Hey, Windy, I need to talk to you," he uttered, "Windy, I don't need to talk to you tonight. I said all that I needed to say earlier." That Babe was always the true-blue friend.

At practice the next day, Sterling pulled me aside and said there was no reason for me to sacrifice the game. Prove a bigger point. Play to win the game for the team, and—indirectly—I would be winning the game for him. I reflected on his and Anne's commentary. It was all about the best decision for the sake of the team to him and the image and selfish limited thinking for her.

I listened to Sterling's advice and played one of my finest games, scoring two touchdowns and dragging the defensive players into the ground in all four quarters. After the game, I went to dinner with Anne's family and told her I wouldn't date her anymore. We just didn't have as much in common as I thought previously.

Uncle Herbert attended the game and talked with me after the dinner breakup. He told me there was great similarity between Mother and that girl. I understood him and inquired why he never married. He had a very similar circumstance when he was in college and vowed to never marry conveniently. He knew many wealthy debutantes and pretty faces, but the main reason was the Victorian upbringing that left him somewhat indifferent to the whole matter. But then he added he was "married" to teaching, and he was satisfied with it over these years. He finished by telling me to be patient and the right woman would come along and I would be very happy.

I have one more special story to share when Babe came to visit me for his first trip to New York City over spring break in 1923. I thought I was excited when I went to his farm. You should have seen the expression on his face the moment he stepped off the train in Grand Central Station. He couldn't imagine the size of the buildings, the subway transportation, the large crowd of people on so many busy streets, all the honking cars, all the merchant stores, people hanging their clothes to dry on clotheslines between windows, and so many impoverished people living within a short distance of opulent mansions. He commented on everything: how he had never met a Chinese person, a community of Negroes in Harlem, the Woolworth Tower, the world's tallest building, and five daily newspapers to read about national and international news.

He loved the Ziegfeld Follies at the Amsterdam Theater on Forty-Second Street, featuring Fanny Brice and Victor Herbert's music, but his biggest thrill was sitting in the box seats behind third base and the New York Yankees dugout on Wednesday, April 18, to see the first home game played in Yankee Stadium. Babe Ruth had been his hero since 1920 when Ruth became a Yankee. The Yanks had shared ballparks with the New York Giants at the Polo Grounds in Upper Manhattan, and the owner realized he needed his own. He built the first three-tiered facility in America. The multipurpose stadium's dimensions were designed to showcase their drawing card: Big Babe. We were part of a 62,000-fan crowd even though the seating capacity was 58,000 and nearly 25,000 had been turned away.

The opening ceremony included the great march king, John Phillip Sousa, conducting the Seventh Regiment Band in the National Anthem. New York Governor Al Smith threw out the first pitch, and the game between the New York Yankees and the Boston Red Sox began. The score was tied at zero until the fourth inning when Ruth would get his one hit of the game: a whopping three-run homer into the right-field bleachers. The final score was 4–1, Yankees winning. That night, the sports page of the New York Evening Telegram called Yankee Stadium "the House that Ruth built."

After we returned to school, Babe could not stop talking about his stay with me in New York. With his usual "I need to talk to you, Windy," he kept reliving some experience he had in the city each day until we graduated.

Whenever the Yankee game was mentioned, I would say, "Your idol—Babe #2—really put on a great show for us."

He would correct me, saying, "No, he's Babe #1."

I would say over and over again, "No, he's Babe #2 because no one will ever replace you as Babe #1 to me!"

He'd laugh and go to sleep, and I would just smile. Babe Ruth could have hit one hundred home runs that year—but he was not going to replace my old reliable Babe.

Father's Affiliation with the NAACP (Event 13)

I had already stated that Father stayed busy with the demanding schedule of his practice after he recovered from the Spanish influenza, but I did not discuss the other activity that preoccupied his thoughts as well as his financial backing and burning passion for human justice: his involvement with the NAACP.

Since its conception on February 12, 1909, Abraham Lincoln's hundredth birthday anniversary, and incorporation in the state of New York in 1910, the national office of the NAACP had frequent visits and a committed family in Grandfather, Mumsie, and Father. I already mentioned the pleas from Grandfather and Father to President Theodore Roosevelt to openly support the ideology of the organization during our White House visit.

The NAACP's main purpose was to vindicate the Constitution for all American citizens by abolishing legal segregation. Although most of the original supporters, the "committee of sixty" were wealthy white liberals, both men and women, the biracial inclusion of W. E. B. DuBois, Reverend William Henry Brooks, and Bishop Alexander Walters set the stage for some of the most powerful Negro minds the twentieth century would produce. Besides DuBois, James Weldon Johnson and Walter White brought an added dimension to the understanding of how best to battle injustice and inhumanity.

After Grandfather's death, Father worked closely with Mr. Johnson and Mr. White, being particularly concerned about the horrors of the lynchings and mob violence toward Negroes throughout the South and parts of the North. Father accompanied Walter White—who had blond hair and blue eyes and could "pass" as a white man down South—and witnessed several of the lynchings firsthand to collect information for the NAACP's public awareness agenda.

In 1919, Mr. White gathered enough information to show there were approximately 4,130 documented lynchings from 1882–1919. Father's ties to Mr. Johnson and his father-in-law, John Bennett Nail, as well as Mr. White remained close through the remainder of his life. I knew that Father had seen this brutality and bestial behavior, but he had not shared the full picture until I came home on spring break in 1921. I was shocked in disbelief about how awful these events truly were.

I passed by my father's desk at the house and saw two newspaper articles, one from the *Memphis Times* dated January 27, 1921 and an article entitled "The Lynchings of May 1918 in Brooks and Lowndes Counties, Georgia."

"The Lynching of Henry Lowery" from the *Memphis Times* gave this account; the details were quite undeniably shameful and immoral:

> It took place during the end of 1919 but somehow was not reported in this paper until 1921. More than 500 persons stood by and looked on while the Negro (Henry Lowery of Nodena, Arkansas) was slowly burning to a crisp. A few women were scattered among the crowd of Arkansas planters, who directed the gruesome work.
>
> Not once did the Negro beg for mercy despite the fact that he suffered one of the most horrible deaths imaginable. With the Negro chained to a log, members of the mob placed a small pile of leaves around his feet.

Gasoline was then poured on the leaves, and the carrying out of the death sentence was under way.

Inch by inch, the Negro was fairly cooked to death. Every few minutes, fresh leaves were tossed on the funeral pyre until the blaze had passed the Negro's waist. As the flames were eating away his abdomen, a member of the mob stepped forward and saturated the body with gasoline. It was then only a few minutes until the Negro had been reduced to ashes.

Even after the flesh had dropped away from his legs and the flames were leaping toward his face, Lowery retained consciousness. Not once did he whimper or beg for mercy. Once or twice he attempted to pick up the ashes and thrust them in his mouth in order to hasten his death. Each time, the ashes were kicked out of his reach by a member of the mob.

Words fail to describe the sufferings of the Negro. Even after his legs had been reduced to the bones, he continued to talk with his captors, answering all questions put to him.[30]

If that wasn't enough cruelty, I then read Walter White's essay describing the lynching of Mary Turner in a town about five miles from Valdosta, Georgia. Here were the most gruesome, despicable acts I have ever encountered in my entire life:

Hampton Smith, a white farmer, was killed. He was the owner of a large plantation who had a very poor reputation in the community because of ill treatment of his Negro employees ... There was talk of a conspiracy among a number of Negroes to kill Smith and reports were circulated that the group involved had met at the home of Hayes Turner, another Negro who had suffered at the hands of Smith and his wife, Mary Turner, whom

Smith had beaten on many occasions. The first and second victims of the mob were lynched; afterwards, certain members of the mob admitted that over 700 bullets were fixed into the bodies of these two men. Hayes Turner was captured and lynched with his hands fastened behind him in handcuffs and allowed to hang there until Monday. On Sunday, while still hanging, hundreds of automobiles, buggies, and wagons bore "sightseers" to the spot while many more tramped on foot.

The murder of the Negro men was deplorable enough in itself, but the method by which Mrs. Mary Turner was put to death and the details so horrible that it is with reluctance that the account is given. Mrs. Turner made the remark that the killing of her husband was unjust, and if she knew the names of the persons who were in the mob, she would have warrants sworn out against them and have them punished in court.

This news determined the mob to "teach her a lesson" and she was captured. The grief-stricken and terrified woman was taken to a lonely and secluded spot. At the time she was lynched, Mary Turner was in her eighth month of pregnancy. Her ankles were tied together and she was hung to the tree, head downward. Gasoline and oil from the automobiles were thrown on her clothing and while she writhed in agony and the mob howled in glee, a match was applied and her clothes burned from her person. When this had been done and while she was yet alive, a knife, evidently one such as is used in splitting hogs, was taken and the woman's abdomen was cut open, the unborn babe falling from her womb to the ground. The infant, prematurely born, gave two feeble cries and then its head was crushed by a member of the mob with his heel. Hundreds of bullets were then fired into the body of the woman, now mercifully dead, and the work was over. The article ended with "all of the facts outlined above, including the names of mob leaders and participants were given in a memorandum on July 10 to Governor Hugh Dorsey. He promised to take action on the evidence submitted."[31]

I was nauseated and chilled. At that point, Father walked in, saw the article in my hand and the disgust written all over my face, and tried to console me as best as he could.

I cried out loud to him. "How could any man in his right mind endorse, enforce, and consciously acknowledge an act so heinous, barbaric, and savage?"

Father looked at me with a reflective stare as if he knew more than what I had read. He said, with deliberate hesitation, that he had just received the *Memphis Times* article and was going to put both of them away in the file where he had several other writings, and he didn't expect me to see it beforehand. He continued, saying that he was with Walter White on that southern trip, and though they both did not actually see Mrs. Turner's lynching, they did witness others where the entire white community would come as "spectators" to watch as they would a Sunday picnic-style fair. Instead of watching a horse race or a wheelbarrow race and receiving balloons or ribbons, they would bring the family, including the children, to witness the lynching and pass out the victim's bones as souvenirs.

"Sit and realize I did not intend to share this knowledge until a more suited time. But revelation, when it comes unexpectedly, can instill a message with more impact and long-term meaning. Trust me, from personal experience. You see that older file cabinet? You thought it was one of my medical file drawers all along. But it really was your grandfather's files on all pertinent information about civil rights, women's rights, and legal inquires for injustice and lawless behavior. Hence the file on lynching since the post-Civil War period."

He then explained the origin of Lynch law and the underlying irony. Somewhere in Piedmont County of Virginia, there was limited criminal jurisdiction because there was basically no formal law enforcement around. Conflicts and arguments were brought to the attention of respectable men who exhibited sound judgment and impartiality as well as high integrity. One such man was known as Judge Lynch. His reputation became quite well broadcasted throughout Virginia and most of the country, hence, the honorable distinction of being called Lynch Law.

Somewhere around the Civil War, and immediately afterward, the law took a reproachable turn, with violent, undisciplined men who Judge Lynch would have gladly punished, took the law into their own hands, thirsty for revenge and usurping the laws of the courts of justice. That is the current understanding of lynching. He pulled out one large file marked "Friends' efforts to combat the absurdity of lynching." He then shared some of the more detailed information from friends of both Grandfather and himself to give me a broad appreciation of the problem and how long it has been denied by "deaf mutes."

Pleas of protection and legally preventing the perpetuation of lynching through enforced law were ignored from Presidents William McKinley through Woodrow Wilson, and now Warren Harding. Strong advocates, both Negro and white, presented scathing, fearless words, both written and spoken, denouncing lynching at public gatherings and personal letters to government officials to address the magnitude of the problem and appeal to their "better judgment."

Pleas from determined, honorable, and upright citizens continued, from Ida B. Wells, whose publication of "The Red Record: Tabulated Statistics and Alleged Causes of Lynching in the US" in 1895 speaks out so uncompromisingly, clearly, and directly, but it was basically unaddressed by the white establishment and remains that way twenty-six years later. She wrote:

> The Southern white man was in a manner compelled to give excuses for his barbarism. His excuses have been outlined by Frederick Douglass in which he shows that there have been three distinct eras of Southern barbarism to account for which three distinct excuses have been made. The first excuse given to the civilized world for the murder of unoffending Negroes was the necessity of the white man to repress and stamp out alleged "race riots." It was always a remarkable feature in these insurrections

and riots that only Negroes were killed during the rioting, and that all the white men escaped unharmed. Then came the second excuse ... The Southern white man would not consider that the Negro had any right which a white man was bound to respect. It was maintained that "This is a white man's government," and regardless of numbers the white man should rule ... The government which had made the Negro a citizen found itself unable to protect him. It gave him the right to vote, but denied him protection which should have maintained that right ... The murderers invented the third excuse—that Negroes had to be killed to avenge their assaults upon women. Humanity abhors the assailant of womanhood, and this charge upon the Negro at once placed him beyond the pale of human sympathy ... During all the years of slavery, no such charge was ever made, not even during the dark days of the rebellion ... While the master was away fighting to forge the fetters upon the slave, he left his wife and children with no protectors save the Negroes themselves ... To justify their own barbarism, they assume a chivalry which they do not possess. True chivalry respects all womanhood, and no one who reads the record, as it is written in the faces of the million mulattoes in the South, will for a minute conceive that the Southern white man had a very chivalrous regard for the honor due the women of his own race or respect for the womanhood which circumstances placed in his power ... Virtue knows no color line, and the chivalry which depends upon complexion of skin and texture of hair can command no honest respect.[32]

From W. E. B. DuBois, the first Negro PhD from Harvard, there were continued efforts through the NAACP and as editor of *Crisis Magazine* to address the injustice and the inhumanity. His awareness of the problem was summarized clearly in an open letter to President Harding after his inauguration last month, March 1921:

Sir: We appeal to you: we the outcast and lynched, the mobbed and murdered, the despoiled and insulted; and yet withal, the indomitable, unconquered, unbending and unafraid black children of kings and slaves and of the best blood of the workers of the earth—WE WANT THE RIGHT TO VOTE. WE WANT TO TRAVEL WITHOUT INSULT. WE WANT LYNCHING AND MOB-LAW QUELLED FOREVER ... We know that the power to do these things is not entirely in your hands, but its beginnings lie there. All the cruelty, rape and atrocities of slavery; all the theft and degradation of that spirit of the Ku Klux Klan mob that seeks to build a free America on racial, religious and class hatred—the weight of all this woe is yours ... You sir, whether you will or no, stand responsible. You are responsible for the truth back of the pictures of the burning of Americans circulated in European drawing rooms; for the hypocrisy of a nation seeking to lend idealism to the world for peace when within its own borders there is more murder, theft, riot and crucifixion than was ever even charged against Bolshevik Russia ... If races cannot live together in peace and happiness in America, they cannot live together in the world.[33]

From Frederick Douglass, who bridged the era of slavery through the Civil War, Reconstruction Period, and Post-Reconstruction came endorsement of Ida B. Wells in his preface to her *The Red Record*:

Let me give you thanks for your faithful paper on the lynch abomination now generally practiced against colored people in the South. There has been no word equal to it in convincing power ... Brave woman! You have done your people and mine a service ... If the American conscience were only half alive, if the American church and clergy were only half Christianized, if American moral sensibility were not hardened by persistent infliction of outrage and crime against colored people, a scream of horror, shame and indignation would rise to Heaven wherever your pamphlet shall be read.[34]

Moorfield Storey, Harvard Law School scholar, who was highly influenced by Senator Charles Sumner and who went on to become the president of the American Bar Association, raised a similar plea. Mr. Storey became the NAACP's first president; furthermore, he did legal counsel for the NAACP pro bono. He was also personal friends with all of the U.S. Supreme Court Justices. He spoke to a Harvard University audience in March 1920, presenting one of the prestigious Godkin lectures. It was a series of five presentations on "The Problems of Today." One was entitled, "Racial Prejudice":

> Race and class prejudice is a fruitful source of danger to this country. The true principle by which government by the people should rest is expressed in the phrase, "Each for all and all for each." The enlightened citizen should learn to put himself in his neighbor's place, see with his eyes, and thus instructed consider what is good for his neighbor's interest as well as his own. Any other course is blind selfishness.
>
> No greater dangers threaten today than those that arise from the treatment of the Negroes all over this country. Bred in the bones of the whites who were born in the slave states is the conviction that the Negroes are their inferiors, intended by nature to be their servants and that they must never be allowed to escape from that subordinate position. Hence they are denied justice in the courts, they are killed with impunity, if charged with a crime, or frequently with a trifling offence, they are lynched and often with hideous cruelty while no attempt is made to prosecute or punish the lynchers ... Ignorance brutalizes a people and an ignorant and brutal element in society is a menace to the whole community.[35]

Storey continued, quoting Henry Watterson, the Kentucky journalist:

> Lynching should not be misconstrued. It is not an effort
> to punish crime. It is a sport ... A lynching party is
> rarely made up of citizens indignant at the law's delays or
> failures. It is often made up of a mob bent upon diversion
> and proceeding in a mood of rather frolicsome ferocity to
> have a thoroughly good time. Lynchers are not persons
> who strive from day to day toward social betterment.
> They are ruffians wholly sober, but highly stimulated by
> an opportunity to indulge in a spectacular murder when
> there is no fear that the next grand jury will return murder
> indictments against them. College festivals come and go,
> but what college president, what orator at commencement,
> takes the evil of lynching as his subject? The universal
> silence disgraces us more than the acts themselves.[36]

Storey clearly understood the baseless premise of the inferiority of the
Negro when he wrote these irrefutable questions:

> If the Negro is so hopelessly inferior, why do whites fear
> the effect of education? Why do they struggle against his
> progress upward? The attempt to prevent him from rising,
> by violence or by adverse legislation, is a confession that
> the assumption of white superiority is unsafe.[37]

James Weldon Johnson, executive secretary for the NAACP, observed the
lynchings and race riots at unprecedented frequency that had been stirred
by the postwar rise of conservatism, Ku Klux Klan mentality, and spiritual
fundamentalism, especially throughout the "Red Summer of 1919." Father
asked if I remembered the news account of the riot in Chicago, but I only
had vague recall. A few months prior to the Chicago Riot, Johnson spoke
at the May 1919 National Conference on Lynching in New York City:

> The veil of self-satisfaction has got to be torn away from
> the face of this nation, and it must be made to look at itself
> as it is ... The raw, naked facts of lynching must be held

up before the eyes of this country until the heart of this nation becomes such, until we get a reaction of righteous indignation that will not stop, until we have swept away lynching as a national crime.[38]

James Weldon Johnson worked tireless in lobbying the Capitol for support of the only anti-lynching legislation presented to Congress from Missouri Representative Leonidas Dyer, a white man representing the Negro population of Saint Louis. The Dyer Anti-Lynching Bill will be introduced in the House of Representatives, holding states liable for failing to protect against lynching.

And finally, our next-door neighbor, Joel Spingarn, chairman of the board of directors of the NAACP, was equally active in being intolerant of the acceptance of the practice of lynching. He endorsed the NAACP's program in the South against lynching, which he described as a "stain on our civilization." His role in the organization has been invaluable. He is deemed the great pacifier and an interpersonal leader who skillfully facilitates communication between the members. Without him, the organization's success would be compromised, to say the least.

Not only is lynching an unjust problem the Negro faces—and the Wilson administration boldly declines to face—but an equal "Negro problem" exists in the armed services, notably the army's handling of Colonel Charles Young.

After facing the most intense racism and intimidation in the "hallowed" halls of West Point Academy as the third Negro graduate in the school's history, Charles Young served his country with distinction. When the war broke out, Lieutenant Colonel Young was recommended to be promoted to brigadier general by several of his superior officers. Southern sentiment, including President Wilson, acted to find ways to counter any promotion. During his physical, he was told he had high blood pressure and he was "asked" to resign, even though Wilson himself had high blood pressure most of his life and a paralyzing stroke and remained president.

Undaunted, Colonel Young, after returning to his home of Xenia, Ohio, decided to demonstrate his true state of health and at the age of fifty-four, in June 1918, rode his horse nearly five hundred miles to Washington, DC. He completed the ride in sixteen days. With the Negro press proclaiming

Young's capabilities, the War Department "conveniently" stationed Young to noncombatant service in Camp Grant, Illinois. Colonel Young was an officer who followed orders. His example of courage, determination, and leadership served as a model for future Negro officers who would hopefully get an opportunity to demonstrate their capabilities and put an end to this maddening injustice. Father was profoundly emotional as he told each event; it was obvious how personal and passionate he was in our discussion.

The biggest puzzle to Father—with all these real issues concerning lynching and inhumanity being presented to our governing officials that were blatant violations of our Constitution—was that they chose to direct their energies and time passing Amendments 18 and 19. Amendment 18, based on the Volstead Act, dealt with prohibiting a cultural practice that had been legal for thousands of years and a very normal part of life experience as well as discarding the need for the vital source of government revenue from taxes on alcoholic beverages. He had no idea how long people would tolerate Prohibition, but he knew the writing was on the wall with regard to organized crime being endorsed by a black-market demand.

Then the suffrage for women was finally passed in 1920 with opposition from both men and women. It made no sense to my father who said that the Fifteenth Amendment allegedly granted voting rights to men "regardless of race, creed, or previous servitude" should have also included women, but it was blocked for the usual myopic reasoning.

I saw my father emotionally torn as he closed the file and shook his head. Tears were swelling in his eyes, and as he took off his glasses, he put his hand on my shoulder and apologized for bringing up such a numbing discussion.

I reassured him that I needed to have a clearer understanding of this problem. I paused for a moment and asked when the acts were going to end. What would it take to place such uncivilized behavior behind us?

My father's facial expression changed from pain to an almost serene acceptance of matters. He shared two stories that Grandfather and Mumsie told him when he asked the same questions many years earlier.

Grandfather said when a passenger train pulls into a station, it has many cars attached that give it the meaning of a fully serviced mode of transportation. The engine is up front, before the coal car, the coach cars, the sleeper cars, the dining car, the mail car, and the well-regarded club car with its fantail and passengers waving to their loved ones who were left behind.

But the beauty and fascination of the train would be far less if any of the cars was missing while in the station. And if the engineer, conductor, porter, or steward were unable to participate in the excursion, there would not even be a trip. While traveling, if the cars were to somehow derail, you would not make it to your destination either. In order to have a successful journey to your destination, all the passengers and personnel must be on board, all cars must be present, and no side-track delays can impede progress.

The model of the train is analogous to American life today. Once born, we should all be welcome passengers aboard the train of life, destined for an unknown station. We will be directed when it is time to depart; some people are destined toward a very long trip, while others will seem like they just got on board and have to leave prematurely. Certain cars are reserved for "first-class" passengers, but everyone aspires to be in these plush, luxurious private compartments where they are treated like royalty. Unfortunately, these passengers are designated the privileged few; many of the others barely have enough to occupy the overcrowded standing-room-only coach near the coal car or in the back of the train. At least they are on the train. Even though everyone should be allowed on the train of life in America, many participants are denied access.

With the system of Jim Crow for the Negroes and other groups denied their civil and voting rights, the American socioeconomic and political systems deprived these "passengers" an opportunity to ride. They have to walk on their journeys, dealing with much harsher conditions and minimal opportunities to receive sustaining nutrition. Those who are on the train scorn and ridicule those walking, telling them to walk faster, carry heavier loads, and don't stop to take a rest break—even though many of these "lowest-class" people were responsible for building the very train they ride and take for granted.

It seems as if those on the train miss the point where they are heading, and they have to be subconsciously or consciously miserable that they voluntarily accept that circumstance as "right." It's a shame they can't see that the train is doomed to collapse without the full passenger list.

He told me he remained optimistic. One day, a new train is going to pull into the station. All the cars will be present and accounted for, and all the passengers can get on board and move forward to fulfill their destinies. "One of these days, maybe not in my lifetime, I feel it will happen, and it will be a joyous occasion. We just have to keep working at it, one battle at a time and plan accordingly to be better prepared the next time." Father added that the poor man burned alive in Tennessee, Mrs. Turner, and the others deprived of basic human rights never had a chance to get on board the train. "They are in God's hands now, hopefully in a better place. We have to keep trying to let the next one have the opportunity."

Father offered Mumsie's insightful words as well: "When you look at the bigger picture of iniquity throughout time, let us look no further than the treatment of Jesus by the Pharisee high priests. Here was a man, a gentle, nonthreatening, peaceful human being helping his fellow man and teaching lessons of humanity and brotherhood. Yet he was accused and sentenced to death by a ruthless crucifixion for charges of wrongdoing that the murderers, thieves, and other criminals would, at most, have been banished or imprisoned. These priests and their community supporters were cowardly and gnarled thinkers. And we are facing the same cowardice at the present time. But I believe Frederick Douglass when he wrote the preface in Ida B. Wells's *The Red Record*:

> But alas! Even crime has power to reproduce itself and create conditions favorable to its own existence. It sometimes seems we are deserted by earth and Heaven and yet we must still think, speak and work and trust in the power of a merciful God for final deliverance.[39]

Father looked deeply inside of me and touched my heart and soul. "All the hard work and sacrifice of the great people who have stood up and openly declared their intolerance of unfairness and indecency has not been in vain. What Mumsie and your grandfather did to contribute to this noble cause was a commitment that I feel was important to follow. This is why we all joined the NAACP, why we represented the homeless and impoverished at the shelters, why we understood that the Indians, the Asians, and other minorities were indignantly left out of cooperative ventures with white

Americans, why wrongful, shameful thinking has no place in a civilized existence, and why God's message to live in peace and respect and help your fellow man has to continue to be our utmost priority in living each day. Mumsie, your grandfather, Uncle Herbert, Uncle Joel, Soulange, and the others who have voiced their like-minded thoughts will count on you. We know the substance that lives within you will sustain you as it has done for us."

I want to summarize our talk with the final paragraph of Moorfield Storey's great message on race prejudice. In only a few sentences, he could not have given a more concise truth of how human beings should conduct their lives and receive their most just rewards:

> If we will only recognize our common humanity, abandon our contemptuous phrases and our irritating stories, at each other's expense, cease to doubt the good faith of our neighbors and not give vent to every hasty suspicion which arises in our minds; in short, if we treat our fellow citizens as ladies and gentlemen should treat each other, class and racial prejudice will begin to disappear and our melting pot will better fuse the varying elements which it receives and in the end turn out a purer metal.[40]

It was one of our most memorable moments together. I had admired Father for his genuine guidance, his medical influence, and being a great comforter, but that day, in my mind, he stood ten feet taller. He had put me on the road to becoming a true man.

I took the early train back to Amherst that Sunday after the break was over, thinking about our conversation and all of its importance. While walking back to the campus, I saw a Negro family heading into the AME church. They smiled and waved kindly, and something in me told me to follow them. I had never been there before. I stayed for the service and shared in the spirit of brotherhood I felt surrounding me. There were other times I went back, and I was happy that I did.

Amherst Graduation and the Phi Beta Kappa Key, June 1923 (Event 14)

The four years at Amherst went by too quickly, but throughout that time, I could feel all the responsibilities and hope for a productive future at hand. Before my family arrived, I attended the baccalaureate sermon on June 17, given by the school president, Alexander Meiklejohn. It was entitled "Is our World Christian?" I kept a copy of my program here and underlined the most helpful commentary:

> To see the way to go, and then to go that way—that is the life of man. Man is the animal who sees his way, can tell the better from the worse and so can choose the better path.
>
> But if man sees the way and does not go; if he has found a principle and does not follow it—what shall we say of that? Life is broken in two ... Men do not see all the meaning of the thoughts they have. There is a sense in which men do take principles, do claim them as their own, and yet deny them in their acts ... Here is the break

in human nature that brings the prophets to despair. They give men principles by which to live and men transform them into shibboleths instead of rules of action. Men cry aloud in praise of freedom, and murder those who will not join the cry. Men dream of insight, and shut their eyes in blind intoxication of the joy of being wise. Men talk of love of man for man, and hate the man who will not share the talk. When deeds belie our words, when even the very saying of words themselves belies the meaning which they bring, then life is cut in two, a gulf is fixed, and we must speak of "world" and "other world" and make our choice between them ... Jesus said "Thou shalt love thy neighbor as thyself." And men agreed ... and teach it to our children. But do we practice it? Only in part ... We live in luxury and ease while others starve. We fight like beasts of prey when interests clash; we have made the Western world just now a place of bitter, hopeless, grinding hatreds. Is this the world of which we speak when we describe ourselves as Christians? Members of the graduating class ... I send you out, not in the search for things that men can own, but in the search for self, for your own lives, and for the lives of other men ... I bid you as you go keep fellowship with other men; no matter what they do, no matter what they say or think, they are your fellows in the common task. You should regard then as you do regard yourself.[41]

After I heard his message, I felt a broader question that needed to be raised. Is our world spiritual? The answer would then have been more inclusive, regarding all the world societies.

The entire commencement week was preoccupied with the news that Dr. Meiklejohn would resign at the end of this school year. There had been some conflict of interests toward him from the board of trustees and many of the faculty members. Dr. Meiklejohn diplomatically decided to resign rather than fight an uphill battle.

At the graduation itself, the first announcement made was that President Meiklejohn had been elected an honorary member of the class of 1923. It provided little solace to several of my classmates who refused to accept their diplomas in a "gesture of protest" to what they perceived as Dr. Meiklejohn's "disposal." His departure from the campus was a bittersweet memory; I was grateful I was leaving as well.

On the morning of June 20, while preparing to attend the Phi Beta Kappa installation, I thought back over my four years. There were keepsake memories to recall and cherish for the rest of my life. There was Bill Casey down at Paige's Livery Stable who would drive the horse and buggies for the celebrity visitors and many of the Amherst College friends and alumni. When I had a few hours, he used to take me on a ride to several of the beautiful back roads leading out of Amherst, retelling fifty years of scenery and the people living in those parts. After returning, we would go to Deuel's Drugstore for a refreshing ice cream.

I took numerous hikes with Babe and a few other friends in the Pelham Hills. We explored the muddy hollows, visited several abandoned farms and untended old cemeteries, and listened to the songs of birds and the scattering of rodents through the leaves. The sun setting over the top of Monadnock, and looking north to Mount Toby, offered breathtaking views.

Looking out my dorm window, I saw female factory workers coming to Leonard Hills Hat Factory between Main Street and College Street. The thick smoke poured out of the tall factory chimneys, and the morning whistle resonated throughout Amherst from Monday through Saturday, every day, at six o'clock. I never needed an alarm. The whistle blew five more times throughout the day as well as the clanging and coupling of the railroad cars in the nearby station yard. When the train and factory whistles overlapped, it was a piercing sound that we all had to accept as part of the day.

Father, Mother, Uncle Herbert, and Soulange came to the graduation. It was not surprising that Mother had invited George Arthur Plimpton, class of 1876, to attend the graduation exercises and "show her the campus." His son, Francis T. P. Plimpton had graduated in 1922, but she had to be seen, escorted, and displayed by a notable alumnus.

The ceremony began with a discussion about the emblem of Phi Beta Kappa, OBK, which stands for *philosophia biou kubernetes*: "the love of learning is the guide of life." Phi Beta Kappa, the nation's oldest academic honor society, advocates "freedom of inquiry and expression, disciplinary vigor, breadth of intellectual perspective, the cultivation of skills of deliberation and ethical reflection, the pursuit of wisdom and the application of the fruits of scholarship and research in practical life."

They went on to remember Ralph Waldo Emerson's Phi Beta Kappa lecture at Harvard in 1837:

> The hope of the future was the American Scholar and the scholar was man thinking … College teaches elements, but they can only highly serve us when they aim not to drill, but to create; when they gather from far every ray of various genius to their hospitable halls and by the concentrated fires, set the hearts of their youth on flame.[42]

It was the eightieth anniversary for the Amherst chapter to distribute the key to the nine class members, including myself. The award is a golden key engraved with OBK, the image of a pointed finger of a hand in the right lower corner aimed toward the lettering, and three stars in the left upper corner to represent the ambition of young scholars.

After the recipients were all announced, everyone stayed for a little while before the full commencement began. I showed Father, Uncle Herbert, and Soulange the key, and they all said how proud Mumsie and Grandfather would be to see this occasion. Uncle Herbert told me that I had joined the ranks of scholars, in particular, a young Negro by the name of Wiley Lane, a graduate of Amherst who was elected to Phi Beta Kappa in 1879. He later went on to be Howard University's chairman of the Department of Greek Studies. He died after contracting pneumonia at the young age of thirty-two, but his academic acumen was praised in his obituary. He was a man described as a "bright star in the intellectual sky and a model of pure, unadulterated character, richer than gold, yea, than much fine gold." I smiled; Uncle Herbert always had a special pearl to offer at the right moment.

I took out my pocket watch and attached the key to the fob. I opened the dustcover and reread the inscription: "Forsan et Haec Olim Meminisse Iuvabit." Perhaps, in future times, it would be pleasant to think on these things. I felt Mumsie and Grandfather's presence; I knew they were happy.

Afterward, while walking with my fellow recipients, I overheard a discussion from one boasting about his intelligence and that he "earned" the privilege of feeling "superior." I said nothing until the fellow made the mistake of bragging to me directly. I told him how, in my understanding of higher learning, there are three points to consider. My father and godfather believed and demonstrated that the more you apparently have learned, the more you are convinced about what you don't know. They made it clear that there is so much to learn in this world that it is enough to make a new world. However, it would require the notion of a mindful thought to fully appreciate that statement.

Secondly, intelligence is not about your acquisition of a key, a robe, a crown, a scepter, a title, or a stuffy fraternity association deeming you worthy. True intelligence in any society would promote all of us to embrace Socrates's awareness of his own limitations and thus become wiser men. According to Plato's *Apology*, some colleagues of Socrates asked the Oracle at Delphi if anyone was wiser than Socrates. The oracle said there was no one wiser. When the colleagues approached Socrates with this answer, Socrates felt it was a paradox of sorts. He believed he did not have the wisdom the Oracle claimed he had. He then went out questioning the "wisest" Athenians, who proclaimed they knew a great deal, but in time, he found many flaws in their thinking. Then Socrates realized he was the only man aware of his own ignorance, and for this insight, he understood the Oracle was correct. Keeping that in mind, we would all know that wisdom is an ongoing journey, never reaching the "top."

Finally, there should be no assumption that your formal education at an academic institution would be "superior" to someone else's self-taught training. There are capable scholars in all walks of life—some with no formal degree or training. They are self-educated, self-disciplined scholars. Robert Frost was on the faculty and never finished college, yet he was given a full professorship at Amherst. It is not about the ability to claim superiority because you receive some award; it's more what you do to apply your talents when you offer service to the cause. I said, "By the way, did you remember any of the sage advice that Dr. Meiklejohn offered in the baccalaureate sermon?"

The student left sheepishly.

After assembling for the commencement, the procession began with the faculty entering with their caps and gowns flowing, displaying all the splendor of the different universities' colors and braids: the crimson red from Harvard, the flaming orange from Princeton, the royal blue from Yale, the beaver braiding on the Oxford robe, and the wonderful King Henry VIII velvet hats with their ornamental tassels. It was a regal event in College Hall. All of the speakers stood in front of the podium with a banner of the school motto—Terras Irradient—(Let them Enlighten the Land). It was a glorious sunny day. There were eighty-five graduates, including myself, at the ceremony. Only three others were bound for medical school.

I looked over at Babe and started to smile. He was heading to the New York State College of Agriculture at Cornell for an extra year's training in soil management for crops. He wanted to learn the best treatment in preserving and replenishing soil nutrients and higher crop yields as well as fertilizer chemistry and natural pesticides. He was going to take that knowledge back to his community to help local and outlying farms have more productive seasons. When I shook that powerful hand one final time, I would miss him and all the genuine support and friendship he extended those four years. We stayed in touch until he passed away in 1951.

At the ceremony, they called my name, stating that I had received my bachelor of arts degree in biology, magna cum laude, final honors in Biology, and the Hyde Prize for best oration as well as acknowledging my piano recitals, receiving several athletic awards, and tutoring many of my fellow classmates. I knew there was much more to achieve. I was heading to Father's alma mater, Harvard Medical School, and would keep Mumsie and Grandfather's dream alive. I had a promise to fulfill.

Summertime at the Ethical Cultural School Camp, 1923 (Event 15)

After graduation, I received a letter from the Ethical Cultural School asking if I would be one of the counselors for a newly organized summer program for two weeks, starting Saturday, July 21. Uncle Herbert "volunteered" my services, and he and Father thought it would be a good "life" experience. I had not made any plans so I agreed to do it.

The campsite is located near Cooperstown, New York, in Otsego County, home to the novelist James Fennimore Cooper and named after his father, Judge William Cooper. The campgrounds overlook Lake Otsego; it was also called Lake Glimmerglass by the novelist. The campers were boys and girls, eight to fourteen, who represented a diverse background primarily from the public schools in New York City, but also some of the current students who attended Ethical Cultural School.

This camp was a pilot to expand the philosophy of the school in a scenario where children of different ethnic and religious backgrounds would gather together and live together for two weeks. For many of the campers, it would be the first time they had left New York City and/or had any interaction with other races and religious groups. The camp needed supportive counseling and supervision so they could have a future plan to continue.

Having to deal with the usual hot and muggy summer days at home, I was eager to go initially, but once I arrived, the conditions would soon change my opinion. Don't get me wrong; it was a marvelous learning experience and one that I would never forget. There were several circumstances and a host of true characters, both campers and camp personnel alike, who made this tough and seemingly long two weeks worthwhile. There were friendships developed and some other participants I would not want to continue seeing. The conditions set up a great deal of the experiences, and I will start with those facts.

The physical surroundings of the camp by the lake were breathtaking, and at times, I thought I was walking in what seemed to be the Garden of Eden: luscious trees, flowers, wildlife (geese, ducks, bumble bees, butterflies, and precious deer), and the moon sparkling over the waters of the lake. There were moments of peace threaded through nature's offerings, and I look back with utter reverence. God created a special place there to feel alive and content. In the early morning, just after dawn, I would come to the lake and feel a calmness overwhelm my thoughts. I would toss a small stone into the lake and watch the ripples disperse serenity to the entire body of water. The sun's rays would accompany the even flow of the tide, and I would wave so long until we meet again.

But then, there was a constant reminder that we were outdoors and away from the amenities we had taken for granted. Electricity was not available. There were no bathroom facilities or light leading to the dreaded outhouse area. The days and nights were just as muggy as they were in the city. Sleep was interrupted with the frogs and crickets having a "session," arguing who had the loudest voice, and the food (that is what it was called allegedly) had the worst preparation and taste. I went to bed hungry many a night, only to go outside and learn to eat the grass beneath my feet to fill my stomach with something other than air.

Nothing, however, was more annoying than those confounded man-eating mosquitoes. There were so many of them that came to attack during early evening hours. They were so big that you felt you could have placed a saddle on any of their backs and ridden into the sunset just by reaching out and grabbing one. And I don't want to forget the summer thunderstorms that lit up the sky accompanied by several cannons rumbling their fury as the rain poured over and into those airy cabins. They were scary for the kids, and I got slightly nervous myself.

Now I can bore you with some of the specific highlights that made this event distinct in my recollections. The cast is colorful. I just needed a camera and subtitles—no script or director. I would create a film to compete with any of Charlie Chaplin's shorts.

Let me start with one of the memorable characters whose commentary would lighten the atmosphere daily, whether it was about that awful food, the outhouse, other camper's mishaps, camp personnel, or even his candid words about me. He had me laughing so hard that, whenever I became depressed or disappointed about something during medical school or training, I thought back on this guy and would just laugh out loud. His vernacular was not the most Victorian, but it got the point across clearly.

"Something you can relate to, Jasper?"

Jasper, in his usual manner, retorted, "Now, Water Pump, why do I get this assignment? I don't know Verna, and I don't know Victoria."

Everyone just laughed, and I continued.

Tyrone was one of the older campers, and a little coarse in his expressions that the younger campers or any other camper need not hear. But there was something distinct, something to tolerate in his behavior, even when I reprimanded him. He had a way of turning it into "Hey, I know I'm not perfect, but neither is anyone else around here. Accept me. I'm human too." I had to look away; I would just start laughing again if he kept talking.

One of the regular breakfast items was this lumpy, tasteless, overcooked oatmeal. After several days, Tyrone came to me and said, "Windy, dammit, I think some shit salesman shows up here at night and leaves his samples for breakfast. As a matter of fact, he shows up at all these damn meals. I'm sick and tired of it."

We also had to deal with the outhouse, which had three holes in the ground. You had to walk on a dirt pathway through the trees, a tall-grassed area, and navigate down a small hill until you reached it. The outhouse was a good quarter mile from the cabins. They had separate girls' and boys' facilities in opposite directions. There was no paper except some old Sears and Roebuck catalogs that you tore a page out to use for wiping. The smell could kill a mule, and if you thought the mosquitoes annoyed you, you got double annoyance with the flies swarming around in "fly heaven." Tyrone called it the "shit pit." It was bad enough to have to go during the day or evening, but if you had to go at night, you had the worst-case scenario to face.

Part of the activities involved learning a skill working with your hands. The boys had a wood shop instructor and auto mechanics. We had an old Ford Model T donated, and the girls had a sewing instructor. The wood shop instructor was a native from Cooperstown. He was probably in his early sixties, and he was very slow and difficult to understand. He had several teeth missing, and the few he had were rotten. He would whistle his *s*'s and leave off letters to any word with more than three letters in it. He had missing fingers on both hands—second finger on his left hand as well as his third and fourth fingers on the right. I couldn't tell if he was left-handed or right. I asked Hugo if he would incriminate himself if his incomplete set of fingerprints were found at the scene of a crime.

Hugo answered without hesitation, "Yes, he would be caught right there at the scene. How quickly could he finish a job with that handicap? The police would have arrested him before he even turned around to leave. They wouldn't need to worry about those fingerprints."

His name was Gus Ruff, and he was as smelly as the outhouse. The flies would follow him religiously while he was working down at the wood shop.

Tyrone said, "Gus should not be amongst us. I don't think that old bastard has had a bath since his mother's water broke."

Aside from Gus, many of the campers learned to work with the wood, paying attention to fine craftsmanship. When Gus was busy, I helped with the instruction. Grandfather and Father had taught me how to repair fences, level a window sill, smooth a door to fit its hinge in opening and closing properly, and build a table, so I had good experience.

One specific camper had a particular natural talent working with the wood. He carved a replica of the airplane used to deliver airmail service. He had meticulous detail in the engine, the propeller, the wings, and the cockpit. The wings looked so authentic that if he had installed a small motor, the plane would probably fly from Cooperstown back to Manhattan, carrying the letters written by the fellow campers. He had such steady hands.

I told him that he could be a skilled carpenter one day. I imagined this boy in Jerusalem accompanying Jesus as his apprentice before his teachings began. After seeing his talent, Jesus would have said, "Use these hands and tools wisely. Build shelters, wagons, wheels, and other needed products for the purpose of sharing your gift with the lives in your community. Your hands speak with determination and serve with dignity. Go forth and do your work."

At the end of camp, he gave me a wooden owl perched on a tree limb that he constructed. He thanked me for my encouragement, and he thought the owl represented me best with wisdom. I believe I still have that owl somewhere in the attic, although I haven't seen it for a number of years.

Despite all the inconveniences, the daily activities brought out the best in the campers and all the staff. It was the first time that many of them listened to stories by a campfire, went hiking, took in all the beautiful landscape, went swimming and canoeing, created artwork to be exhibited, and participated in musical plays and sing-alongs. We had an old, out-of-tune donated piano, and I played it daily. Some of the keys wouldn't produce any sound, so I had to fake it regularly. Certain songs ended on a high C, but there would be no sound to accompany the voices. Sometimes, I played a higher note since it was so flat that it would offer some kind of "harmony."

But with so many activities planned, the one we all found to bring out the most pleasure was the music. Even with an old piano in poor condition, it remained the highlight of fun. Children who did not feel comfortable singing at first developed a quick change of heart and started to sing whenever they had an opportunity. We had cabin contests to see who could sing the loudest, the lowest note, the highest note, and who could imitate an animal sound the best. We composed funny songs, and had "song-a-thons," singing an entire afternoon from lunch to dinner. The music seemed to make everything more tolerable and satisfying. All of the campers and staff smiled, and I think back on this experience as an appreciated lesson of life.

I developed a greater love of music through those young campers. Music is the universal language through the ages. It connects the joys and sufferings, war and peace, feast and famine, history and current events, and man and God. It has woven a life tapestry with each thread—each song, voice, and expressive instrument—lighting the way with hope and heartfelt gladness. Music is, and shall remain, a steadfast, reliable friend.

Along with the music, I had a good friend in one of my fellow camp counselors who was one year behind me at Ethical Cultural School. I was quite pleased when I learned he would be one of the counselors. Nelson Buckworthy was a caring, thoughtful, and remarkable young man. We called him Nellie. He was the winner of the school's top prize, the same honor I was given the previous year. He was a fine athlete and an excellent tutor, and he was always helping someone get things done. His parents were hardworking, good people. He was given a scholarship, and after graduation, he attended City College in Manhattan with a major in business finance. He told me that he wanted to be a banker at one of the People's Banks so he could help assist lower-income and poor families financially. He definitively had the intellectual capability and the caring to reach his goal.

In those two weeks at camp, we were assigned adjacent cabins, and during our free time, we would discuss ways to improve the lives of each of our campers and make sure they were happy. Several of the boys missed their families or were afraid of the night's sounds, especially when the dark sky, heavy thunderstorms, or inconsiderate frightening tales given by the older campers around the campfire. Most of the time, they "toughed" it out, but they did need reassurance and a shoulder to cry on occasion.

Nellie was very patient with the campers, even when they made mistakes. He was constructive with his commentary and passion to build their self-esteem. He took the extra time to ensure all his campers were regarded, including the less popular ones. When they were emotionally unsettled, he would tell them some adventure story and change their mood from sad to glad. He had a wonderful sense of humor, and he never used it to make fun of anyone. Unfortunately, there was an unexpected circumstance that happened one night where, ironically, he was the one who suffered the brunt of being laughed at.

I already mentioned that the outhouse was not the most desired experience. If a younger camper had to go at night, he would awaken the counselor to accompany him. They had to walk that dirt pathway and hope there was enough moonlight or shining stars to see where they were going. One night, when the moon was barely visible and the sky had few stars, one of Nellie's campers needed to go but did not awaken him; he went by himself. One of the other campers knew he left. Time went by, and the camper did not return. The other camper woke Nellie who went out looking for him. He took the pathway and finally heard the boy crying for help in the outhouse. To Nellie's surprise, the boy couldn't see and slipped into one of the adult holes on the bench and couldn't get out. Poor Nellie couldn't see but finally got a hold of the boy's arm. His grip pulled the boy full force against Nellie, embedding the stool on his right side and arm. He managed to get the boy and himself outside, but what condition were they in to return to the cabin?

The other camper awakened me around dawn, and by the time I got there, the two of them were sitting next to each other. As much as I wanted to be sympathetic, the look on Nellie's face and his commentary made me laugh out loud: "Man, I thought this was a big nightmare, and here you are making this a bad case of reality. Look at us. Just don't try to smell us!"

I told them to meet me down by the lake, and I would bring some soap and clean clothes.

I couldn't stop laughing while walking back to the cabin. I didn't say anything to anyone, but the event spread throughout the camp, including Tyrone. He was unmerciful. He called Nellie, "Smellie" or he'd say, "Nellie's been Gusified Ruff!" I tried to tell him to be sensitive, but he replied, "Now, Windy, you know and I know if that happened to us, we'd be the butt end of laughter. Hey, butt end! Now that's something to wipe your ass with an extra sheet of the Sears catalog!"

The young camper apologized to Nellie repeatedly, and they both got over it. It was an event that no one would wish on his worst enemy.

During the day and evening, after all the campers were settled in bed, Nellie and I would sit around and talk about Babe Ruth and the Yankees, the latest songs—Fanny Brice singing "Second Hand Rose" and " I'm Just Wild about Harry" from the Broadway show, "Shuffle Along"—the Hollywood idol, Rudolph Valentino, the flapper rage with

Clara Bow, Theda Bara, and Joan Crawford, the college football rallies and some of Knute Rockne's motivational commentary to his Notre Dame players: "The best of any team is based on team play and sacrifice, unselfish sacrifice … I want you to analyze before you move and when you get them on the run, keep them on the run." We marveled over the radio broadcasts from WEAF in New York City. Nellie didn't have a radio at his home, so he was quite eager to hear about the program selections.

We also brought up horse racing, especially the recent news. Jockey Frank Hayes, twenty-two years old, was riding Sweet Kiss at Belmont Park, and during the race, Hayes had a heart attack, but he remained in the saddle while the horse ran to victory. He was declared dead when he slumped off the saddle after crossing the finish line. That was the first time a jockey died during a race. Six days later, the thoroughbred Zev went on to victory at the Belmont Sweepstakes. He had won the Kentucky Derby but finished twelfth at the Preakness. Zev was a notable horse, but Nellie and I agreed he was no comparison to Man O' War. In 1919 and 1920, Man O' War won twenty of his twenty-one starts, including the Preakness and Belmont; he never ran in the Kentucky Derby. The Kentucky Derby was not as famous a race then as it is now, and they did not have the Triple Crown honors, although Sir Barton had won all three races in 1919. He was a proud horse, large and strong. He ran in the Lawrence Realization Stakes at the Belmont and beat the second-place horse by one hundred lengths and in a record time that has not been broken; it was tied forty years later.

The eminent New York *Herald Tribune* sports columnist Grantland Rice had been familiar with thoroughbred horses for nearly twenty years before Man O' War and kept his opinion about him over the next thirty-four years until his death:

> I took little interest in the track until Man O' War arrived. Man O' War was different—he had a furious desire to win. He started running from the post, and he was still giving his best at the wire—all the way with all he had. Looking over all the great horses since, the most savage competitor of the lot was Man O' War. He was described as "the mostest horse" by his groomer. Nicknamed "Big Red,"

he had a racing stride that measured nearly twenty-seven feet between leaps … During my time, I've witnessed a half dozen great "Match" races. The Man O' War—John P. Grier affair at Aqueduct (New York) in July 1920 was one … they scared the rest of the field back to the barns … As these two magnificent thoroughbreds lined up at the barrier, the sky seemed alive with heat lightning—not generated by the heavens but by the flame-red chestnut who was raising his inordinate amount of hell, bounding and leaping about before Kummer could get him squared away on all four feet … near the end, John P. made a lung-cracking stretch challenge and was neck and neck with Man O' War as they thundered toward home. Man O' War drew away by perhaps two or three lengths for a new world record of 1:49 and one-fifth. Many claim Man O' War broke John P. Grier's heart in that struggle.[43]

Since Nellie and I shared an interest in music, I had to tell him about the time my father met Louis Armstrong and the King Oliver Creole Jazz Band. Father was attending a medical meeting sponsored by the AMA in Chicago during the summer of 1922. One of the waiters was talking about some great jazz that was playing at the Lincoln Gardens in South Chicago. That evening, Father went and saw King Oliver and his new band associate, trumpeter Louis Armstrong. Father raved about the quality of musicianship and original sound coming from Armstrong's horn. He had an opportunity to meet the band personally after the show and told them how much he hoped they would come to New York to perform. He bought one of the 78-rpm recordings of "Weather Bird Rag" that following April, and he loved it. Little did Father or any of us know that Louis Armstrong would redefine the standard of jazz within a few short years.

There were some remarkable similarities at the Buckworthy and Waterbury homes that we shared with each other. Nellie had an older brother who was lazy, disrespectful to his parents, and a conniving, manipulative man with all his teachers and most of his parent's friends over many years. I revealed the disconnected mishaps of my own mother. He said, with a puzzled look, "You can never figure out why people do things that are detrimental to others, let alone the fact that these traits are a disservice to themselves."

We discussed ambitious goals to serve people. He wanted to be a banker to distribute loans to lower-income families as A. P. Giannini had done in San Francisco following the 1906 earthquake disaster. We had so much in common despite the differences in our socioeconomic upbringing. He made the camp experience more meaningful and gave his campers valuable lessons in friendship, trust, hard work, and consideration of our fellow man. He was a positive, nurturing force in the lives of those campers and the other staff members, including myself.

The last day of camp came, and we all proceeded to the Cooperstown train station for the ride home. The ending was bittersweet. Yeah, no more outhouses, mosquito rampage, or bad food, but I knew I would miss Tyrone and his nonsense, all the young, spirited campers, the lake, the music, the laughter, my fellow staff members, and Nellie. He was like a brother to me—until I met you, Jasper. We had unity, camaraderie, dedication, and a purposeful offering to the rest of the camp participants.

As the train clanged toward the city, I couldn't help but think about Bill Murray singing "That Old Gang of Mine" and wishing I could recapture some of the memories that had gone by. It was August 4. Father and Soulange greeted me at Penn Central Station. They saw that I had lost several pounds; when I got on the scale, I had lost fifteen pounds.

Father showed me the *New York Times* newspaper headline for August 3, reporting the sudden death of President Warren Harding. He came into office with the optimistic inaugural message of returning the country to *normalcy*: "Our supreme task is the resumption of our onward normal way" and his campaign speech in Boston, 1920:

> America's present need is not heroics, but healing; not nostrums but normalcy; not revolution but restoration; not surgery but serenity; not the dramatic but the dispassionate; not experiment but equipoise; not submergence in internationality, but sustainment in triumphant nationality.[44]

But our country was clearly not "normal" before, during, or after the Great War. His term was shrouded in secrecy, but the impression he gave the American public was quite positive.

During the four-day journey by train from San Francisco, where he died, to Washington, DC, the newspapers reported the deep reverent tributes while millions of Americans flocked to their local railroad stations, in blazing, humid weather, and thunderstorms in Omaha, Nebraska, waiting hours and hours before the train was scheduled to pass. Military honors and twenty-one-gun salutes expressing deep patriotic sentiment echoed throughout the towns. Church bells and courthouse bells tolled. The country had not seen such a display of mourning since the assassination of President Lincoln; Harding even had a commemorative US stamp issued within one month of his death.

It wasn't until six months after his death that those deep, dark, and scandalous secrets emerged. During his administration, he maintained popularity with the voters because he had such favorable coverage by the White House news correspondents. He was a former newspaper editor in Ohio before his political career and had strong personal relations with all his assigned reporters. It was truly amazing that, after his death, his image tarnished rapidly. He had been drinking and smoking regularly, even though he voted in favor of Prohibition; the law obviously did not apply to him. He had private poker games at least twice a week with several of his cabinet members, including Albert Fall, Edwin Denby, and Harry Daugherty, his campaign manager and then attorney general. These individuals were later involved in bribery and oil lease and veterans' affairs corruption. There were blackmail payoffs to many of Harding's mistresses, married, unmarried, and juvenile. He also fathered an illegitimate child when he was a state senator. His memorial, an elaborate mausoleum, was finished in 1927, but it was not dedicated until 1931 by a begrudged President Hoover, who happened to be a member of that Harding administration as the secretary of commerce.

And many more secrets were kept locked away permanently by his wife who spent endless nights and days destroying many of Harding's personal letters and government documents in the White House fireplace. She herself was dead within a year, and neither of them would have to face any investigation. Harding had deliberately placed a veil over the American public. He rode the wave of illusion to hide his cowardice and fear; he basically felt he was above the need for accountability and responsibility. I believe he had a genuine interest in appearing to be everyone's friend, but his incompetent management of his affairs, both professional and personal, dominated his being and left him broken and dishonored. He wore a mask to deceive the public he served, but the mask was solely intended to protect him from criticism and guilt. "It would be better for him that an ass millstone were hanged on his neck and that he were drowned in the depth of the sea" (Matthew 18:6). His charade would be his downfall and a crushing blow to the leadership of our nation. There was a bit of irony; he had no concept of "normalcy."

At this point, Elizabeth with all her innate awareness, brought up the difference between Grandfather and Warren Harding. "This whole idea of secrecy is quite interesting when you look at Harding's life and Great-Grandfather's life. Great-Grandfather clearly understood he was given a directive by his visionary mother to go forth wearing a mask to enable him to do constructive and beneficial things for many people. His mask served as a protector, as a shield to defend the disregarded and neglected people of the nation. He had no cowardice or fear; he had nothing to be ashamed of. He had a strong commitment and great confidence to accomplish his goal with Mumsie's support. He maintained his secret identity from you, Father, because he did not want the possibility of ridicule, as Thaddeus had demonstrated, nor did he want that revelation to influence any of your future decisions that you had to make or offer you any regret or disappointment.

"Great-Grandfather was trying to protect you with his secret. He had best intentions to make your life a good and happy one. Once his secret was revealed, your respect and reverence for him were questioned initially, but after you fully comprehended his motive, your impression of him soared beyond the atmosphere. Secrets need to be examined patiently and quite thoroughly before reaction, judgment, and opinions are formulated and fixed. What appears to be true may not always live up to appearances. Take time to reexamine any secret, well intentioned or illusive. The former stands the test of time while the latter becomes an error that fails all tests."

I took a moment to reflect on Elizabeth's analysis. Secrets possess mystery and information that can be revealed or remain unknown during a person's life. Sometimes, the information is revealed at an inappropriate time or should never have been disclosed. Sometimes, the information disclosed may not necessarily be true. Some secrets, truthfully, are best kept concealed; the information might be unnecessary or promote pain and suffering that could have been avoided. Sometimes, time is required to understand the true meaning of a secret. Sometimes, secrets are deceptive, but not all secrets are meant to deceive; a deceptive quality, however, would require secrecy. But throughout time, certain secrets of life are kept hidden for reasons beyond our most capable conscious understanding.

Grandfather's secret was kept to protect me, whereas Warren Harding's secrets had no grounded motive. The whole review of hidden truths led me to reopen an ugly wound—a secret about Nellie that would not be revealed until years later when I worked in Harlem; this was an unexplainable mystery. I looked over at Jasper, and he gave me the look that it was not the time to discuss that painful transformation.

I quickly changed my thoughts back to the 1923 summer experience.

The camp gave me a good lesson about friendship, success, and—in spite of harsh conditions or circumstances—a greater appreciation of how resilient and balanced the children are. I would go to medical school with a dedicated call to service and the joy to seek a better understanding of myself and my fellow man. It sure was wonderful to return from camp to electricity, a working toilet, and some good home cooking. Those pioneers and first settlers had quite the challenge to make it day to day and year to year. Who was I to complain about a petty, short-term inconvenience?

Harvard Medical School, 1923–1927 (Event 16)

That September of 1923 was quite a remarkable transition from the quaint town of Amherst to Boston, the well-landscaped "hub of the solar system." A visitor would be fascinated with both historic architectural wonders as well as the splendid greenery sprinkled throughout the city's forty-five square miles. The city was incorporated in 1630 (New York was incorporated in 1664) and included amongst its native born, a veritable who's who—Benjamin Franklin, John Adams, John Hancock, Paul Revere, Ralph Waldo Emerson, Henry David Thoreau, and Edgar Allan Poe, to name just a few. As exciting a place as it was, with its rich history and influence, I was most in awe of the similarities between the two cities, and that was the privilege of experiencing autumn in New England.

Autumn, with all its magical power and glory, is described so well, poetically, by the nineteenth-century literary critic, Richard Stoddard. Entitled "Autumn," he begins:

> Divinest Autumn! Who may sketch thee best, forever changeful o'er the changeful globe? Hark, Hark! I hear the reapers in a row, shouting their harvest carols, blithe and

loud. Cutting the rustled maize whose crests are bowed with ears o'ertasselled, soon to be laid low; Crooked earthward now, the orchards droop their boughs with red-cheeked fruits, while far along the wall, full in the south, ripe plums and peaches fall in tufted grass where laughing lads carouse; And by and by, when northern winds are out, Great fires will roar in chimneys huge at night while chairs draw round and pleasant tales are told: And nuts and apples will be passed about until the household, drowsy with delight, creep off to bed, a-cold! Sovereign of Seasons, Monarch of the Earth! Steward of bounteous Nature, whose rich alms are showered upon us from thy liberal palms until our spirits overflow with mirth! Divinest Autumn! While our garners burst with plenteous harvesting, and heaped income, we lift our eyes to thee through grateful tears. Worldwide in boons, vouchsafe to visit first. And linger last along our realm of Peace, where Freedom calmly sits and beckons on the Years![45]

As I displayed my reflective thought of appreciation on my face for such a beautiful imagery, Jasper uttered, "Man, Water Pump, you always have that high-style use of words. Don't get me wrong. I like 'em. I just don't know what they mean sometimes."

Pamela responded, "Jasper, Stoddard's poem requires a few readings to sense his full insight on autumn. He asks the simple, but provocative question: Who may describe it best? As if in a meditative state of mind, he hears the harvester singing joyfully, cutting the ripened corn, picking the tasty apples, plums, and peaches, and enjoying the rewards at home as his family gathers around the fireplace in the evenings, telling stories into the wee hours of night with chilly winds suggesting the approach of the winter season. The last stanza of the poem is the most powerful and spiritual, defining the core of autumn. It is God's gracious offerings, "worldwide" blessings, reflecting peace and freedom through the eternal years. Autumn brings us God's gifts, showering millions of kisses upon man and all other beings. We all need to give thanks for the richness of autumn; it is truly the ruler of the seasons!"

"Thank you, Pamela, for your interpretation. Jasper was not the only one who needs clarification. I read it many times to embrace its deeper meaning. Well, now that I've shared my philosophical talk on Boston, let me shed some light on the Boston people."

Although the population is composed primarily of the Irish immigrants who arrived after the Great Potato Famine in the 1840s, as well as Italians, Negroes, Chinese, Jews, and French Huguenots, the sector that commands the ship. Those people "who did not just happen, but were planned," are the quintessential Yankees—the proper Bostonians.

The vast majority of the proper Bostonians, also known as the Boston "Brahmins," appear to have descended from many generations, dating back to the Mayflower Puritans—at least the early-eighteenth-century families that combined wealth with high social status. This package—the wealth and social status—made each component interdependent sources of inherited positions in the upper economic and social order. These privileges indirectly gave them political power and control.

According to Colonel Henry Lee, one of their "shining" own, these proper Bostonians had the "satisfying belief that New England morality and intellectuality had produced nothing better than they were; they were contentedly intermarried with the sure faith that in such alliances, there can be no blunder." As a matter of fact, Harvard President A. Lawrence Lowell was married to his cousin, and so was Endicott Peabody, headmaster at Groton Academy. Their status was so clear that a folk poem was recited at a Holy Cross College class reunion in 1910 by Dr. John Collins Bossidy: "And this is good old Boston, the home of the bean and the cod, where the Lowells talk to the Cabots, and the Cabots talk only to God!"

If you live on Beacon Hill, your front view faces the Common, Boston Common Public Park, or you own an enclosed park, Louisburg Square, with the other twenty-plus families who do not have any city government interference. If you are not living in Boston proper, then you live in one of the privileged suburbs of Brookline, Chestnut Hill, or Milton.

However, of all the institutions in Boston, including its banks, churches, office buildings, and historic landmarks, it is "Fair Harvard" that has a proper Bostonian's highest regard. Incorporated just six years after the city in 1636, it has been the training grounds for generations since. There have been at least eight generations of Saltonstalls and Wigglesworths, six generations of Cabots, and five generations of Lowells, just to name a few. The money kindly donated by the alumni has given Harvard the largest university endowment of any school in this country, and they intend to keep it that way. The son of one of Harvard's former presidents would show his Harvard catalogue, listing all Harvard graduates since 1636, and state proudly, "If a man is there (in the catalogue), that is who he is. If he isn't, who is he?"

How ironic to learn that Harvard had quite a different beginning to what is projected today. Originally established with the land and personal library of Reverend John Harvard for the purpose of training "literate clergy," the trustees of Harvard declared, "Let every student be plainly instructed and earnestly pressed to consider well, the main end of his life and studies is to know God and Jesus Christ which is eternal life (John 17:3)." The original motto on the shield read: "Veritas Christo et Ecclesiae (Truth for Christ and the church), but in the early twentieth century, it was shortened to "Veritas." In the embedded shield on Harvard's Widener Library, Memorial Hall, and the lion head at Harvard Medical School, one sees the top two books on the shield face up while the bottom book is facedown, symbolizing the limits of reason and an ongoing need for God's revelation.

Father had told me about the Final Clubs at the college. There were no fraternities, but membership in these clubs was based on social privilege. These clubs were the stepping-stone to the gentleman's clubs in Boston. The Porcellian Club, the "Porc," had the distinction of being the oldest and most exclusive. Theodore Roosevelt spoke quite fondly of his membership there while a student at Harvard. The Porcellian Club members would join the Somerset Club; the AD Club would become members of Boston's Union Club.

Such was the background of several of my classmates as well as their attitudes about anyone who was not of their "position." I was fortunate in my relations with most of the faculty; my father graduated in 1896

211

and knew several of the members personally. Both Dr. David Edsall, the dean of Harvard Medical School, and his assistant, Dr. Worth Hale, who was director of admissions, were encouraging when I applied the previous year. I stayed in the newly built Vanderbilt Hall, which was on the opposite corner of the new Boston Lying-In Hospital (the BLI) for women. Both buildings were on Longwood Avenue, across from the medical school's green quadrangle. The endowment at the medical school was aided substantially by the Rockefeller General Board and the Rockefeller Foundation. Their interest in clinical research would play a meaningful role in my postgraduate years.

The basic curriculum included anatomy in the first and second years, histology and embryology, physiology, biochemistry, and medical psychology in the first year. There were lots of quizzes, but nothing like the second year. We were taking anatomy, bacteriology, pathology and clinical pathology, neuropathology, and parasitology. It seemed like we had a test, both practical and written, daily, and there was so much information required to learn. We also had introduction to medicine, surgery, neurology, obstetrics, and pediatrics. The third and fourth years were in the hospitals learning psychiatry, preventive medicine and hygiene, dermatology and syphilology, gynecology, laryngology, pediatrics, orthopedics, genito-urinary surgery, general surgery, neurology, otology, ophthalmology, and obstetrics. By the end of the fourth year, you were prepared to go into hospital training in the specialty you selected and go out into practice for a fulfilling career.

I had developed cordial relations with many of my classmates, including James Whitaker and Euclid Ghee, who were both Negro. Robert Wilkinson, who was a Negro and Howard Gray joined our class during our third year. Over the past few years, the university had created controversy over the number of Jewish students admitted as well as the banning of Negro students from the freshman dormitories in the Harvard Yard. In January 1922, President Lowell proposed a quota of no more than 15 percent of the student body would be Jewish, even if they were fully qualified above another "acceptable" student. He rationalized his belief, saying, "The anti-Semitic feeling among students is increasing, and it grows in proportion to the increased numbers of Jews."

The burden of addressing Harvard's "Jewish problem" was handled by Harry Starr, class of 1921, who was a Jew. Through several meetings between Jewish and non-Jewish students as well as faculty and administrators, he courageously and outwardly stated that the Jew could not look upon himself as a problem. "The first need of seekers for the truth is understanding and tolerance, but tolerance is not to be administered like castor oil, with eyes closed and jaws clinched."

Lowell received a great deal of criticism as he did in banning the Negroes from the dormitories. In the fall of 1923, the highly qualified Roscoe C. Bruce Jr., a student at Exeter Academy, was not allowed to stay in the Yard as a freshman. He was the son of a Harvard alumni, Roscoe Sr., class of 1902, and grandson of Blanche Bruce, the first Negro elected to the US Senate, serving a full term in the post-Reconstruction years. Lowell's letter to Roscoe Jr. was published in the Boston newspaper. "I am sorry that you do not feel the reasonableness of our position about the freshman dormitories. We owe to the colored man the same opportunities for education that we do for the white man; but we do not owe to him to force him and the white man into social relations that are not … mutually congenial." Many retaliatory remarks from several distinguished Harvard alumni—as well as James Weldon Johnson from the NAACP—were sent to Lowell, but the attitudes remained the same.

I had to deal with this very irrational thinking for four long years in one of my classmates, Tillman Merritt, from Charleston, South Carolina. Tillman came from an old, wealthy family—former slave owners with a large plantation before the Civil War. He was named after his godfather, Benjamin Tillman, an acidic US senator who was an openly, demonstrative racist in the senate chamber as well as his hometown in South Carolina.

During classes, nearly every day, I would hear him say out loud, looking at Euclid or James, "Why are those coons still allowed to come into this class? They have no business here other than to take out the trash or mop the floor."

I confronted him one day and asked what his problem was. He looked at me, and if looks could kill, I would be in a coffin.

"Where I was raised, any respectable white man knows that a nigger has no place in an academic institution. I am part of a long line of sophisticated, intellectual, and successful businessmen who know the nigger is unworthy, lazy, dull of mind, and incapable of performing anything more than a menial task. I agree with my late godfather—may he rest in peace—when he said, 'I believe that niggers are men, but some of them are so akin to the monkey that scientists are yet looking for the missing link.' I believe all of them are akin to the monkey!"

"Well," I replied, "you make a clear point. All the scientists need to do is stick a mirror in front of you—and they will have found that missing link!" I just walked away after my commentary; I didn't want to start any discussion because I knew it would be pointless. I tried to stay away from him as much as I could, but his presence and those crude remarks kept ringing in my thoughts.

I found out later that Senator Tillman's father had attended Harvard College, but he didn't graduate. The senator then urged his godson to come here for his medical training before he died. By all accounts, Tillman was educated, charming around his southern constituents, and was capable of performing well on his exams and clinic work during the third- and fourth-year courses. He was a decent-looking fellow—a head full of blond hair, blue eyes, five foot ten inches—but he always rubbed me wrong.

He was an undermining whiner and manipulator. He took every opportunity to blame James or Euclid or any of the other "undesirable" classmates for anything that was a "problem," even if they weren't there to create the problem. By the time we got to the ward, I called him the "White Weasel." I told James and Euclid, and they laughed. Pretty soon, we just called him "W squared." It got to the point where James asked me if the "W squared" stood for "white squared" or "Weasel squared." I said, "Both shoes fit, and he wears them well."

Jasper blurted out, "Now, Water Pump, you were too nice to that cracker. If I was there while you were talking to James and Euclid, I would have added: 'Both of my shoes would have fit well up his ass!'"

I just shook my head. What could I say? "Jasper, really?"

When Father was a student here, he had told me about a few of his teachers who greatly influenced him in medicine. Dr. Frederick Shattuck was an impeccably dressed master of diagnosis and a genuine advocate for student learning. Father also praised Dr. William Councilman, a transplant from the Johns Hopkins Pathology Department. He had great teaching skills, but he had a well-known stuttering impairment. Once, when he asked a student a question, the flustered young man, looking for an adequate answer, started stuttering back. Dr. Councilman was offended and told the poor lad to leave the class.

I, too, was quite impressed with the encouragement and clinical capabilities of a few of my faculty members. My experience with Dr. Alice Hamilton was quite memorable. Dr. Hamilton was appointed to Harvard Medical School in the fall of 1919 as assistant professor of industrial medicine and the first female faculty appointee to the chagrin of several members of the Harvard Corporation. But it was made clear that she had no privilege in using the Harvard Club, which was specifically designated for use by all Harvard faculty as well as being told that she would not march in the commencement procession of the faculty or sit on the platform during the exercises, even though she was sent an invitation to participate yearly.

Her job was divided with six months of teaching at the medical school and six months working with outside industrial committees. She became a principal investigator for workers exposed to industrial toxins and a real advocate for preventive measures to reduce exposures and the devastating effects of these toxins. Her work revealed conditions that promoted lead poisoning, mercury poisoning, white or yellow phosphorus, and benzol, a coal-tar solvent used in the chemical plants to manufacture rubber cement and tin cans for food. She would have many personal conversations with me about these toxic effects. She described accumulated lead in painters and bathtub enamellers causing severe colic, paralysis in several joints, muscle wasting, and mental disturbance. Mercury accumulation in felt hatters, miners, and manufacturers of amalgam caused swelling and pain in the gums, reflexive jerking of the extremities, and the inevitable psychosis, causing mood changes—depression, anxiety, irritability, and anger. White phosphorus accumulation in the female workers in the matchmaking industry caused a jaw abscess leading to swelling pain and horribly disfiguring facial changes. It was known as phossy jaw. And the workers exposed to benzol had a slow, insidious chronic poisoning, causing anemia and hemorrhaging, which led to bleeding gums and noses and susceptibility to infection.

Her work in post-World War I took her to Europe to remedy the plight of the starving German civilians, especially the children, the infirmed, and the elderly. There was a deliberate blockade of the needed food. This politically motivated indifference and inhumanity of the American, British, and French leadership was a true thorn in Dr. Hamilton's side.

Dr. Hamilton had spent time at Jane Addams's Hull House in Chicago. Mumsie had known Miss Addams for many years, and I told Dr. Hamilton of the similarities of these great women. Dr. Hamilton described the Hull House as a "bridge between the classes, helping both the socially privileged as well as the poor." Miss Addams "offered a place for young people of education and culture where they could live as neighbors (to the poor) and give as much as they could of what they had … and in the knowledge they acquired, they would be better equipped to fight against the evils."

The next teacher was Dr. William Hinton, "instructor" of preventive medicine and hygiene at the medical school. Here was a man, graduated from Harvard College in 1905, who worked as a teacher in biology, chemistry, and physics for the next four years in Tennessee and Oklahoma, accepted at Harvard Medical School, and despite his four-year hiatus from full-time academic study, was able to complete the medical school degree requirements in three years instead of the usual four. He graduated cum laude in his class in 1912, and he won the prestigious Edward Wigglesworth Scholarship two consecutive years for academic achievement. He was openly praised for his meticulous work ethic by Harvard faculty notables: Dr. Richard C. Cabot and Dr. Elmer Southard. But none of his outstanding qualifications allowed him entry as an intern in any Boston hospitals because of the color of his skin. He was first and foremost a highly qualified physician denied the ability to treat patients.

Undaunted, he pursued a career in laboratory work, volunteering at the Department of Pathology at Massachusetts General Hospital and eventually becoming the director of the state lab for communicable diseases (the Wasserman Lab was part of the Massachusetts Department of Public Health). His knowledge of syphilis impressed Dr. Southard who arranged for his instruction to students at Harvard and was appointed instructor in

1919. In addition to his outstanding research at the Wasserman Laboratory, he spent twelve long years developing a more efficient testing of patients with syphilis. At the time of my graduation in 1927, the "Hinton test" was perfected, allowing a more accurate test to determine the diagnosis of syphilis than its predecessor, the Wasserman Test. Realize the importance of this work on a national level. In 1910, approximately 10 percent of the total United States population had syphilis disease. Dr. Hinton taught general bacteriology and immunology to the students. He was thorough, engaging, and quite inspiring as a teacher.

I got a chance to know Dr. Hinton personally and was invited to dinner at his house in Canton, a suburb about fifteen miles southwest of Greater Boston. Canton is home to Paul Revere's Copper Rolling Mill and the Canton Viaduct for the Boston and Providence Railroad. While enjoying the hospitality of the Hinton family, I was so amazed at his beautiful garden. He built a lily pond and planted a magnificent display of flowers, fruit trees, corn, beans, and tomatoes. Many of his wooden cabinetry and furniture pieces were made by Dr. and Mrs. Hinton's own hands.

I owe a great deal of gratitude to the influence Dr. Hinton had on me; he was one of the most encouraging physicians to steer me toward a career in infectious disease. I was also quite in awe of his courage, determination, and stamina; he was intrepid to the obvious racism and disregard for his medical brilliance. But like Father, he was a modest man whose interest was to serve humanity, advance scientific research, and raise the standard of public health.

Although he remained on the Harvard faculty for thirty-four years and had written a classic text on "Syphilis and Its Treatment" that was recognized worldwide as a standard reference in medical schools and hospitals (1936), he did not become a clinical professor until 1949, one year before he retired, the first Negro to attain the rank of professor at Harvard. Thanks are given to Dr. Hinton, once again for envisioning loftier ideals of a good scientist, physician, teacher, and a good human being.

I could not leave the discussion of influential teachers without mentioning one of the great spirits of medicine whose premature death rang a note of sadness and yet reverence for the opportunity of feeling the greatness of his soul.

Dr. Francis Weld Peabody was destined to be a shining torch among the greats of early-twentieth-century physicians and researchers. Both his paternal grandfather and father were Unitarian ministers; the grandfather presided over King's Chapel from 1847 until 1856, and his father was a Harvard professor in the Divinity School and Harvard University minister. His aunt (his father's sister) was married to former Harvard President Charles Elliot, and close relatives included the Derby family, descended from Elias Hasket Derby, a wealthy sea merchant from Salem, Massachusetts. In a household of great social status and influence, young Francis learned in a "lovely Christian home," the principles of close friendships, family values, ongoing refinement of study, and a conscious awareness of his fellow man.

After graduating from Harvard College, cum laude, he attended Harvard Medical School, becoming his class president and vice president of the Boylston Medical Society, a prestigious Harvard medical "club" whose members advance the graduate medical education through papers of current medical research. Unlike the vast majority of classmates, he pursued training in academic medicine and clinical research. He understood the principles of biochemistry and physiology and applied them to the diseases. By 1921, he was offered the dean of medicine at the University of Chicago and the chaired position of medicine at Johns Hopkins, Columbia, Yale, and Stanford. He turned all of them down to remain at Harvard as full Professor of medicine and chief of Harvard services at the Boston City Hospital, which was a public hospital, as well as director of the newly built Thorndike Memorial Laboratories. He wanted to provide "the best possible medical care in a public hospital" as well as a comprehensive nursing care and social services to follow patients after discharge from the hospital. He attracted outstanding physicians to carry out his mission. With all these responsibilities, he was a consummate teacher, offering wisdom and empathy for each of the patients. I watched this man, as I had watched my father, provide that comfort. In his essay entitled "The Public and the Practitioner," Dr. Peabody made it clear: "The truth of the matter is that the practice of medicine is intensely personal and no system or machine can be substituted for a personal relationship." It was evident in every aspect of his brilliant career.

In the summer of 1926, at the height of his contributions, he was diagnosed with inoperable cancer. From that moment until he quietly passed away on October 13, 1927, Dr. Peabody combined working, teaching, writing (he completed his last letter to his friend, Dr. Longcope, which would be published as a paper entitled "The Soul of the Clinic" within twenty-four hours of his death), influencing, and living. His most famous remembrance came from a simple lecture given at the medical school for the students. I was so fortunate to be present at this memorable occasion about "The Care of the Patient":

> Hospitals, like other institutions, founded with the highest human ideals, are apt to deteriorate into dehumanized machines ... in the hospital, one gets into the habit of using the oil immersion lens instead of the lower power and focuses too intently on the center of the field ... thus the physician who attempts to take care of a patient while he neglects this factor is as unscientific as the investigator who neglects to control all the conditions that may affect his experiment. The good physician knows his patients through and through ... Time, sympathy and understanding must be lavishly dispensed ... One of the essential qualities of the clinician is interest in humanity.[46]

A copy of his lecture is given to every Harvard Medical School first-year student since that time, and it was published with full text in the *Journal of the American Medical Association*. His final statement has been quoted through the years in all medical circles: "The secret of the care of the patient is in caring for the patient."

Although I was a student, Dr. Peabody talked to me as a colleague and friend during my last two years of medical school. I spent as much time as possible at the Boston City Hospital ward as well as doing research projects with him at the Thorndike Laboratory. He had a great sense of humor, which seemed to be even more evident as his health declined. He was also quite spiritual in exploring his awareness of patient care and the caring of his patients.

In my written correspondence with Father or my telephone conversations with him before his death in 1926, I would refer to Dr. Peabody as well as Dr. Hamilton and Dr. Hinton as the physicians I wanted to emulate in my delivery of care for my patients. I had been impressed with my father's work since I was a boy. It was nice to have like-minded human beings convincing me that medicine could be all that it is supposed to be—and I did my best to try to make it happen.

It was truly a shame that Dr. Hinton could not have worked with Dr. Peabody in the Boston City Hospital and the Thorndike. The two of them would have made extraordinary contributions together; together, medicine could be more like it was supposed to be.

In addition to the impact of these great teachers, I was equally moved by my patients during the ward experience in third and fourth years, and a few examples are worth recalling.

One evening, near the beginning of my clinical rotation in the Emergency Service at Boston City Hospital, I was approaching the main desk when I heard the supervising nurse raising her voice to an elderly Chinese patient. "I already told you that you can't get care here. No Coolies are allowed. Go back to Chinatown where you belong." I couldn't believe my ears. This poor man, with prominent kyphosis and scoliosis, standing on old, mismatched crutches with threadbare padding, in obvious pain and fatigue and in need of immediate attention was commanded to leave. I told her to get a bed for him. "The hospital policy states—"

"I don't care what your policy says. This man needs care, and I will give it to him. If you have any sense, you will get that bed I requested for him." In the meantime, I found a wheelchair and placed him in a room with all the other patients staring at both of us. There was dead silence except for the coughing and respiratory effort my new patient displayed.

While sitting in the wheelchair, I knew he had Pott's disease, tuberculosis of the spine. Besides the striking curvature and vertebral deformities, his face spoke of prolonged hardship and despair. He had a sallow complexion, drawn due to emaciation. His skin was coarse, and his eyes were dark and sunken to the depths of the ocean floor. His queue was whitish-gray, and his voice was hoarse with labored speech, but he managed a faint smile of gratitude as we waited for admission.

Father had several Chinese patients when I was a boy. He told me that the term coolie meant indentured servant, probably from the Chinese characters "Ku" and "li," which translated to English as "rented muscles." He went on to say that Charles Crocker, a prominent Californian businessman who was in charge of operations at the Central Pacific Railroad, needed the hard work of the Chinese laborers to lay his railroad track in treacherous mountain areas through Truckee, California, Donner Pass, and other dangerous points leading to Provo, Utah. Once the construction was completed in 1869, the Chinese laborers were removed from the picture at the celebration of the final transcontinental link as well as fired immediately from the company.

Sentiments from the president, to the governors, to the local mayors, sheriffs, or any "assumed" law enforcement were crystal clear: the Chinese were a threat to white "purity" and classified as an inferior on the level of the Negro or American Indian. In addressing the "Chinese problem," politician John Miller stated at the 1878 California Convention:

> Were the Chinese to amalgamate at all with our people, it would be the lowest, most vile and degraded of our race … a hybrid of the most despicable, a mongrel of the most detestable that has ever afflicted the earth.[47]

And New York Governor Horatio Seymour agreed:

> Why let the Chinese barbarian stand in the way of civilization? We already do not let the Indian stand in the way. We tell them plainly they must give up their homes and property, and live upon corners of their own territories because they are in the way of our civilization.[48]

The legislation cemented these sentiments. Congress passed the Chinese Exclusion Act in May 1882, not allowing any Chinese immigration for ten years. The act remained in policy until 1943 with fairly strict enforcement on the West Coast. It was the first immigration law to exclude a population strictly based on race. The biggest blow came, however, when the Geary Act was passed in 1892. All Chinese in the United States would be forced to carry a photo identification, a domestic passport, to show at any time requested by a US citizen or face deportation. It extended the Exclusion Act as well as a total banning of citizenship against all Chinese immigrants. Resistance was bravely shown, but unfair treatment persisted. Deportations and lynchings took place, and the whole thing remained so unfortunate and so unnecessary.

After getting the patient fed and bathed, he was placed on the tuberculosis ward. I spoke with him the following morning. He told me it took all his effort to walk the nearly two miles down Harrison Avenue from Beach Street to the hospital. He also thanked me because no one had taken any interest in him since he left his family in California in 1877. In fact, he had never slept in a real bed before last night—only cots, alleyways, or wherever his head was allowed to rest.

Qing King So was born in China in 1858. Both his mother and father had lost their parents, and with the help of financial savings, they went to California when Qing was one year old. His father was a fisherman but an industrious man who could build and do any odd jobs. He had friendly ties with a member of the Chinese Six Companies, based in San Francisco who arranged their travel. His family learned to tolerate the racism and settled in Monterey, but they moved to the railroad town of Rocklin when Qing's father worked on the Central Pacific Railroad until 1869.

They stayed in Rocklin until they were forced to leave in 1877, just before the entire Chinatown area was deliberately burned to the ground. They moved back to the San Francisco area, but Qing left in 1881 to find a better existence in Boston. He found a small basement room on Oxford Place and had several jobs waiting in the restaurants, helping in the laundry shops, or assisting one of the family associations.

In October 1903, Boston's Chinatown experienced an immigration raid with more than three hundred Chinese arrested for not carrying their immigration documents. They were victimized, and Qing was one of those arrested. Fifty men were deported; Qing was saved by one of the restaurant owners who knew he was a good worker.

Qing developed tuberculosis in the winter of 1921. He had brief periods when he felt better, but overall, his health declined. Eventually, he developed spinal pain and disfiguration in 1924. After suffering for four long years, he thought he could see someone to get help. I was glad I was in the right place at the right time.

As I listened to Qing So's story, I was transformed back to the theater, watching the 1922 Lon Chaney classic, *Shadows*, which was based on Wilbur Steele's 1916 short story, "Ching, Ching, Chinaman." It was the first time a Chinese character was the protagonist on film, and Lon Chaney did an outstanding portrayal to show the injustice, hypocrisy, and disregard given to the Chinese by the people in a small New England town.

The townsmen found him and another local fisherman after surviving a wreck at sea. When one of the influential members asks everyone to pray for the other fishermen who had died in the storm, Lon Chaney's character, Yen Sin, does not kneel. They said, "Pray or get out. We are all believers in Urkey. We want no heathens." He is called the "Chink" and is ridiculed, but there are three kind inhabitants—the minister, his wife, and a neighborhood boy—who show him respect. Throughout the movie, he is an observer of truth and is portrayed in the end to be a decent and upright man. At the beginning of the movie, the words forecast the significance of the plot and its development.

> To every people, in every age, there comes a measure of God to man through man. Wisdom may dwell among us in humble disguise, unknown, despised, until its mission is fulfilled, and it steps back into the mystery from whence it came.

Mr. So came into the hospital when I needed to care for him, offering me a piece of wisdom that was neither despised nor unknown. It was taken graciously. I would never forget this decent human being. I only wish I could have given him care sooner. He died a few days later.

My pediatric experience was exciting for two good reasons. The Infants' Hospital facility (which took care of children from newborn up to the age of two years) had become attached to the Children's Hospital grounds in 1925. Dr. Kenneth Blackfan was physician-in-chief and the Thomas Morgan Rotch professor of pediatrics, one of only two faculty-appointed positions at Harvard Medical School that were exclusively training in pediatrics. Dr. Blackfan's bedside teaching and his caring for the children were exemplary. The Infants' Hospital had a premature infant nursery, a sunroom, and individualized feeding cribs with an excellent nursing and volunteer program.

Pediatrics was a newly developing branch of medicine. The US Children's Bureau, in the Department of Labor, was the first nationally organized group to represent the welfare of the child and acquire data on infant mortality. Funding was provided to educate women about prenatal and post-delivery care of their infants. By 1921, the important Sheppard-Towner Act, the act for the promotion of the welfare of maternity and infancy was passed in Congress. Visiting nurses and preventive health clinics developed in rural, southern, and western states, examining children from infancy through pre-school. Although the program was viewed positively by the mothers, the state medical societies, including the AMA, opposed it as an "intrusion of private practice … an imported socialistic scheme" and led to the act's funding cut in 1929.

I remember several of the patients with malformations, diphtheria, scarlet fever, rickets, and tuberculosis meningitis, but the image most clearly viewed in my mind is that of a longtime volunteer who rocked many of the most irritable babies, with deafening cries, agitation, and profound suffering into a state of tranquility and contentment. Though elderly and somewhat frail, this woman's role was purposeful. She was one of the hospital's most stable and reliable fixtures; her name was Bessie, but she was affectionately called Grandma.

Born a slave, she moved up North somewhere in her mid-twenties after the Civil War ended and eventually settled in Boston in the 1870s. She never married, but she did domestic work for a number of families. She was a regular at the Columbus Avenue AME Church, but she was present at the hospital the other six days from 8:00 a.m. to 3:00 p.m. She had a special wooden rocker that she used while holding the infants and children.

The nursing staff told me a little about her when I came to the pediatric floor. The first impression was quite striking. Here was a peaceful older woman with snow-white hair, pulled up and back, tucked under her straw floral sun hat. The hat was well worn with scattered, tattered openings around its top and a faded yellow velvet border supporting a small bouquet of carnations on the left side of her hat. Her chestnut brown complexion displayed a forehead etched with lines carving out years of hard labor and wear. There were deep, furrowed laugh lines surrounding dry lips that receded into a mouth of several missing teeth, and an extended prominent mandible with white coarse hairs on her chin. Her vision was clouded, but even through her thin, gold-framed, thick-lensed glasses, you saw a genuine awareness of her faith and joy in her soul, right there, right there in those ageless eyes. As you gazed into those eyes beyond her glasses, it was as if you were walking through the mist of the rainforest—and the break of dawn suddenly and gently lifted the mist. Her eyes and penetrating smile melted my heart. I felt her living presence each time she rocked any of the patients in her arms.

As I approached her, she was always humming or softly singing a Negro spiritual. When she spoke, she would rest the baby in her lap and hold your hands with a rhythmic up and down gesture until she finished speaking. After each of many conversations, she would end with a sweet and soft "I love you." She told me about the Boston Riot of 1903 that occurred in her church when Booker T. Washington was a guest speaker. William Monroe Trotter—prominent Boston Negro newspaper editor, Harvard class of 1895, magna cum laude, Harvard's first Negro Phi Beta Kappa member—confronted Mr. Washington on a number of controversial questions, eventually leading to his arrest after that meeting. She said that Mr. Trotter raised some important matters that should have been addressed by Mr. Washington and had no business being arrested.

She also told me that she had been a volunteer at the Infants' Hospital since 1891 and had met another doctor, a few years later, who showed concern about her welfare as I did. She didn't recall his name, but he was no ordinary white doctor. She said, "He cared about everybody, like you. The two of you have the same thoughts. I see it."

I told her it was probably my father.

"I knew you two were the same." She asked about my grandfather, and I told her he was the inspiration for my father and me. She inquired where he was from, and I told her down South in Georgia and he came North during the Civil War. She wanted to know about his hands, and I told her he had a scar on his left palm.

She hesitated and then said, "Your granddaddy was given a great opportunity from God, and he used it wisely. He taught your daddy and you the right way. You keep him near in all your work. God blessed all of you, and I am blessed to know you." Bessie pulled me closer and said, "You will face many battles ahead, but your belief will get you through. Stay strong and be patient on the Lord! Never give up—and never give in to temptation." It was nearly 3:00 p.m. She asked me to place the baby back in the crib and get her cane from the corner. I went to get the cane, which was quite heavy and sturdy. She walked away with that cane, convincing me that she knew more about my family than I knew.

There were times when I would see a fussy baby who had seizure activity, poor feeding, or some infection be placed in her arms, wailing in distress, inconsolable, and within five minutes, would be silent, settled, and ready to sleep. There was no clock in the sunroom where her rocking chair was located. Sometime, I would jokingly ask her what time it was, and she would always answer, "Oh, it's a good time to praise the Lord."

One morning, I asked her for the time and she said it was a quarter past nine o'clock. I looked at my pocket watch, and it was 9:15 exactly. I asked her how she knew, and she said, "The spirit keeps me in time." A few days later, I asked her the time, and she said, "Ten minutes before ten o'clock." My watch indicated 9:50. There was no special time when the nurses came by or any regular routine planned; she just knew what time it was without a clock.

On my last day of pediatrics, I went to say good-bye to Bessie. She placed the baby in her lap, put both of her hands on her cheeks, and a great smile erupted. She took my hands with the usual rhythmic sway. "You is on your way to being a great doctor. I know. The Lord told me. Don't let the storms move your feets from solid ground. Remember what I told you— stay strong and be patient on the Lord. Time will tick, tick, but answers will come when time says it's ready, when time says it's ready. I love you."

"And I love you, Bessie."

I got up off my knee, and she went back to rocking that baby who needed her solace. We all needed her solace.

As I left the sunroom, I looked at my pocket watch. It was 2:15 p.m. I thought of John Keats's succinct quotation about time: "Time, the aged nurse, rocked me to patience." From that moment on, I have fondly called my watch "Bessie." I could not have given her a more fitting tribute.

Obstetrics was a medical discipline that had recently gained its reputation as an important service in hospital training. Prior to the 1920s, most of the births in the United States took place in the private homes by private physicians. The high incidence of post-delivery sepsis was more common in the hospital deliveries than the home. Also, the hospital would not allow the husband, the grandmother, neighbors, or other supportive friends to attend the birth; these ancillary members were very helpful in the homes. By the 1920s, better delivery service and fewer complications were reported in the hospital deliveries. The use of forceps was coming back into popularity after a forty-year hiatus of unfortunate complications and inept technique.

Dr. Franklin Newell was the obstetrician-in chief at the Boston Lying-In Hospital. My rotation there allowed me to deliver many beautiful babies, and the joy on the faces of the new mothers and their families was priceless. Several of my delivering mothers named their sons Windsor. I could not have been more honored. It was unfortunate, however, that several of the white women patients complained to the professors that they did not want "any Negro doing an examination on my privates." But the school allowed James, Euclid, and Robert to do their rotations at Boston Lying-In.

There was further conflict that became quite inflammatory when Tillman Merritt had to do his obstetric training with James Whitaker and new transfer student, Robert Wilkinson, who was also a Negro. Thank goodness Euclid was on his medical rotation at Massachusetts General Hospital. Tillman was angry enough during the first two years in the classroom. Taking care of or the thought of either of them delivering a white woman was too much for him to accept. He went to Dr. Newell and Dr. Edsall and wrote a petition to prevent either of them from setting foot into Boston Lying-In. It was ironic that both James and Robert were from his home state of South Carolina, but that fact probably placed more fire in his heart.

I approached Tillman, reminding him that they were competent students, and he looked at me and said, "I won't allow any nigger to look at a white woman or any part of her personal body."

"Well," I replied, "when you are in charge of the Tillman Merritt Hospital, and you are in charge of selecting which doctor sees which patient, then you have something to say. But this isn't your hospital, your rules, or your decision about anything other than you doing your assignment."

Merritt hit the ceiling. "Why don't you just go back to New York and take care of all the niggers?"

"Well, at least I'd be giving the service I signed up to deliver as a doctor. I don't know what kind of white-only service you'd be pretending to do. Just don't do it near me."

"I'd rather burn in hell before that happened."

I said, "You don't have to worry about that. You are already there."

From that moment until we graduated, he remained scornful and resentful, and he looked at me as he viewed the Negro, the Jew, the Chinese, the Catholic, or the Indian. I felt sorry for a man so locked in hatred, so unaware of his own misery, and so unappreciative of his own limitations of humanity, decency, and all the things that make a heart open and sound.

He continued to make comments to those classmates who thought like him, and they would laugh and agree with his maligned thoughts, but I wasn't going to offer anything to give him further reason to think he even mattered. It wasn't worth any effort. He was the White Weasel. What more could I expect of him?

Outside of my medical school experience, there were many social and political events that were happening in Boston, at Harvard, and in other parts of the country that reflected many of the hard, inflexible attitudes displayed by Tillman Merritt. The time leading up to World War I, during the war, and the postwar years sustained an undesirable faction in the population. Influenced by Bolshevism and Communism, the anarchist—usually assumed in the newly immigrated Slav, Italian, Portuguese, Bohemian, or Hungarian—was labeled a "threat" and "un-American." A great divide was created in the United States. The patriotic banners waved, and if you didn't join in, something was wrong with you. You were unpatriotic.

This sentiment was promoted by Wilson's lead, and everyone was expected to embrace it. A fundamentalist mentality pervaded American psyche through the "majority" Christian teachings of fear, evil, heaven, and hell. The renowned preacher, Billy Sunday, delivered a Christian outcry, claiming that Christianity and patriotism, like hell and traitors, are synonymous.

In one of his many remembered sermons given in Indiana in 1922, "Nuts for Skeptics to Crack," he stated:

> The vast majority of mankind of all ages, of every phase of civilization and savagery, from the refined and brilliant Greek to the savage North American Indian, has fallen into many errors regarding creation. They believe in a plurality of Gods. In the beginning, God, G-O-D; not plural, created the heavens and earth ... Some people believe that though there is a God, we know nothing about that God. They say they don't believe what they can't understand. Then you are a fool. If you only believe what you can understand, you will be dumbfounded to discover how little you really know ... Can you tell me why it is that a black cow can eat green grass and give white milk?[49]

Fundamentalist persuasion, with Sunday's classic "Get on the Water Wagon" sermon preached throughout the country, supported the temperance amendment in 1920 and also supplied the fuel for the riots, lynchings, and dramatic resurgence of the KKK after the war. When Harding was promoting normalcy, he did not want any rust scraped off the conventional "manners" to create attention to the real problems being faced.

The limitation on immigration and job opportunities for all minorities and the propaganda of eugenics all fueled further discontent. Eugenics was promoted as legitimate science, even though the eminent Columbia University Professor Franz Boas had refuted any validity of these studies of white superiority over the non-white inferiority in 1903. The propaganda was clear: "Every fifteen seconds, one hundred dollars of your money goes for the care of persons with bad heredity such as the insane, feebleminded, criminals, and other defectives." There are four types of mental deficiency: Idiocy has a mental age between zero and three years. Mongoloid imbecility (Down's Syndrome) and imbecility have a mental age between three and seven years. Moron (high-grade feebleminded) has a mental age between seven and eleven years.

The popular nonfiction promotion of Madison Grant's *The Passing of the Great Race* summarizes the collective understanding throughout the country. In the preface, Columbia Professor of Zoology, Henry Osborn, wrote:

> The moral tendency of the heredity interpretation of history is in strong accord with the true spirit of the modern eugenics movement in relation to patriotism ... This conservation of that race (the white race) which has given us the true spirit of Americanism is not a matter either of racial pride or of racial prejudice; it is a matter of love of country, of a true sentiment which is based upon knowledge and the lessons of history rather than upon the sentimentalism which is fostered by ignorance.[50]

And, of course, let us not forget the distinguished head of the Department of Anthropology at Harvard, Professor Ernest Hooton, who for forty years—along with eight other Harvard faculty as members of the American Eugenics Society—rallied openly to embrace the "science" behind segregating the biologically and socially unfit from the "better stock."

This inflexible, unreasonable state of mind was highly favored throughout my years in Boston, and it was affirmed quite dramatically after the deaths of Sacco and Vanzetti in August 1927. Closed thought is driven by judgment and an ego-boosted sense of illusionary superiority. It is promoted to secure a position of control. Many unsubstantiated allegations plagued the Sacco-Vanzetti trial, but it did not matter. These were "uneducated, unworthy, and guilty" people before and after the verdict had been deliberated. It was very convenient to address a judicial case with all the chips stacked against you.

Even though quite influential voices from Boston and throughout the country and world, including my college president, Alexander Meiklejohn, Felix Adler, Dr. Alice Hamilton, Jane Addams, and Pope Pius XI pleaded to reverse the decision. I read later that Judge Webster Thayer, who presided over the case, would not allow a retrial even when new hard evidence to support the innocence of these men was brought to him. He had no one to be accountable to on all his decisions. He singlehandedly laid down a sentimental judgment; there was no justice given. A closed mind will always feel the limitations of entrapment, which leads to compulsive, irrational actions based on those feelings.

These closed-minded thoughts lingered many years after the executions, but they were of the same thought that the Pharisees and Sadducees had about Jesus, Hitler had about the Jews, President Andrew Jackson had about the American Indians, and the Southern slave holders and Northern business owners had about the Negro.

I stopped a moment to reflect on that very stressful time. Besides the civil imbalance during those years, and the routine demands of medical school, I had to face the reality of losing two of my close friends and mentors, Father and Uncle Herbert. I felt I could get through any challenge with the words of wisdom and encouragement that each of them gave me. Then, they were gone. I was devastated, and a horrible feeling surrounded my soul; its impact was vast.

I had to continue living and using the wonderful principles they so generously shared with me. They knew how to consider people whose thinking was closed—people who justified their thoughts on human nature. Man is born to make errors, to feel hatred, and to possess shortcomings. Yes, it is true that man is not perfect in any sense of the word, but he is a creature of thought. The voice of reason maintains its ground, but it could not be steadfast if all the fallacies, described above, were caused by human nature. The nature of man is good; how we think, speak, and act on it is our individual choice.

The 291st Harvard Commencement was on June 23, 1927. A bright, sunny day greeted us and warmed us while the candidates for the various degrees assembled at their designated areas for the full processional. Mother was too "busy" to attend the graduation; she was being entertained by her socialite friends in Washington, DC. Besides, she was told that women and children were not permitted in the Yard activities and didn't feel "obligated."

I graduated number one of 135 students in my medical school class, and I should have walked behind the class marshal who led us into the

Sever Quadrangle. But I refused to walk in front when the school "position" placed James Whitaker, Robert Wilkinson, and Euclid Ghee in the back of the rest of the candidates. James had graduated cum laude from the medical school, Euclid had graduated from Harvard College cum laude, and Robert was elected to Phi Beta Kappa at Dartmouth College in 1924. In good consciousness, I voluntarily walked at the back to honor those who deserved a better "place" in the processional.

Even though I had good relations with most of my classmates, Tillman Merritt continued displaying his contempt toward me. He graduated tenth in the class ranking and openly stated his disgust that I was a member of the Alpha Omega Alpha Society and one of the recipients, along with my friend Howard Gray of the Boylston Medical Prize for original research in medicine.

When I walked toward the back, I could hear Merritt speaking to one of our classmates. He said, "Look at that Waterbury loser—always sticking his neck out for those niggers. I hope he never comes to South Carolina. He wouldn't get off the train before he was lynched."

I'm sure he was pleased that I walked "behind" him.

As the line formed to march, I was placed near the entrance to Hollis Hall, one of the freshmen dormitories. I looked up and realized that we were in the north part of the Yard, which was the oldest part. Room 8 was on the second floor, facing the front, and was occupied by Henry David Thoreau when he was a freshman there. All of these buildings had great history; it is a shame that they would be closed to so many contributing, capable minds based on race, religion, or other arbitrary difference.

The ceremony finally began with President Lowell being seated with the governor of Massachusetts, Alvan Fuller, as well as the mayor of Boston, Malcolm Nichols, the other dignitaries (the governing board of the university), and the recipients of the honorary degrees.

As I sat patiently listening to the four Latin orations, I couldn't help but think about Father and Uncle Herbert not attending. I know they were pleased that I chose medicine as a profession, and I was convinced they were smiling down on me that day. However, there would be tough decisions to make in the next few years, and I had to be prepared to face a harsh reality as well.

The Deaths of Father and Uncle Herbert—June 1926 and August 1926
(Event 17)

While in training during medical school, I saw and cared for many patients who suffered physical and/or mental hardships. Some of them had longstanding pain, and others had short-lived pain, leaving their families and loved ones devastated and remorseful. And at times, I witnessed parents losing two of their children within weeks of each other to diphtheria, pertussis, cholera, TB, or scarlet fever. The emotional burdens were indescribable. The acceptance, however, had to be a harsh reality, and the families had to pull together to move forward because another setback was surely going to come into their future.

Although I went to several of the patients' funeral services and felt their family's losses sincerely, I was particularly overwhelmed with the sequential deaths of Father and Uncle Herbert who had both been such shining lights and pillars of strength and wisdom. They were close friends and contributed so consistently in molding the very foundation I walk upon as a man today.

Father continued working hard even though he still experienced frequent headaches and fatigue attributed to the influenza back in 1918. He never complained to anyone, but it was clear that his "engine" did not have the capability of using that high horsepower it had relied on for so many years before. It was more evident over the winter of 1926 when Father was ill with a routine cold and needed to stay in bed for a few weeks to recover.

Soulange would faithfully give him the same nursing care she administered when he had the Spanish flu. Even after recovery, he was much slower, and the headaches became more intense and prolonged. Aspirin was partially helpful, but he could not examine a full day of scheduled patients. He was increasingly in need of rest. His will to do his work kept him from feeling completely helpless, but each day brought further compromise. He saw his last patient in May; he had been seeing Father for many years. He had been a bespoke tailor with Brooks Brothers and a frequent visitor to London, Paris, Rome, and Milan to see the latest styles. He had made a custom suit for Father several years earlier for saving his right hand in a fall from a ladder.

He saw Father pause to recommend a treatment and gently said, "Dr. Waterbury, God was kind to direct me under your care. You kept these hands of mine sturdy and useable all these years. My hands have been able to tailor suits and other clothing. But your hands have been able to work many miracles, and they are hands that deserve a rest now." He held Father's hands inside of his own for an extended moment. "You go home and rest. Your hands gave me the treatment I needed today."

I heard that story tearfully remembered by the tailor himself at Father's funeral. He passed away in June from complications of a stroke. Soulange had called me at school to come home to see Father right after I finished my final exams. She always knew what to do, when to do it, and how to take care of Mumsie, Grandfather, Father, and me.

When I arrived home, Mother was conveniently at her social club. Father was in bed, but he was lucid enough to smile and run his hand along my face. "I have studied your face for nearly a quarter of a century, and each time I look at it, I learn something new and fortifying. When your grandmother and grandfather passed away, you gave me an uplifting boost to get through both of those storms. When I almost died from the Spanish flu, it was your and Soulange's care that gave me the strength to hold on. And now your presence is a comfort for me. Thank you, Son, for always offering a ray of sunshine to navigate a road of challenge as well as to feel satisfaction. And when tested, you will need to look inside yourself for worthy answers. You have learned how to take the test; along the way, you absorbed much to your credit.

"Opportunity knocks and medicine awaits you at the door. Medicine walked with me these thirty years and gave me great rewards. It will open your life as the thunder and lightning open the sky. I trust your judgment and your sound principle. You will have God's guidance throughout your career.

"You are in charge of this household now. I am confident you will make all the appropriate decisions when they need to be made. Rely on Soulange. She will be by your side as she has always been for our family. Your mother will probably remain unsupportive and indifferent toward you. You will have to find the means of steering through those *icy* waters as I had to painfully learn. My headache has intensified. Let us have a long talk tomorrow. Good night."

Tomorrow appeared, but Father's stroke placed him in eternal sleep during the night.

Soulange came to my room and told me the news and that he appeared peaceful. When I came into the room, she was whispering in his ear, as she had done during his illness with the Spanish flu. It was as if she was calling the angels to come and take Father "home" in regal splendor.

The service was quite moving with many of his colleagues, patients, and friends all offering one unanimous voice praising Father for being the man he was. I gave his eulogy with tremendous effort to deliver it as he needed to hear it.

I began with a quote from John Donne:

Bring us, O Lord our God, at our last awakening into the house and gate of heaven, to enter into that gate and swell in that house, where there shall be no darkness or dazzling, but one equal light; no noise or silence, but one equal music; no fears or hopes, but one equal possession; no ends or beginnings, but one equal eternity; in the habitations of thy glory and dominion world without end.[51]

I then read a William Penn quote:

> We give back to you, O God, those whom you gave to us.
> You did not lose them when you gave them to us and we
> do not lose them by their return to you. Your dear Son
> has taught us that life is eternal and love cannot die, so
> death is only a horizon and a horizon is only the limit of
> our sight. Open our eyes to see more clearly and draw us
> close to you that we may know that we are nearer to our
> loved ones, who are with you. You have told us that you
> are preparing a place for us; prepare us also for that happy
> place, that where you are we may also be always, O dear
> Lord of life of death.[52]

The final quote was from Proverbs 15:30: "The light of the eyes rejoices the heart; and a good heart makes the bones fat."

The highlights of the text read as follows:

> Dear Friends, colleagues, patients, hospital staff associates,
> and others fortunate enough to have known my wonderful
> father. We are gathered here to pay homage to a man
> who lived life to its fullest and left an indelible imprint
> on the hearts of those who loved and admired him. He
> indeed carried a light within, which darkness can never
> extinguish. He was the consummate physician and
> promoter of well-being. He would take the unconventional
> walk in his patient's shoes, appreciating firsthand what it
> felt like to be in their condition right up until the time he
> quietly left us. His compassion and deep feeling for others
> epitomized the standard of care my father offered to all of
> his patients: the well to do and the desolate, poor patients
> in the clinic. He was a meticulous and true scientist in the
> tradition of Louis Pasteur and Robert Koch. He always
> questioned his work, and he always tried to refine it. He
> welcomed ideas to improve his already successful work.
> He was dedicated to sharing his knowledge for the good

of mankind. He was a diligent worker who embraced the very essence of a standard work ethic; he knew no lesser option. He never let anyone really know how much pain or suffering he endured. At night, when everyone else's work has ended, you would find my father laboring over a patient or counseling one of his colleagues.

He was a humble servant of God. For a man to reach the heights in his scholarly achievements and his stature in the medical community, one would imagine him to feel more than a common man. But he did not; he was genuinely unassuming, always smiling, always concerned about someone's feelings, and always selfless.

His legacy will be engraved on the minds and hearts of many generations to come. He carries a light within his eyes that can never be extinguished, a good heart that makes the bones fat and lasting memory that shall bring us no more pain. As we send you off to be greeted by the angels with the sounds of trumpets celebrating your return, take time, my dear sweet father, to serenade your reunited family with your melodious violin and hold their hands while comforting them as you treated your patients and loved ones here and then look down and see all the great things you left behind for us to cherish and love forever.

After the burial at Greenwood, I remained paralyzed for a day or so, trying to realign myself and blend the sorrow with the conscious insight that I had been privileged to have had such a strong and positive father whose legacy would continue to serve in a helpful capacity.

I was also disturbed with the bitterness I saw on both Mother's and Uncle Thaddeus's faces throughout the service. They showed no emotion or expression of grief, no caring words exchanged, no love lost, and no biologic or conjugal sentiment. They both looked like hungry crocodiles skimming the surface of a stilled river with those dark black, haunting eyes and those ugly, tough-skinned mouths ready to devour its prey. I wondered why they even came.

They didn't say a word to me throughout the service, but at the burial, Uncle Thaddeus spoke briefly to me. Then, I saw Uncle Thaddeus do something I had never seen him do. He spoke to Soulange privately, and when he finished, she appeared unmoved, but he was outwardly frustrated. He went away without being outraged, but I knew he had no nice words for her. Mother left on a trip that evening, appearing "excited" to get away. I said nothing and let her be.

I did talk to Soulange—who was always faithful and soothing—to get me through this setback. She told me to think about some of the personal things that Father and I shared, and it would help give me a close presence to him now.

I thought about a conversation we had just a few days before heading to medical school in September 1923. He said that, in his typical day seeing patients, there would always be a challenging case that might require several visits before finding a definitive diagnosis or patients who had unsolvable conditions.

Then there were the unpredictable but expected devastating effects during the Spanish flu epidemic. But all of these circumstances are a part of life that we came to realistically accept. However, he told me about being called to three tragedies, not expected or very acceptable when all of them were the result of human error, irresponsibility, and poor judgment.

Father had just opened his office for the morning on January 8, 1902 with the winter's cold and snow flurries already starting to accumulate. His first patient of the day was scheduled for nine fifteen. He was surprised to hear a knock on the front door at 8:55. A Western Union telegram message arrived with the urgent message: "Come to Park Ave. and Fifty-Sixth Street. Train crash in tunnel, heading to Grand Central Terminal. Terrible tragedy."

Father knew it couldn't be anything except disaster. It was rush hour, it was dark and smoky underground, and access for help would be terribly limited. Father had said the layout of the steamed locomotives coming in and out of Grand Central was unsafe for many years. Several people trying to walk across the tracks were killed inadvertently, but the matter of safety remained unaddressed until then.

By the time he arrived, there was mass confusion. The rear car of the motionless train had been jolted by the impact into the adjoining car, creating an accordion effect. To see the poor victims in those two cars crushed, mangled, and scalded by the broken steam pipes in the engine was one of the horrible memories he faced. There were others on both trains who were frozen in shock and required smelling salts and a comforting hand to get them through this nightmare.

The following day, the *New York Times* reported:

> Unaccountable blunders of an engineer who disregarded signals are held to be responsible for the accident—the worst railroad disaster that ever occurred on Manhattan Island. Fifteen people were killed and 2 score (40) more severely injured as a result of the rear-end collision.
>
> All of this loss because the engineer failed to slow down or heed several warning signs before the full impact. Most of the dead were residents in New Rochelle, a city just north of the Bronx. Most of the dead would have been killed instantly but those who survived would have been burned and frightened in that dark tunnel, trapped and deprived of clean air or any escape alternative.[53]

After reading the article the following morning, Father learned that one of the victims was Mr. William Leys, one of the general managers at B. Altman's Store on Sixth Avenue and Nineteenth Street in Manhattan. He had met this wonderful man when he needed to purchase a new trench coat a few years before. Mr. Leys was a model employee, offering fine service and a gentle demeanor. Father went to the well-attended funeral service at his home in New Rochelle on January 10 and then to his interment at Woodlawn Cemetery. He was loved and would be duly missed by his fellow employees at B. Altman's and his friends in New Rochelle. It was sad that this productive man was denied an older life because of careless ways and inattentive behavior. While coming home, Father was reminded that it was one of the few times in his career that a sense of helplessness and inadequacy gripped his conscious thought. It was a horrible feeling that he knew I would have to face and deal with straightforwardly in my career.

The second incident was even more tragic on a much grander scale. A chartered steamboat, *General Slocum*, was used for a summer outing on June 15, 1904, with 1,300 Lower East Side German immigrant families with children on board, heading to Empire Grove off the Long Island Sound. It was their annual Saint Mark's Lutheran Church event, and the weather and the waters could not have been more favorable. The thirteen-year-old ship had not been properly inspected since its inaugural trip in 1891; the life preservers and water hoses had not been changed or used. When they left the dock at the lower end of the East River, it was an uneventful day like any other.

Fifteen to twenty minutes into the excursion north, a fire broke out in the forward storage room and was not contained. Inexperienced crew members did nothing to prevent the spread of the fire when it was first discovered, and to make matters worse, the captain made a terrible, illogical decision to speed the flaming boat to a nearby island off the Bronx shore. The flames grew out of control. With the lifeboats inaccessible due to the fire, and the weatherworn, non-useable life preservers unable to preserve any of the passengers, the flames continued to engulf the ship—and 1,021 people were dead within minutes. My father was called from his office that day to North Brother Island where a temporary morgue was set up for the bodies and the horrified survivors searching for their loved ones.

The minister of the church had fallen into the water with his wife and daughter holding the hands of both of them, but the ongoing pressures of so many other people falling on top of them, jumping from the ship, caused their hands to open, and they were separated. He struggled to keep afloat, but panic may have prevented his ability to help any other people surrounding him, including his family. A tugboat worker saved him from drowning.

By the time Father arrived, the race to help the unconscious people who were washed ashore or brought by the rescue boats was over. They had drowned because they had taken too much water in their lungs. A few were fortunate and did revive with chest compression and back blows to expel the water.

He joined the minister, Reverend Haas, who was dazed walking by the corpses that lay in the grass for identification. It was close to noon, and the hot sun intensified the grim view. Rows of bodies, some burned, some mothers clutching their young children, some maimed, but mostly lifeless from the drowning, stared at them with a mocking, chilling reflection. There had to be something, some inner voice, some tranquilizing whisper within themselves, to keep those survivors from walking straight into the water and ending it all to join their departed.

Father was familiar with this scenario, but Reverend Haas was devastated. He stuttered words to Father, saying that he was looking for his wife, sister, and daughter amongst this awful spectacle. But he was a man, true to his ministry. In spite of his personal pain, his congregation called on him for support and comforting during their own search through the mass gravesite. Father had a moment to share his admiration of Reverend Hass's courage, his inner fortitude, his sense of duty, his genuine ties to his congregation, and a reminder of the hope that the reverend relied on would never fail him.

As Father offered his words of solace, Reverend Haas looked in his eyes and showed that he received Father's words with the same thoughts that had to flow through the minds and hearts of his church members who sought similar advice and counseling from him at his church and more urgently, in the midst of this hysterical fiasco. Like so many of the other families, Reverend Hass suffered through the loss alone but grateful that God had not taken away his faith.

The final "avoidable" tragedy happened on a cold and windy Saturday afternoon, March 25, 1911 when the city faced its deadliest industrial disaster. It was known as the Triangle Shirtwaist Factory Fire at the Asch Building in Greenwich Village, east of Washington Square. One hundred forty-six young women, mostly aged sixteen to twenty-three, met their death by smoke inhalation, burning, or jumping from the eighth or ninth floors, windows, or the tenth floor roof. Father was at his office that day and was about to finish when a policeman, who knew him, came to his door, saying there had been a huge fire and could he come to take care of the survivors. When he arrived, most of the fire, which swept through the seventh, eighth, and ninth floors was contained, but what he saw and heard from the survivors lived on with horrible remembrance.

241

Before he gave me the personal account, he wanted me to appreciate why this setting was the perfect setup, not just for potential fire, but a predictable tragic ending for these workers. Many of the factories in lower Manhattan were housed in loft buildings. From the front of these buildings and the stairways, similar to the Asch, you sensed that you were walking into a "fireproof" edifice. As you went up the elevator though, you would hear a constant humming sound, and when the door opened to a designated floor, the sound amplified to a dissonant roar behind wooden partitions. The area behind the partition was the loft, a single large room with men and women working on top of each other at sewing machines and other pieces of machinery. Sometimes there were up to five hundred people in one crowded room.

At the time, the New York factory law required each worker to have 250 cubic feet of air. A tenement ceiling was eight feet high, but a loft ceiling was ten or eleven feet high. The more space above each worker (the higher the ceiling) the less space a proprietor would have to use between adjoining workers. These loft rooms were usually located on the seventh floor or higher, and the fire department's equipment was unable to reach higher than six stories. The buildings were not required to have any fire escapes, and the passageways in the stairs were purposely made narrow so that each worker's hand purse could be checked at the end of the day to ensure that no thievery occurred. Paper patterns and other flammable cloths and baskets lined the windows, tables, and the exit doors. Oil was needed for the machines, and it constantly spilled on the floor. Most of the workers smoked their cigarettes in the break area, but some also sneaked a puff while working at their stations.

The fire was thought to have started on the eighth floor in the Asch building, secondary to a match or a burning cigarette. There were 1,500 workers that day, and because the fire spread so quickly, panic, pushing, shoving, and hysteria blinded any rational judgment. The door on the eighth floor was locked, and several women were trapped into the corner by the window. The fire department arrived within two minutes of the alarm going off. While they were setting up their hoses and safety nets, many of the women, clinging to another, leaped from the eighth, ninth, and tenth floors, ablaze in fire. They landed on the equipment or tore through the canvas of the nets, leaving the firemen helpless.

One young woman who escaped down the Washington Place stairway told Father a few more details. She saw many women burned and falling over each other trying to get down the narrow, unlit, winding stairway. Women were pulling at other's hair or clothing so they could get through the doorway first, but the doorway was already jammed.

Father could not be very helpful except to give some pain medication to several of the survivors who had injured themselves or had mild smoke inhalation cough. He looked at those faces of the dead and the survivors, and it reminded him of the other two tragedies. He had seen death and witnessed bad circumstances for many patients, but he was most upset knowing this nightmare could have been prevented.

New York City Fire Chief Croker was at the Triangle Fire and resigned one month later. He wrote in September 1911 that:

> New York is paying 8 million dollars for the maintenance of the fire department and about $15,000 dollars to prevent fires. There are certain things that should be done at once, not requiring either new laws or building alterations. Every exit should be plainly marked and all employees familiar with every exit. No locked doors during work hours. Compulsory fire drills. The drill would show whether the old stairways were capable of emptying the building in an adequate time for safety.[54]

"Prevention, prevention, prevention!" my father stated emphatically. But it is not just for fires. It applies to medicine as well. When treating your patients, always remember to keep recommending ways to prevent their illness or injury and reduce their accidents. We live in a society where everyone's emotions are stirred after the fact, and they do not give too much active thought beforehand to promote better outcomes. Remain an advocate to reduce these perpetual "errors" that have no defense or rationalization.

Whenever Father had his insightful conversations, they would inevitably reflect his axiom to practice what you preach. His written thoughts would reveal that same theme. I have already shared the story of my graduation from Amherst, but I did not talk about the gift that Father gave me that day. It was a copy of Joseph Conrad's *Heart of Darkness* with an inscription on the cover page.

> For my dear Chip on your graduation from college and matriculation to medical school,
>
> In the past four years, you have taken the time and effort to increase your knowledge and prepare yourself to walk down the road leading to a career in medicine. It is written that with the increase in knowledge comes an increase in sorrow—a deeper awareness of the opportunities missed to ameliorate the suffering all around us.
>
> *Heart of Darkness* is a chronicle of such missed opportunities. It parallels other chronicles that we have shared and will continue to share.
>
> In the novel, Joseph Conrad uses the protagonist to reveal the exploitation of goods (ivory and rubber for exports) in the Congo in Africa and the tortuous treatment of its people under the ruthless ruling of the Belgium's King Leopold II. Leopold, in real life, used the deception that it was his "association" that had anti-slavery intent for public support—and not his personal views. Indeed, he lied, seized the land, and enslaved its inhabitants for personal aggrandizement and power.
>
> The countries of Europe as well as the United States watched as Leopold continued this abuse with no interference or realistic attempt to bring this crime to a halt. Conrad's book, written in 1902 by a native Pole who did not learn English until he was twenty years old, was acclaimed as a great novel, but its urgent message and plea were conveniently ignored.
>
> This missed opportunity reflects in a similar way to our own country's presentation of equality and democracy,

but not representing the true intent. Where as many of the founding fathers of our country spoke, and wrote that "all men are created equal," in so many cases, this was spoken and written primarily for public consumption in their personal campaigns for the advancement of only a small minority. The words matched neither their thought nor the actions that stemmed from those thoughts outside the small circle.

And nearly 150 years later, our leaders have spoken words that were incongruous with their thoughts. We find ourselves still struggling to articulate the need for a matching of word, thought, and deed. This is the unbroken silver thread that continues to run through our lives as father and son, friend to friend.

With every affectionate good wish for our shared struggle and attempt to find our opportunities to ameliorate the suffering all around us.

Your loving and proud father

Pamela looked like she wanted to interrupt me, but she paused for a moment and then she said, "This man truly offered a life that was worth emulating."

Jasper chimed in and said, "Like father, like son! I know them both, and you couldn't find a more dynamic duo. You know, like Batman and Robin."

I added, "Are you the Joker?"

"Not me, Water Pump. I stay clear of that mess."

I smiled, "Well, good for you. Let's get back to the story. I saved this remembrance for last because it bridges the past with the present and future in a special way. We already talked about Mumsie's and Grandfather's deaths, but I needed to add that, every year afterward, Father and I would discuss some personal memories of each of them on their birthdays."

I happened to be home from medical school on Mumsie's birthday in April 1925, and we were in Father's study when he surprisingly locked the door. He told me he had some very important items to go over and did not want to be disturbed. He went in his lower desk drawer and pulled out the old black wood box with the embossed C engraved on it.

I recognized it immediately. I had not seen it since Mumsie showed it to me just before she died. He opened the pouch with the diamonds and the handwritten letter and told me there wouldn't be a better time to discuss the full story behind the treasures, especially when it was a remembrance of her birthday.

He began by saying that precious diamonds had a unique character and many admirable qualities besides being placed as a showpiece for a lady's finger. "The very name diamond comes from the Greek word *adamas* which means unbreakable and unalterable. It is composed of simple carbon atoms, very similar to graphite, but they are arranged in a strong covalent bonding to create a lattice, a cubic structure that is crystallized. Under tremendous pressure, a hundred miles deep in the earth, the diamond is formed and released upward through volcanic eruption to cool but still remain buried in the upper regions of the earth's crust. The diamond's formation is a slow process and is estimated to take one to three billion years. The end result is the hardest known natural material on earth, one of the toughest, one of the most beautiful in its cut state, one of the most versatile in color, one of the most sought after, one of the most expensive, and ironically, one of the least appreciated.

"Here is a product of simple carbon structure, like common graphite, but formed under distinct conditions and over a long period of time. A diamond does not get dug up conveniently from the ground or reproduced over a season to excavate. The process takes time, tremendous pressure, and skilled, meticulous cutting after mining to obtain the finished, polished, and admired stone. Diamonds come in all colors of the rainbow—blue, white (colorless), yellow, green, pink, red, brown, orange, purple, and almost black; they would be likened to the iris flower. One of the least known properties and distinctive features of diamonds are that they are hydrophobic; they cannot be made wet by water.

"Look throughout history when the first diamonds were discovered in India and later when Marco Polo brought word of the quality of diamonds to Europe. There was a great demand for possession, including the diamonds in Mumsie's collection. Royalty and other wealthy patrons assigned set values to each piece and paraded around with the notion that they were privileged and powerful because they could own it. But did they really understand that the rarity and beauty was not to be displayed but as a symbol of one's character to emulate?

"Remember in the letter that Mumsie wrote when she showed you these jewels? 'Life involves a series of burdens, obstacles, challenges, injustices, imbalances; in other words, a series of errors that need to be corrected. We could not change them all ... but we've made an effort to improve these errors. These jewels are symbols of love and commitment to basically reach that goal. They have no monetary value for us. They are priceless. They represent that worthy post. Our focus remained to nurture a more steadfast character in each other.'

To keep their interest alive, Mumsie and Grandfather used these cherished properties of the diamond—the durability, the great pressure it endured, the extended time to make it what it needed to be, the diversity of colors, its simple structural makeup, its inner and outer beauty, and its universal usefulness—to represent the superior qualities of man's character to longingly seek. Mumsie knew what she saw in your grandfather, and he knew what he saw in Mumsie. Remember the Charles Wagner quote:

> The great thing is to belong to humanity through the heart, the intelligence, and the soul. Then an unknown power takes possession of us ... and yielding to its irresistible impulse ... men of all times and places have designated a power that is above humanity but which may swell in men's hearts. And everything truly lofty within us appears to us as a manifestation of this mystery beyond. To serve it is their pleasure and reward. They are satisfied ... well knowing that nothing is great, nothing overall, but that

our life and our deeds are only of worth because of the spirit which breathes through them.[55]

"These diamonds are a symbol of that power above humanity; they are rare and priceless. They are priceless because of the immeasurable spirit that breathes through them.

"Mumsie summarized her instruction when she told you to be 'colorless.' The most valuable diamonds are the colorless diamonds. They are the clearest and the most desirable. Like the colorless diamond, the most valuable quality of character in a human is to be colorless and truthful to yourself and others. It is a rare quality but nevertheless, one to aspire to and one to continually refine. This quality promotes the clear thinker, the clear learner, and the clear being.

"Remember that feature of diamonds where they do not get wet in water. They are immune to the crashing waves, the turbulent seas, and the unsettling thunderstorms that rage at times throughout our lives. All during the struggles, the tragic losses, personal injustices, or other complications that arise, always look at these diamonds and be mindful how they uphold their qualities in all conditions, especially in the 'waters' of life.

"Mumsie and your grandfather felt that way, and they felt you would have similar appreciation. I have felt it in you as well, so I give you this priceless box to utilize accordingly. Continue to incorporate the influences of Uncle Herbert and Soulange. They symbolize the character of these diamonds—just like Mumsie and your grandfather. Son, don't you just wish they were still with us? Don't you miss them at certain times?"

I couldn't agree with him more.

Father's life had sadly ended, and even though I had strength to get through the service and burial, I was worried about Uncle Herbert. I had gone to talk with him as I had done with Father; he had consoled and taught me so much that I thought, at times, that he, Grandfather, and Father were one mind. However, over the past six months, he had slowly shown signs of fatigue, highly unusual emotional outbursts, and a constant runny nose. At the funeral service, he was irritable and unsettled and had lapses of memory, forgetting the names of Father's friends and associates he had known for years.

I received a call from Soulange when I was back on clinical rotation in early August. Something was terribly wrong with Uncle Herbert. He came by the house looking for Grandfather, and when she told him that Grandfather had died, he asked how that could have happened; he was not informed. He was congested, and his mouth looked like he had bleeding gums. He acted as if someone had taken his mind away. When I thought about it more, I remember having a patient who had a sudden mental impairment and fatigue, but he was diagnosed with mercury poisoning. Uncle Herbert didn't work in a hat factory or any other known exposure area.

I came to see him, and Soulange was very accurate in her description. I looked in his mouth, and several areas of his gums were bleeding. He had an ulcerative area on the lining of his cheeks, and he had a few new silver fillings. I remembered his toothache at Christmas 1925. When I asked him about the dentist visit, he could not remember. He had the tremors as well. I took him to the hospital, and within forty-eight hours of admission, he died with me by his side.

The day had been somewhat hot and muggy, but when he passed, the clouds formed very quickly and the lightning and thunder roared as a rain shower beat down on the city. It was as if God had announced the arrival of one of his true spirits; it could not have been coincidental. I was still in a painful state from Father's death, and now I would have to lead another service to honor my mentor.

I chose two special quotes: a poem that he shared with me when I was in Amherst and one of his favorite Bible quotations.

> To Herbert Horace Huntington, ancient friend, guardian of wisdom, thinker of open thought, and intellect extraordinaire:
>
> Now I remember that you built me a special tavern ... with yellow gold and white jewels and we were drunk for month on month, forgetting the kinds and princes ... And we all spoke out our hearts and minds and without regret. And then I was sent off to South Wei and you to the north of Raku-hoku, till we had nothing but thoughts

and memories in common. And then, when separation had come to its worst, we met and travelled into Sen-Go, into a valley of the thousand bright flowers ... and my spirit so high it was all over the heavens, and before the end of the day we were scattered like stars, or rain. I had to be off to So, far away over the waters, you back to your river-bridge. And one May you send for me, despite the long distance ... and what a reception: food well set on a blue-jeweled table, and I was drunk, and had no thought of returning ... And you would walk out with me to the dynastic temple, with water about it clear as blue jade, pleasure lasting, with the willow flakes falling like snow ... and the wind lifting the song, tossing it up under the clouds. And all this comes to an end ... And if you ask how I regret that parting: It is like the flowers falling at spring's end confused, whirled in a tangle. What is the use of talking, and there is no end of talking. There is no end of things in the heart.[56]

"Exile's Letter"

Rihaku (Li Po), translated by Ezra Pound

I then read from Philippians 2:2–4; 13–15, paraphrased from the King James Version:

Complete my joy by being in one accord and one love and one soul and one mind. Do nothing through strife or vainglory; but in humility let each regard his neighbor better than himself. Let no one be mindful only of his own things, but let everyone be mindful of the things of his neighbor also ... For it is God who inspires you with the will to do the good things which you desire to do. Do all things without disputing and doubting. That you may be sincere and blameless ... in the midst of a crooked and perverse generation, among whom you shine as lights in the world.

The text of the eulogy could be summarized quite clearly.

> Here was a man who had such a powerful command of his mind and heart, and blended that unique gift with common sense to generate a presence—humble and yet memorable—an aura that allowed you to touch and feel him but not fully reach him. He drifted frequently amongst the heavens and stars, or would be drinking with the muses deep in the Pierian Spring, and then share his precious gifts to all who chose to learn and be enlightened. Old sage, you will be missed but your memory and thought will linger like the blue sky above. Zeus has released his thunderbolt and all the ancient Greek thinkers are happy you have returned.

I was emotionally empty that night. I went to my room, still trying to accept these two great men had gone. Soulange knocked and came in; she soothed me and understood my pain. She told me to think about the remembrances with Uncle Herbert as I had done with Father. When she left the room, it was painfully clear that she was my last surviving connection, my last vital link to all my memories and all that I held dearest to my heart. She would understand what I needed when I needed it; I have relied upon her for these forty years. I don't know what I would have done without you.

Soulange smiled. "You would have done all the splendid things that you have accomplished."

During the late evening, as I lay in bed contemplating all of the illuminating times I shared with Uncle Herbert, my thoughts were transformed into a vast grove of fruit bearing trees, offering their nectar of knowledge. In each of our "meetings" since I graduated from the Ethical Cultural School, he selected a new "tree," a new topic for nourishment.

While visiting at Amherst over lunch, Uncle Herbert asked me about some of my friends' hobbies outside of schoolwork. We talked about athletics, music, art, singing, drama, automotive mechanics, dance, coin and stamp collecting, and Babe's enjoyment with fishing and arm wrestling. After listing these hobbies, he inquired further by asking what one favorite thing I felt most passionate in doing.

I told him I was happy in all of these wonderful activities.

He paused, so I repeated the question back to him: What one thing was he most passionate about? His inquisitive look became a radiant stare, his eyes opened wide, and his eyebrows rose. He said, "Windy, people of all ages will tell you they have many varied interests and say they do each thing passionately when it is a strong interest. Did any of them ever say to you that they were passionate about thinking? With open thought, your energy and excitement will rise even further with any of the endeavors you mentioned."

The closeness that he shared with my grandfather and me, believe it or not, was from the mutual exchange for the passion of thinking. He and my grandfather were conscious of this understanding. He and I have had it on an intuitive level. He wanted to bring this underlying tie that we had to my attention. My passion for thinking resonates deeply. He felt it in me when I was a boy, during my classes with him, and even more as I was maturing. He wanted to thank me and emphasize that I was given a great gift with the passion for thought.

There are many worthy examples in classical Greek times of how this thinking promotes the good life. Aristotle and Plato were passionate in their thoughts. They felt it was incumbent on us to seek, to consciously attempt, to live the good life. In *Nicomachean Ethics*, Aristotle clearly and simply defines what is "good" for man: an open review of happiness, moral virtue, intellectual virtue, practical judgment, friendship, pleasure, and making the wisest, most purposeful choice of action with these principles. All of these virtues promote a good, stable character and a refinement of decent habits throughout a complete lifetime.

"Young man, continue to rely upon passionate thinking. It will be your closest friend in your darkest hour. It will guide you through the good life you are living."

He then shared something personal, which gave his discussion of the good life even more meaning. He had been an assistant professor in the Classics Department at Yale, and in his moral philosophy class, "Introduction to Greek Thinking," he advocated for the students to practice the virtues of ethics in their day-to-day interactions with the next person. Although his class was quite popular, the department felt he veered away from the conventional "wisdom" they were promoting. Therefore, when his tenure was being considered, the voting was not very supportive, and he left without any recommendation for a faculty position elsewhere. Disheartened, he came to New York and applied to the Ethical Cultural School. Grandfather was on the committee for hopeful candidates, and they became instant friends. Over time, Uncle Herbert told Grandfather that several of his associates in colleges throughout the world had no tolerance for open thought. How ironic when you teach a class on moral philosophy and engage it passionately in your classroom, but then be told this is not the way we do things around here.

Conformity is the acceptable order of business with the obvious example of his friend, Harvard Professor George Santayana. Although tenured and quite renowned as a philosopher, essayist, and literary critic, he was designated as an "outsider," not a conventional careerist as many of his colleagues in the William James "circle" chose to be. Santayana was led away in 1912 to Oxford and Rome, never to teach in the United States again. How noteworthy that people are quick to quote his aphorism, "Those who cannot remember the past are condemned to repeat it," but cannot fully appreciate that complacency/conformity lies at the core of perpetuating repeated conflict.

He told me these things because he saw the painstaking effort my grandparents offered in their fight for social justice, world peace, and human rights—and the detours they were forced to take. As powerful a social position as they were given, and as truthful as their appeals were made, they did not succeed in penetrating the "powers of influence." However, they thought with passion, lived the good life, and had no regrets for any of their visions. Uncle Herbert would have liked to have used the university platform to speak of these "truths," but God had other plans for him that he did not regret. One of his greatest rewards as a teacher was watching me grow and think in the like-minded direction of my grandparents and father. He told me the satisfaction was as great as his friendship with Grandfather.

"Your father and I had this same discussion when you graduated from Ethical Cultural School. I also reminded him to continue living the good life. He was the one who told me to tell you when it was an appropriate time. I felt it was right now!"

We had reviewed the insights on the good life and his friendship with Grandfather and Father, but he wanted to add an extra, deeper appreciation of what they shared and felt about each other. He said that there were no other words to fully express their ties except that they had an identical friendship. Identical twins look alike and are difficult to set apart physically; identical friendships think alike and are difficult to distinguish as they speak. They have independent opinions and likes as well as dislikes, but they have a oneness of heart and soul that cannot be denied.

When Father met Uncle Herbert, they had similar conversations between themselves and Grandfather. However, Father added another dimension to their shared thoughts. His training in science and medicine was blended with their philosophical, historical, and spiritual discussions and gave all three of them a clearer view of the good life and a strengthening of their identical bonding.

The four disciplines—science, philosophy, history, and spirituality— have been categorically separated in textbooks, teaching, political arenas, churches, hospitals, businesses, courtrooms, opinions, leadership decisions, beliefs, and overall thoughts and deeds. This separation dampens the opportunity to seek broader thought and divides the essence of a good life. When all four subjects are amalgamated, they promote a purer thinking. So let us place the whole concept into a summarizing statement: Good thinking encourages good habits throughout a lifetime, which builds the making of a good man with a good heart, living the good life.

I told Uncle Herbert that Father had given them great enlightenment. I wished I could make such a worthwhile contribution for all that they collectively had given me.

Uncle Herbert looked with an assuring smile. "You could not have made anyone of the three of us stand any taller, feel more honored, or be more convinced that your contribution matches anything we have given or shown you. It has always been a two-handed 'cleansing,' one hand washing the other, and you have given us the cleanest hands that anyone would want to inspect."

He smiled, reached over to pat my head, and placed his hand in mine as he had done when I was a boy. I thanked him and told him that his glowing presence served me continuously. Looking back on all those treasured conversations, it seemed he was most fulfilled when we spoke—even more than either of my graduations or other accomplishments.

Another conversation evolved after we went to see the silent film classic, *The Big Parade*, down at the Astor Theatre on Forty-Fifth Street and Broadway, only a week after its opening in 1925. I was visiting the family for the Thanksgiving holiday, and Uncle Herbert treated me to the movie for my birthday gift. The movie had tremendous favorable critical acclaim. It was the first realistic wartime story based on a true account. Laurence Stallings had served as a marine in the trenches of northern France and lost his leg in one of the battles. Silent screen star John Gilbert gave his most famous performance as the protagonist, Jim Apperson.

The movie was a lengthy two hours and twenty-three minutes, and the storyline was divided into two parts. The first seventy-five minutes set the stage for the life experiences of three inductees destined for the battlefront. American participation in the war is declared. For Jim Apperson, a young, carefree, well-to-do man reluctantly joins the army to serve his country. He is accompanied by two newly acquired friends from very different backgrounds as they go off to France and wait for orders in the town of Champillon. A very passionate love develops between one of the local town farm peasants and Jim. Their relationship is complicated because Jim doesn't speak French, and Melisande doesn't speak English. But they manage to convince each other that they are truly in love. The bugle sounds, and the men are called to gather their belongings and go to war. Before the end of the first section, Jim and Melisande embrace for one final kiss before he is carried away. On the truck, he reveals his deep love. He tosses his watch, dog tag, and a shoe to her, saying he will return when the war is over.

The second section begins with a distant camera shot of a long single-file line of military trucks leading up an endless hill filled with troops. This was the "big parade," and Jim and his two friends are about to face the grim atrocities of war. They are dropped off and march another twenty or thirty miles into the Belleau Wood area. The troops are marching through the woods where German machine guns and snipers are hiding in camouflaged areas. They reach no-man's land, where the combat occurs in open trenches. Scattered corpses and continued sniper attacks surround the three soldiers. The battle gets fiercer as the explosions increase, and gas attacks force the soldiers to wear their masks.

An order is given to extinguish enemy fire in a nearby machine gun nest. When his friend is gunned down, Jim summarizes the complete madness of war: "Orders! Orders! What the hell do we get out of this war anyway! Cheers when we left and when we get back. But who the hell cares … after this?"

Jim fearlessly goes forward with his other friend, and after taking a bullet to his leg, he drags himself to a wounded German and pulls out his bayonet to kill him, but he can't complete the deed. The inhumanity, the closeness of death surrounding him, and the futility of war were carved on the face of Jim. It was one of the most powerful, dramatic scenes in the entire two hours and twenty-three minutes.

He is taken by ambulance to a local hospital where he is trying to recuperate when he is told that he is only six kilometers away from Champillon. He hitches a ride and hobbles into a ransacked city to find his sweetheart. While visualizing the bomb-shelled place where he had met Melisande, another bomb explodes. His wounded leg is hit again.

In an unforgettable scene, Jim is brought home to his family on crutches. His left leg has been amputated to the knee. His mother embraces him, realizing the sacrifices and the bigger impact the war has had on so many of the brave young men, but the most important view is the horror of the war still etched on Jim's face. The movie ends with Jim going back to France and finally reuniting with Melisande. Love conquered all, but did it?

When we left the theater, I told Uncle Herbert about one of the patients I had seen at Massachusetts General Hospital. A World War I survivor had been hit by gas and lost his right hand during a battle. He was in the great New York Giants pitcher, Christy Mathewson's platoon. Mathewson died in October 1925 due to pulmonary complications from the gas and infectious tuberculosis. The patient told me what a waste to see such a good man die. He talked about many of his army buddies who died at the mercy of cannons, rifles, and gas. When I asked him about his own adjustment, he acted as if he just needed to move on and forget as much as he could. "We all enlisted for the cause, but we never know what the cause was all about. I still have to go on. It's no use in complaining over spilled milk."

We walked to a restaurant for coffee, and our conversation recaptured the whole point of the movie as well as my commentary about the patient.

Uncle Herbert started by shaking his head with a puzzled look and then talked about war psychology since ancient Greek times. "Nothing has changed even with the belief we have become more *civilized*." He referenced the justification for entering a war with a modification of Plato's well-known "Allegory of the Cave." I had read *The Republic*, but in Uncle Herbert's usual way, a bigger insight was presented.

The dialogue between Socrates and Plato's brother, Glauson, develops a setting of the "real" world in a cave where men are chained to a wall facing another wall. They are able to see mere shadows on that wall, projected by a fire behind them and what appears to be a bridge with figures passing in both directions and muffled conversations between the figures. The imprisoned men take the shadows and sounds to be real, and the most "clever" is the one able to figure out who would appear next on the bridge or what the best interpretation of the conversation might be understood. The men, in time, learn to depend on the shadows presented on the wall and the opinions of the designated "leaders."

One of the prisoners is released from the cave and is exposed to the blinding light of the sun. Initially, he would rather look back toward the "comfortable" shadows, but as he acclimates to the brightness, he sees things around him more clearly than he ever saw in the cave. What would the current, enlightened thought be for this man? What passed for wisdom and praise in the cave would now be considered a false impression. And if he returned to the cave recounting the "realities" he had witnessed, how supportive would his fellow cave dwellers be toward him? Would they feel he had returned with a "corrupted" view of things and not be taken seriously or truthfully? He would try to share the truth, but confusion, ego, or indifference would block the open message. The dilemma is very real—how can justice prevail in such a condition as staged by Plato?

This allegory is very similar to Jim Apperson's circumstance in life. He was quite content in the realm of his "world'—his cave existence—before the draft. He then was taken out of the "apparent" secure environment and dropped into a "nightmare"—the constant realness of horrible gas effects, the pointless disregard for another human being, the pain of lost friends, and the permanent loss of a leg, arm, eye, or a balanced mental state. He returned home to a "hero's welcome" and was praised for his patriotic support for the "cause." In his case, he found his true love, and we can only assume he tried to forget the "reality" of war. He tried to fit back into the cave, and go about a familiar routine.

It was obvious that Jim recognized the absurdity of war, and it was even clearer that King Vidor, the director, recognized it as well. But the flag-waving, martial bands and the "glamour" of a fighting soldier lured a man's grip on reality to sway just enough to perpetuate the battles, the confusion, and the devastating consequences over and over again. The stories come home, just like a patient, the accounts are accurately revealed, books are written against war, and this movie revealed the downside of war graphically and yet, these reminders fade away over time and we regroup into the cave.

Wouldn't you think that somewhere, sometime, someone would want to choose living out in the sunlight to see things as they really are, and learn to get along with his fellow man because that would be in his best interest as well as his fellow man's? Any war, like the cave experience, can never be in anyone's best interest, but that ego and propaganda machine can create a buyable justification to appear to make it in our best interest. What is your choice—the cave or outside? What are we willing to sacrifice to remain on the pathway of truth? It takes a lifetime to consider.

I pondered Uncle Herbert's analysis with a heavy heart. It made sense, but I did not have a full appreciation of his final thought until I was in World War II. And I still wonder, after the Korean War and our current involvement in Viet Nam, what cause could justify the insanity of the losses—and who ever really wins?

The final remembrance to share came at Christmas in 1925. I visited Uncle Herbert at his home because he was suffering from a toothache. He lived alone in the beautiful Osborne Apartment at 205 West Fifty-Seventh Street, on the third floor in a spacious living area in the front of the building, facing Carnegie Hall. At the entrance of the foyer, he had an original bronze sculpture of an American Indian on a horse done by his friend Frederick Remington. In the parlor, he had a copy of the original mission statement of the Sierra Club in a framed picture:

> To explore, enjoy and render accessible the mountain regions of the Pacific Coast. To publish authentic information concerning them and enlist the support and cooperation of the people and government in preserving the forest and other natural features of the Sierra Nevada Mountains.[57]

It was dated June 4, 1892, and signed by his friend, John Muir. Uncle Herbert had been an original charter member. He also had several pictures of landscapes painted by George Catlin and Albert Bierstadt.

While walking from the door to his chair in the parlor, Uncle Herbert was in obvious pain. He was holding his jaw with a warm cloth and trying to sit still, but movement and chewing intensified his pain. He was delighted that I came. I am sure he saw me admiring everything on the walls and stands.

"Anything you would like to discuss, Windy? It doesn't hurt as bad to speak."

Father and Grandfather had told me about Uncle Herbert's passion with nature, conservation, and preservation over many years, but on this particular visit, I was curious how he developed such an interest.

"Windy, you could not have asked a more meaningful question." He put down his warm cloth and proceeded to take me on a journey through the last fifty years and how science revealed a greater understanding of the relationship those living organisms, particularly mankind, have had with each other and their natural environment. "The term *ecology* evolved in the middle 1860s. Its Greek origin, *oikos* and *logos* mean the study of the household. It is clear that the principles set in any individual or his or her household (family) can be applied to the bigger *house*, the planet earth. The key point to consider with regard to successful relationships in all three cases (individual, family unit, and the planet) is a practice of preservation and order. Everyone should have some responsibility to maintain the integrity in them or in a whole family. If not, there will be an erosion of sorts, which will eventually become a disservice to you and your loved ones. The preservation of the wilderness, water, wildlife, and the landscape is needed to keep the framework of the earth's *house* intact for future generations. You, as an individual, and your family need to stay in good health as long as possible. The earth and its environment require the same *treatment* to keep everything moving forward in an orderly fashion.

"So the *house* has great importance on several levels. It can be a structure used as a shelter or habitation. It can involve household affairs or domestic concerns in any given family under one roof. It can be the individual's body (habitation for one's soul—your *mortal* house). It can designate a lineage of descendants from the same stock (e.g., a noble family—the House of Hanover). It can represent a constitutional body united in a legislative manner (the House of Representatives or the House of Lords). It can be a commercial establishment, a public house, or an inn. It can be an assembly or audience gathered to hear a concert or a lecture (the ovation brought down the house). It can have an astrological meaning (the sky is divided into twelve houses to denote twelve distinct areas of life). Finally, it can mean the grave when the adjective *dark* or *narrow* precedes it as in the 'narrow house.'

The point of mentioning these nine definitions is that a *house* in good working order appears to be the most stable house—the house that will stay preserved over the longest time. To create a stable house, one has to take a lifetime to become familiar with it and respect it, become familiar with it and respect it, and become familiar with it and respect it."

He said that three times in our conversation.

"Henry David Thoreau had a clear understanding when he studied his internal *house* in Walden. *Walden: Life in the Woods* gives an account of his life for two years in a simple cabin he built near Walden Pond, which is near Concord, Massachusetts, on Ralph Waldo Emerson's family property. By living amidst nature, he hoped to gain personal insight through simple living and self-reliance of the essential facts of life: 'I wanted to see if I could not learn what it (life) had to teach, and not, when I came to die, discover that I had not lived.' The book encourages solitude from time to time to promote deeper thinking and develop *closeness* to nature.

"The 'House Divided' speech given by Abraham Lincoln in 1858, before his presidency, foresaw the writing on the wall with the Northern and Southern differences over slavery and the coming of the Civil War. 'A house divided against itself cannot stand. I believe this government cannot endure, permanently, half slave and half free.' Lincoln's theme was inspired by the Mark 3:25 passage in the Bible: "And if a house be divided against itself, that house cannot stand." Lincoln's reference to the country's division has the same truth and validity whether he was speaking about an individual, family unit, community, country, continent, or the planet itself. All of these *houses* need to be in order, in order to go on."

During our class in Greek mythology, Uncle Herbert told me that I was always fascinated by the stories of the Gods on Mount Olympus as well as the adventures of humans like Perseus or Theseus. I did not recall very much about Hestia because there were not many stories about her. Uncle Herbert reminded me that her contributions and influence, though relatively obscure, have great impact and greater relevance to our discussion about the house.

"Hestia was a mythological goddess who represented the very core, the *being* of any house. Her qualities are the ingredients of good human beings: peacefulness, loving, forgiving, impartial, gentle, dignified, stable, hospitable, dependable, trustworthy, comforting and her most rare virtue of equanimity (balanced thought). With all these desired traits, she was given the most responsible position in Mount Olympus. Zeus personally gave her the keys and appointed her *manager* of their *house*.

"Hestia was recognized as the center of the home, the family, the community, and the world itself. Her name means the *essence*. She was the sacred fire that lit the hearth of a home and a community. The Olympic torch is dedicated to Hestia, though few realize this tribute today. The ritual of bride and groom bringing two flames to unite a *new* family is taken from the ancient custom of bringing Hestia's fire from the bride's mother's home to receive Hestia's blessing on the couple.

"Hestia's intuitive awareness of any *house* was that it is a place where an individual took the time to be one with body, mind, and spirit, and when guests came, they too would be regarded. In other words, the house is a place to be familiar with yourself and hopefully offer these qualities to your guest to nurture both the giver and receiver. This mutual cordiality is how Hestia treated all the inhabitants of Mount Olympus and was the intent of her eternal fire to burn in every home and public place in the communities. The outcome would bring order and prosperity to all of the *houses*.

"And so, Windy, to bring these references back to the original question that you raised about how I got interested in conservation, preservation, and ecology, I will add a tenth definition to the meaning of house. It is the bigger *house*—the earth itself—that also needs constant order, respect, and familiarity. The conservationists hopefully appreciate the tenth definition and are consciously aware of the other nine definitions. It would make Hestia happy and I am happy with it as well.

"You have been a lucky man, Windy, to have had two women in your life who represent that core character that Hestia possessed. Mumsie and Soulange remained faithful in guiding you and nurturing your *essence*. Keep the meaning of Hestia's offerings close to your *hearth*. Mumsie and Soulange could not have given you more assurance. I will let you in on a little secret. Your grandfather had the same gift of Hestia in his mother."

My eyes must have been as big as golf balls when I heard his last comment. Grandfather had briefly mentioned his mother to me when I was younger. I saw how tired Uncle Herbert was, and any further talk would probably aggravate his pain. I hugged him good-bye, and he promised he would schedule a dental appointment as soon as possible.

I went out on the street where the sky was now cloudy and looked like snow would fall soon. I said hello and Merry Christmas to people as they passed. Some acknowledged me, and others kept walking by with their faces looking down on the ground—lonely and empty. It was as if Hestia's flame had died, and they had nothing to look forward to. It is sad to see a drafty, old deserted house where a greeting at the front door echoes throughout the rooms—and nobody home to hear it.

That conversation I had with Uncle Herbert was one of the last great times I had with him. I was busy at school and didn't realize the slow but progressive neurological changes. I did not see him until Father's funeral and noticed his confusion, but I attributed a certain amount to the shock and pain of Father's death.

Over the few weeks after Uncle Herbert was buried, I kept thinking about the cause of his death. Even after reading on his death certificate that cardiac failure was the cause of his death, I knew there was a further explanation. I went to the medical library and reviewed mercury poisoning. I found a newly published article in German by a dentist named Dr. Alfred Stock. He identified silver amalgam as a source of mercury vapor and concluded with the statement:

> Dentistry should completely avoid the use of amalgam for fillings. There is no doubt that many symptoms— tiredness, depression, irritability, vertigo, weak memory, mouth inflammations, diarrhea, loss of appetite, and chronic catarrhs (nasal discharges) are often caused by mercury, which the body is exposed to from amalgam fillings, in small amounts, but continuously. It will likely be found that the thoughtless introduction of amalgam as a filling material for teeth was a severe sin against humanity.[58]

Uncle Herbert had died from a slow poisoning—no different than the hatters or other workers exposed to mercury. Father's death was inevitable, but Uncle Herbert's was preventable. I thought back to Father's remembrance when he discussed New York City former fire chief's recommendations for prevention and Father's emphasis on prevention in medicine.

The whole matter—their deaths and the discovery of mercury poisoning—left me numb and depressed. I had to remain strong because my schooling continued and life had to go forward. But it was an ordeal that I had to face and conquer. I had been knocked down by a one-two punch, but I wasn't going to stay down for the full count of ten.

Relationship with Talize, 1926–1928 (Event 18)

Everyone was silent, reflecting on the loss of two strong mentors in a relatively short period of time. But Soulange, who was as close as any family member could have been, spoke to share a broader insight on these humble and positive influential motivators.

"This was a sorrowful experience for both of us. The Waterbury family had been kind to me from the moment I arrived. Though I was Windy's guardian, I was given the privilege of deep friendship with Windy Sr., Mumsie, Deuce, and Mr. Huntington. With our relationships so well connected, it was tough watching Deuce and Mr. Huntington face their challenges at the end of their lives, yet they asked for nothing and remained steadfast until their transition. While you were away at school, your father's headaches raged night and day, but every evening, we would talk about you—your progress, your intent to help others, and your constant inquiry as to how to do the right thing for as many as you could. He saw great promise in your life, and during those moments, it seemed his headache would be lifted temporarily so he could rejoice in peace. He had no regrets, no anger, and no bitterness—even toward Rose. It was as if he knew better, he knew what would be, would be, and he accepted all circumstances with courage and dignity.

"Your father was not fully appreciative of Mr. Huntington's deteriorating condition, trying to deal with his own limitations. As you said at your father's funeral, you knew Mr. Huntington's behavior was strange, atypical, but it was difficult to really take time to examine him at such a time of grievance for us.

"I was concerned about you losing both of them within two months, having to return to school, and keeping your mind on your medical studies. But then, a ray of hope shined on your heart within a few weeks of your return to Boston. Everyone needs to hear about your unexpected good fortune in meeting a very fine, dynamic woman whose strength and love still resonate within the core of your soul—Talize Morning Star. You know that my fondness and respect for her was immediate. I can still feel her presence after these thirty-seven years."

It was quite clear that Talize was uniquely special and dear to many people. Our first meeting was not expected, but I was deeply appreciative of making the right decision to go to her lecture. I was invited to attend an informal discussion given at Boston University Medical School. I was still in a somber mood that fall, but my medical student friend told me that an amazingly knowledgeable person would be speaking. An American Indian female medical student was interested in topics that would help educate the community to have a better understanding of their health problems and preventable exposures. I decided to go, and I was quite impressed with her insights, her confidence, and her genuine appeal to get this information to the general public.

Her topic was entitled "Twentieth-Century Warnings against the Continued Use of Lead in Houses and Gasoline: The Detrimental Effects on Our Children and Industry Workers." I had been somewhat familiar with this issue in my conversations with Dr. Alice Hamilton at the medical school, but Talize included the 1904 studies done in Brisbane Hospital for Sick Children in Queensland, Australia, which showed the noxious effects of the white lead paint. The pathologic effects included abdominal cramping, pain in all extremities, seizures, hearing loss, and developmental/motor delay in toddlers. Apparently, the white lead's sweet taste appealed to youngsters who were exposed to it.

In the 1920s, there was a worldwide campaign to ban the use of lead paint; the most popular pediatric textbook, Holt's *Diseases of Infancy and Childhood*, reported the complications of lead ingestion, but money was still driving the industry. The discovery of tetraethyl lead for use in automobile gasoline efficiency became commonplace. When one of General Motors' top engineers working on that project became severely affected by the lead exposure, the surgeon general appointed an investigating committee with Dr. Hamilton as one of its members. The 1926 final report could not find "sufficient information" to ban the use of lead. The record did include the following prescient words:

> It remains possible that, if the use of leaded gasolines becomes widespread, conditions may arise very different from those studied by us which would render its use more of a hazard than would appear to be the case from this investigation … Longer experience may show slight storage of lead … which may lead eventually to recognizable lead poisoning or to chronic degenerative diseases of a less obvious character … a more extended use of this fuel … may constitute a menace to the health of the general public.[59]

After the lecture, the small audience—made up of personnel in the pediatric department and social workers—left without further inquiry. The few medical students did ask some relevant questions, but I was most drawn to the paralleled detrimental long-term effects of lead and mercury. I went to Talize with my review of mercury and realized she was familiar with my citations. She felt there was a definitive association of the untoward effects on the brains of people exposed to both elements. She stated that mercury's vapor effect from the silver fillings in those mouths was like hidden termites underneath a wooden-structured house. The destruction would not be evident until it was too late and irreversible damage had occurred to the very foundation of the house. She compared the foundation to the nervous system in the body.

She told me she wanted to be a physician, but more importantly, a humanitarian first to serve people who were given limited resources and opportunities. While making her point, I was brought back to my childhood listening to Mumsie sharing her experiences in the shelters and Henry Street Settlement. I thanked her for a well-prepared presentation, and quite out of character, I built up the nerve to ask if I could see her again to discuss some of the other public issues she wanted to address. She was kind enough to say she had some free time the following Sunday. I thought that would be perfect; there was a haunting appeal about her that I couldn't define clearly, but it was certainly there.

She made arrangements to meet me at a diner for lunch. That morning, while looking for a nice shirt to wear, I uncovered a letter that Father had written that previous spring. It was encouraging and supportive of the wonderful friendship we developed. I was once again feeling blue. The thought of seeing Talize elevated my feelings somewhat. I would much rather go to see her instead of dwelling on Father's death.

When I arrived at the diner, Talize was reviewing some notes at a table. I was still preoccupied with thoughts of Father and Uncle Herbert, and as I sat down, there had to have been an open expression of bewilderment on my face because she directly asked, "Is something troubling you? I get the sense you are not yourself, even though we have met only once before."

I felt awkward, paralyzed for a second, yet not violated or interrogated. I was aware of her sincerity; in the back of my mind, Mumsie was encouraging me to give her a straightforward reply. I reviewed the agony of the two deaths, and she listened intently.

She listened so well that her eyes spoke with serenity and resolution. Before she opened her mouth, I knew she would offer useful and kind words; I was not disappointed. She started telling me an American Indian story, a tradition used for thousands of years. The folklore, myths, and storytelling have expressed the pulse of their creation and symbolized a connection to the earth, the waters, the sky, the plants and trees, the mountains and rocks, and all the living creatures sharing in the whole existence of life. The stories share a code of important lessons and valuable tools to consider when a challenge is faced, a good decision is needed, a conflict is to be resolved, and a way to live on "higher ground."

She added that the stories were quite reverent, and it was important that certain stories could only be told at certain times—and only to certain people. And some of the stories were not meant to be repeated by the listener. She looked me in the eye and gently uttered, "You come to me now with deep forlorn feelings about the death of your close loved ones. This particular story helped me through the loss of my mother and father who died within six months of each other when I was a freshman in college. It is entitled 'Coyote and Eagle Visit the Land of the Dead.' I will add some personal thoughts that will give the message a little more uplift."

She explained how the coyote and other native animal and bird symbols represent people with distinctive qualities to give a message, a physical guidance to make the story more resonating. It is similar to the use of allegorical stories that Jesus shared in the New Testament. The coyote plays several roles, including Creator and a mischievous, cunning spirit. He is spiritual at times and selfish and greedy at others, but his presence is felt to be magical in a positive way, so he remains an endeared animal symbol. The eagle portrays strength and courage, and the frog is likened to springtime, sensitivity, and stable being.

A long time ago, when animal people walked the Earth's pathways, the influential Coyote grieved over the people including his loved ones, who had passed on and now resided in the land of the spirits. He had recently lost his sister and a few dear companions, and his friend Eagle had lost his wife as well. He commiserated with Eagle, offering words of assurance:

> The dead shall not remain forever in the land of the spirits. They are like the leaves that fall in autumn, brown and lost in the wind, but in the spring, the new grass grows and the new leaves return to the trees. The birds even sing once again. The departed shall return.[60]

But Eagle was too impatient to think his wife would not return for several months.

So they both went out immediately, searching for the land of the dead. As time went by, they came to a body of water. They called out for a boat to cross, but no reply was given. They waited until darkness, and Coyote began to sing. Four spirits came over the water in a boat to greet them. They brought Coyote and Eagle back in the boat with them. When they arrived on shore, they could hear drums beating. They pleaded with the spirits who initially wanted to keep them away from their festivities, but they eventually gave in and allowed them entrance. Once inside, Coyote and Eagle were amazed with the splendor of their ceremonial robes and the beauty of the lodge. Everyone was having a good time, dancing and singing to the beat of the drums. The lodge was lit with the bright moonlight, and Frog was monitoring the activity of the moon. He stood close to it to keep everything illumined.

Eagle and Coyote recognized some of the spirits, but they waited unnoticed with a basket that Coyote brought to contain the spirits at an opportune time. The moment arrived at dawn when the spirits left the lodge to return to their sleeping grounds. While Frog was preparing to leave, Coyote struck, killed him, and took his clothes.

The following night, Coyote, cleverly disguised as Frog, stood next to the moon while the spirits began dancing and enjoying themselves. At the height of the frivolity, Coyote swallowed the moon, creating total darkness. Eagle swooped down on the spirits, grabbed them, placed them in the basket, and closed the lid tight. Coyote and Eagle met outside, crossed the river in the boat, and started their journey home—mission accomplished.

But at what expense? After they traveled for some distance—and only a little way from home—the spirits started transforming into people. The weight of the basket became too much for coyote to carry them further. They complained that they were cramped and uncomfortable and needed to be freed. Coyote was tired and felt they had gone far enough away from the spirit's grounds. Eagle cautioned not to open the basket until they were home, but Coyote didn't heed his advice. The lid was released, and all of the people took their spirit forms again and returned to their island as swiftly as the wind would carry them.

Eagle was irascible, but he slowly settled, remembering Coyote's original plan to wait until spring when the leaves and flowers were in bloom to return to the island of the spirits to try again. But Coyote was more pensive. He said to let the spirits lie in peace and not disturb them. There was good reason that they returned upon their release from the basket. The leaves and flowers depart and return every spring, and we celebrate the magnificence of the transformation, but the spirits need their freedom, their eternal peace, and their heightened enlightenment to move on. Their imprint remains perennial, like the blooming leaves and flowers, in the hearts of those left behind. Their *fragrance* and beauty linger in our thoughts. They return, just like the flowers and leaves, but in their spiritual forms instead of their physical forms. But we don't have to wait until spring to feel their presence; they are with us always. They are content, and they want us content. Unbeknownst to Coyote, he did the right thing—as the Creator had intended it to be.

I was in the realm of a trance: purged, cleansed, given water to quench my aching thirst. The depth of her understanding and inner wisdom was so powerful yet so naturally flowing from her. Before I could respond, she offered additional pearls for me to give thought.

The Wampanoag tradition of presenting evergreens—the pine needles or a cut branch—and seashells or conch shells takes place at a burial ceremony. With the evergreens, each family member or friend of the deceased feels his or her departed soul will be *evergreen* and vibrant on the journey. The journey takes them to the stars, their final destination. The Muskogee Indians call it *Spirit Road*. They are guided along the way until they reach the sky.

Talize said, "So, every night, your father, mentor, and other loved ones watch over you and shine brightly to be recognized as beacons. As they were once guided, you will be guided. You will acknowledge them regularly, and you will be given the Creator's blessing."

I came to have lunch and friendly conversation with Talize and got the added bonus of her caring heart. I forgot to mention that her presence was striking enough—an attractive, soothing face with a smile broadcasting a gorgeous set of teeth, silky smooth skin, and expressive, dark, magnetic eyes. I thanked her for meeting me for lunch, and I told her my deepest gratitude for bringing some sunlight back into those last few months of lingering clouds. I shook her hand, and I felt her being. Her appeal remained haunting, but at least I knew that Father must have brought that letter to my attention that morning for a good reason. I was certain of that understanding. I asked if I could see her again. She said yes. Boy, was I pleased.

We met at the same diner a few weeks later, and she told me about her background. She said her parents were members of the Wampanoag and Muskogee tribes. The Muskogee Indians were traditionally farmers and usually settled near the Coosa and Tallapoosa Rivers and its outlets, forming the Coosa Valley in what is now Alabama. The whites called them the *Creek* Indians because of their close proximity to water. She was born in Johnstown, Pennsylvania. Her family relocated near Harrisburg when she was five years old. Her Muskogee maternal grandfather was a very young boy when his family moved north to Pennsylvania in the early 1830s when the ongoing unrest with the Alabaman white settlers became more and more ominous. Talize's mother and father met while students in the Carlisle Indian School. They learned a Western education, but neither of them was willing to abandon their traditional Indian upbringing completely. They named their only child Talize, the Muskogee name for *beautiful waters.* Though originally spelled Talise, they changed the *S* to a *Z.* Her father liked it because there was no *Z* in the Wampanoag language. And Morning Star was her second name because she was born around the break of dawn, and when her father looked up in the sky, a star was shining brightly, signifying a new life, and a new day with the promise of their ancestors' approval.

Talize was able to attend the local public school in Harrisburg and did well; she skipped the first and fourth grades. She attended college at Temple University and then one year at the Women's Medical College of Pennsylvania in Philadelphia and transferred to Boston University at the beginning of her second year. She was going to graduate the same year that I would. Her mother died during the winter of 1920 from complications of influenza, and her father passed away within six months; he was also the victim of flu. Since there was no immediate family remaining, Talize was *adopted* by her father's Wampanoag family near Plymouth, Massachusetts. She became close to the medicine man and the chief and sought their counsel regularly.

Our visits became more frequent during our "spare" time. We had so many common interests. I told her about my love of history and the many discussions I shared with Mumsie, Grandfather, and Uncle Herbert about the plight and injustice of the American Indians. She was curious to hear about my thoughts on the Indian dilemma. I was told that approximately ten million Indians inhabited the North American continent for more than ten thousand years before the first white explorers came to Florida in 1540. Over the next three hundred years, the Indian population was reduced by 90 percent due to disease, starvation, or fighting conflicts brought by the white population.

Tension developed early with the white-Indian relations, creating wars that forced many of the eastern tribes to relocate west. But the more land acquired, the more land desired, and general policy from the government was issued in the form of "treaties." After the Louisiana Purchase in 1803, more pressure was placed on the Indians to move west of the Mississippi River. Resistance was inevitable, but by 1830, with President Jackson enforcing the Indian Removal Act of 1830, all the years of negotiations broke down to a horrible injustice: the Trail of Tears. It was clear that from colonial times onward, the European settler used religion and modern "civilization" which they assumed they possessed, over the "unworthy" Indians who "lacked" these virtues, to justify their crusade of dominance and control over the Indians' welfare and fate.

I had learned the horrors of broken promises as a boy listening to the detailed review of Helen Hunt Jackson's *A Century of Dishonor* (she was not related to the president):

> It makes little difference, however, where one opens the records of history of the Indians; every page and every year has its dark stains. The story of one tribe is the story of all, varied only by differences of time and place. The US government breaks promises now as deftly as then, and with an added ingenuity from long practice ...

> There are hundreds of pages of unimpeachable testimony on the side of the Indian; but it goes for nothing, is set down as sentimentalism or partisanship tossed aside and forgotten. President after president has appointed commission after commission to inquire into and report upon Indian affairs, and to make suggestions as to the best methods of managing them. The reports are filled with eloquent statements of wrongs done to the Indians, of perfidies on the part of the Government; they counsel, as earnestly as words can, a trial of the simple and unperplexing expedients of telling truths, keeping promises, making fair bargains, dealing justly in all ways and all things ...

In 1790, General Washington had said to the Six Nations of the East, "In future, you cannot be defrauded of your lands. No state or person can purchase your lands unless at some public treaty held under the authority of the United States. The general government will never consent to your being defrauded, but it will protect you in all your just rights. You possess the right to sell and the right of refusing to sell your lands. The United States will be true and faithful to their engagements."

In less than 40 years, after giving up lands to appease the white settler's lust, the Indian Removal Act of 1830 was implemented to force the Southeastern tribes west of the Mississippi River. The Cherokee nation extended along the Tennessee River, and in the Highlands of Georgia, Carolina and Alabama. It was the most fertile and valuable land east of the Mississippi River.[61]

Miss Jackson went further:

What imagination could have foreseen that the Chiefs of the Cherokee nation would be found piteously pleading to be allowed to remain undisturbed on the very land they were born and raised? In the whole history of our Government's dealing with the Indian tribes, there is no record so black as the record of its perfidy to this nation.

Talize was impressed with the knowledge base I had, but she would add some very meaningful thoughts from the perspective of her loved ancestors. I listened as I did to Mumsie and Grandfather when they shared their life stories during my childhood. She told me how honored she felt to talk about her heritage in a constructive, beneficial way to another set of ears that treasured the truth and yearned for the whole concept: the precious root of its foundation that has led a common people on a traditional ten thousand-year sojourn of life, appreciating the "Great Spirit" that created and kept it beautiful for all to share with one another. Everything changed in all the Indian nations once the white settlers and the "righteous" missionaries came to dominate and strip the collective tribes of their land, their resources, and their way of living. The Indians were assigned the labels of *barbaric, pagan, savage, heathen,* and *primitive,* and issued treaties, almost four hundred of them between 1778 and 1871. The treaties were meaningless words that faded like the ink on the yellowed, cracked parchment they were written on.

The Greek word for barbaric is *barbaros,* which means a *foreigner* or *alien.* The Latin root for *pagan* is *pagus,* which means village or country dweller. *Savage* comes from the Latin *Silvaticus,* which means wooded area or forest. *Heathen* is of Old English origin, meaning inhabitants of the open countryside, the moors of Northern England or Scotland where the heather plants grow. The inhabitants were called heathens, as a person from Egypt is called an Egyptian. *Primitive* is from the Latin word *primativus,* which means first of its kind. All of these innocuous words took on a convenient, negative connotation as the white missionaries and settlers described the red race while they were spreading their religious values and fulfilling their Manifest Destiny, respectively throughout the US territories.

Several tribesmen, famous and unknown, recorded their awareness of the true picture present by white America in memorable words that should evoke disappointment, irresponsibility, distrust, and discontent in all readers. I felt shame as I listened to Talize, even though I was not directly a part of those people's actions. The gifted orator, Tecumseh, spoke to the Osage Indians in the Great Plains around 1811:

> Brothers, we all belong to one family; we are all children of the Great Spirit; we walk the same path ... we are friends; we must assist each other to bear our burdens. The blood of many of our fathers and brothers has run like water on the ground, to satisfy the avarice of the white men ... When the white men first set foot on our grounds, they were hungry; they had no place on which to spread their blankets, or to kindle their fires. They were feeble; they could do nothing for themselves. Our fathers commiserated their distress, and shared freely with them

whatever the Great Spirit had given his red children. They gave them food when hungry, medicine when sick, spread skins for them to sleep on, and gave them grounds that they might hunt and raise corn … The white men are not friends to the Indians: at first, they only asked for land sufficient for a wigwam; now, nothing will satisfy them but the whole of our hunting grounds, from the rising to the setting sun … My people wish for peace; the red men all wish for peace; but where the white people are, there is no peace for them, except it be on the bosom of our mother.[62]

I was suddenly transported back in time, over one hundred years, as if I was hearing the great warrior's message personally. Talize went on saying that Tecumseh was described by a white contemporary, Sam Dale, as he spoke impassionedly to the Muskogee tribesmen:

His eyes burned with supernatural lustre, his whole frame trembled … His voice sounded over the multitude … hurling out his words like a succession of thunderbolts. I have heard many great orators, but I never saw one with the vocal powers of Tecumseh. Had I been deaf, the play of his countenance would have told me what he said.[63]

She mentioned Corn Tassel, elder Cherokee facilitator speaking on behalf of his people to the US Peace Treaty commissioners in 1785:

Indeed, much has been advanced on the want of what you term civilization among the Indians; and many proposals have been made to us to adopt your laws, your religion, your manners and your customs. But, we confess that we do not yet see the propriety, or practicability of such a reformation, and should be better pleased with beholding the good effect of these doctrines in your own practices than with hearing you talk about them, or reading your papers to us upon such subjects … the great God of

Nature has placed us in different situations. It is true that he has endowed you with many superior advantages, but he has not created us to be your slaves.[64]

Talize added two elder Indians whose wisdom was worth spreading throughout the white civilization. One spoke poignantly of his inner reflections on the destruction of the Indian world:

My sun is set. My day is done. Darkness is stealing over me. Before I lie down to rise no more, I will speak to my people ... The white man came to our hunting grounds, a stranger. We gave him meat and presents, and told him to go in peace ... His fellows brought among us the mysterious iron that shoots, the magic water that makes men foolish ... his numbers were greater than blades of grass. They took away the buffalo and shot down our best warriors. They took away our lands and surrounded us by fences. They wiped the trails of our people from the face of the prairies. They forced our children to forsake the ways of their fathers. When I turn to the east I see no dawn. When I turn to the west the approaching nights hides all.[65]

The other, an elder Hopi man, responded to a missionary who tried to convert the man to Christianity. The missionary told him that his sacred beliefs were "foolish," and the elder retorted:

We may be foolish in the eyes of the white men, for we are a very simple people. We live close to our great mother, the Earth. We believe in our God as you believe in your God, but we believe that our God is best for us. Our God gave us the rain cloud and the sunshine, the corn and all things to sustain life before we ever heard of your God. If your God is so great, let him speak to me as my god speaks to me, in my heart and not from a white man's mouth ... Our God is all-powerful and all-good, and there is no devil and there is no hell in our Underworld where we go after we die.[66]

On another visit, we discussed nature and its intricacies in the sacred rites celebrated with the Great Spirit. There are so many testimonies found among the tribes and so much reverence for all of nature. The insight of Charles Eastman clearly summarized the connection of nature to the spirit:

> Whenever in the course of the daily hunt, the red hunter comes upon a scene that is strikingly beautiful or sublime—a white waterfall in the heart of a green gorge or a vast prairie tinged with the blood-red of sunset—he pauses for an instant in the attitude of worship. He sees no need for setting apart one day in seven as a holy day, since to him all days are God's.[67]

Talize brought up the distinctive symbolism of water. It is the root of life on earth, the mirror of the universe, the connector of life and death, the bearer of historic secrets, and the shaper and transformer of the past and present civilizations. It possesses the extremes of behavior, ranging from calm and serene motion to raging and furious tides. It nourishes all created living things. It has had many stories to tell since time was recorded.

Water has its own spirit with many tribal ceremonies performed in or by its borders. At the time of death, close family members go down to the river to be cleansed for seven days to respect the dead while the newborns are dipped in the flowing river waters for seven days to wash away any impurities. Prayers are given by the waters, gifts are offered to the waters, and you feel the silence of life and listen and watch the birds and fish show their appreciation of the Spirit represented through the waters. One human being is an insignificant drop in the majestic waters throughout the world, but an included drop, sharing in its power and beauty.

Talize told me she had a deep commitment to live up to the origin of her name: beautiful water. I told her she had shown it to me each time we were together. After several visits, she gave me the sobriquet, Chowilawu, which means "joined together by water." The name made me feel very personal to her. How ironic that I also had to live up to my family name: Waterbury?

We shared a mutual love of music. She was an accomplished cellist. I told her that her instrument was the "grandfather" of the orchestra and that it was the most versatile in its range of notes. We eventually learned to play Rachmaninoff's "Prelude in F Major," Op. 2, No. 1 for cello and piano together. What a passionate piece! We liked the opera, symphony, and the ballet. We went to a few concerts at Symphony Hall to hear Serge Koussevitzky conduct the Boston Symphony Orchestra during the 1927–1928 season.

We ventured to the Museum of Fine Arts, Haymarket Square, and Faneuil Hall to get some fresh produce on weekends, and one of our favorite spots, the ever-exciting Scollay Square. We would get off the Scollay Square subway station and come upstairs through a unique kiosk that had a very stylish appeal in the middle of Court Street and Cambridge Street. The memorable station was demolished to a simple street-level entrance in 1927 due to increasing traffic whose drivers were unable to see pedestrians around the tall structure. What a loss to the city's landscape.

But other activities flourished on all the adjacent streets. We would go to Patten's Restaurant for a delicious meal, then to Epstein's Drugstore for an egg cream dessert, stroll through Jack's Joke Shop, and up Cornhill past the Sears Crescent Building to look at the many wonderful bookstores. Sometimes we would stop at the Oriental Tea Company. The enormous brass teakettle that hung outside its door was one of Talize's favorite landmarks in Boston. At times, we went to the Olympia or Star Theaters for movies, but the best entertainment was the spectacular comic acts at the Old Howard Theater. I had been many times before I met Talize, and each time, I left with a great smile on my face.

Months went by, our friendship grew, and we started dating. I invited her to attend my medical school graduation party at Harvard in June 1927. Talize always looked attractive, but that evening, she was a knockout. She had a gorgeous cranberry-colored dress, her hair was styled like the actress Clara Bow, and her face was photo perfect. How elevated I felt as we came into the reception room. Everything was quite lovely, and a talented band played good dance music.

The conversations were light and gay until one of my classmates who had a reputation for drinking came staggering up to me and shouted, "Hey Waterbury, who's the glamour girl with you?"

I told him her name, and he said, "Oh, a real red-skin girl? I thought they had to be home in their teepee before dark. Did her daddy, Sitting Bull, say, 'You got-tum permission to take-um my daughter to the party. Have-um a good time. Don't be-um late!' He was laughing hysterically, and I was ready to take him outside.

Talize spoke quite assuredly for herself, saying, "My fine man, the day you find a 'red-skin' who fits your description given, tell him you will try to learn the truth when you are sober, but if you still don't understand, your ignorance will continue speaking loudly, unaddressed, and you will remain a miserable being, trapped, lonely, and afraid of your own shadow!"

The man slowly walked away and said nothing to anyone for the rest of the evening.

That night, while walking Talize home, I reviewed the injustice and the arrogance that white America has for all the colored races. I felt embarrassed.

Talize looked at me and said I had nothing to be embarrassed about. She said, "Do you love me?"

I said, "With all my heart."

She smiled and said, "I know why you love me. You have taken the time to examine that part of what you love most about yourself and what love you offer to your fellow living creatures, including man. You have also taken time to review what it is within me that you love about me and what love I offer my fellow living creatures. You have recognized that our thoughts and heartfelt expressions are quite aligned, and your love for me has been nurtured through that alignment—as I feel my love for you. As time goes by, the bond will become more and more convincing that we are on a road, traveling together, directed toward the same destination. We may not get there at the exact same time, but God will see us through and give us the patience and strength to feel fulfilled and not live in vain. Both of us are truly blessed."

I left Talize that night, looked at the sky and moon, and counted my lucky stars that I had met her. She was the best woman I could ever meet; Mumsie, Grandfather, Uncle Herbert, and Father would nod in agreement.

When internships started, we were both consumed with patient responsibilities. We didn't get a chance to see each other as much. And when we did meet, there were times I was on edge. The medical demands and the large gaps between our visits frustrated me.

Talize, however, was always balanced, calm, and assuring.

One day, an embarrassing episode evolved between the two of us about the clinical condition of one of my female patients and the treatment and recommendations that I gave her.

Talize asked if I had considered discussing an added point, and I arrogantly assumed there was no need for that point. I argued with her and got stubborn while she tried to reason with me. I persisted, and she got quiet. Our precious time together was compromised with my shortcoming.

I apologized and told her I was not worthy of her consistency.

She reminded me, holding me in her arms, that if she was as "perfect" as I made her to be, she would not fit as well in our relationship, our pleasures, our common dreams or like-mindedness. Times like that made me appreciate the total woman she was.

Talize's birthday was on October 10, and she usually spent time with her Wampanoag "family" as they celebrated Cranberry Day, which was the second Tuesday of October. Cranberry Day is traditionally the last day of the year for the Wampanoag to gather together, and it usually is the start of the full harvest season. As they gather, they also give thanks for the harvest; the gathering has as much significance as our traditional Thanksgiving holiday. Cranberries were a stable part of the meals, especially during the winter months. They were also medicinal; the medicine man used them for laxatives and treatment for fevers, abdominal pain, and childhood diseases.

I planned a special surprise birthday party on Sunday, October 16, 1927, and invited some close friends. That morning was peaceful and not too chilly so we went to the Public Garden to walk around. We enjoyed the swan ride and all the autumn colors displayed on the trees. We stopped to sit and talk on one of the park benches.

Talize sensed something when I reached to hold her hand and kept thanking her for being a part of my life.

I paused for a moment, reached into my pocket, and handed her a letter, which I had memorized. The letter remains etched on my heart:

Let me gulp your kisses, and you gulp mine,
And with our mouths sip each other's bliss.
Each, both beloved and lover can be
Two lives, I in thee, thee in me ...
Louise Labe, *Sonnet*

Love is the sweet and hidden pollen which is nesting in the tender
and sweet petals of your heart waiting to be awakened by the silent and sweet tones of your soul. Its fragrance invites you to a Great feast wherein two blends of wine made from the vineyard that was planted by the hand of God are mixed together, and are
ready to be drunk. And the more is drunk, the more the joys of life abound.
George Lamsa, *And the Scroll Opened*

In happiness and sorrow, hold your standard high and let not your
desire die, and let not the rose which your heart nourished dry. Neither let the flame of your candle vanish into the endless sky.
George Lamsa, *And the Scroll Opened*

I have loved thee with an everlasting love.
—Jeremiah 31:3

Dearest one,

When I look back in my life, I know I was loved deeply by my family and friends. They regarded and encouraged me to be that person who would be caring for others, helping, offering, and living to give his very best. To say the least, I was and still am truly spoiled.

But I wrestled within myself to express a deeper meaning of love, one that could not exist without the opportunity to find "that other half" of me—that soul mate, who like a revealing clear mirror, could see my strengths and flaws, could share her wisdom to guide my doubts and fears into certainty and courage, and teach me a better approach to my daily existence; that friend, with an ever-growing desire to keep our friendship dynamic, unconditional, and resonating. Through college and the first part of medical school, I kept searching and searching, with no one to find. At times, my frustration compromised my ability to remain patient and hopeful. But then, God directed me to you at the presentation that you delivered. Although the lecture shared many enlightening pedantic pearls, I knew there was more to see in you. At our next meeting, I heard your comforting words about facing death of loved ones, and afterward, I was immediately enamored by your charm, beauty, equanimity, and gentle, soothing demeanor. I had the privilege of sharing more conversations, and somewhere during those visits, I realized that I finally understood what true love was, and I knew that it poured from your heart into mine.

I remember all the wonderful talks we shared about our feelings as they were growing, and as much as I wanted you, I knew I needed to be patient and allow time to give us a sustained desire, not just a quick sensation or thrill. Then, one evening, as we came upstairs, right by the door to your apartment, you kissed me ever so passionately, ever so sincerely, ever so completely. I was about to leap out of my skin with joy and excitement. Your smile and your offering were penetrating and so special.

Since that moment, I have felt the flame of love rise high and bright within me—at times sending me to boundless heights and feeling it over and over again. I know many circumstances have interfered with our time together and our sharing of love. But true love has transcended the gaps and filled in the longing and missing with projected caring and steady good intention for each other.

Nothing can or will ever be able to separate us, my dear, except God Himself. We will be given our time one day; no matter how long, it will come to pass. You must know I will take care of you and your needs; you will always have my devotion and commitment. You are mine, and will always be mine; God truly blessed me in my lifetime to have such a wonderful spirit near me.

Thank you for being you, letting me "gulp your kisses and sip your bliss," inviting me to a "great feast wherein two blends of wine were allowed to mix together," holding "your standard high and not letting my desire die," and giving me the privilege of "loving thee with an everlasting love."

May God continue to bless our pathway as we journey in life to receive our ultimate awareness of our tie to humanity and His love.

All of my love,
With admiration and devotion,
Windy

P.S. You just don't know how I count my blessings, giving thanks that you are a part of my being, joined by God, for eternal love, peace, and happiness.

When I finished, I asked if she would marry me—and she accepted. She said she knew I was planning to say something very important by the way I held her hand at that moment. Well, I not only pulled off that surprise, but

I managed to pull off the surprise for her party that evening. We shared the good news with our friends and planned the wedding for the end of 1928.

We decided to have two wedding ceremonies and agreed about the importance of both. The first would be at Aquinnah Cliff with a traditional Indian ceremony in September 1928, and the second would be a "formal" wedding at the Trinity Church in New York around Christmas.

The Indian ceremony took place on Aquinnah Cliff near the home of Talize's father's tribe. She had arranged all the details with the chief and the medicine man. Several of her father's relatives and friends attended. I could not do full justice in describing the power of spirit and the gorgeous backdrop of nature that surrounded us during the gathering. Aquinnah Cliff is on the southwest side of Martha's Vineyard. The Wampanoag call Martha's Vineyard *Noepe*, which means "in the midst of the sea." Aquinnah is also called Gayhead, because of the brilliantly colored clay on the surface of the cliff, which makes everyone very "gay."

The ceremony began about an hour before sunset, and the medicine man performed the service. Two separate fires representing each of us were started. There was a ritual washing of the hands, symbolizing purification. Talize walked up with a female friend and looked marvelous; she wore a beautiful red buckskin dress. The color red offered good luck. She had several bracelets, a necklace of wampum, and moose-skinned moccasins. The wampum was made of quahog shell, a hard, durable clamshell that is purple and white in color, and looked like precious gems; the wampum nurtured one's health. Then the four elements were passed between us— fire, water, wind, and earth. Prayers that we wrote for each other were exchanged as vows; Talize expressed her passion quite vividly. She told me to "see the universe light, hear the universe music, feel the universe love, smell the universe peace, and taste the universe joy of living."

The medicine man offered a prayer from Chief Yellow Hawk that we had to repeat to all the attendees:

> O Great Spirit, whose voice I hear in the winds and whose breath gives life to all the world, hear me. I am small and weak. I need your strength and wisdom. Let me walk in beauty and make my eyes ever behold the red and purple sunset. Make my hands respect the things you have made.

Make my ears sharp to hear your voice. Make me wise so
that I may understand the things you have taught your
people. Let me learn the lessons you have hidden in every
leaf and rock. I seek strength, not to be greater than my
brother, but to fight my greatest enemy—myself. Make
me always ready to come to you with clean hands and
straight eyes. So when life fades, as the fading sunset, my
spirit may come to you without shame.[68]

At the end of the one-hour ceremony, the two fires were brought together,
symbolizing our union, and the gifts we had brought for everyone who
witnessed our marriage were distributed.

After the closing moments, while standing on the cliff, I was
surrounded by the beauty of the Aquinnah Lighthouse behind me and
the unforgettable red-orange sunset in front, blended in the orange-blue
sky with the steel-gray puffs of clouds accenting the scenery until they
faded into the edge of the horizon; it was an artistic masterpiece! The view
was breathtaking, the bride was stunning, and all that was taken in was
magical and serene as I listened to the waves gently brushing against the
shore and felt the wind kissing my elated face. I was deeply moved to tears,
and as I looked at Talize, I was so completely in love.

After we departed Aquinnah the next morning, we took the ferry back
to the mainland and drove to Boston. We packed our bags to spend our
honeymoon at our summer home in Northeast Harbor, Maine on Mount
Desert Island. We called it Merrywood Cottage, which was on South
Shore Drive. In 1887, Grandfather "modernized" the original summer
home owned by his father-in-law and named it Merrywood because the
wooded area surrounding the house made him quite happy—*merry*—
when he went outdoors. Father added several improvements in the early
1920s. The servants would stay most of the year round, but the place was
not routinely used for vacationing during the harsh winter months.

Transportation for Mumsie and Grandfather was on the Bar Harbor
Express railroad from New York to the Mount Desert Ferry. The boat
was a beautiful steamship that traveled with a direct stop at Northeast
Harbor. I remember traveling there as a boy on the Bar Harbor Express;
it was an elegant train of rich blue and gold interior trimmings, detailed,

carved woodwork, and comfortable, spacious seating. We would wait at the ferry terminal, which had an open fireplace, stained-glass windows, and chandeliers hanging from the ceiling. We would board the luxurious steamship, and the servants would come to the harbor to greet the family.

By the late 1920s, the Bar Harbor Express and the ferry were not as popular as they had been at the turn of the twentieth century. Talize and I took the Boston-Maine Railroad heading toward Ellsworth, Maine. The servants came there in a motorcar to take us to Northeast Harbor. The old gravel roads took time to get to the cottage, but the early evening light allowed Talize to take in the spectacular view of the natural landscape and beauty of Mount Desert Island. When we arrived, she did not want the car ride to end.

After Mumsie and Grandfather passed away, I still had an occasional visit with Father. Mother was usually on one of her social trips and did not accompany us. I was willed the summer home; although I came to spend time away in this peaceful setting, I was lonely most of the time. I told Talize that she would bring warmth and comfort, so we would be going there regularly. She fell in love with the place the moment I opened the front door.

As we walked in the large, well-designed door from the landside, we passed the front entry and went into a well-accommodated, spacious living room with enlarged picture windows looking out over a sprawling 150-foot lawn, lined with multicolored flowers and bushes in addition to the surrounding trees and shrubs. A stone staircase led down to the lovely beach sands on the shore of the open Atlantic Ocean.

Talize stopped and stared, frozen, trying to take in all this magnificent beauty. When she snapped out of her hypnotic gaze, she looked around the living room and noted the adjacent porch. The screens were up. We walked outside and heard the birds singing and saw the gulls searching for fish off the shore. As she looked down the stone staircase, she observed the boulders adding to the landscape and the pier for boat docking.

She wanted to go down to the shore, and while we were there, she looked back to see the massive size of the cottage. When I told her there were forty rooms, her eyes opened even wider. She looked at me and said, "This place is some Garden of Eden, some lost paradise."

I responded, "Well, I'm glad it's no longer lost because it is our paradise to treasure."

She kept raving about the manicured flower beds and lawn nestled in the rock and foundation and how carefully the whole structure was crafted to fit into the setting. I told her the skilled artisans who built the house placed the clapboard and shingle meticulously overlapping the upper boards to the lower boards so that none of the unrelenting winter weather would get inside.

We went back through the living room and into the formal dining room, which sat up to twenty people at the lovely table. The adjoining butler's pantry had numerous shelves and drawers stacked with glassware, silverware, and china place settings.

When we walked through to the large kitchen, Talize was in awe of the divisions with stoves and different iceboxes to handle any size meal needed. It was "almost a restaurant." We walked upstairs and came to the bedroom with a veranda looking out with the same view as the living room.

She inquired, "Is this our room?"

I told her if she wanted it to be, it would be.

She nodded with approval. After taking an hour to go through all of the rooms, including the servant's quarters, Talize was so excited. She could barely sit still when it was time to get something to eat.

That evening, while she was upstairs in the bedroom, all of the servants came to me to say that they thought Talize was charming, quite friendly, and a good woman. Their opinion meant a great deal to me, and I was pleased.

The night air had cooled considerably, and it began to rain. Talize and I sat near the fireplace for a while and absorbed all the peaceful surroundings. We finally went to the king-sized bed. I was next to her skin-to-skin for the first time. I asked for her hand, and she placed it on my face.

She looked at me with the expression of a newborn doe gazing upon its mother and said, "I am quite honored to be Mrs. Waterbury. You have made me very happy. You have been patient, kind, considerate, and respectful of my body, mind, and soul. I now want to make you happy. I want to please you, excite you, and make you want to come back for more."

I said, "You make me feel like a king."

"That's because you are my king."

"Well, as long as we share this crown and kingdom, I am at your service, my lovely queen."

The night was one thrill after another, and I could not have been more fulfilled. God gave me a loving angel, and I could not ask for anything more.

We stayed at Merrywood for one week. We visited the Bass Harbor Head Lighthouse, and Acadia National Park, and we sailed on the steamship that traveled between the island and the Mount Desert Ferry. Our time went by too quickly.

We returned to Boston and found a nice place in Brookline. We made plans to have our "formal" wedding sometime before Christmas; it would be done at Trinity Church. Mother was out of town. Talize and I went to the Seventy-Third Street home for a long weekend in October to meet Soulange. The staff greeted us warmly, and Soulange was very pleased.

Talize liked Mumsie's room and felt very special when I said we would move in there. We selected new drapes and other colors for the room. Mumsie's chair at the dining room table needed a new cover, and a new shawl with Talize's initials, TMW, was embroidered on it to place over the chair. The arrangements were all made with the Episcopalian minister. Everything was just perfect.

Talize enjoyed the carriage ride through Central Park, the Metropolitan Opera to see a beautiful performance of the light and cheerful "Martha" by Friedrich von Flotow, and the personal conversations with Soulange and the staff. I showed Talize my 1923 Bosendorfer Grand piano that Father had bought for me when I graduated from Amherst. She loved its sound. I gave her some background to the company's Austrian origin and how it was respectfully played by the composer, Franz Liszt. She had told me previously that he was one of her favorite composers. I had been practicing the "Benediction de Dieu dans la solitude" (The Blessing of God in Solitude), #3 of 10 pieces in his collective work called "Harmonies poetiques et Religleuses" which is based on French poet Alphonse Lamartine's work by the same title. As a preface to the Benediction, Liszt used the quote from Lamartine: "Whence comes, O God, this peace which overwhelms me? Whence comes, this faith, with which my heart overflows?" I told her that the music reminded me of beautiful waters. "When I hear and play this piece, I think of you." I surprised her when I sat down and played it for her. She was quite emotional after I ended the final peaceful notes. It was the best gift I gave her in all our moments together; words cannot describe the joyful expression on her face.

Being lovers of books, I had to take Talize to Book Row in downtown Manhattan, along Fourth Avenue and south of Union Square. We stopped at the relatively new Strand's Bookstore, and while I was looking over the shelves, she bought me a copy of the recently published *Jesus* by Kahlil Gibran to thank me for our New York visit. After opening to the title page—"Jesus, The Son of Man, His words and his deeds as told and recorded by those who knew him"—and seeing Gibran's own illustration of a profile of Jesus in a beautiful pencil etched on the frontispiece, we were captured and inspired by each personal account of the influence of Jesus on themselves and others in his time. After reading the entire book, it has been on my nightstand as a constant source of comfort in times of despair and during the good times.

Before leaving to go back to Boston on Sunday, Soulange said that Mumsie, Grandfather, Father, and Uncle Herbert would all stand proud and overjoyed at the marriage ceremony at Trinity. We thought it would be appropriate to discuss the formal plans over the Thanksgiving holiday with Mother since she was away. Little did we realize the unexpected course of events that would follow our blissful experience in October.

Chapter

33

Thanksgiving Dinner at the Waterbury House, 1928 (Event 19)

As happy as everyone was listening to the enchanting memories after I met Talize, they were all very subdued knowing there was sad news to follow.

Soulange spoke again, being an eyewitness and whose shoulders supported me through the storm. "Windy and I knew that Rose was not going to be favorable in his marriage to Talize. But it was his life and his decision. He was grown and knew how to make a good decision. He truly did not expect to place her in a vulnerable or shameful position, and he never intended to be disrespectful. What came to the Waterbury house that Thanksgiving evening, however, was unjustified, deliberately malicious, painful, and cleverly manipulative. They all need to hear the details. It is not a story to repeat without sorrow, but it is an event to bring truth to our understanding and resolution to any lingering uncertainties."

Soulange could not have been more appropriate in her sentiments. I have always felt that William Congreve's quote from his tragic *The Mourning Bride*—"Heaven has no rage like love to hatred turned, nor hell a fury like a woman scorned"—was a bit exaggerated until I witnessed the transformation of my mother into a beast that even hell could not contain. I had been forewarned by Soulange of her displayed anger after returning home from her trip to find Mumsie's reupholstered chair and the newly engraved shawl over it, and the preparations that were in the making for our formal wedding at Trinity Church. She would not speak to anyone except to make hushed phone calls behind her closed bedroom.

I called during the first week of November to tell her of my plans for Thanksgiving dinner, and she said, rather unexpectedly, "Oh, don't worry about a thing. I'll make sure you have a memorable evening." I couldn't figure out how to take her answer, but I just continued to do my work at the hospital until I got there. Little did I suspect that she would make sure that the memory of that evening would not be a pleasant one for either Talize or me.

We took the morning train to New York and arrived around three o'clock. It was November 22, and the skies were cloudy. The first snow flurries of the season had fallen the night before, but the forecast was for seasonable weather that evening. Talize was quite apprehensive about meeting Mother. I had already told her how cold and withdrawn she was, especially in greeting people for the first time—unless they were some nobility or a famous person and then she would put on the charm with a pretentious smile. Talize took the time to prepare a basket of cranberries for Mother as a gesture of goodwill; it was a Wampanoag tradition. She looked absolutely fabulous.

We got to the house around four. Soulange answered the door, and from her face, I could tell that the clouds outside were going to settle indoors. We removed our coats and were escorted into the dining room where Mother was seated with Uncle Thaddeus and some young woman who was unfamiliar to me.

When I saw him at the table, I had a horrible flashback to our last encounter at Father's gravesite two years earlier. Before the burial was complete, he had the audacity to come to me, wanting to speak about family finance now that I was "the man of the house."

"You know, Nephew, if you pool your financial resources with my investments, we could make quite a profitable deal. I'm in the inner circle on Wall Street. It's time you join me at the Knickerbocker Club so I can introduce you to some of the most important and successful people living in the United States."

I was still numb. I told him I was not interested in any deals right at that moment. I was still trying to get through my father's death.

He responded, smugly, "Oh, I understand. Just take your time, but not too long. You have many valuable pieces in your possession. You don't want to foolishly neglect your fiduciary responsibilities."

He left showing no emotion, sympathy, or concern. But before leaving, I saw him talking to Soulange, appearing disgusted, and pointing his finger in her face. When we returned home, I went to her room to speak to her.

She asked what he said to me, and after I told her, she answered quite deliberately, "Do not get involved with anything that man proposes. He is not to be trusted. Although he is your family, he is not your friend. Stay cautious and avoid his ways."

I had never heard Soulange talk about anyone so bluntly—not even Mother. "And I have something else to tell you, that I dare not have told your father, because he would have gone to jail after killing him." Soulange explained that, on Christmas Day, back in 1911, Uncle Thaddeus came to the house for his usual brief visit, but this time, she did not see him leave. She looked around upstairs, but then she heard noise above in the maid's quarters. As she got closer, she could hear a seventeen-year-old maid, pleasant and hardworking, pleading, "Please don't hurt me."

Uncle Thaddeus responded, "Just give me what I want, and if you say anything to anyone, you will be a colored girl in deep trouble." She left before morning—never to be seen again.

I thought, *This uncouth man took advantage of that innocent, helpless minor for his sexual pleasures. How despicable!* I was speechless, but Soulange looked at me and said, "Your grandfather, grandmother, and father knew that something was very wrong inside his mind, and they couldn't do anything about it. He is not our problem. He is his own problem. Let him deal with it. If he chooses to stay in darkness, he will suffer his own dark consequences."

I listened to her sage understanding, but I was not so quick to accept his unkindly ways. I did not expect him or Mother's young friend to attend this dinner. Talize and I were there to share our wedding plans with Mother and not be involved in any confusion. But the evening did not go as planned; in fact, it turned out to be one of the most heartbreaking, earth-shaking devastations that could happen to a man. It was all deliberate, unnecessary, cruel, and unbelievable. I started to feel that awful suffering I did those thirty-seven years ago, but I glanced over at Soulange, and the reassurance on her face calmed me to continue.

I tried to regain my composure enough to offer cordial greetings, but as I started to introduce Talize who approached Mother politely with her gift of the cranberries, the most rude, impersonal response and gesture was offered.

Those words from my mother's mouth resonated with bone-chilling pain: "I didn't ask for—nor would I want—any of your trinkets. You give that to your tepee friends, and they might whoop and holler in approval." As she pushed the basket aside on the table, Uncle Thaddeus sat with his hand over his mouth, imitating the whoop-and-holler routine of some fantasied "savage." Needless to say, the evening progressed poorly. I became embarrassed and more and more angry as my uneasiness grew.

After Talize and I reluctantly sat down, Mother changed her tone and started talking about her young female guest. "This is Victoria Donelson. She is a Donelson, a direct descendant of President Andrew Jackson's wife's family. The poor man lost his wife just before his election and Emily Donelson, her niece, became the White House hostess through his presidency. Yes, the great Andrew Jackson. He was a heroic general who fought to preserve the blessings of liberty and justice in the United States."

Victoria shyly expressed her greetings and then said she admired a man in the field of medicine; it showed great ambition. It sounded like something Mother would say to impress or flatter someone. I said thank you, and she continued telling me that a doctor is an important leader in the community and someone who deserves respect.

I answered her directly, saying, "Did you know that my fiancé is a physician and someone who would also deserve great respect?"

Mother interrupted, "Victoria is talking about real doctors—not some medicine man passing out roots and voodoo dust. She has been groomed in social etiquette and proper culture. Remember she is a Donelson and a direct contact to a distinguished president."

"Dr. Morningstar's training is as qualified as my own, so your point is specious." Mother's endorsement of Jackson tweaked a nerve in me. "Spare me the hero or great man rhetoric for Andrew Jackson. First of all, during the election, Jackson and his wife were accused of adultery because his wife had not formally separated from her first husband when Jackson married her. He wouldn't wait around for lawful matters to settle; he wanted things to go his way. He took advantage of whatever he needed. His popularity, his fortune, and his ascent to the presidency were aided directly by the very people he hated most: the American Indian. He purchased land cheaply that was originally inhabited by Indians and opportunely taken after his war campaigns down South. He then sold it for a huge profit to other white settlers."

Uncle Thaddeus interrupted, "Well, Nephew, you can't blame a shrewd businessman who knew how to legally get a good deal when he saw it. Besides, those 'injuns' didn't know the value of that land. All they knew to do was to sit around the campfire, 'smoke-um' the peace pipe, and tell worthless stories. President Jackson was far cleverer than all the tribes put together."

I had great difficulty containing myself, and the look of disbelief on Talize's face didn't make matters any better. Dinner was being served, and the conversation shifted to Victoria's interests in art and plans to become a teacher.

As time went by, Talize went to the restroom, and Mother, once again, brought up Victoria's ties to the famous Jackson.

I interjected, "When he was a major general in the War of 1812, commanding troops against British allies, the Creek Indians, he ordered his men to kill the Indian women and children to 'complete their extinction.' Over the course of the next twenty-eight years, almost fifty thousand Indians were gone—either by death or forced removal—and twenty-five million acres of their land was taken."

Uncle Thaddeus said, "Well, what do you expect when you are fighting with bows and arrows against a sophisticated arsenal of real military power? There's going to be some blood spilled. There's bound to be a victor and a loser. Did you expect the president to go to the chiefs and start crying over spilt milk? He's got more important matters to address. Give it a rest, Nephew. President Jackson was great. That's why he's on the twenty-dollar bill—or did you forget that important fact?"

"The man allowed states to violate federal treaties with the tribes—while claiming he was helpless to prevent it. His philosophy was: 'What good man would prefer a country covered with forests and ranged by a few thousand savages to our extensive republic, studded with cities, towns, and prosperous farms filled with all the blessings of liberty, civilization, and religion?'"[69]

Uncle Thaddeus responded, "The man had sound judgment. What else would a strong leader of this great nation do?"

I remarked sharply, "I would not expect him to act as cruel and unjust as he did to the Cherokees on the Trail of Tears."

Victoria said, "I am not familiar with the Trail of Tears."

I continued, "Relations between the Cherokee nation and neighboring whites became more hostile with more land being taken, but in 1819, the Cherokee Council would no longer cede land voluntarily. By 1828, Georgia passed a law pronouncing all prior treaties or laws of the Cherokee Nation were null and void. Gold was discovered on Cherokee land in 1829, and President Jackson implemented his Indian Removal Act of 1830, a broad policy to dissolve any land titles of the Indians and force them all to relocate west of the Mississippi River.

"By 1838, the Cherokees were placed in internment camps in Tennessee and Alabama. There was theft and destruction of Indian property. By the time the land routes were organized, the winter was upon those weary travelers. A snowstorm with freezing temperatures made conditions worse for the Indians who slept on the ground with no fire to warm them, and they had limited, decayed supplies of food. The Indians endured deep suffering and painful death. The journey ended for the survivors around March 30, 1839 with four thousand of the Indians dead. The Cherokee survivors called the sojourn 'Nu na hi du na tho hi lu i,' which means 'the trail where they cried.'"

Uncle Thaddeus kept rolling his eyes in disgust throughout my conversation. "What is your point, Nephew? These mishaps occur. No policy is without a few flaws. But death is an inevitable part of life, and we must all accept our place in the pecking order. Those red men were weak and couldn't stand up and face the hardships. Anyway, if you see one less redskin, it's all the better. They are not worth more than the bones and cowhide around their necks."

At this point, Talize, who had returned to the table in the middle of my discussion about the Trail of Tears, would no longer remain quiet. She gave him a reply he did not want to hear. "Mr. Waterbury, you are a man with no experience and no familiarity with Indian culture or Indian life. You never had to suffer from prejudice, poverty, or total humiliation. You have no idea that your forefathers who drafted the United States Constitution did not dream the Bill of Rights out of the thin air. They were all former British subjects who were only acquainted with British laws. They based the model on the relations they saw that existed between tribes and their conversations made with the tribal leaders. They conveniently took credit for their *vision* and then made sure it only applied to white men—even though they were too cowardly to write that into the Constitution. You can sit there with your smirk, your contempt, and your ego-driven illusion of superiority, but no true justice was given to my people or any Northern Continental tribe. If you had any awareness of humanity, you would not deny the tragedy of the Trail of Tears or the infamy of your hero, Andrew Jackson."

"Well, Nephew, it seems you have a woman who speaks her mind. Maybe one day, Pocahontas could visit President Coolidge before he leaves office. You've seen the picture where Sioux Chief Henry Standing Bear placed an official Indian headdress on him and made him an honorary tribal member last year at Deadwood, South Dakota. Maybe he can have a picture taken with her in his headdress and sign it, 'to one of my favorite squaws.' Ha, ha, ha!"

I was livid. "I have had it! Enough of your insolence!"

Mother interrupted, "Now, Windsor, let's not be rude to your uncle."

I asked if we could be excused. I took Talize into the library to try to calm down. To my dismay, Uncle Thaddeus decided to follow us. I had to go to the bathroom and left for a few minutes.

When I returned, I saw that loathsome man attempting to proposition Talize for a one-night stand, waving a twenty-dollar bill in her face, telling her that the great white father would approve, and if she was good to him, he might consider giving her a second twenty-dollar bill and she would be doubly pleased.

I couldn't take it any longer. I shoved him up against the wall, lifted him with my right arm and my hand around his neck, tightening my grip with each second making me more enraged.

His face was as red as his hair.

Soulange came quickly by my side and said, "I don't need to visit you behind prison walls. Release him and take care of Talize."

"Her simple words penetrated my impulsive hate. If I had killed him, there would be no further story to tell. I would have lost my license, I would not have known any of you except Soulange, and I don't know if I would have ever recovered from the disappointment I would have given the Waterbury name. I was grateful to Soulange."

I finally looked around, and Talize was gone. I rushed to the front. Her coat was gone, and her engagement ring was in the dish where I usually placed my keys. I ran outside, coatless, frantically looking for her.

I went to Central Park West, looking both directions. Not seeing her, I turned around and headed toward Broadway. There was still no sign of her. In a state of disbelief and agonizing pain, I took a taxi to Greenwood to speak to Grandfather, Mumsie, and Father. All the time during the taxi ride, I tried to go over each minute of the evening, each helpless minute created by Mother and Uncle Thaddeus, each torturing statement made to banish Talize from my life, and each twisted, manipulated turn of events so craftily orchestrated to make it a done deal. It was as if President Jackson returned to force both Talize and me on another Trail of Tears.

After my arrival at the front gate, I pleaded with the night watchman to allow me to go in to go to see my family plot. He must have felt my anguish and finally let me enter. Once at the gravesite, I poured my heart out about the unjust circumstances. *What would happen to all of my future plans with Talize? Why did I even suggest a dinner with Mother, knowing her disapproval and knowing what cruel schemes she was capable of creating? My world was literally lifted from under me, and I didn't know what to do to get back on my feet again. Help me, in my hour of despair.*

The wind and sounds of the dried brown leaves seemed to intensify, and the trees were swaying to and fro. My thoughts were taken away to John Greenleaf Whittier's *The Battle Autumn of 1862*:

> And, calm and patient, Nature keeps
> Her ancient promises well,
> Though o'er her bloom and greenness sweeps,
> The battle's breath of hell.
> Ah, eyes may well be full of tears,
> And hearts with hate are hot;
> But even-paced come round the years,
> And nature changes not.
> She meets with smiles our bitter grief,
> With songs our groans of pain;
> She mocks with tints of flowers and leaf,
> The war field's crimson stain.
> Still, in the cannon's pause, we hear
> Her sweet thanksgiving psalm,
> Too near to God for doubt or fear,
> She shares the eternal calm.
> Oh, give to us her finer ear
> Above this stormy din,
> We, too, would hear the bells of cheer
> Ring peace and freedom in.[70]

I was in the cannon's pause. All three of you told me to listen to Nature's thanksgiving psalm, but I was not seeing with a clearer eye or hearing with a fine ear or feeling the eternal calm. I felt broken and downtrodden. But God, like Nature, did offer the eternal calm in the midst of the fiercest storm. *What did I have to do to feel it?*

I remained there through the very early morning hours until the night watchman had come, looking for me, worried that I was out there too long. He brought me back to the gate and got a cab to go home. I was exhausted, cold, and confused. I don't remember anything about the ride.

When I approached the stairs, Soulange opened the door, and I passed out. I had no idea that my decision to physically bear the consequence of my confusion and despair outdoors in winter conditions with no proper, protective garments would shake my soul senseless and create the development of a threatening pneumonia.

My memory is vague on subsequent events until I was awakened by a nurse at the hospital and saw Soulange smiling at me. I will ask her to share that gap in time. Soulange paused for a moment. I saw her thoughts from the whole ordeal etched on her pensive face.

"I want all of you to realize that Rose knew exactly what would occur that evening, and there was not going to be any interference to accomplish her goal. She, alone, could not have pulled it off. She waited until that morning to inform me she had the additional guests and that I was not to speak to you or Talize until the evening was over. I tried to give you a signal by the dining room entry, but you were too focused and preoccupied by all those ugly commentaries. When Talize went to the restroom, I was distracted away and did not get the opportunity to talk to her either. When you walked into the library and I heard you say, "Enough is enough!" so emphatically, I knew what would follow. I really didn't care what Rose would say about my intervention. I did not see Talize leave, but I am sure that Rose did. Her look said it all.

"When you ran out in the cold without your coat, and did not return that evening, I knew you were in trouble. I could not sleep at all that night. I kept looking out the window, and when the taxi stopped, I could not believe how you survived. You were frigid, gasping, coughing, and drained of all energy. You passed out in my arms; I dragged you inside. My assistants helped me put you to bed.

"I nursed you for the first twenty-four hours, but you progressively worsened with fever, short dyspneic breaths, audible grunting, and persistent cough. Your condition was very similar to your father's when he contracted the Spanish flu. I would have continued your care, but Rose was insistent on you going to the hospital. She did not want to be around any exposure. Remember how fearful she was during the 1918 epidemic. You remained in serious condition for four days, and I gave you the care when the nurses were busy with the other patients. On the fifth day, you were more conscious, even though you were still compromised."

I resumed the conversation from there.

I remember opening my eyes and seeing your smile. But the agony of the dyspnea and any movement in bed were both excruciating. When I coughed up the blood-tinged sputum, I knew I had pneumonia. After the doctor came and discussed my case, he confirmed that I had Type I pneumococcus. I remembered reading in Father's 1901 edition of Dr. William Osler's *Principles and Practice of Medicine* that pneumonia, "the most widespread and fatal of all acute infectious disease is now the captain of the men of death to use the phrase applied by John Bunyan to consumption."

I was aware that a Type-I specific anti-pneumococcal serotherapy, a type specific horse serum, was being used on patients at Mass General Hospital. I did see one patient who received the serotherapy, developed a severe allergic reaction to the serum, and died from a progressive anaphylactic shock. My doctor did not discuss giving me a trial or whether it was available or not. After that patient's death, I was not inclined to personally receive it.

The six-week stay at the hospital seemed like an eternity. The illness was a setback, but the emotional and spiritual emptiness from not having Talize and the uncertainty about where she could be was the worst pain— far more than the effects of the most aggressive expression of the disease. I had Soulange call her at her Boston apartment; there was no answer. She called some of our mutual friends, but they had not heard from her either.

What happened to Talize at Thanksgiving in my house was no different than what happened to Chief John Ross at the Trail of Tears, Chief Black Kettle at the Sand Creek Massacre, or Sitting Bull at Little Bighorn. They were all victims of being depicted as one-dimensional, wild, uncivilized savages, not capable of any sophistication, spirituality, or erudition. Media, including newspaper articles across the country and William Cody's *Buffalo Bill's Wild West*, convinced most Americans of a stereotypic impression—the dark Indian aggressor against the righteous white conqueror. The *Wild West Show* displayed the wilderness inhabited by the primitive Indians finally settled by civil and "moral" settlers who knew the value of Manifest Destiny. Cody brought to the audience what they wanted to see, and he knew how to convince them that he knew what was right.

Even Merrill Gates, an alleged "friend and benefactor of the Indian," former Amherst College president and president of the Lake Mohonk Conference of the Friends of the Indian was supportive of the white general consensus opinion:

> We have, to begin with, the absolute need of awakening in the savage Indian broader desires and ampler wants. To bring him out of savagery into citizenship we must make the Indian more intelligently selfish before we can make him unselfishly intelligent. We need to awaken in him wants. In his dull savagery he must be ... discontent with the teepee and the starving rations of the Indian camp in winter ... to get the Indian out of the blanket and into trousers, —and trousers with a pocket in them and with a pocket that aches to be filled with dollars! ... We have found it necessary, as one of the first steps in developing a stronger personality in the Indian, to make him responsible for property. Even if he learns its value only by losing it, and going without it until he works for more, the educational process has begun. To cease from pauperizing the Indian by feeding him through years of laziness—to instruct him to use property which is legally his, and by protecting his title, to help him through the dangerous transition period into citizenship—this is the first great step in the education of the race.[71]

Mother and Uncle Thaddeus were convinced the same way at the dinner table. Talize was more intelligent, civilized, caring, and human than either of them combined. Money could not buy that for them, and remedial training could not be helpful for them. It didn't matter that she was a qualified physician, accomplished cellist, or a worldly thinker; to them, she couldn't fit into any part of their world. And now, Talize and I were the victims of ignorance and were being punished with impunity.

During those six weeks recuperating in that hospital bed, I had an opportunity to think deeply about the treatment, the lack of respect, and the harassment that Mother displayed on Thanksgiving. Although she told

Soulange to tell me to get better, Mother never came to visit. It was very clear that I would directly approach her after coming home.

"I hope you are satisfied with your brutal extermination of the most treasured part of my life. A spider crawling up your leg would have had a more merciful outcome. How could a mother be so deliberately cruel, unjust, condescending, and vindictive to ruin her son's life by destroying his very heart and soul? Are you just plain out of your mind? If God had taken Talize away from me, I would know there was a reason—whether I accepted or understood the reason or not—but there is no sane explanation to rationalize your behavior that night."

Mother, with her usual smug look, acted so surprised with my statements. "You come in here, raising your voice to me in disrespect? I was only trying to spare you the humiliation of marrying this outsider who did not know you, and you couldn't see it. She would have jeopardized the Waterbury name and put us in a terrible position in the community."

I was quick to interrupt. "*Know* me? She knows me far greater than you ever dreamed of knowing me, Father, Mumsie, or Grandfather."

"I was only trying to help."

"Yes, that's right. Help yourself. You knew you couldn't pull this off without assurance ammunition. So you invite Thaddeus—who I haven't seen since Grandfather's death and who couldn't have been more scathing and disregarding of Talize—as well as Victoria who doesn't know anything about me and had no business at my private dinner. Although she presented with ennui, she at least was civil and more decent than you or Thaddeus.

"Do you despise me that much? Don't answer, when I already know too well. I have full remembrance of Father's forceful words that you not be buried next to him whenever you die. Not only will I honor Father's desire, but I will also cut your precious allowance in half again. Say no more to justify any of your actions. I'm sick of your manipulating and your selfish and poisonous disposition. If Father, Grandfather, and Mumsie were still alive, I don't know if you would be allowed to set foot through the front door ever again—and no one would be the worse for it."

Mother remained stoic and proceeded to walk toward her room. She did not speak to me for a few weeks and then only to inform me she had been invited to be a guest at Eagle's Nest with Rosamund and Willie K.

Vanderbilt, at their home in Northport Bay, Long Island, and she would get a personal ride on Willie's yacht, *Alva*, in the summer.

As difficult as it may appear, I felt sorry for both of those miserable people—Mother and Uncle Thaddeus—and their jaded thinking, their illusions of prestige, and their genuine denial of decency.

I blame myself for introducing Talize to my family. I was not ashamed of her; I was quite proud to introduce her to anyone who was president in the White House or the less fortunate, downtrodden man. I had been treated so kindly by her uncle and other family members at Gayhead. I became part of their family, and I was so happy.

We should have left the house when Mother pushed the cranberries aside. I cannot undo the past, and God knows what I wish I could understand. It was a heartache that I still carry today, thirty-seven years later."

Everyone was feeling my sorrow, so I moved on to the next event, which defined a crossroads experience in my professional career.

Career Planning, June 1929 (Event 20)

After graduating from medical school, I thought back to that trip to Troutbeck in upstate New York with Grandfather, Uncle Herbert, and Uncle Joel. While on the pathway, Uncle Joel discussed the underlying unfolding of the seeds in all the plants and trees and their potential for growth and greatness. All the programming within the seed is designated to express itself once planted in the ground. There is time taken by the seed to tap into that source hidden in the soil, to develop the root and remain unseen and quiet, until the full process is complete and a sprout erupts and becomes a mature plant or tree. The greatness of the individual blossoms is dependent on its establishment of that vital root system. The stronger the root is nurtured, the more potential it has to gain heartiness and greater heights. The plant or tree cannot survive a harsh winter, a summer drought, or a massive flood without that deep-rooted connection.

We can apply those same observations in man. After birth, he is "planted in the ground" to be cultivated with the necessary nutrients to develop. He or she needs an education, whether it is in a formal classroom or on the streets of life, to allow the roots to set. Once education has been established, there is a need for independent experience and an ongoing growth to reach the highest potential for yield. After school is completed, and after leaving home, the whole process of maturation moves in the direction you choose to follow:

Tis Education forms the common mind
Just as the Twig is bent
The Tree's inclined
—Alexander Pope, *Moral Essays*, Epistle I, line 149–150

Most important, however, always be conscious of your root system. Neglect it not because it is your security, your worth, and your core as a human being. Surely you will spread your limbs and witness your development evolving, but you are not as resilient when your root is not firmly established in the deepest part of your soul. The root is that connection to life itself.

I had to consider these insightful analogies since I was starting to plan what direction I was going to pursue while my career was taking shape. I had to decide between medical research and a general clinical practice, serving a community in a local setting. Father had the opportunity to remain as a faculty member under Dr. Osler's tutelage, but he chose to go to the clinic in New Orleans and subsequently New York. Father felt an obligation to the people who needed him most, and he had no regrets.

I stayed in Boston and started my internship in medicine at Boston City Hospital in July 1927. I did some research in the Thorndike Lab with Dr. George Minot, who replaced Dr. Peabody as director after his death. During that busy time, I was brought back to the familiar pain of loss at the death of my friend and mentor, Dr. Francis Peabody. He died peacefully on October 13, and I attended the funeral services at King's Chapel. The church was packed. Inside the church, the standing-room-only crowd extended out of the church. Colleagues from all over the United States and the world, medical students, family, and former patients, were all bringing messages of condolence.

Three outstanding tributes were written about him.

1) *The Boston Medical and Surgical Journal*, October 29, 1927: Others, no doubt, will take up his tasks where he left them and carry them forward in the paths he pointed

out; but, however able and worthy, others cannot replace him in the hearts of those who felt his influence. Great in wisdom, he was tolerant; strong, he was patient of weakness; rich in gifts and honors, he was without pride.

2) Dr. Hans Zinsser: One gathers only wonder at the inner symmetry of intelligence and heart which made his life a blessing and his death an inspiring lesson. Death had no triumph in him, and he died as he had lived—with patience and love in his heart, with the simple faith of a trustful child and the superb gallantry of a great soul.

3) Dr. Warfield Longcope: He had learned to know his fellow man, to look with sympathy upon their misfortunes and to use his knowledge wisely for their benefit. He was essentially the good physician absorbed in his patients.

While reflecting on his service now, I have to feel Grandfather's sorrow when he attended Senator Charles Sumner's funeral at King's Chapel fifty-three years earlier.

In his weakened state, Dr. Peabody remained encouraging to me, giving recommendations on career choices. He had worked at the hospital of the Rockefeller Institute in 1911–1912 before returning to Harvard. I saw him for the last time the day after my graduation at his home in Cambridge. He congratulated me for all my honors and achievements, and he felt my internship at Boston City would be a good one. He told me to consider the Rockefeller Institute, Columbia's Presbyterian Hospital, which was newly completed in 1928, Johns Hopkins, or perhaps a year abroad in London, Berlin, or Leiden for research in infectious disease. I stayed at Boston City Hospital the following year as assistant resident physician and did research in syphilology, tuberculosis, and other respiratory disease on the infectious disease ward.

My work was interrupted considerably after the Thanksgiving fiasco, and even though the pneumonia was clinically cured after six weeks, it was not until late spring of 1929 that I finally felt physically recovered. My heart, however, was still in pieces. My persistent inquiries to find Talize, including her relatives in Aquinnah, were ineffectual. By June 1929, I had to face my circumstances without the guidance of my usual and dependable "advisors." There were several points to consider as my Boston City Hospital years neared their completion.

Medicine had undergone a tremendous change toward commercialism and sterile businesses during the 1910s and 1920s. Father had discussed this frightening transition when I decided to go into medicine, and he gave me a series of articles written anonymously in *Century Magazine* in July through October 1922. The first article stated:

> One of the most distressing tendencies in American medicine is the decline of the old-fashioned general practitioner and his replacement by the modern so called scientific physician ... the passing of the "old doc" means the disappearance of a charming character, a wise counselor, a comforter in times of distress, a rock to cling to in the storms of disease and in the presence of death. His twilight must fill one with melancholy, because he was usually a figure of simplicity and sincerity and real dignity in our communities, which are already more than filled with hypocrisy, charlatanism, loud advertisement, meretricious efficiency, pretense, and vulgarity of all kinds.[72]

The author used his own family doctor as an illustration:

> His ability in diagnosis ... showed that combination of careful observation, long experience and rare good sense that led one to consider his judgments to be intuitive rather than based on memory of principles rammed into him in his college courses. He made little use of modern diagnostic paraphernalia. He did not pooh-pooh at them as new-fangled, but seemed impressed with their importance. At the same time, he was never afraid to admit that he was baffled in the study of some obscure malady. This characteristic, so much a part of

his fundamental frankness and honesty, added to the confidence that everyone had in him. He was a firm believer in the power of nature to cope successfully with many diseases. He constantly reminded his patients of this fact, and disdained to take the credit for cures that the universal mother herself had effected.[73]

He criticized the offices of the modern specialists:

The stylish doctors have waiting rooms of expensive, luxurious furniture and around the walls are arranged bookcases, garnished with fat medical tomes and with endless ranks of bound volumes of medical periodicals ... The business organization of the group is usually conducted with a truly American efficiency, and with an impersonality and heartlessness necessary to all sound economic enterprises. For it is this, in fact, that medicine is rapidly becoming. This materialistic element is essentially foreign to the spirit of a true physician. Like the functions of the educator and the priest, that of the good doctor has been one of self-abnegation, of devotion to ideals. These ideals, which are necessary to a calling which should be altruistic and partly religious in its nature, have been rudely upset by the entry of economic enterprise ... In addition to the rich, the services of the super-doctor are available occasionally to the very poor. These he attends as a teacher in a hospital clinic. For the title of "clinical professor" is an important adjunct to prestige, and, by the same token, a business asset.[74]

And then he offered his analysis of the scientist and the physician:

There is confusion of the art of healing, which is the true function of the physician, with the science of the study of disease, which is the duty of the biologist, physicist and chemist, and it is wide-spread and a disastrous tendency.

The physician should be venerated not for supernatural knowledge or scientific acumen, but for his understanding of our ills and troubles, for raising his patient's morale and last, for applying, as a technologist, the therapeutic discoveries furnished him by the small group of scientists who actually study disease ... his relationship to his patient should be that of a comrade coming to the aid of a stricken friend ... Humanity in general is certainly not ready for a martyrdom to the progress of knowledge. It is not ready to take the place of the laboratory guinea-pig.[75]

He concludes by saying:

It is unsound to consider the doctor as a scientist in his relation to the patients or to think of medicine as an independent science. The practice of medicine is something of an entirely different nature. It is to the greatest extent an art; it is part craft; it begins to smack of a technology or applied science ... The last and most important function of the physician is still his art, which consists largely in the emotional relationship he must bear toward his patient. In this all good doctors, from Hippocrates to Osler, have been proficient. This is in its nature antipathetic to the scientific attitude.[76]

I discovered that the anonymous author was the microbiologist, Paul DeKruif, PhD, who was fired from the Rockefeller Institute after the *Century Magazine* publication. His straightforward accusations were not taken with agreement. He went on to collaborate with the author, Sinclair Lewis, to write a novel, *Arrowsmith*, which was published in 1925.

Although the story is fictitious, Lewis and DeKruif used the protagonist, Martin Arrowsmith, to openly discuss the triumphs and defeats of the physician and the scientist doing medical research during contemporary real times. The surrounding characters—his mentor (Max Gottlieb), his medical school dean (Dr. Silva), his wife (Leora), fellow medical students, and the less influential, but still important community citizens interacted with Arrowsmith and gave him an analytic awareness throughout the story. As he struggles to seek the "truth" delivering medical care to the community and making conclusions to his scientific results, Arrowsmith finds his most rewarding experiences while he is alone in the laboratory or with his understanding and supportive wife. In his interactions with colleagues, fellow scientists, and the community folks, he appears unaffected on the surface, but an underlying ego boosts his pride after he is judged successful in his work.

Eventually, he learned a hard lesson: To survive in the world of scientific research, everyone must align with one of the well-established institutions and be at the mercy of their objectives, which may not be quite fitting for an individual longing for a greater truth. There was a time when Arrowsmith questioned the validity of his research project, but the director of the famous "McGurk Institute," Dr. A. Dewitt Tubbs, forced him to discuss his discoveries. After hearing the new discovery, but sensing Arrowsmith's hesitancy to publish his results immediately, Tubbs glibly remarked, "Nonsense! That attitude is old-fashioned. This is no longer an age of parochialism, but of competition, in art and science just as much as in commerce."

By the end of the novel, Arrowsmith realized that the scientist who maintained a truthful search and steadfast vision on any particular discovery may not gain the fame or success of a scientific "breakthrough," but he or she will be satisfied with the clear understanding of being truthful to oneself and being patient during all failures. The novel won Lewis the Pulitzer Prize in 1925, but he declined it. He accepted the Nobel Prize in 1930 and was the first American to win that honor in literature.

Even though *Arrowsmith* was a novel, there was a great distaste for the way medicine was evolving during that time as written by a physician with the highest clinical knowledge, the formidable Dr. William Osler. In the *International Clinics Journal*, 4, 25th Series (1915), he wrote:

> The burning question to be settled by this generation relates to the whole-time clinical teacher. It has been forced on the profession by men who know nothing of clinical medicine, and there has been a "mess of pottage" side to the business in the shape of big Rockefeller cheques

at which my gorge rises. To have a group of cloistered clinicians away completely from the broad current of professional life would be bad for teacher and worse for student. The primary work of a professor of medicine in a medical school is in the wards, teaching his pupils how to deal with patients and their diseases. His business is to turn out men who know how to handle the sick. His business, also, is to bring into play all resources of the laboratories in the investigation of disease, for which purpose he must have about him active young men who will stay for years in the clinics ... His business, further, is to get into close touch with the profession and the public and with both to play the missionary; and this he can only do if engaged part of his time in consulting practice. There always have been of choice whole-time clinicians ... By all means let us have them in the special hospitals attached to institutes of research, as in the Rockefeller; but spare the medical schools an experiment, which may be successful now and then, but which—from my point of view—cannot but lower in type and tone the work of the clinical professoriate.[77]

During all that criticism, a true bright light, like the beacon from the North Star, Polaris, the navigational star which marked the way due north for the ancient mariners who were guided by the stars at night, would shine on the medical world and change the course of medicine forever; it convinced me that I had made a good decision in selecting infectious disease as my special interest. An article I read in the *British Journal of Experimental Pathology* in June 1929 was written by a physician from a lab at Saint Mary's Hospital in London. Dr. Alexander Fleming found a species of mold that was able to inhibit growth in particular bacterial colonies on a culture plate. He named his mold species, Penicillin, after the penicillium organism. In his summary, he stated:

A certain type of penicillium produces in culture a powerful antibacterial substance ... The action is very marked on the pyogenic cocci (staphylococcus) and the diphtheria group of bacilli. Many bacteria are quite insensitive … Penicillin is non-toxic to animals in enormous doses and is non-irritant. It is suggested that it may be an efficient antiseptic for application to or injection into, areas infected with the penicillin-sensitive microbes.[78]

But to his great disappointment, after presentation of his paper on Penicillin was given to the world's foremost bacteriologists, there was no support and no suggestions for further collaborative work mentioned. The use of penicillin remained dormant for ten long years.

All of these useful references presented greater insight to help me make a commitment to either general practice or scientific research, but I still had some soul-searching to do. Whenever I needed an introspective review while I lived in Boston, I went to a place that would expand my inner sanctum, offer guidance, and find much-needed peace of mind. I went back to the Jamaica Pond and the Arnold Arboretum where I took many wonderful walks by myself and with Talize during our internship year. While I was at Boston City Hospital, Talize interned at the New England Hospital for Women and Children in Roxbury.

Jamaica Pond was the former summer home to the Mattapan Wampanoag tribe. It had been a melted glacial water body and became incorporated in Frederick Olmsted's "Emerald Necklace" parks, which were designed to spread greenery from Boston Common over six miles of outlying areas in the 1880s and 1890s. These parks were connected by major boulevards along the Fenway, Riverway, Jamaicaway, and Arborway. Olmsted recognized Jamaica Pond's natural beauty and only added walking trails and park benches around the entire perimeter.

South of Jamaica Pond is the Harvard-owned Arnold Arboretum, a 265-acre botanical garden, which is also a part of the Emerald Necklace. Once inside the beautiful stone pillars, adjacent to the front gates, you are taken away from the crowded, urban life of Boston to a land of meadows, ponds, and multiple varieties of plants, trees, and shrubs. It is so impressively green in the summers and so dazzling with color in October's Indian summer.

Talize and I had many discussions about nature, including my trip to Troutbeck, and we spent time talking about our future plans to build our charitable services together. We did talk a little about career opportunities, but she always felt we would be directed to the post most needed and most suited for what we wanted to share.

She clearly stated, "Never worry about any decision you have to make, important or trivial. Even if it appears wrong at the time, there will be a greater understanding later to say that you made the decision meant to happen. It will eventually turn out without regret if your intentions were good and you were unselfish in how the outcome would affect you." She did not favor either decision. She wanted me happy and doing work to serve the community unconditionally.

As I took time overlooking the wide view from the Jamaica Pond, I paused for a moment and reflected on the beautiful Ralph Vaughn Williams song, "Linden Lea." It was his first published composition (1902), and it was based on a poem by nineteenth-century English clergyman, William Barnes. The first verse reads:

> Within the woodland, flow'ry gladed,
> By the oak trees" mossy moot;
> The shining grass blade timber-shaded
> Now do quiver underfoot;
> And birds do whistle overhead,
> And water's bubbling in its bed;
> And there for me the apple tree
> Do lean down low in Linden Lea.[79]

I was grateful for the peace I felt. I was lifted away. Though brief, it was appreciated. I smiled and returned to my thoughts about a career.

There was good reason to do either research or general practice. The idea of Rockefeller Institute was intriguing or an assistant professorship of medicine at any of the good medical schools. I could walk in the footsteps of Dr. Peabody, but I knew I still had to make my own footsteps and make my own contributions.

Without any explanation, I suddenly lost my composure. I cried out, "Talize, you said you did not favor either decision. You wanted me happy, but I still want your thoughts, your counsel, and your love. The time away has been agonizing. Can I make the best decision without you?"

I did not feel a reply. I had to accept my circumstance, and I realized there would be more challenges ahead. Grandfather had to accept his circumstance, yet he endured. I had to allow Fate to be my guide, but in my weakened emotional state, was I strong enough?

I glanced at Soulange, and she looked as if I had said enough and needed to end the conversation.

I looked at everyone and felt their sympathy and sincere understanding of my dilemma.

They all left, and I got ready for bed. My thoughts were reflective. There was more of my life to review and more secrets to unfold. But those setbacks—those toughest, painful moments, those times when Sallie Ann, Miss Charlotte, Grandfather, Mumsie, Uncle Herbert, Father, Soulange, Talize, and I were placed in what seemed like an intense fiery furnace— were the evolving stages to further our awareness of what we were made of as human beings, and our connection to life and its glorious Creator.

Yes, there is more to reveal. I am looking forward to our gathering and the remembrance of the subsequent experiences. I would like to paraphrase what my father said to me the night he passed away, and one of the stories that Uncle Herbert had mentioned. Let us have a long discussion tomorrow. But for now, and during the interim, give conscious consideration to the lessons shared; it is a practical matter to preserve and keep order in your *human* house, which has a divine connection. Become familiar with it and respect it. Become familiar with it and respect it.

Endnotes

1   Unidentified biographer of Saint Vaclav, Duke of Bohemia

2   "Old Christmas"—Paragraph 2,3,7,8,11—Washington Irving (1820)

3   Paraphrased from unidentified abolitionist

4   "Uncle Tom's Cabin"—Harriet Beecher Stowe (1852) pg. 493

5   "Speech on the Reception of Abolition Petitions"—US Senate Speech—1837— by Senator John Calhoun

6   Comments quoted from Reverend Thornton Stringfellow—1856 in "The Bible Tells Me So" by Jim Hill and Rand Cheadle (1996) pg. 4

7   "Mudsill Speech"—US Senate—1858 by Senator James Henry Hammond in "The Arrogance of Race" by George Fredrickson (1988) pg. 23

8   The New York City Draft Riots—July 1863 Exhibit at the Museum of The History of New York City—2015 and "The Epic of New York City: A Narrative History" by Edward Robb Ellis (1966) pg. 236

9   "What The Black Man Wants" by Frederick Douglass (speech given in Boston in April 1865).

10 "Equal Rights of All" Speech—Senate Floor—February 6, 1866 by Senator Charles Sumner pg. 32

11 "A Memorial of Charles Sumner" by Carl Schurz (1874) pg. 26

12 "A Memorial of Charles Sumner" by Samuel Johnson to the Twenty-Eighth Congregational Society (1874) pg. 4,13

13 "The True Grandeur of Nations" speech in sections entitled "The Bloody Heel of War" and "Victories of Peace" by Charles Sumner (July 4, 1845)

14 "A Memorial of Charles Sumner" by Carl Schurz (1874) pg. 34

15 "The Battlefield" by William Cullen Bryant (1839)

16 Speech by Thaddeus Stevens, seen in "The Unknown Architects of Civil Rights" by Barry Goldenberg (2011) pg. 36

17 Speech by Thaddeus Stevens, seen in "The Unknown Architects of Civil Rights" by Barry Goldenberg (2011) pg. 39

18 "Measure for Measure"—Act 2 Scene 2 Lines 110-123, William Shakespeare

19 "American Folklore and Legend"—Readers Digest book (1978) pg. 263

20 Newspaper article from the Springfield Illinois Independent Newspaper—September 3, 1908 by William Walling

21 "The Simple Life" by Charles Wagner (1901) pg. 65

22 "Optimism Within" by Helen Keller in "The World I Live In"—Helen Keller, edited by Roger Shattuck (2003)

23 Watch description from "The Watch" by Catherine Cardinal (1985) pg. 201, 207

24 "The Myth of Er" in "Republic"—Book 10 by Plato

25 "Hetch Hetchy Valley" essay by John Muir; "Writings of John Muir," Library of America (1997) pg. 813

26 "The Faerie Queene" by Edmund Spencer (1596)

27 "When Lilacs Last in the Dooryard Bloom'd" by Walt Whitman (1865)

28 "The Six Mistakes of Man" by Marcus Tullius Cicero

29 "What Does a College Hope to be During the Next 100 Years?" Centennial Day speech at Amherst College by college President Alexander Meiklejohn, June 21, 1921

30 "The Lynching of Henry Lowery"—Memphis Times article on January 27,1921

31 "The Work of a Mob" by Walter White from "The Crisis Reader," edited by Sondra Wilson (1999) pg. 345-350

32 "The Red Record—Tabulated Statistics and Alleged Causes of Lynching in the US" by Ida B. Wells (1895)

33 Open Letter to President Warren G. Harding By Dr. W.E.B. DuBois (March 1921)

34 Preface to "The Red Record" written by Frederick Douglass (1895)

35 "Problems of Today—Race Prejudice" by Moorfield Storey—talk given at the Edwin L. Godkin Lecture at Harvard University in March 1920. Pg. 103

36 "Problems of Today—Race Prejudice" by Moorfield Storey pg. 118

37 "Problems of Today—Race Prejudice" by Moorfield Storey pg. 118

38 Speech given by James Weldon Johnson at the National Conference on Lynching in May 1919

39 Preface to "The Red Record" written by Frederick Douglass (1895)

40 "Problems of Today—Race Prejudice" by Moorfield Storey pg. 148

41 "Is Our World Christian?" Baccalaureate Sermon at Amherst College by President Alexander Meiklejohn on June 17, 1923

42 Phi Beta Kappa Lecture at Harvard by Ralph Waldo Emerson—1837

43 "The Tumult and The Shouting—My Life in Sport" by Grantland Rice (1954) pg. 267-272

44 Campaign speech in Boston by Warren G. Harding—1920

45 "Autumn" by Richard Henry Stoddard in The Collected Poems of Richard Henry Stoddard—1880

46 "The Care of the Patient" by Dr. Francis Peabody in the Journal of the American Medical Association, Vol. 88 (March 19, 1927)

47 Remarks addressing the issue of the "Chinese Problem"—Senator John F. Miller at the 1878 California Convention in "A Different Mirror" by Ronald Takaki (1993) pg. 205

48 Remarks addressing the issue of the "Chinese Problem"—Former New York Governor Horatio Seymour in "A Different Mirror" by Ronald Takaki (1993) pg. 205

49 "Nuts for Skeptics to Crack"—sermon of evangelist Billy Sunday in Indiana—1922

50 Preface to "The Passing of the Great Race" by Madison Grant (1916); preface written by Professor Henry Osborn, anthropologist at Columbia University

51 Prayer by John Donne from the Doubleday Prayer Collection (1992) pg. 218

52 Prayer by William Penn from the Doubleday Prayer Collection (1992) pg. 221

53 The New York Times newspaper—January 9, 1902

54 "The Fire Question in the US"—Editorial by former New York City Fire Chief Edward Croker about the March 1911 Triangle Fire in New York City in the McClure Magazine September 1911

55 "The Simple Life" by Charles Wagner (1901) pg. 66

56 "Exile's Letter" by Rihaku (Li Po), translated by Ezra Pound (1915)

57 Sierra Club Mission Statement—1892

58 "The Hazards of Mercury Vapor" by Dr. Alfred Stock in Zeitsch Angew Chem (Volume 39) 1926 pg. 488

59 1926 Final Report from the US investigating committee's recommendations on lead exposure in the EPA Journal, May 1985—article written by Jack Lewis

60 "Coyote Story" from "The Story Telling Stone," edited by Susan Feldman (1965) pg. 213

61 "A Century of Dishonor" by Helen Hunt Jackson (1881) pg.337, 274, 270

62 Speech to Osage Indians by Tecumseh in "Native American Testimony" by Peter Nabokov (1978) pg.96-97

63 Description of Tecumseh's oration by Sam Dale in the American History Illustrated from the National Historical Society (February 1972) pg. 6

64 Reply to the US Indian Commissioners by Cherokee statesman Corn Tassel in "Native American Testimony" by Peter Nabokov (1978) pg. 122

65 Comments by elder Indians—"My sun is set …" in "Native American Testimony" pg. 181

66 Comments by elder Indians—"we may be foolish …" in "The Sacred: Ways of Knowledge, Sources of Life" by Peggy Beck, Anna Lee Walters and Nia Francisco (1977) pg. 165

67 "The Soul of the Indian" by Charles Eastman (1911) pg. 46

68 Chief Yellow Hawk's quote in "A Garden of Prayer: A Family Treasury" edited by Jenna Bassin and Jane Lahr (1989); pg. 16

69 President Jackson's quote in "A Different Mirror" by Dr. Ronald Takaki (1993) pg. 88

70 "The Battle Autumn of 1862" by John Greenleaf Whittier (Atlantic Monthly Magazine—October 1862)

71 Commentary by Indian Commissioner Merrill Gates in "Americanizing the American Indian: Writings by The Friends of the Indian 1880-1890" by Francis Prucha (1973)

72 "Our Medicine Men" by Dr. Paul DeKruif in Century Magazine (July 1922) pg. 416, 417, 421-422, 423-424, 426

73 "Our Medicine Men" by Dr. Paul DeKruif in Century Magazine (July 1922) pg. 416, 417, 421-422, 423-424, 426

74 "Our Medicine Men" by Dr. Paul DeKruif in Century Magazine (July 1922) pg. 416, 417, 421-422, 423-424, 426

75 "Our Medicine Men" by Dr. Paul DeKruif in Century Magazine (July 1922) pg. 416, 417, 421-422, 423-424, 426

76 "Our Medicine Men" by Dr. Paul DeKruif in Century Magazine (July 1922) pg. 416, 417, 421-422, 423-424, 426

77 Commentary by Dr. William Osler in "The International Clinics, Journal 4, 25th Series (1915)

78 Article by Dr. Alexander Fleming in "The British Journal of Experimental Pathology"—June 1929 pg. 236

79 "Linden Lea" by Reverend William Barnes (1859)

About The Author

Daniel McCrimons, MD is a Harvard College and Columbia University trained pediatrician who has a passion for blending his thirty-five years of clinical experience with family values, science, and spirituality to create stories that encourage self-improvement. He currently resides in Sacramento, California. Diamonds in the Water is his first book.